SEARCHING
~FOR~
ETERNITY

Books by Elizabeth Musser

FROM BETHANY HOUSE PUBLISHERS

The Swan House

The Dwelling Place

Searching for Eternity

OTHER BOOKS

Two Crosses

Two Testaments

Two Destinies

ELIZABETH MUSSER

SEARCHING ~FOR~ ETERNITY

BETHANY HOUSE PUBLISHERS

Minneapolis, Minnesota

Published by Bethany House Publishers
11400 Hampshire Avenue South
Bloomington, Minnesota 55438

Bethany House Publishers is a division of
Baker Publishing Group, Grand Rapids, Michigan.

Printed in the United States of America

ISBN-13:   978-0-7642-0372-5
ISBN-10:   0-7642-0372-X

Library of Congress Cataloging-in-Publication Data

Musser, Elizabeth
    Searching for eternity / Elizabeth Musser.
        p.   cm.
    ISBN-13:   978-0-7642-0372-5 (pbk.)
    ISBN-10:   0-7642-0372-X (pbk.)
    1. French—United States—Fiction.   2. Self-realization—Fiction.   I. Title.

    PS3563.U839S44   2007
    813'.54—dc22   2007023562

This story is dedicated to my wonderful son, Christopher Alan Musser.

How incredibly thankful I am to be your mother!

God has gifted you with compassion and joy that are contagious and have so often spilled over into my life. Your love and humor have encouraged me on many, many days. What a delight to watch you grow up in Christ. I am so proud of you. Keep seeking Him and never fear. The best is yet to come. . . .

I love you,
Mom

ELIZABETH GOLDSMITH MUSSER, a native of Atlanta, Georgia, now living in France, is a novelist who writes what she calls "entertainment with a soul." Her novels have been acclaimed in the United States and in Europe. Her bestselling *The Swan House,* set in Atlanta in the early sixties, was named as one of Amazon's Top Christian Books of the Year (2001). Her French-Algerian trilogy, which takes place during Algeria's War for Independence from France (*Two Crosses, Two Testaments, Two Destinies*), has been a bestseller in Europe.

For over twenty years, Elizabeth and her husband, Paul, have been involved in missions work with International Teams. They presently live in Lyon, France. The Mussers have two sons.

To learn more about Elizabeth and her books, please visit her Web site at *www.elizabethmusser.com.*

| *prologue* |

*There is a time to
search and a time to
give up as lost . . .*

January 29, 1983, Nashville, Tennessee

I am watching the evening news, alone in my house,
hungry and tired from the day's work, eating a piece of leftover pizza
and wishing it were *blanquette de veau*. The story comes near the end
of the NBC program.

Jessica Savitch is standing in a town square, talking excitedly over
the commotion around her. "It appears that the infamous Butcher of
Lyon, Klaus Barbie, has been located here in La Paz, Bolivia. Living
under the assumed name of Klaus Altman, the former Nazi official
who was responsible for thousands of assassinations and deportations
during the Second World War has at last been located, after having
disappeared nearly forty years ago. . . ."

I try to concentrate on what she is saying, but my breathing is
coming hard. I scoot close to the screen, catch a glimpse of the monster, and shudder. Maybe now it can be over. Finally, it can be over.
For so many of them. For us. For me.

I dial the phone number in Atlanta automatically. "Mama, turn
on the news! Hurry!"

"We're watching, Emile," she whispers.

"Maybe finally we'll get more answers."

"Maybe, son. Time will tell."

I want to remind her that time does *not* tell. At least in this matter, time keeps secrets, many secrets. Twenty years of secrets.

Then it is Grandma Bridgeman's voice I hear in my mind, the voice of twenty years ago. *"Emile, you know there is more to life than looking for answers. Some answers you will never find—some you will. As long as the most important question is answered, the 'not knowing' of the others doesn't seem so unbearable."*

Of course I am thinking about *him*, but at the same time, I am thinking of *her*, wondering if she is down in Bolivia, if she helped them locate the Butcher. *"You may never see me again, Emile, but I will do this one thing for you. I promise."*

I cannot eat stale pizza or grade finals or anything else. I sit as if in a trance while the TV screen switches to a commercial.

I did what you said, Grandma. I gave it up. Left it for years. But it is back. I cannot ignore this.

I get off the couch, grab my raincoat, and head for the door as if I can just simply drive to the airport and catch a plane from Nashville to Bolivia.

What am I thinking? But I have to do something.

I go to the bedroom and take out a thin, hardback comic book, the size of a three-ring binder. Tintin, my boyhood hero. I let the book fall open to the middle, stare at the mutilated pages, cut in the shape of a knife, squeeze my eyes shut, and, as if in prayer, I say out loud, "Let it be over. Please let it be over."

———————

But it is not over. The next night Klaus Barbie's atrocities fill the TV news: "When somebody bombed Barbie's favorite restaurant, he had five prisoners machine-gunned and left their corpses on grisly display as a warning. When German airmen were shot nearby, Barbie opened an entire cell block as if to permit an escape. As the prisoners ran, all twenty-four were gunned down. . . ."

Somehow, having this man's heinous crimes displayed on national TV seems wrong—as if the pain that ripped my family apart is only an image on a screen, flickering and flat. No news report can measure the depth of the wound.

"As the war progressed toward Germany's defeat, Barbie lashed out at entire villages. Among his prime targets were Lyon's Jews, many of whom had fled to the region for sanctuary after the fall of Paris. Barbie's secretaries confiscated jewels and other valuables from people brought in for questioning. Many Jews never lived to see the Auschwitz train platform because Barbie packed them into cattle cars with no food or water. Since the trip took weeks, everyone died. The Germans had to wear gas masks to get rid of the bodies."

I do not want to hear any more. I turn off the TV and find the Tintin book—my escape mechanism. Perhaps I am wishing for another of my father's spy stories. How many times over the past years have I imagined him coming into my room with the comic book in hand, the switchblade concealed inside? But there will not be another story, of that I am sure.

Unless perhaps I tell it.

I sit down at my desk, open the book, and once again trace the outline of the cut pages with my fingers. I put a piece of typing paper in my old Smith Corona, advance the roller until the pure white paper appears.

I know how to begin the story, even though I have no idea how it will end. I begin to type. *Smack, smack, smack,* the keys hit the paper, staining it black with these words: *Searching for Eternity.*

PART I

*A Time to Plant, and a Time to
Uproot What Is Planted . . .*

| *one* |

"You will love America, son," my mother had always predicted. "Someday we'll go there, and you'll love it."

My French grandmother, I called her Mamie Madeleine, was less enthusiastic. "It's a land without history, proud and young with much to learn. Beware of America, Emile." Still, the day before I left my native France, she held her head high, the proud, harsh regard so familiar to me, and whispered through a tightening in her throat, "It will be all right, Emile. Be brave." She had kissed me twice, once on each cheek, and refused to shed one tear.

The next day my mother, Janie Bridgeman de Bonnery, and I boarded the Delta plane at the Orly airport with no one there to see us off. For the entire eight-hour flight, I did not utter one word to her, did not try to calm the fury pulsing in my temples, did not once think about how she might be feeling.

My mother was relieved, I was sure; she was escaping France, escaping an existence that had suffocated her for fifteen long years. I felt no pity for her. I felt only a gradual boiling anger that would have exploded if I had dared to open my mouth.

The way the plane landed at the Atlanta airport that late September day foreshadowed perfectly the next nine months of my life:

bumpy—so bumpy, in fact, that I reached for the pocket in front of me, grabbed the paper bag, and puked right in it.

"Emile, you're green!" my mother announced to the whole cabin of passengers.

"Gross!" offered the kid across the aisle.

I glared at my mother, no longer trying to disguise the fury I felt inside, and seethed to her in French, "It's all your fault! Everything is your fault!"

She knew I was referring to a lot more than my throwing up on a plane, but she said nothing in her defense. She just continued to turn a white handkerchief over and over in her lap, as if she could wring out the pent-up tension from the past few days.

I wish a voice had floated out of heaven as we were wildly vibrating up there in the plane and whispered, "Everything will be different now, Emile. Everything in your whole life is going to change."

I was two months shy of fourteen when I moved from France to America with my mother. I'd been waiting for change, hoping for it for the past year—to grow taller, to develop muscles, to find hair forming under my arms and above my upper lip. But on that particular day, as we stood in the Atlanta airport surrounded by mounds of luggage, I didn't want change. I wanted to run back to what I had always known, what was familiar and safe.

"For goodness' sake, Emile, help the man with the bags!" my mother ordered.

I glared at her and halfheartedly began retrieving pieces of luggage from the conveyor belt with the help of a black man in a blue uniform.

Mama lifted her share. Despite her size and manner—she looked like an ad for some French perfume in her pale yellow suit and high heels—my mother was a very determined lady. She shoved the suitcases, some almost half her size, along the floor to where the baggage man was haphazardly stacking them on a long metal pull-cart. We finally made it out the door to a waiting taxi.

"Ain't no way all this is gonna fit, ma'am," the porter offered a bit apologetically.

A round spot of deep crimson appeared on each of Mama's cheeks, her brow creased slightly, and she said, "Well, we'll just have to take two, then. Can you fit them into two taxis?"

"I can try, ma'am." He signaled for another taxi to pull over to the curb, and the three men began loading up the cars.

I stood on the curb, arms folded tightly across my chest, and watched.

When my mother was particularly upset, she'd bark out orders to anyone who would listen, all the while furiously tugging at one of her perfectly plucked blond eyebrows. On this day, she was tugging for all she was worth, intermittently wringing her hands. She was wearing her sunglasses—the ones that looked just like the glasses we'd seen Mrs. Kennedy wearing in all the photos since her husband had been shot a year ago in Dallas, Texas. Mama wore those glasses so that the whole world wouldn't know that she'd been crying—bawling her eyes out, if the truth be told—although you could still sort of tell, the way her nose was a little pinker than her cheeks and her lips trembled slightly.

I stood beside her, sweating and wondering what in the world I had come to.

"I'm sorry. It looks like you will have to leave France." Those were the words Mamie Madeleine had used the day before, her voice high and agitated, her eyes fierce but filling with tears, her hands trembling as I brought suitcases into the yard of the family estate—a thirteenth-century château that had been painstakingly restored through the years and handed down from generation to generation.

My father had disappeared, and we were going to America, my mother and I. Mama tried to explain. She held me tight and said, "Emile, I can't stay anymore. It's too hard. Your father . . . your father has found someone else, and . . ."

It had happened just like that. Two days later we were on the plane, along with thirty-three bags and boxes, my mother's face all swollen and red from crying and me yelling at her, "I don't want to leave! I will not leave. Papa will be back soon. He always comes back. I'm staying here!"

I didn't quit. "You don't force people out of their country all of a sudden! I won't go! I'll stay with Mamie Madeleine. I will not leave."

But it was no use. Although normally archenemies, the two women who ran my life had agreed on this one thing: my mother and I had to leave Lyon immediately.

My French father, Jean-Baptiste de Bonnery, had a long history of disappearing for weeks at a time. Mama always came up with some excuse about a business trip, but I was never fooled. Papa was a spy. He supposedly worked at a government office, directing people who made important decisions. But I had read enough detective stories to see that this was merely a cover-up.

"He's involved in counterespionage, isn't he, Mama?" I'd confronted her six months earlier. "I'm not a little kid anymore. You can tell me the truth."

She had stared at me, bewildered, then forced a laugh. "Emile, where you come up with your ideas, I'll never know. Quit reading those books and do something sensible, will you? Your father is away on a business trip and will be back in ten days."

Up until quite recently, she had always been right.

The porter was jamming bags into the trunk and back seat.

"We should have waited on him, Mama. He always comes back. Why is this time any different? Tell me!"

I shouldn't have spoken to her like that. If Papa had been there, he would have slapped me across the face for showing disrespect to my mother. But that was the whole point. He *wasn't* with us, and this time something *was* different. Still, I would not accept Mama's explanation.

All my life I'd believed her, so it seems ironic that the one time I had almost unshakeable proof that she was telling the truth, I didn't believe it. Surely she knew a lot more than she was telling me.

But I knew more than I was telling her, too. I knew more than I could bear to tell anyone. It didn't occur to me that this was hypocritical, keeping my secret from Mama while expecting her to reveal hers to me. I was on a mission to find out about my father, and everyone knew that a noble cause justified a few inconsistencies along the way.

I traipsed obediently out to the cars while Mama handed the driver an envelope with an address scribbled on the back. "Can you find this street? It's on the north side of town, I believe."

The black man tipped his hat and said, "Yes, ma'am. I'll getcha there."

She'd said it nonchalantly enough, but I could tell that Mama was relieved by his answer. My grandmother had moved since my mother left for France.

"And also," Mama added firmly, "we want to eat lunch at the Varsity on the way. Are you gonna charge me extra for sitting in the parking lot for fifteen minutes?"

He looked at Mama as if she'd asked him to pay for her plane ticket back to France, but before he could say anything she added, "I'll pay for y'all to have a frosted orange and fries, and you can order them at the curb."

"That'll be fine, then, ma'am," he answered with a smile and a shrug as he glanced at the other taxi driver.

The two taxis moved onto the freeway, and little by little the Atlanta skyline appeared outside the window. It was nothing like Lyon, with its two rivers that met in the south, shook hands, and continued together along the way. I saw no water at all near Atlanta, only four-lane highways and modern skyscrapers and cars. Lots of big, fancy cars.

My mother seemed undaunted by this big city. "We're going to get a bite to eat first, Emile," she told me as the taxi driver pulled into the vast parking lot of a restaurant painted red and yellow, with a tall vertical sign that read *The Varsity*. It was midafternoon in America, but my stomach thought it was nighttime, and food was the last thing that interested me.

"Honk the horn, for heaven's sake," she called to the driver so the other taxi driver caught sight of her wildly signaling him to turn into the lot. Mama and I got out of the car and went inside.

"This is called the world's largest drive-in restaurant," Mama explained. "For years you could only order from the carhops at the curb, but now you can order inside, too."

The restaurant—if you could call it that—was loud and crammed with people and smelled of grease. I'd never been to a restaurant where I had to wait in line to order my food, but Mama directed me as if she'd been doing this all her life. Despite my lack of appetite, I was intrigued by the prospect of American food.

An enormous black woman wearing a red paper hat with *The Varsity* written on it leaned over the tall counter and said, "What'll ya have?"

My eyes grew wide, and I thought at first she must be speaking a different language. I mumbled "Excuse me" in English, my face turning red, and she repeated the same unintelligible phrase.

I glanced at my mother, feeling panicky, sure that she too must be baffled. Instead, she laughed for the first time in days, smiled good-naturedly at the woman, and said, "Emile, tell the lady what you want to order."

When no sound came out of my mouth, my mother pointed to a board behind the counter that advertised the menu. She whispered, "It's not like France, Emile. But you'll get used to it," and she ordered for me. "A hamburger, onion rings, and a Coca-Cola."

She pronounced the words slowly in English—as if she could already taste the food and it was delicious—which confirmed to me that, in spite of her tears and trembling lips, my mother was still relieved to be back in her hometown.

"I couldn't understand what she was saying, Mama," I complained when we'd taken our seat at another long counter and perched ourselves on two black vinyl-cushioned stools.

"Don't worry, Emile. It just takes getting used to."

The lunch was unlike anything I had ever tasted. My father often poked fun good-naturedly at American food, but when he was away on a business trip, my mother would fix fried chicken or something else fried, so that I'd acquired a taste for some Southern food. But this was so greasy that my hands looked sweaty after I'd picked up a handful of the onion rings.

I nibbled at the hamburger and swallowed one of the rings whole, washing it down with a gulp of Coke. The same queasy feeling I'd had on the plane twittered in my stomach, so I excused myself, following the sign proclaiming *Restrooms* that hung at the end of the long hall. On the door in bold black letters was written *Whites Only*. That struck me as odd because some of the waiters were black.

When I got back to the table, I asked my mother, "Where do black people go to the bathroom?"

Mama seemed flustered for a moment, then she shrugged and said, "Things are different here, Emile. I'll tell you about it later. Finish your lunch. I don't want you showing up at your grandmother's house starving."

She didn't have to explain anything, I thought. It was obvious: in America, white people thought they were superior to black people.

"Time to go, Emile," she said, and she stood up and walked down the hall of the restaurant. The taxi drivers were standing beside their cars, munching on French fries and talking with each other. They seemed happy enough with the bargain.

As soon as we were out of the parking lot she started rummaging through her purse. She pulled out a small case of rouge and peered into the tiny mirror.

"Are you nervous, Mama?" I asked.

She gave a forced little laugh and said, "Well, Emile, I guess I am. I haven't seen your grandmother in fifteen years."

So that was that. After fifteen years of silence, my mother appeared at her mother's door with a thirteen-year-old son, thirty-three pieces of luggage, and no warning.

My grandmother's house sat back from the wide shaded road on a slight hill, the front yard an expanse of green grass and tall trees. The breeze made it look as if the trees were waving to me, welcoming me to their house. In fact, that is how my grandmother's house looked— comfortable and at ease, like someone you wanted to get to know better, someone who was inviting you over to play.

The exterior was covered with gray shingles. French houses were made of cement bricks covered with stucco or of stones dating back to the Middle Ages. On the left side of the shingled house was a projection that Mama called a screened porch. It looked like a happy, airy place, a compromise between being inside and outside.

The two taxis pulled into the driveway and cut the motors. Mama didn't budge for a minute.

Serves her right to be terrified, I thought.

Finally, when the driver looked back at her, she gave a deep sigh and said, "Well, let's see if she's home. Come on, Emile."

I followed her along the gray flagstone path winding from the driveway to the steps that led up to the entrance. Mama hesitated again, then pulled open a screened door, something I'd never seen in France, and knocked on the door behind it. She gave me a thin smile, wiped a finger under her sunglasses, and waited.

The woman who opened the door was pleasantly plump—one of Mama's American expressions—with gray hair pulled up off her neck. Not only was she pleasantly plump, but to me she looked just simply pleasant. She was wiping her hands on a faded apron, not really paying much attention to who was at the door, when Mama said, "Hello, Mother."

My grandmother let out a soft cry. "Janie! What in the world. . .!" Then she burst into tears and reached out to her long-lost daughter.

It looked to me like Mama wilted there by the white door, letting herself be drawn into her mother's hug. I thought she'd be stiff and proud, the way she'd always described herself as a teenager, mad at her mother. But here she was, crying right along with the stranger in the apron and wiping a handkerchief across her eyes and paying no attention to the black smears her mascara was making on the handkerchief and on her face.

She kept saying, "I'm sorry, Mother. I'm so sorry. I wasn't very good at answering your letters. But I read them all and kept every one. I'm so sorry. And now here we are."

My grandmother took my face in her hands. "Emile. You must be Emile. Oh, Janie. Your son," she whispered softly. "Your beautiful child."

My French grandmother was a woman whom I respected, but I had a feeling right away that my American grandmother was a woman I could love. She would have rocked me on her lap when I was little, I thought, and baked me cookies and read me storybooks. I liked her immediately, and knew that if we were going to survive this change of cultures, it would be because of her.

Mama was sniffing and wiping her eyes and folding up her sunglasses. "There's so much to explain, Mother . . ." she began.

"That can wait, Janie. Let's get your belongings inside."

"Then it's okay if we stay with you for a few days? Just until we get things worked out?"

"Of course, Janie. Of course you can stay here."

Soon the hallway was filled up with our suitcases and bags, and Mama was handing the two taxi drivers a wad of green bills, which I knew were American dollars.

We walked through the hallway into a room my grandmother called the den. It was filled with worn, comfortable furniture, a fireplace, and best of all, lots of books, arranged in no particular order—paperback novels next to ancient books with leather covers. They filled the shelves on either side of the fireplace.

"Have a seat, please," this grandmother said.

I could tell she had a thousand questions in her eyes, but she didn't ask any of them.

"Now, Emile, you must be starving. Can I get you a glass of milk and a peanut butter and jelly sandwich? Just the thing for a growing boy."

I looked warily at Mama, who smiled at me and gave a wink.

"That sounds great, Mother. But you have to realize that Emile doesn't know a thing about peanut butter and jelly."

My grandmother looked shocked and pretended to be horrified. "Really? Imagine that!"

"We don't have peanut butter in France. Children eat baguettes stuffed with chocolate for their snacks."

"Well, I'm afraid I'm fresh out of baguettes and chocolate, Emile." There was a twinkle in my grandmother's eyes.

I almost grinned in spite of myself and, although my stomach was still trying to recover from the onion rings, I said, "That's okay. May I try the sandwich, please?"

I followed her into her kitchen and took a seat at a small, white rectangular table, and soon the sandwich appeared on a blue and white plate in front of me. I examined it, pulling apart the two squares of flat, white bread so that I could see the contents inside. The peanut butter looked like a darker colored *paté*, the goose liver my French grandmother bought at the market each week. It was smeared with something deep violet in color, smooth, shiny, and jiggling, that came from a jar labeled *Welch's Grape Jelly*. I was suspicious. In France, grapes were used for wine. This substance certainly didn't resemble the jellies and jams that Mamie Madeleine made with fresh fruits and berries from her garden.

"American food is processed, Emile. You never know what you're putting in your mouth." I could hear Mamie Madeleine's warning as I placed the squares back together and hesitantly took my first bite. In France, it was a very big sin to combine something sweet like jelly with something salty like peanut butter. But the moment my taste buds were introduced to peanut butter and jelly, I decided that for this at least, I was glad to be in America.

"Well, let me show you to your rooms," my grandmother said.

Mama and I followed her up the curving wooden staircase. There were two bedrooms on either side of a long hall that overlooked the stairway.

"Here you go, Emile. This can be your room."

I was amazed that with absolutely no warning my grandmother could have a room ready in her house. In Lyon, it was always a great affair to have *des invités* even for a meal; it was a feat that took the better part of a week to prepare for. But here was my grandmother offering me a completely furnished room and saying, "I hope you'll be comfortable here. I'm sorry for the wallpaper."

I wondered then, *Maybe this grandmother has been waiting for fifteen years for her daughter to come back home. Maybe this room has been waiting just for this moment.*

There were little yellow flowers on the wallpaper and, hanging on the walls, framed prints by great French artists I had studied in school—Monet and Pissarro and Toulouse-Lautrec—along with framed photos of my mother when she was young. The bed looked like it was meant for a little girl—with a yellow bedspread and a frilly white canopy above.

"You can put your clothes in the closet here," my grandmother said, motioning to the doors on either side of the bed.

As I set down one of my suitcases on the floor, she added, "There is a little attic space beside the dormer window. You can use that, too."

"Thank you, madame," I said as she turned to leave.

She turned back around, took my hands in hers, and said, "And you can call me Grandma, if you'd like."

"Thank you, Grandma," I repeated. I liked the taste of that word on my lips—maybe even better than a peanut butter and jelly sandwich.

What Grandma called the dormer window turned out to be a vertical window in a projection built out from the sloping roof. The result on the inside of my room was a little alcove where a desk had been built in under the window. I stared out this window at the front yard, its tall trees, and the wide street beyond with the sidewalk where a young woman was pushing a baby carriage.

I sat down on the bed, feeling suddenly very sleepy. *I'll just lie down for a minute,* I told myself, listening to my mother's and grandmother's voices disappearing down the hall. But my eyes closed themselves, and before I knew it I was dreaming of an old château and a different grandmother and my father, walking away in the distance, glancing over his shoulder to warn me, "Emile, watch out for those peanut butter and jelly sandwiches."

When I awoke, the late afternoon sun was coming in the dormer window and the room felt stuffy. Groggily I opened my eyes and went out of the room and across the hall where I found my mother in a similar position to what mine had been moments ago, lying fully clothed on the bed, sound asleep. I tiptoed back toward the stairs and went down to find my other suitcases in the pile that the taxi driver had left by the front door. Grandma was nowhere in sight, so I carried the bags upstairs and decided to start unpacking.

Carefully I removed neat stacks of clothing from my biggest suitcase until I uncovered my set of Tintin comic books in the bottom. There were nine of them, hardback, each the size of a three-ring binder. I always pretended that I was a lot like Tintin, the young hero—small and resourceful with a mind that wanted to solve mysteries. I used to think that if only I had a dog like Tintin's trusty Milou, all would be just perfect.

I put the books on a low shelf beside the dormer window. Then, after closing the door, I began removing the clothes from the next suitcase and unwrapping what I thought of as "my collection." I placed each item on the bed. First there were the old yellowed newspapers, then the thumbtack tin, the writing pen, and the bicycle pump. Next I lifted out a small oilcan and a wooden hairbrush and one more comic book.

I studied the yellow room for a good place to hide these things. Mama could not know that I had brought them. She had never approved of them in the first place.

———

Mama strode into the room where Papa and I were seated on my bed, and grabbed the oilcan from me.

"I thought we agreed you wouldn't give him any more gifts like this for his birthday! Are you crazy, Jean-Baptiste? I will *not* have Emile touching these things. You will not train him to be a revolutionary!"

"Janie, please, calm down! He's a boy. Boys need a little adventure."

"He's nine. Nine years old, do you hear me? He's a child. I will not have you influencing him with your gruesome war stories. I will not!"

I watched wide-eyed as they exchanged heated words, my father's in French, my mother, as always, replying in tearful English, her lips trembling with rage. I was furious with her for interrupting one of the few private times I had with my father. Eventually he calmed her down, assuring her he would not corrupt her darling son, but even I could hear the condescension in his voice, and the humor, too.

From then on, I kept the oilcan and the other strange birthday gifts Papa had given to me, starting when I was about five and continuing on every birthday since, hidden from Mama. I don't think she ever saw them, and she certainly never heard the stories that Papa shared with me in hushed tones.

———

I went over to the dormer window, bent down, pulled on a small brass knob, and opened the little door that was part of the wall, revealing an attic-like space that apparently ran the length of the house until it reached another dormer window in the bedroom down the hall. I took each article on the bed, placed them all in one of my smaller, empty suitcases, and carefully carried the suitcase, holding it out flat in front of me, over to the window. Then I set it inside the attic space, satisfied that my greatest treasures had made it from France to America and were safely out of sight. Mama didn't know it, but I was sure that this collection was going to lead us back to my father.

Then I reached into my pants pocket and pulled out a wristwatch, a cheap, old timepiece that nevertheless was ticking. I turned it over in my hands, gripped it hard, and then dropped it onto the bed. My throat went dry. I picked the watch up again, thinking *He didn't even have a chance to explain it.*

Just three days earlier, Papa had come into my room before I went to bed, ruffled my hair, and said, "Happy Birthday, *mon grand.*"

"But my birthday is two months away, Papa."

He stared at me for a moment, his pale blue eyes translucent, his thick black hair falling on his forehead. He looked pained. "Yes, I know," he whispered, taking a small wrapped box from his suit pocket. "This year it's coming early."

Quickly I tore off the wrapping, excited, intrigued. The box held a watch, a very plain watch with a leather wristband.

"Thank you, Papa. Thank you."

"It still works, Emile. Still tells time as well as it did back in 1943."

"And I can keep it?"

"Of course. You can wear it if you want." He forced a smile.

I waited expectantly for the story. Every year, when Papa presented me with my "real gift," the one I dreamt about for weeks before my birthday, he would reveal to me another part of his harrowing past.

I don't know why telling me horrific stories about the war made him feel at ease, but his manner changed on those nights. He relived his past with all the pride and joy of a teenager bragging to his friends.

But this night Papa said nothing for the longest time. He fingered the watch and then caressed my face, his lips drawn into a thin, tight line. Again he looked pained.

I turned the watch over and over in my hands, trying to summon the courage to ask him about it. Suddenly there was a knock on the door. Without thinking, I thrust the watch into my father's hands, and he put it back into his pocket.

"Jean-Baptiste," my mother said, cracking the door open. "I'm sorry to disturb you, but you have a call . . ."

"Just take a message, Janie, and I'll call back."

I let out a sigh of relief. The phone call would not interrupt my special time with Papa.

But my mother didn't go away. Instead she came over by the bed and whispered, "Dear, I think it's important. A man named Rémi said to tell you he is very sorry to bother us at this hour, but it's about a shipment—"

Before my mother even finished the sentence, Papa was on his feet. "Janie, tell him I'm coming."

All I could manage to say was, "But, Papa!"

He closed the door, came back to the bed, and knelt down, his face filled with remorse.

"So I won't hear the story tonight, Papa?"

I could see his chest heaving, see the way he swallowed. "No, not tonight, son." His voice was raspy, as if he were going to sob.

I felt a mixture of alarm and pride at his emotional reaction.

Then he did something he had never done before. He grabbed me and held me in a tight hug. "Emile, I have to leave again."

"You just got home."

"Yes, I know, but I'm going to have to leave."

"When?"

"Tomorrow, before you are even awake."

"It's okay, Papa. You can tell me the story when you get back."

"Yes." But this he said as if choking. "You're almost fourteen, Emile. Almost a man. You take good care of your mother while I'm gone, you hear?"

"Sure, Papa."

He held me for a moment longer, then kissed the top of my head and left the room.

It was only later that I realized he had not given me back the watch.

I must have drifted off to sleep then, because suddenly I was awakened by the sound of crying and muffled words—angry words. It was pitch-black outside. I tiptoed out of bed and listened by my door. My parents' room was down the hall.

My mother was crying, my father was talking forcefully. "Janie, you must calm down—it will be better for everyone. You mustn't lose control. Please."

The talking and crying continued for a good while, but I could make nothing else out.

I finally crawled back into bed and fell asleep. The next morning, my father was gone.

I went to school and was thankful that we had a field trip planned to visit the Roman ruins and museum near Vieux Lyon. I had seen them several times, but I enjoyed history, and I knew it would keep my mind occupied.

We walked down one of the cobbled pedestrian streets in Vieux Lyon. The sun was bright, a perfect early autumn day, and my friends and I joked and laughed and teased the girls. People all along the streets were sitting in outdoor cafés, eating and drinking.

As we sauntered past a café, I stopped dead in my tracks, letting my friends go ahead. At a table not twenty feet from me sat my father. I could see his profile. He was wearing the same business suit as the night before, but the worried expression was completely erased. He was smiling, leaning forward, thoroughly enjoying himself as he talked to a young woman across the table, his hand on top of hers. Something in his manner was terrible and intimate.

I had not seen my father look like this in a long time—carefree, happy. I felt a falling sensation in the pit of my stomach and thought I would vomit. I stood there, unable to move. I wanted to greet him, call out at least, but my dread was too great.

For one brief second our eyes met, my father's and mine. His showed great surprise—but only for a second—and then studied indifference, as if I didn't exist, as if he had never seen me before in his life. Through that one calculated glance, I heard him shouting in my ears *Go away! Go away!* and I ran to catch up with my friends.

I knew about mistresses. France's history was peppered with spicy stories about them. All the kings of old had them. But somehow I could not fathom that my father had one, and that I had just seen her.

I felt the sharp pangs of betrayal, remembered my father's tight hug from the night before, the look of love in his eyes—and now, the look of indifference, complete unconcern.

Still, I was sure he would come into my room that night and explain it all to me. He had not gone on the trip—he had run into an old friend, just a friend, and they had lunch together. He would explain it, I knew.

But my father did not return, and the next day my mother packed our bags, and the following day we were at the Lyon train station, headed to Paris and then America.

At the train station Mamie Madeleine, eyes red, face tight, gave me another round of kisses on the cheeks and handed me a small box. "This is for you, Emile."

As the train sped toward Paris, I opened it and found my father's watch.

I fingered it now as hot tears ran down my cheeks. I was almost fourteen years old and acting as if I were five. There was no mystery to why we were in America. Anybody could figure it out. My father had a mistress; my mother found out, and she wanted to escape. Or perhaps she had known about his affairs for a long time, and she had finally had enough.

Poor Mama. I should have felt sorry for her, but all I wanted right then was to hurry back to Lyon and find my father and listen as he told me a riveting story about his days in the war and why he had given me this wristwatch two months before I turned fourteen.

I followed Mama from room to room on that first afternoon, both of us moving in slow motion. I helped her unpack her
bags, watched her eyes, normally pale blue and defensive, now tinged
with red, and wondered what she would whisper to my grandmother
after I went upstairs to bed. I could not imagine why they had not
talked in fifteen years or why now, sitting side by side on the worn
sofa, they seemed so much at ease, why my grandmother seemed to
hold no bitterness toward her daughter or why Mama offered no
explanation for all the silent years.

It wasn't that we couldn't afford to travel to America. My father's
was a real bourgeois family; they had enough money for the whole city
of Lyon. But never had we gotten on a plane and flown to America,
and all the stories of my mother's past life were superficial and quickly
told.

That first night at my grandmother's house, I fell asleep around
nine o'clock, but then awoke in the early hours of the morning. After
I had read several of my Tintin comic books and gone through the
names of every soccer player on the French national team at least five
times, I was still wide awake, the little ticking alarm clock on the table
by my bed proclaiming one o'clock.

I tiptoed down the winding stairs, gripping the smooth wooden railing, and wandered into the entrance hall. I stood by the archway that led into the den, surprised to hear voices talking softly.

"So he doesn't believe you?"

"No. He won't accept that his father has . . . has someone else."

"Really, Janie, he must have suspected something all along. He's old enough and intelligent. Surely he has noticed—"

I sneezed, unfortunately, and Mama turned a startled face toward the door.

"Emile, what are you doing here? I thought you were in bed!"

"I woke up and couldn't get back to sleep. I tried reading and dreaming of soccer and a hundred other things. I'm sorry."

"Well, that's perfectly normal—it's exactly what happened to your mother," Grandma interjected. "Jet lag is terrible. Always takes me a few days to recover."

"Have you been on a plane, Grandma?" Somehow my grandmother, with her pinned-back gray hair and blue bathrobe, did not seem like a world traveler.

My mother and grandmother exchanged glances, Mama's eyes darting from one thing to another, as was her habit when she was worried.

"Well, of course I've been on a plane, Emile. I've been on quite a few."

I wanted to ask why she'd never come to see us then, why this was the first day in all my life that I'd met her, but something stopped me. Maybe it was my mother's ashen face, or the way Grandma held out her arms to me so that I sat down beside her on the couch and felt immediately comfortable. At any rate, I didn't ask.

But in my mind I was asking loud and clear, *Where is my father and why have I never met you before and what was my mother telling you about that pretty woman in the café?*

I didn't fall back asleep until half past five, and when I awoke, the hands of the little clock proclaimed ten-thirty. I felt as if I had suddenly gained fifty pounds, and I could not lift any of this new weight from the bed. After another thirty minutes of dozing and wrestling with that annoying heaviness, I finally struggled from bed, found the bathroom, threw cold water on my face, and stared at my reflection in the mirror above the sink.

At almost fourteen, I looked more like ten, maybe eleven at most. I was a head shorter than any of the kids in my class. Plus I was skinny and pale-skinned with very blond, curly hair, something you don't see a lot of in France. On this morning, the hair on one side of my head was flat where I must have lain mashed against the pillow, but on the other side the blond curls stuck out, giving me the look of a lopsided Bozo, the circus clown Mama told me about as a child. My blue eyes were streaked with red.

It was no mystery where I got my looks. One glance at my mother, and you saw an older, female version of me. She was the perfect *petite*—if she had never opened her mouth, she could have been French, with her tiny figure and fashionable clothes. But her size and style were the only things that worked for her in France. She did open her mouth, way too often, in my opinion and that of Mamie Madeleine. She had an ugly accent, one that was learned on the spot as an adult, with no formal training—she had studied Spanish in school. It hurt my ears and made me squirm when she addressed my friends. She had a temper that flared when criticized. And unfortunately for my mother, almost everything she did in France was criticized.

When I walked into the kitchen, my mother and grandmother were sitting at the white table, steaming cups of coffee in front of them.

"Good morning, Emile," Grandma said pleasantly. "Poor dear, did you finally get to sleep?"

"Yes, thank you."

"Are you hungry?"

"Yes, I am."

"What would you like?"

"Anything will be fine," I said.

"Your grandmother went to the store bright and early this morning and bought you some cereal, Emile," Mama said, as if warning me that I'd better like it.

Soon I was dipping my spoon hesitantly into a bowl filled with cold milk and what Grandma called "kids' cereal." It tasted as if I was just spooning liquefied sugar into my mouth and slurping it down. I didn't much care for the cold milk or the cereal or the orange juice that Grandma made by opening a little can of frozen stuff, emptying the icy chunk into a pitcher, adding water, and stirring until the orange ice became liquid. This, to me, did not seem much like orange juice, but I drank it just the same.

Grandma was saying, "It's probably the best thing to get Emile into school, Janie, even if classes started up a month ago. It will help him feel more settled."

"That's what I was thinking, except . . . what about all the trouble with desegregation? We read about the murders in Mississippi last month. Made the front page of Lyon's newspaper."

"There is a lot of bad stuff going on. Fortunately Mayor Allen has handled things well in Atlanta. He's very sympathetic to the plight of the Negroes."

"Too bad there aren't more like him."

"Yes."

My mother raised an eyebrow. "Do you agree with him?"

Grandma put down her coffee cup slowly, deliberately, and looked at my mother. "Yes, Janie. Now I do. It's been very gradual, over the past ten years. It was after your father's heart attack, after we moved here. I couldn't see it before."

My mother eyed her own mother suspiciously. Then her eyes got teary again and she said, "I wanted to come for the funeral. I . . . I . . . tried, but . . . it got complicated." She sniffed. "And then it was too late."

"Yes. I gathered," Grandma said in a suddenly subdued voice.

I wasn't sure whose funeral they were talking about, but I guessed it was my grandfather's. It must have been a sensitive subject because Mama let it go and asked, "Are the schools here integrated?"

"No, but a few Negro families have tried to enroll their children in white schools. It hasn't gone over well. It hasn't even been an issue at the school Emile will attend—you know, Northside. Not yet, at least. Go on and register him, Janie. It'll be hard at first, I know." Now she was addressing me. "You'll have to get used to all your schooling being in English—everything will seem different for a while. But you'll do fine."

"Of course he'll do fine. He's survived the French school system; why wouldn't he do well here?"

"And don't you worry about your accent, Emile. Young people can be so unkind. Maybe they won't—but you'd best be prepared."

Although I read and understood English well, I knew I had a very pronounced French accent, which was a shame to my father. He said that with a mother who was American, my English should be impeccable, and had sent me to the best schools to make sure it was. But since I spoke almost solely French at home, even answering my mother in French when she addressed me in English, the strong, stubborn accent had remained.

"Don't you worry, Emile," Mama said. "Soon you'll sound just like everyone else."

But that was the problem. I didn't want to sound American. I missed France, the fresh *baguettes* in the morning that we smeared with real butter, and the *confiture* that my grandmother had made from the apricots and plums on the trees in her orchards, and the yogurts of a thousand kinds.

I felt the familiar anger inside and cursed my mother silently. I was determined to discover why we had fled, and I was afraid—very, very afraid—when Mama assured me that I would get used to America.

How could she! She wants to wipe away the last fifteen years of her life.

I was not about to wipe away anything. When I looked in the bathroom mirror after breakfast as I was brushing my teeth, what I imagined was my father's face—my father, the perfect Frenchman, with the prominent nose pointed down at the end, the high forehead, the coffee brown eyes accentuated by thick black brows. Then my father's face changed, wearing the tense, remorseful look of four nights earlier, the look that replaced all cynicism and confidence. I imagined him lying dead, shot through the heart, somewhere in an alleyway of Lyon.

I looked in the mirror again and saw that woman's face, her dark, laughing eyes, her black hair falling casually over her shoulders, her delicate hand under my father's. I saw the look of surprise and then indifference on Papa's face.

Liar! Traitor! I screamed in my mind. I was not going to get used to America. I was going to get on a plane and head back to Lyon to find my father—and the other woman if I had to. The look of remorse and then of devotion and love that I had seen in Papa's eyes that night could not be replaced by indifference in sixteen short hours. My father loved me; the wristwatch was proof.

He knew he was meeting the woman. He planned it all and sent Mama away.

I wondered if the dark-haired woman was sitting in front of the fireplace in the *salon* of Mamie's château. I wondered if her head was resting on Papa's shoulder. I wondered if Mamie Madeleine stood in the doorway watching, secretly approving, relieved to be rid of my mother at last.

———

The next day was Sunday. At a little after nine o'clock Grandma ushered us out of the house and into her old green and white Chevrolet to go to church. My mother was dressed up in her pretty peach suit with the little matching hat with the funny veil on the front and white gloves. She forced me to wear a pair of khaki trousers with a suit coat that was two sizes too small and a tie that might have been fished out of the back of Grandma's closet—something from the 1940s, I imagined with a grimace.

I thought the whole business extremely odd. We had never gone to church in Lyon. Occasionally we went to Mass at the Catholic church in Caluire. We'd sit stiff and uncomfortable on the wooden pews in the dank cathedral and listen to the priest drone on and on. Fortunately for me, this only happened two or three times a year, at Christmas and Easter and maybe some other special occasion.

It annoyed me to have to go to church, especially when Grandma could plainly see that I wasn't over jet lag. I don't think it mattered to her that I'd be fighting to keep my eyes open. "Going to church" was clearly something that happened way too often for my grandmother, maybe even every week. I was sure that Mama would explain that we were good Catholics now, and we weren't very interested in going to a Protestant service.

But she said nothing, and Grandma Bridgeman announced that I was going to Sunday school. She led me through a maze of carpeted halls and down some stairs to a classroom, where she deposited me with ten other boys and girls about my age and said, "We'll find you in an hour."

This was the first and perhaps only mean thing my grandmother ever did to me.

I didn't doze off at Sunday school or during the church service afterwards. I found it fascinating, this big Baptist church with its white steeple, wine-colored carpet, and choir all dressed in wine-colored robes, sitting expressionless behind the pulpit. The funny pastor boomed out a sermon, his face getting all splotchy and red when he talked about the "wages of sin" and the "threat of eternal condemnation." It was almost like attending a play.

The strangest part was "taking the Lord's Supper." This was something like receiving the Sacrament, only we didn't file to the front of the church where a priest would put a thin wafer on our tongues. Instead we passed around a plate of tiny little squares of hard crackers. This was Jesus' body. Each of us was supposed to pick up a square and hold it until everyone had been served. Then we stuck it in our mouths and pretended not to chew it while the pastor mumbled a prayer.

Next was Jesus' blood, only in the Baptist church in Atlanta, His blood was passed around in little individual glass cups—Mamie Madeleine would have called them "jiggers" and served some strong *digestif* in them. At the cathedral only the priest was allowed to take a sip of Jesus' blood from a silver chalice, but I'm pretty sure it tasted like wine. In Atlanta His blood tasted all sugary, like the grape juice that Grandma had given me for breakfast that morning.

All kinds of people came up to greet us after the service, saying things like, "Oh, Maggie! Your daughter and her son!" "So good to meet you, Janie and Emile. We've heard so much about you!" "All the way from France! My, my!" Or occasionally to my mother, "Janie

Bridgeman, well, I never! It's good to see you after all these years. And this must be your son."

And Mama just played right along, a big smile on her lips, extending her hand in its white glove and saying in her Georgia accent that was much more pronounced than in France, "It's great to see you again, too. Yes, thank you."

And I would shake the men's hands and wonder if I should kiss the cheeks of the women when I was introduced, as every French child knew to do. But according to my mother, I was just supposed to say "Pleased to meet you," and let it go at that.

I heard several women giggle to each other, their gloved hands in front of their mouths, "Isn't that so dear, his cute little French accent," or "Well, it doesn't look like Janie Bridgeman brought that dashing French husband of hers home with her, does it?"

Later that afternoon, as we sat on her porch drinking her sugary iced tea, Grandma asked, "How was Sunday school, Emile?"

I squirmed. "Well, I guess it was interesting."

"Were the children nice to you?"

"Okay, I guess." I wasn't about to tell her what it had really been like.

First of all, they weren't children. They were teenagers. And no, they weren't nice. I sat alone, an empty chair on each side of me, as if I had a contagious disease. The boys looked twice my size and the girls all looked mature, what Mama called "well-developed."

"Some of you know Mrs. Bridgeman. This is her grandson, who has moved from France to live with her—Ameel," the teacher had announced in her thick drawl.

Two girls giggled; one of the boys rolled his eyes.

"Tell us a little about yourself, Ameel," the teacher pursued.

I stared at her, horrified. The absolute last thing I had planned to do was open my mouth. I couldn't speak. The room grew stuffy.

"How old are you?" asked a boy named Ace.

"Thirteen."

The girls giggled again. Ace gave a muffled laugh and whispered loudly to his buddies, *"Serrrteen!"*

"You should be in the eighth-grade class. This is for ninth grad-ers," a boy named Billy added.

The teacher seemed oblivious to my humiliation and merely said, "You'll stay with us today, Ameel, and we're happy to have you."

I vowed to myself that I'd never go back to that class.

But to Grandma Bridgeman I just said, "It was interesting."

"Well, I'm glad it was interesting, Emile. You'll have a lot of friends in no time. You'll see."

––––––––––

The dreaded day came way too soon: my first day of school in America. Mama enrolled me on Monday, and on Tuesday morning she drove me to the school in Grandma's Chevrolet.

Northside High School was a long, red-brick building, three sto-ries high with big glass windows that looked out onto a street appro-priately called Northside Drive. Seven hundred students from eighth through twelfth grade went to this school. I was in ninth grade in France, so Mama enrolled me in the same grade in America. I guess it never occurred to her to consider that the way kids were placed in grades, by their birthdays, was different in France, and I would have doubtless fit better in eighth grade, what was called "sub-freshman" at Northside. After all, I looked more like a seventh grader.

But Mama had not thought these things through. She drove me to school that first day, speaking in her no-nonsense manner. "Your homeroom teacher is Miss Holloway, Emile. I've already spoken to her, and she sounds competent. She'll see to it that you get to your classes and have the right books."

Mama seemed to think that because she had attended high school in Atlanta, I had automatically inherited her knowledge of how things worked. I would have rather spent five days in itching agony with the chicken pox than to walk through the front doors of that school, but I wasn't about to say that to her.

I shuffled into the classroom just as the bell was ringing and went immediately to the desk at the front of the room, where Miss Hollo-way was seated. She wore a dark blue suit and a pinched smile on her round, inquisitive face, and looked as if she could have been a high school student herself, fresh and pretty and inexperienced.

"Hello, madame," I squeaked out. "I'm Emile. Emile de Bonnery."

"Oh, yes! Ameel. How nice to meet you. Your mother and I have spoken. Just stay here with me."

I winced at her pronunciation of my name with the long exaggerated syllables, and waited awkwardly by her desk.

Miss Holloway stood up and addressed the students. "Now, class, I want you all to meet our new classmate. This is A-meel Dee-Bonneree." She looked at me apologetically and said, "I'm sorry, I'm not too good in French."

Then back to the class. "He's come all the way from France. Everybody know where France is? Now I hope you will all be real nice to him, this being a new school and a new country for him."

I could feel the way my face turned crimson, as if I had gotten instant sunburn. Every boy in the room, about fifteen of them, stared at me blankly, as if they were bored by my presence, and the girls giggled and whispered among themselves. I was relieved when Miss Holloway let me sit down at a little wooden desk in the front row.

When the bell rang to end homeroom, Miss Holloway said, "Ameel, I've asked Judy Armsted to show you to your next class. She has science with you."

Before I could even locate Judy, three boys came up to me. Two of them, Ace and Billy, had been in my Sunday school class.

Ace, two heads taller than I and twice as thick, his blond hair in a crew cut, jabbed me in the chest with his finger. "Great to see you again, A-meel. Guess you just couldn't figure out what we meant by eighth grade. This is no place for a runt like you." He motioned with his head, and he and his friends sauntered down the hall as if the school belonged to them.

Judy found me standing in the busy hallway, staring after the boys. She asked, "Ameel, you okay? You look kinda white."

I shrugged.

"Well, follow me then. The science room is in the other building. And the teacher, Mrs. Hunt, is soooo boring. . . ."

Four hours later, my stomach growling and my head swimming

with way too much English, I followed several kids to the cafeteria.

Another boy from homeroom, Teddy, gave me a punch in the shoulder. "Hey there, A-Meal! I bet all you ever think about is food. Your mama must've thought it was real fine since she named you 'A Meal'!"

Half a dozen other boys heard him, and they all snickered together. As I walked through the cafeteria, Ace, Billy, and Teddy followed, chanting obnoxiously, "A meal! A meal! A meal!"

I guess every country has its bullies, I thought.

Standing in a long line of students who were all jabbering and laughing, I had never felt quite so alone. I told myself that my goal that day was to observe very carefully so I wouldn't do something stupid and draw even more attention to myself.

I slowly approached the section of the lunchroom where each student was picking up a plain brown tray, a fork, knife, and spoon, and a paper napkin. I did the same. We stood in line at a long counter that contained deep rectangular trays filled with food, and a hefty lady in a white apron on the other side of the counter ladled heaps of mashed potatoes and some kind of meat with a thick brown sauce onto my plate. Next came the green beans and a funny soft roll, hot and pleated in the middle, placed there by another apron-clad woman who was much smaller in size.

I mumbled *"Merci"* without thinking and saw her surprised look.

We had exactly twenty minutes to eat. At my school in France all the children went home for lunch, and we had a long leisurely meal with our parents.

Holding my tray in my hands, I stood examining the lunchroom. The boys were beside me again, chanting, "A Meal, A Meal!"

"Leave me alone!" I hissed without thinking.

They burst into laughter. "Leaf me alhone," they mimicked. "Say it again, A Meal. That's great!"

It suddenly struck me how my mother must have felt all those years. She had moved to France when she was pregnant with me, and at the time she knew only a handful of French expressions that she'd picked up from my father. She spoke French fine now, but she would often start a sentence in French and end it in English. *"Mon fils! Il faut* get washed up for dinner. Quick."

It had never occurred to me that this was a strange way to talk, mixing together two languages. Now, hearing Ace's cruel taunts, I wanted to run home and listen to her charming *franglais* for the rest of the day.

The girl was sitting alone at a table in the lunchroom. I saw her first from the back, her black hair neatly plaited into one long braid that hung down her very long spine like a zipper on the back of one of my mother's dresses. She sat ramrod straight and seemed to be staring ahead of her, for neither of her arms was moving in any way to hint at her eating.

For some reason, I was intrigued. The rest of the cafeteria was one loud cacophony of giggles and screams and dishes clattering and chairs scraping the floor, every table crowded with teenaged kids, burping and laughing and punching each other and being generally obnoxious.

But this girl sat perfectly still, oblivious.

Maybe she's in a trance, I thought as I headed to her table and sat down. She didn't glance my way, even though I was no more than inches from her and our trays were practically touching.

"Hello," I said tentatively. "Do you mind if I sit here?"

She didn't move in the slightest, but sighed as if she'd just been asked to hand-wash every plate in the lunchroom. "If you have to."

"My name's Emile."

"I know," she replied, still not turning her head.

"You know? How do you know?"

Slowly she turned toward me with eyes that looked sleepy. They were a dark brown, but I could barely see the color under her thick lashes. It was as if those black lashes were so heavy that she couldn't quite get her eyes to open.

"Everyone knows about the misfit French boy," she said without interest.

Her voice was smooth and deep. Her face was chalk-white but covered with lots of freckles, so that the first thought that flashed across my mind was *salt and pepper.* It was a thin, long face, almost angular, with a small, straight nose. Those lazy eyes were wide, like

Cleopatra's in the old movie where they were outlined in thick black eyeliner. It struck me that the most fitting thing in the world would have been for her to produce a cigarette on a thin-stemmed holder and take a long drag before slowly blowing the smoke out into my face, like a movie star from the 1930s.

Her plate held the same food as mine—a "chicken fried steak" and mashed potatoes and green beans—but she had cut up the meat and swirled the potatoes around it and decorated the white and brown mass with green beans in such a way that it looked like a strange landscape. That was what she had been doing, sitting so straight and still. Staring at her work of art.

"What are you thinking about?"

"The planets and the stars and the way it all fits together, and wondering if there is really any life out there. And I'm thinking of the Milky Way and what that Russian astronaut saw when he sped through space."

"Oh."

This strange girl had drawn outer space on her plate with potatoes and tiny pieces of meat. She lifted her right arm, took the fork in her hand, and carefully pierced a piece of meat, moving it onto a glob of potatoes.

"There," she said, satisfied. "That's more like it."

"Aren't you hungry?"

"Not particularly. The cafeteria food is inedible. My name is Eternity. Eternity Jones."

"It is? That's a very strange name. No wonder you like making planets out of your mashed potatoes."

"It's no stranger than yours, *Emile.*" She pronounced my name in perfect French.

"Why are you sitting all by yourself?"

"I'm not. You're here."

I could feel my face reddening, and I wished I had chosen a different table. I was starting to cut my meat into little pieces when she said, "I have a disease. A terrible disease. That's why I sit alone. The other kids are afraid they'll catch it."

She looked healthy enough to me, although I wondered if her eyelids drooped because of some strong medication. Her pale skin did not look sickly, nor did her posture, so stiff, almost rigid. I took a bite of the meat, immediately agreeing with her about its poor quality.

"Aren't you going to ask me about my disease? Everyone always does."

I shrugged. "In my country, it's not polite to ask about a person's private life."

"Oh, well, welcome to America. Everyone tells everything."

"So what is your disease?"

"Culture." She smiled so that the freckles moved, as if in orbit around her nose and mouth. "I bet no one else in this whole school has ever left the South. Their idea of travel is going to Lake Burton on the weekend."

"Culture?" I smiled at her. If there was one thing my upbringing had taught me, it was culture. I didn't say it out loud, not yet, but I thought it loud and clear.

Eternity Jones, I think we're going to be friends.

three

For the rest of the afternoon, I couldn't get Eternity out of my mind. The first reason, and most embarrassing, was that when we stood up I realized that I was more than a head shorter than her. In fact, my eyes came precisely to, well, to her chest. I had blinked and forced myself to look way up into those sleepy eyes.

But the second reason was all about that word she had used—*culture.* If Eternity Jones wanted to meet someone who had culture, well, here I was! France *was* culture, and every French child was expected to be *cultivé* by the time he entered sixth grade.

Conversation around our dinner table moved seamlessly from one subject to the next with Papa directing it. From an early age I had learned to sit still at the table—set with fine Limoges china and sparkling crystal wineglasses—for hours at a time, listening to the adult banter. Sometimes it was politics, sometimes history, sometimes art. Often the subject was wine. The wine bottle was opened an hour before the meal began, giving it time to "breathe." When we were all seated, Papa would pour a small splash into his glass. Then he would lift the goblet and swirl it quickly around and around, all the while commenting on the wine's color. When he stopped, residue of the thick dark liquid would coat the sides of the goblet, and he would stick his nose into it and inhale.

"Strong, earthy taste, obviously a Bordeaux. A fine, robust wine."

I grew used to phrases like these, and I learned to appreciate the subtleties of wine before I'd ever had my first sip.

So I felt a thrill at the possibility of knowing someone else who was "cultivated." I hoped it meant the same thing in English—to be interested in history and art, to talk about wines and regions and wars.

As I was leaving the school building, I literally ran into Ace and Billy and Teddy. Or rather, they ran into me, Ace bumping me hard on the shoulder and walking right on by without even acknowledging my presence. I didn't turn around, but I could hear them laughing. True bullies. I knew that someday, probably soon, I'd have to stand up to them and prove myself. Their meanness scared me, and it also brought back a painful memory from just two weeks earlier.

Ahmad, a boy at my international school, was Algerian, a terrible thing to be in France so soon after the Algerian war. Algeria had gained its independence from France in 1962, and we hated them for it. Ahmad's father had remained faithful to the French army, fighting against his own countrymen. Considered a traitor by his fellow Algerians, there was no place for him in the new state. So he came to Lyon, and Ahmad came to our school—a fact I'm sure he regretted every day of his life.

Day after day I watched him be bullied at school. Then two weeks ago, as I was waiting on my bus after school, a group of boys in my grade found Ahmad right outside the school gates. Jean-Jacques, the biggest and meanest, shoved him hard against the chain fence.

"You stink, Ahmad. Get out of here. Go back to your stinkin' country. You think they're the only ones who know how to slit throats? We're pretty good at it, too!" He'd even produced a sharp pocketknife as proof.

They had taunted the poor kid for no reason except that his skin was olive and his name was Ahmad and they didn't want his race in our country. When Jean-Jacques hit him in the chin, I knew I should step in and say something. But of course, I didn't. I was small for my age even in France. Instead I watched them take turns punching him until another kid ran back into school, calling for help.

I wished that had been an isolated incident, but unfortunately I had plenty of memories of my inability to stand up to bullies. I had never let myself think about them much before, but now, standing in the hallway at Northside and rubbing my shoulder where Ace had just "accidentally" run into me, they came back to me. I wanted to bolt out of the building and take refuge at Grandma Bridgeman's house. Instead, I forced myself to calmly follow the crowd of students outside and across the street to where they waited at a bus stop.

Soon I was boarding the yellow school bus, along with way too many other students. I found a seat near the back, gazing out the window as the bus started and stopped, depositing students on streets in residential neighborhoods. Houses of every kind—red-brick, painted wood, one-story, two-story—sprawled out on either side of the streets. Each house had a well-manicured grassy yard, with only a driveway to show which patch of green grass belonged to which house.

In France every house with its yard, no matter how small, had a wall around it, and the higher the wall, the richer the house's occupants. We hid behind our walls, valuing privacy and independence. Mamie Madeleine's château was surrounded by a wall, centuries old, made of beautiful yellow stone from the Mont d'Or. I found the openness of these American neighborhoods strange and inviting.

I got off the bus at the correct stop, feeling a kind of gentle relief when Grandma's house came into view, pleased that it had no walls around it, that the trees seemed to beckon, that life seemed simple for this grandmother. I imagined that she would open her door to anyone who appeared on the doorstep, greeting the stranger with a warm smile, just as she had me.

I knocked on the screen door. No answer. I found it unlocked, opened it, and stepped inside. The house was empty. I went through the long hall to the kitchen and looked out the window onto the back-yard. Grandma was there, in her garden, kneeling beside a flower bed, using a trowel to remove the weeds. I stood by the opened back door and watched her for a moment, noticing how comfortable she looked in her wide-brimmed straw hat and her worn overalls and faded cotton shirt, her gray hair swept under the hat, the sturdy green rubber of her garden shoes faded by the sun. She was intent on her task, seemingly lost in thought and in no particular hurry to remove the stubborn weeds.

I set my books on the kitchen table and wondered if her knees were sore where she knelt in the dirt, if her fingernails were brown beneath the garden gloves that surely had holes in the tips of the fingers. I wondered if it would be difficult for her to lift her body back up, if she would give a small grunt, the way Mamie Madeleine did when she gardened.

My French grandmother approached her garden as she did every other aspect of her life, as if the trees and flowers and shrubs were soldiers and she were the general whose goal it was to whip them into shape, and fast. Mamie Madeleine yanked the weeds; she clipped and pruned at a dizzying speed, gathered roses and within minutes had made a perfect bouquet. She never gave me time to volunteer. She'd thrust a spade in my hands, point to a flower bed, and give me orders.

I called out to Grandma Bridgeman, "Do you need any help?"

"Why, good afternoon, Emile. I see you made it back okay on the bus. How was your first day of school?"

I nibbled my lip, wondering what to tell her. Should I mention Eternity, or the way everyone called me "A Meal" and made fun of my accent, as Grandma had known they would? Or should I talk about the three bullies? Finally I found the right words.

"It was interesting."

She glanced up at me, wiping perspiration off her face and swiping at a stray hair. Squinting at the sun, she studied my face and saw my grin. "Interesting, did you say? As interesting as Sunday school?"

"Oh, much more so!"

We both laughed, and then she said, "Well, I'm eager to hear about it. And yes, that would be nice, if you'd like to help me. Have you had a snack? A peanut butter and jelly sandwich? You must have a good snack before you start the yard work."

"That sounds like a good idea."

She started to get up, but I said, "Don't worry, I can fix it. And then I'll come back and help you."

The backyard of Grandma's property started out as simply a small flagstone terrace surrounded by a low brick wall. On the wall sat all different sizes of clay pots filled with every imaginable flower. Beyond the wall on the right, her driveway led to the garage—a small shed with an opened front where her old Chevrolet was usually parked. The carport stood to the left of the garage, behind the brick wall, and then the actual yard opened up beyond, with grass and tall trees on one side, shrubs and rosebushes, a vegetable garden, and a wrought-iron table on the other. The yard gave the feeling of happy abandon, but I knew from experience with Mamie Madeleine that its carefree exuberance had been preceded by a lot of planning and sweat.

We weeded, she hummed, and we passed the time in silence otherwise until finally I asked, "Where's Mama?"

"She's out looking for a job."

I hesitated, let the spade drop from my hand, then scrambled to pick it back up.

A job! Impossible. Not this soon! We aren't staying here in Atlanta. She can't give up on my father and France this soon.

I wanted to scream this at my grandmother, but I didn't know her well enough to show my temper. In my head I said, *Don't you see? She doesn't care about me or my father or you. She's just using you to have a place to stay. She has not talked to you in fifteen years!*

But I said none of this. I kept my head bent down, dutifully pulling up weeds. The peaceful spell of Grandma's backyard was broken.

"Would you like something else to eat, Emile?"

"No, ma'am." Mama had taught me how to answer politely, with ma'ams and sirs. I could be polite. I could hide my emotions, but sometime soon I would use them to their fullest effect.

The silence between us lasted several minutes, well-rooted, like a stubborn patch of weeds. Grandma pretended not to notice, but after a while she looked over at me and said, "I know it's hard for you, Emile, at a new school. Everything is new. It will get better, I guarantee."

She was trying to gain my confidence, but I was too angry to give in. "Yes, ma'am. I'm sure you're right." I stood up. "I'm going to my room to rest for a while."

"You do that, Emile."

I flopped onto my bed, then got up again and paced around the room. Nothing made sense. Why would my mother look for a job? Surely we had plenty of money. At least it always seemed that way.

My temples were pulsing with anger, and in an effort to gain control, I took one of my comic books from the shelf under the dormer window, lay down on the bed, and began to read.

Most boys my age were not still reading Tintin. They had graduated to something racier. Actually, back in France I read all kinds of literature, both for school and pleasure. But I didn't have any other French books with me in America, and I did not plan to tackle Grandma's shelves of novels in English—at least not until I'd gotten over jet lag. So for the time being, Tintin suited me just fine, especially since, in real life, I had found myself in the middle of a mystery.

I went over again the three possibilities of why Papa had disappeared. The first one: he was a spy and was suddenly required on a secret mission. This theory seemed perfectly logical to me, considering the stories he'd told me about his involvement in World War II. His expertise had been needed, and of course the mission was secretive. Mama couldn't know, Mamie Madeleine couldn't know, and I couldn't really know either. But I had good reason to suspect.

The second possibility was that some war criminals, the old Nazis, had caught up with my father and captured him and were going to force him to talk. I had no idea what about, almost twenty years after the war. Perhaps they wanted information about Indochina or Algeria. It didn't really matter. What mattered was that my father had been kidnapped and now he desperately needed help.

The third possibility was the one that any adult would tell me was the most likely. Another woman. But I would not let this be true, no matter what I'd seen and heard. I would not believe that my father could abandon Mama and me for someone else. This was simply not possible. And yet . . .

I opened the little door by the dormer window, slid out the suitcase, and took out the one Tintin comic book I had hidden in there. I brought it back to the bed with me and let it fall open to those familiar pages, the ones with a long slender hole sliced straight through to the back. I fingered the hole and said to myself, "Papa is a spy, and he needs my help. Mama, you have got to understand." I closed my eyes and felt the heaviness descend.

———————

It was my eighth birthday, and I waited expectantly for the present from Papa. I understood by then that it would always be this way—waiting, hoping for something modern, something appropriate for a boy my age and receiving nonetheless a strange gift, a stack of yellowed newspapers, a tin for thumbtacks, a fountain pen that didn't work, the gifts I had received when I was five, six, and seven. I had learned to wipe the disappointment off my face, learned dutifully to get up from the floor with the wadded tissue paper looking like discarded clothes and walk over to where Papa sat in the thick leather chair smoking his cigarette.

"*Merci, Papa,*" I would say, placing the kisses on his cheeks, mine flushed with embarrassment and maybe fear, his eyes carrying that bemused look, that faraway stare that turned to an almost impish grin when he looked at me. Self-satisfied, he was, or as Mama said, "Full of himself. Again." She would groan and roll her eyes and say, "Really, darling, he can hardly be expected to be excited about *this.*" *This* being the thumbtack tin or the fountain pen or whatever.

And Papa's predictable reply, "Of course Emile is excited, *n'est-ce pas, mon fils*? He doesn't understand the significance of these gifts yet, but he understands mystery and intrigue. When he is old enough, I'll tell him. It will be our little secret, Emile's and mine."

Mama always gave an irritated sigh, rolled her eyes again, and said, "Well, open this one now, Emile," and would hand me another gift. My French grandmother often scolded my mother for giving too many gifts. "You'll spoil the child," she'd say. In bourgeois French culture there was one gift, usually something elaborate and costly, but one gift. My friend Théo had received a brand-new bike for his eighth birthday and the rest of us, his *copains*, were intensely impressed and jealous.

But my mother refused to be limited to one gift, especially when, in all probability, the gift was likely to be some enigmatic tool of my father's picking.

However, when I unwrapped his present for my eighth birthday, I was delighted and surprised to find a hardback copy of the Tintin comic book *The Black Island*. It was the first color edition from 1943, the only book in the series lacking from my personal collection and the most sought-after comic book among boys my age. I jumped from the floor and spontaneously threw my arms around Papa's neck, a distinctly American gesture usually reserved for Mama. *"Merci, Papa! Merci! C'est genial!"*

Papa's eyes were twinkling as he drew in on his cigarette and patted me on the head.

There were other presents to open and then the birthday meal, complete with the usual four courses and the very American birthday cake and ice cream, a real *mélange* of cultures. So it was late by the time I gathered up my gifts and took them upstairs to my room. The adults were still talking and drinking coffee and laughing good-naturedly after the bottle of red wine had been consumed.

I brushed my teeth, changed into striped flannel pajamas, turned off the overhead light, and switched on the tiny light by my bed, snuggling under my covers with the prized Tintin comic book. On the cover Tintin, dressed in a blue sweater, striped Scottish kilt, and a blue hat that covered most of his red hair, was seen from behind, walking on rocks, the little white dog Milou staring up at him. An island with a gray castle on it sat off in the distance.

I opened the first page and began to read. I knew the story almost by heart, but I had never owned the color edition. I was halfway through the book, right on the page where Tintin had discovered two of the counterfeiters, when disaster struck: I came upon a hole, a long, thin oval, carved through the remaining pages of the book, from page twenty-five to the very last page.

I sat in my bed, dumbfounded. He had ruined the book! For some spiteful reason, known only to him, he had bought me a prized copy of Tintin and cut a big hole through it. Indignation crept over my face, then the hot burning feeling of anger and then the tears. I squeezed my eyes shut to rid them of the shameful wet substance, but to no avail. Rivulets of warm tears ran down my face and onto the desecrated pages of Tintin.

I felt a pure and innocent hatred of my father, a deep wounding and a helpless resignation that I would never understand him or the way he expressed affection. I switched off the light, tucked the book under my pillow, and would have cried myself to sleep if it had not been for a knock on my door.

"Emile?" It was my father's voice.

Terrified and humiliated, I wiped my face with the backs of my hands and kept my eyes closed. Perhaps he would go away. He opened the door just enough for the light from the hallway to seep across the room, throwing shadows on the floor, outlining him so that he appeared tall and spooky.

Then he was beside the bed, kneeling down on the floor, pushing my thick, curly hair from my forehead, no doubt feeling the wet stain on my cheeks. "Emile, son, have you looked at the book?"

I shook my head no.

"Where is it, then? There is something I must show you. You're old enough now."

Apprehensively, I slid the book out from under my pillow.

"You *were* reading it, Emile!" my father scolded good-naturedly.

"I was until I came to the pages you had cut up! It isn't funny, Papa! I don't like your jokes! I don't like your presents!" This came out in a soft rage that surprised me, that scared me. I expected a *gifle*—a slap across the face.

But Papa was shaking his head, looking almost repentant, and saying, "No, my son! No, I don't suspect you do. But that is because you don't understand them. And now, for the first time, you are old enough to know, to hear the stories, to know the truth."

As he spoke, he fumbled in the pocket of his jacket, retrieved something with his left hand, and quickly, deftly, before I could really notice, placed the book back in my hands. "Try again, son. Try to read it now," he said.

Obediently I opened the book, turning automatically to the middle of the book and the ruined pages. And there, wedged in the cut oval of the pages, sat a thin, shiny silver object.

I sat up in bed, wide-eyed. "What is it?"

"Take it out. Hold it. You'll see."

I pried it out. It felt light in my hands and cool and smooth. "It's a tiny pocketknife!"

Papa smiled. "Yes, Emile. But it's much more than that. It's a dangerous weapon."

My anger melted, liquefied into a puddle of anticipation, of fear and of raw excitement.

My father sat down on the bed beside me and took the silver knife from my hands. He held it carefully and pressed something on the side. Immediately a sharp blade shot out of the front. "It's a switchblade."

I reached over to touch it, but my father shook his head. "As I said, it could be dangerous." He pushed the spring again, and the blade disappeared. He placed the switchblade in his pocket.

I swallowed hard, suddenly wide awake, heart pounding. Papa began to talk in the dark shadows, the perfect atmosphere for a scary story. He reached over and took my hand.

"There was a war going on in France when I was a boy, not too much older than you are. All wars are terrible, and this one was no different."

"There were good guys and bad guys?"

"Yes. France was at that time no longer a free place to live. The bad guys who came from Germany told us what we could do and couldn't do. And these bad guys, these *boches*, decided that Jews shouldn't be allowed to live in Europe."

"Why not?"

"Mostly hate and fear and prejudice against people who were different. So the bad guys started treating the Jews very badly."

"Like the bullies at school?"

"Yes. But there were many good French people who wanted to do something to get rid of the bad guys. They were called *résistants*. They were normal French citizens—not soldiers—who worked in secret to try to stop the *boches* and help the Jews. And Lyon was the capital of the Resistance."

"Why, Papa?"

"Because of its location—close to the Swiss border, a big city with lots of trains coming and going."

I nodded as if I understood this talk of war perfectly.

"I was one of those *résistants*," he whispered.

"You, Papa! But you were a boy!"

"Even boys can help fight evil, Emile. And since I was a boy, the bad guys didn't suspect me. I worked with some very brave men."

"Are they still alive?"

"Some of them are. Some very good men died trying to fight the *boches*, trying to protect Jewish families."

"Did the *boches* come after you, Papa?"

"Sometimes they did. But I was usually safe because of how well I knew Lyon. We would hide out in the *traboules*."

I smiled. "There are lots of very good *traboules* to hide in," I conceded.

I knew the *traboules* well. My class at school had taken a tour of these hidden, interconnecting passageways earlier in the year. There were over three hundred of them in the sections of Lyon known as the Croix Rousse and Vieux Lyon.

"We were always afraid of being followed. Once, when I was delivering a message in Vieux Lyon, I became aware of someone following me. I was sure of it, though each time I looked around, I saw no one. It was after curfew, and the message was urgent. Although I didn't know what it said, I knew I was in for double trouble if I was caught out after curfew and with a message.

"I walked quickly to St. Jean's Cathedral and on to Rue St. Jean and stepped inside the first open *traboule*, rushing through the passage in the pitch dark. I heard the door open, saw a shaft of light, heard footsteps running. But fortunately this *traboule* was complex. I ran in and out of the streets, and the man never found me."

"So you delivered the message safely?"

"That time I did." He squeezed my hand.

I looked into my father's eyes. "Can you tell me about the Tintin book, Papa? And the switchblade?"

"In the fall of 1943—I was fourteen at the time—I was given this Tintin book and sent on an official mission. The leaders felt it would look less conspicuous to have a young teenager carrying the book."

"Was the switchblade hidden in it?"

"Yes, Emile."

"Why did it have to be hidden in a book? Why couldn't you just carry it in your pocket?"

"That's a very good question. You see, at that time, carrying any kind of weapon was very risky—even something that looked like an ordinary pocketknife. In fact, several of these switchblades had already been found on *résistants*, and they had been arrested. So this one was hidden in a Tintin book, and I was given the job to deliver it."

"What was it used for?"

"A very important mission. A special raid to free a captured *résistant*. My job was simply to deliver it to a house. Other people took over after that."

"Papa! Mamie Madeleine would have been very angry if she'd known about you carrying a switchblade!"

He grinned. "Oh, Emile. Mamie and Papy were very much a part of the Resistance themselves. They weren't afraid for me. They taught me!"

I swallowed hard, not sure I believed him.

"So I was walking down the Rue St. Jean, past the cathedral. It was in the afternoon, a bright autumn day. I tried to look casual, but I was trembling. All I had to do was take the book to an address near the cathedral and leave it at the secretary's desk, telling her it was for the good doctor's son. But that day the Germans were out all over town, raiding the stores of Jews. And as I was walking down the street, a German guard caught me by the arm."

I gave a sharp little cry.

"He jerked me hard and said, 'You pick up these old things. Throw them into the fire.' They were breaking the glass windows of the shop, tossing all sorts of old books into the street where they had lit a bonfire. The old shopkeeper with the yellow Star of David sewn onto his shirt stood by, wringing his hands, his head down. Once in a while a *boche* would slap him across the head and laugh.

"I was terrified. I hesitated, and the German hit me hard, so hard I stumbled forward and the Tintin book fell from my hands. It landed on the cobblestones and flipped open precisely to the page where the switchblade was hidden."

"They saw it, Papa!"

He put his finger to his lips. "Shh, Emile, listen. At this point in the war, many young Frenchmen were being rounded up and forced to work for the Germans. Many were sent to work camps in Germany, and some never returned. I was afraid my time had come. But the officers didn't notice the Tintin book. It was just another book to them. I pushed the cover closed with my shoe. Then, as I dutifully threw books into the fire, I made my plan. I kicked the Tintin book into the stack of other books, under them. At last I reached down and picked it up, pretending to throw it into the fire. Instead, I turned on my heels and ran for my life.

"I heard them shouting after me, but I had a plan. I knew there was a *traboule* only a hundred yards away. I turned into it, ran through it. Two *boches* followed me inside. One went up the steps to the apartments. There was a door that closed off the rest of the *traboule*, and I was hiding behind it. It looked like an entrance to another apartment. When the other *boche* tried to open the door, I was holding it closed. I heard him step away, calling to his friend that the door was locked. 'Kick it down!' his partner ordered."

"Oh, Papa! Did they get the door open?"

"I didn't stay around to find out. I ran through the *traboule*, which twisted in and out of three different streets. When I finally came back outside, I ducked into the *boulangerie* right next door to the *traboule* entrance on that street. The owner was a friend of my parents and also was working in the Resistance."

"That was lucky."

"Yes, it was, Emile. But not just lucky. You see, the Resistance workers in Lyon knew these *traboules* perfectly. I did, too. We knew every shop in the city where there was someone who worked for the Resistance. It was a very complicated and well-thought-out system."

"And the *boches* didn't find you?"

"No, they didn't. I waited at the *boulangerie* until dark, hiding in the back of the shop, eating bread. And then I delivered my book with the switchblade to the doctor's house. And from that day on, I knew that I would have to go underground."

"Underground? You lived underground, Papa?"

He chuckled. "No, Emile. It's an expression that means that I knew I would always have to work in secret. Lots of times even Mamie Madeleine and Papy Pierre didn't know what I was doing. It was safer that way."

"Safer?"

"In case we were caught and tor—" He stopped mid-sentence. "In case the bad guys caught us and asked us questions. We wouldn't be able to give away important information about the Resistance—and about each other."

"Were you ever caught, Papa?"

He ruffled my hair. "Shh, Emile. That's enough for tonight. You know the first story. Someday you will know others."

"But, Papa! Tell me now! How did you get the Tintin book and the switchblade back? How do you have them now?"

"Another day, Emile. I cannot tell you all the stories in one sitting."

"Does Mama know?"

"She knows some things."

"And I will, too?"

"Yes, Emile. Some things. But not everything. Not yet." He kissed me on the forehead and left the room.

———

The memory of that night haunted me as I held *The Black Island* in my hands and ran my fingers along the oval hole in the worn pages. My father was a man of integrity and courage; even when he was only fourteen, he had put himself in danger to help others.

Now he needed my help. I was determined to give it to him.

| *four* |

I had the dormer window opened and heard the gentle rumbling of my grandmother's green and white Chevrolet turning into the driveway. I stuffed *The Black Island* back into the suitcase and closed the little door. I had laid the stack of schoolbooks given to me on the desk; I quickly busied myself flipping through the strange math book.

The screen door slammed, and Mama's high heels clicked across the wooden floor. "Emile? Ehh—meele," she called.

I didn't answer.

Soon she was tiptoeing up the stairs. She poked her head into my room. "Emile! There you are! How was school? Did you find the school bus okay?" She spoke in English, walking over to where I was sitting, kissing me on the top of the head and then taking a seat on the bed.

"It was fine. Everything was fine, Mama," I commented in French, without enthusiasm, without meeting her eyes.

She cleared her throat, and I knew without looking that she'd started tugging on an eyebrow. "Well, that's great. Can I hear about it?" She was trying to sound cheery.

"Nothing to report that you don't already know about wonderful

American schools." My sarcasm was thicker than peanut butter, but I couldn't help it.

"Emile—look, I know it's not going to be easy at first—"

"You don't know anything!" I said, shifting in my chair to face her. "No, that's not it at all. You *pretend* that you don't know anything! No, that's not it either. You say you know *everything* about America and *nothing* about why Papa left! Well, I don't believe you! I don't believe anything you say to me anymore!"

"Emile, *cheri*, please don't do this. I know this has been hard on you, but—"

"And don't you dare tell me I'll get used to it! I don't want to get used to anything!"

"No, of course you don't right now. It's all too new. I'm sor—"

"And don't tell me you're sorry! You're not one bit sorry! You're glad to be gone from France!"

She got off the bed and came toward me, but I swiveled around in my chair and stared out the dormer window.

"Please just leave me alone."

Mama placed a hand on my shoulder, gave me a squeeze, and waited for my reaction. I didn't budge. Finally she sighed dramatically, turned, and left the room.

"Dinner, Emile!" Grandma Bridgeman called at six o'clock.

I was back to perusing Tintin and didn't respond.

"Emile! Dinnertime!" This was Mama.

I heard her start up the stairs and then heard Grandma Bridgeman saying, "Janie, let him be. He's dealing with a lot. He must be completely worn out after his first day at school."

"But he has to eat!"

"I assure you he will, dear. When it's time, his stomach will speak louder than his temper."

I didn't go back downstairs at all. Complete exhaustion overtook me, and I crawled into bed still wearing my clothes.

I awoke again around three, changed into my pajamas, and lay in bed staring at the ceiling. After an hour of sleeplessness, I crept across the hall to where I saw a light in my mother's room. Her bed was empty. She had placed a photo on the bedside table—one of my favorites. Papa was behind Mama, his arms encircling her while she cuddled me, infant Emile, in her arms. Their faces were happy, more than that: delighted. His was not the face of a man who had decided to abandon his family for someone else, no matter that the photo was taken years ago.

I went back into the hall, heard soft music coming from below, and crept down the steps.

Just to the left at the bottom of the stairs was Grandma's bedroom. The door was closed, and there was no light coming from under the door. I was sure she was sound asleep, perhaps snoring lightly. The music floated through the hall from the den.

"I'll be seeing you in all the old familiar places that this heart of mine embraces all day through . . ."

I listened to the words and was transported back to a night in my childhood. Bing Crosby's voice was crooning from the record playing on the old Victrola in the *salon* of the château. I was supposed to be asleep, but had crawled down the stone steps and sat with my face pressed against the iron banister, looking down and through the hall to where I could see the silhouettes of my parents moving back and forth, arms around each other. My mother's soft-pitched giggle sometimes broke smoothly over the music as my father guided her effortlessly across the floor, leaning so close and whispering something in her ear. He was holding her tightly, holding her around her tiny waist, her full skirt swirling out as he twirled her.

I fell asleep there on the stairway, with the sound of Bing Crosby and Mama's and Papa's laughter intermingled. I was safe.

Now I could hear the record player in the den playing the same melody in the hidden hours of the night, and I stood by the door, observing my mother from the hall. She was wearing pale pink pajamas and fluffy pink slippers, and she was dancing, alone. She had her arms out and her eyes closed and she was singing along with the words on the record, "I'll be looking at the moon, but I'll be seeing you. . . ."

After a few minutes I went into the den. When she caught sight of me, Mama stopped in her tracks and brushed her hands across her eyes. I pretended not to notice.

"I couldn't sleep either," I offered, and then I took her hands in mine and led her in the dance, led her as I'd been taught at my school. We shuffled across the floor, barely missing Grandma's coffee table, Mama's steps light and delicate, so different from the silly girls in class who giggled and tried to take the lead and said such foolish things while I held them at an awkward arm's distance.

Mama gave me the sweetest smile and held my hand, and I put the other on her waist and we went around and around like that until the song ended. Then she folded her arms around me, resting her head on mine, and I knew she was crying.

"You miss him, don't you?"

She sniffed. "Yes, Emile. I miss him very much."

"He'll come and get us, Mama. I know he will. It will be just like the other times. In a few weeks he'll be back. You'll see."

She held me even tighter. Maybe she was imagining all the other times of Papa's homecoming after his being away for a week or more. They celebrated—the candles, the perfume, the music, the dancing, and I was whisked off to bed.

Never in all those years of Papa's sporadic absences had Mama alluded to another woman. Never had Mamie Madeleine said, "I'm sorry. It looks like you will have to leave France." Never had we even thought of coming to America. And now that we were here, my mother was already looking for a job—even though my father's family had loads of money. I couldn't make sense of much that had happened during the last ten days.

I was sure of one thing, though. Mama was madly and completely in love with my father, no matter what and in spite of everything. She had danced that love before me just minutes ago. As she held me and cried, I wondered if from now on this would be my new role . . . dancing with my mother while she dreamed of him.

———————

My eyes still heavy with sleep and my stomach still grumbling, unsatisfied by the bowl of cereal, I took the yellow school bus to school on Wednesday. This strange American convenience allowed only children inside, plus one poor driver who had to endure the chanting and screaming and flirting. I found a seat right up front and sat scowling for the whole ride. My plan worked—no one even ventured near me.

However, Ace and Teddy and Billy were waiting at the homeroom door, glowering. First they eyed me up and down.

"Great clothes, Frenchy Fry," Ace said. "Perfect for a faggot."

I had noticed yesterday that my clothes were as un-American as my accent. My pleated blue cotton pants and button-down shirt looked very out of place among the blue jeans. The boys' clothes were rumpled and unkempt, but their hair was shiny with some kind of grease, and parted on the side.

"Great looking shoes, Goldilocks," Teddy said with a smirk, kicking my leather loafers with his toe. The American boys wore Keds, a type of canvas gym shoe.

They were determined to humiliate me, but I didn't care; I had planned my own strategy in the middle of the night. Mrs. Harrington, the guidance counselor, had explained the school regulations to me in boring detail the day before. *"We have a very competitive sports program here at Northside, but all athletes are expected to maintain at least a C in every class in order to be eligible to play."* As luck would have it, I had seen a scribbled note about Ace's failing grade in French on Mrs. Harrington's desk as she spoke to me.

"Bonjour, les gars," I said, holding out my hand to Ace, Teddy, and Billy.

They narrowed their eyes and curled their lips and laughed.

"I said *Bonjour, les gars,*" I repeated, this time pronouncing the French words very slowly.

Ace ignored my outstretched hand and came up to within inches of my face. "Shut up, you French sissy," he spat, literally spraying my face with his saliva.

"You're not even trying, Ace. Say, *Bonjour, les gars.*"

"Shut up, I said!" he fairly roared.

Miss Holloway was out in the hall in a flash, consternation on her face. "Ace McClary, what in the world! Is he bothering you, Ameel?"

I had my answer ready, "Oh, no, ma'am. Ace asked me to help

him with his French, and I was trying to teach him a few important words."

"What a nice idea, Ameel! Mrs. Smith will be thrilled. Well, good luck, boys. Come on in; the bell's about to ring."

Ace shoved me as soon as Miss Holloway's back was turned, but it didn't matter. I was safe inside homeroom.

Once all the students were seated, Miss Holloway started distributing something called *Tiger Tales*. "This is our very own school newspaper, Ameel," she explained. "All the articles are written by students."

I nodded, wishing she'd quit pointing out to the whole class that I was completely illiterate in the way life worked at Northside.

The students, their heads hidden behind copies of *Tiger Tales*, paid no attention to Miss Holloway's announcements that followed. I did likewise, diligently reading the articles: sports news about the first two football games, along with a picture, several cartoons, a report on an art exhibit, and a book review. Then a headline caught my attention.

JIM CROW, GO HOME!
By Eternity Jones

Try as I might, I cannot find a law in our Constitution that justifies the hatred of blacks. Perhaps I am not looking in the right places. If someone can advise me, I would be most grateful. I am not necessarily for integration or opposed to segregation. These are sticky issues, tricky questions. Would busing unwanted kids halfway across town really help them, I wonder? But I am opposed to hatred and prejudice. Daily I hear remarks of condescension and disrespect that are not appropriate for students from Northside.

In this monthly column I will tell true stories of students from other areas of Atlanta, in hopes of getting us thinking about what we do and say and why.

Laetitia Lemons is a thirteen-year-old Negro student who is in the eighth grade at a school not that far away from ours. I met Laetitia last summer and dared to ask her what she thinks about segregation:

"I think what's important is what Dr. King always says—respecting one another, giving each human being an equal opportunity to learn and grow. If that means going to other schools, I'll volunteer. I'm not afraid."

Laetitia could be afraid. After all, her brother was beaten last week for trying to register at the city high school. A white senior threw a brick at him.

Although we have heard many times during assembly hour our teachers supporting peaceful "civil rights" and respect for people of different races, these same teachers find this mandate hard to put into practice. Last Thursday, the school board turned down the request of a Negro family who wished to put their two children into Northside High School. I find this hypocrisy revolting and would like the school officials to address this issue honestly.

Since the Supreme Court's desegregation decision of May 1954, only one school district in Georgia has desegregated. Nine Negro students were admitted to previously all-white schools in Atlanta in the fall of 1961. Nine students in seven years for the whole state! Georgia should be ashamed of herself! The Civil War was over a hundred years ago, putting an end to slavery, and yet we continue to treat Negroes as people of lesser importance and intelligence. Wake up, students of Northside!

The bell signaling the end of homeroom startled me. I looked up quickly, tucked the newspaper under my stack of books, and stood up.

As we left the classroom, several students were laughing among themselves.

"Miss Eternity Jones! Thinks she's God Almighty because of her name," one said. "Well, I say, 'Jim Crow, stay here! We love ya, Jim Crow!'"

I walked right past, hoping my face had not turned that annoying shade of red that let everyone know how I felt about things.

Eternity Jones was right; she did not seem to have any friends. Whenever I caught a glimpse of her, she was alone. And in spite of her scowl and self-assured, almost haughty composure, I guess maybe I felt sorry for her. I took comfort in the idea that she might need me.

It turned out that we had three classes together—Algebra I, English, and, ironically, French. I found her in the hall after English class.

"I liked your article, Eternity."

"What do you mean by 'liked it'?"

"I thought what you said was nice."

"Nice?" She looked disgusted.

"Not nice. I mean *convincing*." I tried again. "You said interesting things," I ended, frustrated with my limited English vocabulary. "Where did you meet Laetitia?"

"What does it matter?"

"I was just asking. You don't have to act suspicious."

She shrugged. "I'm not acting, Emile. I'm not acting at all."

When the French teacher, Mrs. Smith, stood in front of the class and addressed us, I cringed. *"Bownjure, lez enfawnz,"* she drawled. Suddenly my mom's French sounded perfect in my ears.

Eternity was sitting beside me and smiling in her condescending way. She leaned over and confided, "She has a terrible accent, but she's a pretty good teacher anyway. But she's going on maternity leave in two months, so who knows who we'll get then."

I nodded.

"I understand we have a new student, Emile de Bonnery, from Lyon!" Mrs. Smith said in French. "Emile, I don't want to embarrass you in front of the class, but I hope we'll be able to speak French together. And if you wouldn't mind, perhaps you could help me out from time to time?"

"Yes, I'd be glad to help, Madame Smith," I replied in French.

She beamed at me. "I am so thrilled to have you here. Now, whereabouts in Lyon are you from? I've visited there several times."

"The north side, by the Saône, a little village in the Mont d'Or."

"Which one?"

"St. Romain."

"I know it! Charming village with the golden stone."

The entire class was staring at us as we babbled in French. Mrs. Smith gave me a wink and said in English, "Sorry, class. I'm afraid I got carried away. What a great opportunity to have Emile with us. Listen to how he speaks French and you will have a perfect accent."

When we walked out of class, Ace sideswiped me and whispered,

"Brownnoser! A brownnosing French fry!"

I looked after him, bewildered. As he walked away, he hit me hard on the back of the head, yanking my hair in the process. "Get outta my way, Frenchy Fry, ya hear? You're just a Goldilocks fairy anyway. A brownnosing Goldilocks fairy."

"Don't mind Ace. He's always looking for a fight." This came from a boy only a little taller than I with smooth skin the color of *café au lait*.

I'd noticed him the day before because of his skin. He wasn't a Negro, but he definitely wasn't a hundred percent white.

He stuck out his hand and said, "My name's Griffin. Griffin Henderson. Welcome to Atlanta, *Emilio*." He pronounced my name with a slight Hispanic accent, but the rest of his English was as Southern as Ace's.

"Nice to meet you, Griffin."

He didn't smirk at the way I said his name, which came out something like "Greefien."

"So you're French. Nice place, France." His hair was black and straight, his eyes slightly tilted at the corners and the color of good French chocolate, his face a thin oval. His whole manner suggested warmth.

"You've been there?"

"Not yet. My father travels a lot and tells us all about Paris. I'm from Mexico." He pronounced it "May-hee-co."

"Ah."

"My dad is American, my mother Mexican. I grew up in Mexico, but we moved here three years ago. Mom gets homesick. Dad is gone a lot."

I calculated the similarities of our histories. We stopped in the hall, sized each other up, and smiled.

Then Griffin patted me on the back and said, "Just don't answer when Ace and his friends make fun of you. And try to figure out how to talk like the kids around here. You'll get along okay if you do that. Three years ago my accent was thicker than refried beans, and the kids called me Hot Tamale."

I couldn't distinguish even a trace of an accent in Griffin. "How in the world did you do it?"

"Practice. If you want to fit in—or at least not stick out—you'll pick it up, too. It's easy. You already speak two languages. You'll hear it."

"What is *brownnosing*?"

Griffin's face broke into ripples. "It means trying to be the teacher's pet."

"The teacher's pet?"

Eyes shining, he leaned over and whispered in my ear, his arm around my shoulder as if we were already best buddies. "It means sticking your nose in your teacher's butt. Ya know—turns your nose brown."

I grinned. "Oh. I get it."

As we walked to the lunchroom, he added, "And whatever else you do, learn to like football."

"I already like football. I play defense on a team in Lyon."

Griffin laughed. "*American* football. You play soccer—and no one over here cares a thing about soccer." He shrugged. "Except for me. In America, everyone loves football, and Northside has a pretty good team. There's a game this Friday night. Ace is on the team. Just don't get on his bad side, and he'll leave you alone after a while."

"Thanks for the information."

"Sure." We were at the door to the lunchroom, and Griffin turned to greet several of his friends. "Oh, and I might as well tell you. I've seen you hanging around with Eternity Jones. The other kids don't care too much for her. She acts too high and mighty."

"She's smart."

"Yeah, I guess. I'd call it opinionated."

"You don't agree with what she wrote in the school paper?"

"Of course I do. But you won't find many others around here willing to take her side. Kids think she's strange."

"I think she's just really smart and not very outgoing."

"Kids say you're the smart one. Must've skipped two full grades."

"No, I'm not smart. It's just the French system is different."

"Okay, well, I'll see you later, *Emilio*."

"Okay, later."

I watched him saunter over to his friends, and it struck me he would have looked perfectly at home with a sombrero on his head and a serape across his shoulders and a pinto pony waiting for him just outside the lunchroom.

I chose a seat next to Eternity at the otherwise empty table and watched her make a new solar system with her food.

"So why did you come to Atlanta?" she asked, surrounding a small mound of white rice with three or four plump green peas.

"My mother's from here."

"So?"

"So we decided to leave France and move back."

"Got a dad?"

"Yes, of course."

"He come with you?"

"No, not yet. He travels a lot."

"Is he American, too?" she asked without looking at me, intent on placing her corn along the edges of the green peas.

"He's French. He's away for a while, and he thought it'd be good for us to come here." Immediately I wished I hadn't volunteered any information.

She glanced over at me, frowned suspiciously, then shrugged and returned to her artistic use of cafeteria food. "Any brothers and sisters?" she continued, head bent over her plate, her long black braid falling over one shoulder.

"No, I'm a unique child."

She jerked her face up and laughed—the first time I'd heard her do that. "A unique child! Well, aren't you humble, Mister French Fry?"

My face was burning.

"You must be translating directly from French. In English we say, 'I'm an only child.' Idioms are always hard to grasp in another language."

She said it so matter-of-factly that I truly didn't think she was trying to show off, but I was still mad at her for pointing out my gaffe. Then I thought about that little word *culture*, and my anger subsided.

"Do you have brothers and sisters?" I asked quickly, all the while pretending to be enraptured with her creation.

"Yeah, I do. A little sister and a little brother." Eternity's plate became a white rice planet outlined by three concentric green pea halos. "Saturn," she said.

"I know. Looks just like it."

That afternoon, the school bus was late so that I was still waiting for it out by the road when Eternity walked by, grasping the hand of a child on either side of her. She noticed me, nodded, and led the children to me, as if she were tugging the leashes of two reluctant dogs.

"Emile, this is my brother, Jake." She shoved the boy over toward me.

I held out my hand, but he just stared down at the ground.

"Jake's seven. He's in first grade."

He actually looked too big to be in first grade. In fact, he plain looked too big—or parts of him did. His head seemed too large for his body, and his hands and feet reminded me of a puppy's—something he would have to grow into. His dark brown hair was shaved close to his head—making me wonder if he'd had lice—and his ears stuck out awkwardly. His eyes were brown, too, and big and completely empty of expression. He seemed clumsy and slow, and all in all, something about him didn't look quite right.

"Hi, Jake. Nice to meet you. I'm Emile."

Jake didn't respond, but looked worriedly at his big sister. He made an exaggerated grimace with his face and stood on tiptoe to whisper, loud enough for me to hear, into Eternity's ear, "He talks funny."

Eternity patted Jake on the back—she could have been stroking a favorite dog—and said, "Don't worry, Jake." Then she surprised me by adding, "Emile's my new friend."

Next, Eternity took her little sister by both shoulders and moved her to stand directly in front of me. "And this is Blithe. She's five."

She was the exact opposite of Jake, small for her age, with curly blond hair that looked so light and fluffy it could have been egg whites whipped to soft peaks. When she smiled, it took up her whole face, spreading contagiously to her dimpled cheeks and sparkling blue eyes.

"Hello, Blithe," I said, and she grinned and hid behind her sister.

I would have enjoyed talking to the three of them, but the school bus arrived. "I have to go. Nice to meet you, Jake and Blithe. Bye, Eternity."

I watched them from the window of the bus until they disappeared from sight, the tall skinny sister with her two younger siblings.

| *five* |

Mama was waiting for me when I got home. I think she wanted to do penance. She was wearing a light blue suit that matched her eyes and proudly displaying what looked like a squashed-up version of a French baguette with a piece of dark chocolate sticking straight through it. In spite of our early morning dance, I hadn't forgiven her for everything she'd done wrong. Nonetheless, the sight of the baguette made me break into a smile, and I gave her a hug.

"Where'd you get this?"

"I found the bread at the store. *Ce n'est pas comme en France, mais* it's probably as close as we'll get here. And the chocolate is *pas mal.* I tried some myself."

Mama was combining her French and English, which made me sigh with relief. She could not wipe out all connections with France so quickly.

As I munched on the snack, I accused, "You were out looking for a job, weren't you?"

"Yes, Emile."

"That means you're planning on staying here?"

"It looks like it, yes."

"What about Papa's money? Surely he left plenty for us to use until he joins us."

She looked miserable. "I can't get to that money right now, Emile."

"Why not?"

"It's complicated, Emile."

"You're making excuses! Just tell me!" I was speaking quickly in French, agitated.

"Please, Emile. This is hard on me, too. Trust me. Right now, I have to find a job."

"Well, will we stay here with Grandma?"

"For now, yes. But I don't know for how long. She's been great to take us in when she had no idea we were even going to show up at her door."

"She doesn't seem to mind. I think she's real happy to have us here. I think this is about the best thing that's happened to her in a long, long time."

"We'll see about that, Emile." And with a blink of her eyes, she changed the subject. "How was your day? Have you met any nice kids at school?"

I told her about Miss Holloway and Mrs. Smith and Eternity and Jake and Blithe. I mentioned Griffin. But I couldn't bring myself to tell her how hard things were, not with her sitting there looking so pretty and imagining that I was finally in the safe haven of the American school system.

I collapsed on my bed, my head throbbing. From there I observed the sun, shining brightly outside the window. I heard the sound of birds chirping and smelled the scent of early autumn in the air. My schoolbooks were spread out on the desk, representing a mountain of homework I could not understand. My eyes faltered, heavy-lidded, then closed, and I was in another place.

Mamie Madeleine was in her garden, working feverishly at a flower bed, all the while talking to herself, preparing a speech for The Friends of the Resistance. The delicate, buttery *pains au chocolat* that she'd gotten fresh from the *boulangerie* were waiting for me in the kitchen, where my first bite of the crusty layers of pastry would shatter into hundreds of tiny, delicious flakes as I chewed contentedly, discovering the rich dark chocolate inside.

Soon I was asleep.

When I awoke, yawning, my mind sluggish, the clock on the bedside table displayed four-thirty. A school day in France lasted from eight in the morning until five-thirty in the afternoon. Here I had finished a full day of school, had an afternoon snack, and taken a nap before I would even be starting my last class in Lyon. This was one thing to like about America—the long, lazy afternoon free from classes.

I wandered downstairs, unable to focus on anything except the warmth and weight of the fall weather. In slow motion I found the kitchen, opened the screened back door, and leaned against the doorpost, watching my grandmother at work in her garden.

At length I made my way up to her. "Emile! Welcome home from school. You look exhausted."

"Yes, ma'am. I am." Then I asked, "Are you always so happy and peaceful in your garden, Grandma?"

She sat back on her heels, wiped a glove across her sweating brow, and said, "I am now, Emile. Yes. Almost always."

"That's nice."

"Yes, it is nice, Emile. Contentment is a gift."

"Haven't you always been content?"

"Heavens no! I've only learned it the hard way, with age. I used to have a garden simply so I could show it off. I spent my days making sure everything looked perfect—my husband, my daughter, my house, myself. And of course, my garden."

"Why did it have to be perfect?"

"Appearances. If things looked perfect, they were perfect. Of course I knew that wasn't true, but still we felt we needed to keep up appearances."

"My French grandmother believes the same thing," I noted. "She orders everybody around, even my father." Somehow I could not imagine this grandmother as intimidating or haughty. "What made you change?" I asked, not realizing that she might think I was asking about things that were not my business.

But she answered. "My husband got ill. Very ill. Our life of appearances and his work were killing him. I was losing him and . . . losing other things."

"My mother?"

"Yes."

"She ran away from you, didn't she?"

Grandma cocked her head, like a dog listening for a sound. "In a way, yes. I suppose you could say that."

"Why did she run away?"

"It's simple, Emile. She got tired of trying to be perfect. I chased her away."

"But she found the same thing in France. Another kind of perfect."

"So I gather."

"Do you think my father is a good man?"

"I don't know your father."

"But you've heard of him?"

"Yes. Yes, I've heard all about him."

"Do you hate him for stealing Mama away from you?"

Grandma had gotten off her knees, with the anticipated grunt, and stood up slowly. "Dear Emile! You do have a lot of questions."

I followed her to the shade of a hickory tree.

"I guess I was upset with your father for some time, in the early years. Hate is too strong. But even then I knew in my heart that he didn't steal your mother. I drove her away. Now I don't blame her. I understand better what the wrong kind of love can do."

I was turning these phrases over in my mind, trying to piece together my mother's early life, trying to imagine this grandmother with the wrinkled skin, bright eyes, and mussy gray hair as someone who at one time was "perfect."

"The wrong kind of love grabs and holds and chokes and demands and expects."

With every word she pronounced, I was seeing my French family, Mamie Madeleine ordering, my mother cowering and then stubbornly refusing, my grandmother threatening and then shaking her head exasperatedly, my mother's silent tears in her room, and my father . . .

where was my father? Where had he been in the midst of this?

"Do you think the wrong kind of love drove my father away?"

I could tell that she did not want to answer. She removed her garden gloves and twisted one in her hands. "I don't know, Emile."

"But you must know something! My father didn't abandon us. He didn't. He's coming back, and if he isn't here now, it's because he is in danger. In some sort of terrible danger, and we have to find him."

She wiped the look of pity off her face as quickly as it came, but I saw it. Then she took me in her arms and held me against her sweaty blouse, under the shelter of the big straw hat, while I cried my own silent tears.

Eventually she said, "I think I have just the thing for both of us. Let's go out on the screened porch, and I'll bring you something to drink." She appeared minutes later offering me a tall glass of her extra sugary iced tea, a welcome respite from the late afternoon heat.

"Now I want to hear about you, and your life. Tell me something about Lyon, Emile."

I had no idea where to begin. After a few awkward seconds, I said, "Well, Lyon is a very nice city. It has two rivers, the Saône and the Rhône, running through it. Up above the Saône River is a steep hill where the Fourvière Basilica is perched. Have you heard of it, Grandma?"

She shook her head, no.

"Well, it's a very famous church. It was built at the end of the nineteenth century and dedicated to the Virgin Mary—because she saved the city twice—once from the plague and once from being invaded by the enemy. There's even a really big gold statue of her on top of one of the steeples. And inside, there are hundreds of mosaic sculptures of the Blessed Virgin's life.

"And the best thing is the Festival of Lights on December eighth; it's known throughout France. Have you heard of that?" I asked hopefully.

"No, no, I can't say I have, Emile."

"Every year, on December eighth—that was when the cathedral was finished—the people in Lyon place small candles along their windowsills to commemorate Mary."

I remembered staring out the window from my cousin's fourth-floor apartment beside the Saône River and seeing the shimmer of thousands of candles reflected on the river's surface, and far up on the hill, Fourvière, ablaze in lights.

"Mamie Madeleine loves the Festival of Lights. When I was little, she would take me out into the streets on December eighth, to look at the lights everywhere and eat roasted chestnuts. The children drink hot chocolate and the adults drink *vin chaud*." I struggled for the translation. "It's hot wine—you drink it from a mug, and it is sweet and spicy. Anyway, Mamie loves the festival because she loves the Virgin Mary."

I watched my grandmother carefully. I'd heard that Protestants didn't like the Virgin Mary, didn't even believe in her.

Grandma just smiled and patted my hand. She said, "Can you imagine the responsibility of Mary? A young girl really, finding herself suddenly pregnant even though she was a virgin? How she must have trembled and wondered, and yet she accepted the destiny God had for her."

"So you believe in the Virgin Mary, Grandma?" I asked, intrigued. I was thinking, *That's not what Papa and Mamie Madeleine always said.*

"Well, yes, of course I 'believe in' her, Emile. I admire her. The Virgin Mary is a very special woman, but she was only human. I just don't believe we should pray to her."

"Well, that's not what Mamie Madeleine thinks." Then, afraid that I might have offended this Protestant grandmother, I added, "But I guess she thinks a lot of strange things."

"Your Mamie Madeleine sounds like a very nice woman, smart and sensible and a good gardener. I'm sure I'd enjoy meeting her."

I made a face. "I don't know about that. You two don't seem very much alike."

"Perhaps not, but you don't have to be alike to get along. Surely you've had friends who were different from you?"

I thought of my international school in France, how several of my friends had lived in so many different places they didn't have a clue which one they considered as home. "Yes, ma'am, you're right. But the problem is that Mamie Madeleine knows exactly what she thinks, and if you ever disagree with her, well, she gets really . . . unpleasant. It's happened to Mama a lot of different times, and it was not very fun to watch."

Grandma chuckled and said, "No, I suppose that wouldn't be much fun. It was never very fun to watch when your mother got into trouble with me either. And you know, Emile, she was pretty good at getting into trouble!"

We'd finished our iced tea, and Grandma was headed back out to the garden. "Just a few things to finish up before I start getting supper ready. Your mother should be back from the store soon. She wants to fix fried chicken, and I'm making my famous biscuits."

"That's super!" I said, trying out a new word I'd heard at school. "I love fried chicken."

I followed her back outside, my head filled with so many more questions I wanted to ask this grandmother. Finding a vegetable bed that needed weeding, I bent down and got straight to work. "What was my grandfather like?" I managed after a few minutes of silence.

She thought for a moment, the spade poised in her hand. "He was a very fine man and a good husband. He put up with a lot."

"What do you mean?"

"It took us a long time to learn how to appreciate each other. That's what I mean. I just about drove him crazy."

I used the trowel to dislodge a stubborn weed and didn't look at her, hoping she'd explain.

"I guess I was one of those wives, and there are lots of us around, who gained pleasure by trying to control my husband. Don't get me wrong. He was the head of the house; he was the brilliant business-man. But I nagged him about everything, about our house and our social circle and our friends and even his business, and little by little there was a wedge between us. That's how it was while your mother was growing up. Each of us busily involved in our own important matters, tiptoeing around the other, relieved not to be together. He started staying late at work. Played a lot of golf, took business trips, accepted more and more responsibility at the office. And then he had a heart attack. Fifty-one years old, and he had a massive heart attack and almost died in my arms."

"*C'est terrible.*"

She must not have heard me, because she said, "It was the best thing that ever happened to us, Emile. When you realize someone is about to be taken from you, all of a sudden you start looking for the good things, remembering how much you needed that person, whether you ever said so or not.

"After his heart attack, we changed our lifestyle, got to know each other again. Forgave each other for so many things."

I thought I heard a catch in her throat.

"And we reinvented our marriage. We really did start over. Moved out of the big house, moved out of the fast social lane, calmed down. Drew together." She looked back at me and flashed a smile. "I'm sorry to be boring a thirteen-year-old boy with grown-up problems."

I didn't say a word. I wasn't bored. I wanted to hear it all.

"I was fortunate enough to have your grandfather for another ten years. Ten years almost to the day. I should have asked for twenty."

She glanced toward the sky, and I imagined her imploring not the Virgin Mary, but God himself for ten more years with my grandfather.

"We learned contentment through giving up a lot of things that weren't that important anyway. Someday you will understand it, Emile. The wisdom of the ages."

But I wanted to tell her that I already understood, that I knew what it was like to lose someone I loved and regret not having had more time with him. I wanted another ten years with Papa. I felt very sure that I had already learned my lesson well, that I would not take Papa for granted if only he would come back. I wondered if perhaps the heavens would listen to me, too, if I asked the right way.

But I just kept pulling weeds.

After dinner, Mama proclaimed that she was wiped out, and when I gave her a blank stare, she explained, "*Epuisée, crevée.*"

"You go on up to bed," Grandma suggested. "Emile and I will get things cleaned up."

Mama kissed me on the forehead, bent down, and looked me in the eyes. "You have everything ready for school tomorrow?"

I nodded.

When she'd gone upstairs and Grandma had her arms down in the soapy water of the kitchen sink, I retrieved a picture in a silver frame, obviously a professional photo, from a shelf in the den and brought it into the kitchen.

"Who is this?" I asked.

The woman in the photo was *éblouissante*—yes, that was the perfect word. Stunning. She was very young and had a smooth, oval face. Her lips were closed—they were full in the middle, and showed just a trace of a smile. Her nose was straight and pointed down. Her eyes I imagined to be a beautiful blue-gray, although the photograph was black-and-white. Her dark hair was short and wavy, barely covering her ears, on which I could make out two small pearl earrings, and she wore a pearl necklace, too. Her eyes were laughing, almost in a mocking sort of way, as if she knew some kind of secret.

I tried not to stare too long at the photo, because my eyes were just naturally drawn to the low-cut V on the front of the young woman's dress.

"Oh, that's me when I was nineteen."

Immediately I felt a little sickish twinge in my stomach, embarrassed to be staring in that way at a photo of my grandmother. I set it on the counter and picked up a dish towel.

"That's you?" It came out as a thinly veiled accusation of disbelief. I didn't see any resemblance.

She laughed good-naturedly. "It doesn't look much like me now, does it?"

She was right. And it wasn't just the age. The sophistication and aloofness of the woman in the photo simply could not belong to the same friendly, kind woman standing with her hands in the dishpan.

"I keep it to remind me of how I was back then—as shallow and flat as that photo in its frame."

"I don't think you look shallow, Grandma. I think you look, um, beautiful, and . . ." I tried to find the right word in English. *"Mysterieuse."*

"Exactly, Emile. I wanted to look mysterious and intriguing. It was all planned, down to the shade of lipstick and the way I let my hair curl slightly above my left eye. All planned to attract attention."

"I'll bet it worked!" I said too enthusiastically, and then blushed.

She let out a soft chuckle. "Oh, yes, Emile. It worked—for whatever it was worth."

"Anyway, you were very pretty."

Grandma dried her hands, gave me a quick hug, and said, "Thank you, Emile. Don't mind me. It was nice to be pretty. It felt marvelous at the time to be noticed and valued. Oh, there's nothing the matter with good looks, in and of themselves. It's just what I did with them that was . . . was unhealthy, foolish."

She gave me a kiss on the head and said, "It's about time for bed, young man, if you're going to catch up on your sleep."

I placed the silver frame back on the shelf in the den, staring at the striking young woman in the photo. I still couldn't quite imagine that *that* was my grandmother. But I could imagine it being my mother. I could see a resemblance to her now. The main difference was that Mama never wore a look of aloof assurance. My mother always looked to me as if she were surprised by the daily drudgery of life. Not big disasters, but little disappointments that drained the spark out of her eyes, that stole away what my father had called spunk, so that even when she laughed, I could hear the effort behind it.

But I'd noticed, even by the fifth night of our stay at my grandmother's house, some of the hardness leaving my mother's face, the subtle creases across her forehead dimming, the tight, determined look of her jaw softening.

Mama is thawing, I thought, *like the ice on the pond in the courtyard of the château when the midday sun of March warms it.* I learned the American expression for this quite by accident: she was letting her guard down.

Eternity had used the phrase when referring to our English teacher, Mrs. Chalkin.

"She's a really swell teacher," I'd whispered to Eternity during class that day, trying out a piece of American slang.

Eternity shrugged. "Yeah, she's okay. But you should have seen her at the beginning of the year—a real witch—before she let her guard down."

Mama had never been a witch. She had been a tightly wound

spring, a bundle of nerves—another great American expression—fidgety and apprehensive. That's what living with Mamie Madeleine had done to her. I could see in vivid detail her clenched jaw and fists, the anger in her eyes when Mamie corrected her in front of the family. Corrected her French, corrected the way she set the table or made the vinaigrette salad dressing or cut the bread. The silliest details, but Mamie always let my mother know, in her slightly mocking way, that my mother would never get it right.

Where was Papa? Absent. Or, on the rare occasions he was present at these silent battles, he would stand between the two women, with a forced smile on his lips and say, "Now, Janie, don't pout. Mamie is only trying to help,"

"You always take up for her!" Mama would hiss, when Mamie left the room.

"Keep your voice down, Janie! Please!"

"This is my house, too! Do you have an inkling of an idea what it's like living in this *château* with your mother? She thinks I'm her slave! And you always take her side—if you're even here, that is. I swear to you I'll go crazy, I will!"

I couldn't see my father's face, but I imagined the twitch on the left side and the way he clamped his lips shut—a habit I had inherited, if habits can be inherited—and then him reaching out to Mama and her spinning on her heels and turning away.

"Don't! Don't try to make it better with a sly grin and a hug! It won't get better. It is hell for me, can't you see it? When are you going to do something about it?"

As far as I could tell, my father had never done anything at all about it. Then I thought of something, and it sent shivers down my spine.

Oh yes, he did. He finally did something about it. He abandoned us, so we were forced to come to America.

six

I slept hard, but woke early once again, this time at five
o'clock. Mama was still asleep in her room. I tiptoed down the stairs,
listened by Grandma's closed bedroom door until I was convinced she
was inside, and went to the entrance hall where the telephone sat on
a small table. I sat down in the chair, picked up the receiver, and dialed
a zero.

"Operator."

"I'd like to call France."

"Excuse me?"

"I'd like to call France," I pronounced more slowly, in my best
English.

"Number, please."

I gave it to the operator and listened until the French ringing, so
different from the way the phone rang in America, sang through the
receiver.

At length there came a voice. *"Allo?"*

"Mamie! Mamie, it's Emile!"

"Emile, *mon cheri*! What are you doing?"

"I wanted to hear your voice." A pause. "Mamie, has he come
back?"

"Non."

"You've not had any word from him?"

"No, Emile. Nothing."

"He didn't run away with another woman. I know he didn't! Mamie, he's in danger."

"Emile, stop worrying. Do what your mother says."

"But you've never wanted me to do what she says before."

Mamie chuckled into the phone. "You're right. But this time, you must listen."

"Is there another woman, Mamie? Did Papa leave for someone else?"

"Shh, Emile."

"Will you tell me when he comes back, Mamie? Will you call or write? Please."

A pause. "Yes, of course, Emile."

"I miss you, Mamie. I miss France."

"I miss you, too." It was the softest her voice had ever sounded.

"He will come back, won't he, Mamie? He always has before."

"I hope so, Emile."

Then she asked me about America, about the food and the school and my American grandmother. She didn't say a word about Mama, but she told me about the calls she'd had from my friends, Jean-Marc, Cyril, and Bastien. We chatted away in French for probably fifteen minutes. I didn't want to hang up, for when the connection stopped, my link to France would be severed, replaced by a dial tone.

I trudged up the stairs, a hollowness swelling in my stomach, expanding until it hurt. I thought of Mamie—stylish, elegant, even in her garden clothes. I heard the worry in her voice, an unfamiliar sound, frightening, coming from her lips. I imagined her hanging up the phone and hurrying outside, trying to forget my voice. I missed her.

I missed my life in France. My family, my friends, the food. I missed the real butter and the rich, creamy sauces served over well-seasoned meat, the fish straight from the Saône, the vegetables from the garden. And of course the cheese, the soft Brie and the firm but tender Camembert and the hard Comté and the strong *bleu* and the warm goat cheese served with crusty bacon bits over fresh salad with vinaigrette made with hot Dijon mustard. I missed France.

I climbed back into bed and lay down, my eyes wide open. I thought about my friends, how we laughed and joked, our cheeks red from running in the park by the Rhône River during a break between classes. I thought of how my father had laughed with great pleasure when he'd read my grades from last year. *Félicitations* was written across the bottom of my report card. It was the highest honor a student could receive, and I lapped up Papa's approval like a thirsty dog.

For many years, Papa had merely grunted and frowned when he received my report card in the mail. He did not seem embarrassed by me, not even exactly disappointed, although I was far from what he had hoped for.

"Let's face it, Janie, he'll never be a rocket scientist," I remember him telling my mother in the middle of my first-grade year. "We won't set our hopes on *Polytechnique*"—the French equivalent of Harvard, so I'd heard. "But surely he can find a suitable line of work in a technical school."

It always infuriated my mother that French parents predicted gloom and doom for their offspring as early as first grade. If the child was not learning to read quickly, if he had trouble writing his name with the fountain pen in the required tiny cursive, if he could not pronounce the sounds of the complicated French alphabet perfectly and conjugate a verb, he was labeled *en difficulté* and most likely doomed to be a plumber.

I found plumbing to be a perfectly respectable trade, as did my mother.

"Quit projecting his whole future on one dumb grade!" she'd hiss, irritably. "For heaven's sake, he's only six! Don't you think we should give him a chance?"

And my father's patronizing voice, joined by my French grandmother's, "Janie, dear, it's been proven time and again that if your child has a bad year in first grade, then he will get behind and be unable to catch up. By third grade he's struggling, by fifth it's *catastrophique*, and by eighth"—when every French child had to choose what he wanted to do with his life—"it will simply be out of the question for him to continue in the general route for the baccalaureate. But we've known some fine families who produced a plumber, and it worked out okay."

Mama would have none of it. She considered this type of reasoning archaic and degrading and spent many hours telling me about capitalism and the wonders of being entrepreneurial. "Your father has a creative streak as long as the Saône River," she would say. "He's forgetting how school was hard for him at times. Don't listen to any of it. Besides, you'll do university studies in the States, so try your best and never mind what anyone says!"

Mama believed that her calling in life was to get me through what she called "the tedious and cruel" French school system. More than once she had caused me great embarrassment by insisting on seeing one of my teachers and arguing that the grade I had received was ridiculous.

I tried to explain to her that the teachers were always right, that it didn't matter if the kids and parents and whole village rose up to protest a grade, nothing would change. But she wouldn't stand for it. In third grade I made the mistake of telling her that my teacher had ripped up my paper because I had forgotten to underline the title in red ink. Another time, when I had remembered the red ink underlining the blue ink title, but had neglected to use a ruler to make the line perfectly straight, the paper was once again ripped in two. Mama marched into my class the next day and proceeded to bless out the teacher with her painfully thick American accent, the rest of the children looking on in amusement and perhaps disbelief.

Father laughed condescendingly at her feeble efforts to "reform the French," as he called it, which of course infuriated Mama even more. My grandmother considered my mother a scar in an otherwise blemish-free family line, and on more than one occasion I heard her whisper to my father, "*Mon Dieu*, Jean-Baptiste, she is going to be the downfall of the de Bonnery clan. Can't you do something with her?"

Father would humor his mother with a quick *bisous* on the cheek and say, "I married her for her spunk, Maman. You'll see. It will come in handy someday."

Father was right. Mama's spunk was going to help me get through the first days of American school—whether I liked it or not.

Mama was leaning over me, her blond head a bundle of pink curlers, shaking me and saying, "Time to get up, Emile."

October had come overnight, and with it, I noticed golden-yellow tints on a few leaves that flittered on the trees below. I watched them from my upstairs bedroom, perching myself on the desk and staring out the alcove of the dormer window. The oak leaves were five-pronged, like a hand, like my father's hand, big and reassuring. I thought about Papa for the hundredth time, expecting at any moment the phone to ring and Mamie's voice to rush through the line, explaining to me that, right after I had hung up, Papa had walked through the front door of the château.

I took out my suitcase of treasures, thinking if I touched the old newspapers and the tin for thumbtacks and the pen and *The Black Island* and the others, if I held them and turned them over and over in my hands, perhaps they would reveal another secret, something I had not yet considered, something that would lead me to Jean-Baptiste de Bonnery.

But a strange thing happened as I contemplated the objects in the suitcase. The more I touched them, the more I kept seeing Eternity Jones in my mind—her long, thin body, her sleepy eyes with their feigned lack of interest, the way she told Jake and Blithe that I was her new friend. I felt my cheeks grow hot, and every time I tried to plot a strategy for finding my father, Eternity's image intruded into the scene.

In spite of myself, in spite of the way I missed France and desperately did not want to get used to America, in spite of the pressing need to solve the mystery of my father's disappearance, Eternity was crowding in on me, surprising me with the most pleasant of thoughts. I had a new friend.

I didn't hear the knock on the door, so when Mama came into the room, I was still lost in thought about Eternity, still sitting on the floor with the suitcase spread open beside me.

I closed the lid quickly on my treasures. Only the Tintin book remained on the floor.

"Emile! Hurry up! You've got to eat breakfast." Then she caught sight of *The Black Island*. "What in the world? You brought this book with you?"

"Of course I did, Mama. It's part of *him*. I had to. Don't be mad."

She sat down beside me, pulling her bathrobe around her, her thin legs neatly tucked to the side. She placed her thumb and forefinger on either side of the bridge of her nose, pressing hard, looking down. This meant she had a headache coming on. At length she took my hand and squeezed it. "Of course you'd bring that book, Emile."

"When will Papa call or write?"

She nibbled her lip. "I don't know, Emile." It seemed to me that Mama pressed even harder with her thumb and forefinger on her nose. She gave a sigh, and then she looked up at me, her pretty blue eyes all liquid and sad, and said, "Come on down for breakfast," and left my room.

I put the suitcase back in the attic space, then brought it out again. I decided then and there that I was going to show Eternity Jones one of my treasures. Wasn't that what friends did? Shared stories with each other, revealed secrets, confided? I placed *The Black Island* in a pile with my schoolbooks and hurried down to breakfast.

Mama was waiting for me there. "Emile, before long I know you're going to like Northside. You'll see. You'll find it so much easier than that crazy French system."

She'd said it rather innocently, but all my fears for Papa and my anger at leaving France exploded in torrential French.

"Mama, I *am* French. You thought that school was hard in Lyon, but to me it was just school. I was like everyone else. Here, I'm different. I'm small. I talk funny. Just exactly what did you think would be easy for me? Or did you even think about it at all? Maybe that's the problem, you didn't think. Well, you need to know: Every day I wish I were back in France." I concluded my tirade with a spray of milk and half-chewed, soggy cereal.

A soft red spot appeared on her cheek, and she creased her brow. "Oh, Emile . . ."

But I didn't let her finish. "I've got to brush my teeth and get my books before the school bus comes." I threw my bowl into the sink, took the stairs two at a time, and went into the bathroom. I leaned over the sink, staring in the mirror, and said, "I want to go back to France. I hate America!"

But all the while, I thought I could see Eternity's long black braid just out of the corner of my eye.

Homeroom was still tainted by Ace and Billy and Teddy, who continued to call me A-Meal and pop me on the back of the head. Biology came next, an hour of heart-stopping agony as I implored the Virgin Mary to keep the teacher from asking me a question. Griffin sat beside me and whispered answers to me that I could not understand. Fortunately, I made it through class without opening my mouth, which I considered a great success and answer to my prayer.

"See you later, *amigo*," Griffin said, his black hair bobbing as we left the classroom. I stared after him, almost jealous of his friendly confidence.

During the next hour I had study hall, which meant I was supposed to work on homework in the school library. I'd dumped my books on a table and was sitting down when Eternity perched herself in the chair next to me.

"I didn't know you had study hall now," I said.

"Well, now you do." Then she whispered, "Shhh—use a library voice in here, Emile."

"What are you talking about?"

"Whisper."

"Oh."

Then out of the blue she asked, softly of course, "What's it like to live in a château?"

I thought for a moment. "I don't know what it would be like for other people living in other châteaux, but for me, it's like trying to wear one of my father's expensive old suits from the early 1950s. It's out of style and way too big for me and not at all comfortable."

Her eyes were for once wide, and then she grinned. "So it's not fixed up fancy like the Château of Versailles?"

"Oh, not at all. I grew up hearing my father say that this château was the worst liability in the world. He would have sold it for a loss years ago, except he was afraid it might break Mamie Madeleine's heart. It's been in her family, oh, for probably centuries. Anyway, he kept it. But some of the rooms are cold and damp, and in the winter, they're really depressing."

Grandma Bridgeman had driven me around some really fancy neighborhoods in Atlanta, so I added, "It's not like here—not as well cared for."

In truth, I was hoping that someday soon Eternity would invite me to her house. I could imagine it, a large white house, maybe what Americans called a mansion, sitting far back from the road, a perfectly green lawn lined with tall oak trees, the interior of the house filled with everything that came to mind when I heard the word *culture*.

I struggled with a math problem, gave up, and walked over to the section of the library marked World War II. I found a book on the Normandy invasion and took it off the shelf. Eternity scooted her chair beside mine, perusing the book with me. Its pages were filled with pictures of Omaha Beach and Ste Mère Eglise and Arromanches, names as familiar to me as my own.

"Do you know much about the Second World War?" she asked, followed quickly by, "I mean, since you lived in France and all."

"Yes. I guess you might say I know a lot."

"Do you like to study history?" There was a hint of interest, even excitement in her voice.

I shrugged. "Not any kind of history, but World War II, recent history, things that happened on our doorstep—I like to learn about that."

I was staring at a photo of the bunkers on Pointe du Hoc, the ones the Germans had used to hide in as they tried to shoot down the Allied soldiers who were climbing up the cliffs.

I was there, in my mind's eye, with my father, both of us looking past the barbed wire out into the English Channel, what the French called *La Manche*. Papa's hand was draped around my shoulder—he was talking about how the Allies arrived and pointing down below to the blue-gray water.

"They were just sailing in to be massacred, Emile, those brave kids . . ." He'd cleared his throat, a deep, guttural *hmm, hmm, hmm,* and then clamped his lips together and was silent, looking out into the expanse of water, his dark eyes shining, his chest rising and falling.

I'd relived that moment a dozen times, always thinking, *It's like Papa was there when it happened. Like he saw everything from way up here.*

"I've been there," was all I said to Eternity.

"Really? You've been to the Normandy beaches? Cool."

I felt pleased that she said it with a proper amount of awe and respect.

"When did you go?"

"Two years ago. With my father."

"Wow."

"My father and I stood right there and looked over the edge of the cliff, and he told me about the way the Allies came in."

She sat up straight, as if a new thought had just crossed her mind. "Was your dad there when the Allies came to Normandy?"

"No."

I thought she seemed disappointed. As if on cue, I laid *The Black Island* on the table.

"What's that?"

"A treasure," I answered automatically, before I had thought through how childish the response must have sounded.

"A *treasure*," she said, mocking a French accent. "How exciting!"

"Never mind," I grumbled, my face burning with embarrassment.

"Don't 'never mind' me, Emile. Now I want to know. What's so exciting about a comic book?"

"You tell me, Miss Smart Ilic."

"Smart *Aleck*," she corrected.

She could tell I was furious, but she pretended not to notice. She brushed her long pigtail over her shoulder and flippantly lifted the book to inspect. "Hey, there's a hole in this comic book."

"Oh! How surprising!" I mocked her back.

"Okay, I'm sorry. Tell me about it."

"It was a gift. A birthday gift to me from my dad."

She rolled her eyes at me. "Okay, I give up. What's the deal with the hole in the comic book?"

I had her full attention now. "My father fought in the war."

"Which war?"

"The Second World War, idiot."

"Why is that an idiotic question? You just told me that he wasn't at Normandy. So maybe he fought in Indochina, or maybe Algeria. Maybe he was too young for the army in World War Two."

"He wasn't in the Army, Miss Know-It-All. He was in the Resistance."

"Ah."

"You do know about the French Resistance, don't you?"

"Some."

"How much?"

"Forget it, Emile. Just tell me the story."

"Papa was twelve when the German troops occupied Paris—in June of 1940. He was seventeen when the war ended, in 1945. And in those five years, he helped publish an underground newspaper, hide Jewish children and smuggle them to Switzerland, and blow up trains. And a whole lot more."

"Are you serious?"

"Of course. I have lots of other things he gave me, and every one of them has a story to it. Every one except . . . every one."

She overlooked my slip, remained quiet for a moment, then hissed, "Well, I don't particularly care which story you tell me—just start, you pigheaded boy."

"Okay, if you insist. I'll tell you the first story Papa told me, on the night of my eighth birthday."

When I'd finished my story about *The Black Island* and the switchblade and the *traboule* and Papa escaping from the Nazis, I sat back in my chair, feeling rather self-satisfied. Eternity was trying hard to look aloof, but for once failing miserably. Finally, after three or four different expressions had paraded across her normally placid face, she asked, "What exactly are the *traboules* like, Emile? Have you been in them?"

"Some of them, yes. There are hundreds of them throughout Lyon. Hidden, zigzagging passageways that lead from one street to another. Papa's shown me through the ones he used during the Resistance. They're actually quite dirty, and sometimes when you're in one, you almost wish you couldn't smell at all, it's such an awful stench. And there are pitiful stray cats wandering about and rats scurrying in and out."

Eternity wrinkled her nose.

"They were built in the third or fourth century, nobody's sure why. My history teacher last year said the original use was perhaps for people to get water from the Saône River. In later centuries the *traboules* permitted merchants and silk weavers and others to carry their wares from one place to another without getting wet in case of a storm. But the *traboules* could be very deceptive. What looked like just one more wooden-door entrance into an apartment could actually be a door leading into a labyrinth of small pedestrian roads that twisted in and out between buildings. Only a true *Lyonnais* knows the correct route to take."

I could tell Eternity was impressed. I blurted out, "Someday I'll show you around Lyon. You can see the *traboules* for yourself, and lots of other interesting things."

She looked at me as if I told her that someday we'd go to the moon together. "I doubt it." She was examining *The Black Island*. "Do you have the switchblade?"

"No, not here. I left it in France."

She tilted her head a little, perplexed. "But why would your father give you a switchblade on your eighth birthday? No father would do that. I mean, it's downright dangerous."

I knew she wasn't really criticizing my father. She was simply stating the obvious. But it stung. I felt a boiling anger and also the desperate need to rescue my absent father's image. "He didn't give it to me that night, silly. He only let me hold it. He kept it hidden for years."

I thought she'd beg me to tell her more about the switchblade right then, but I was to learn that Eternity Jones had never begged for anything in her life, and she wasn't about to begin with me.

Finally she said, "Well, it's all very interesting. Hey, I could write up an article about your dad's work in the French Resistance for the school newspaper."

"No, don't do that. Just keep writing about civil rights."

"Why not, for goodness' sake? The war's been over for almost twenty years!"

I didn't want to say anything, but it came out anyway. "For my father. For his safety. I can't explain it very well, but I think he's in trouble. I think that's why he disappeared."

"Your father *disappeared*?" That roused her interest. "Really? What kind of trouble?"

"I'm not sure. But I think all the different items from the war that my father gave me are going to help me figure it out. I'm positive they will."

She scooted her chair over closer to mine and skimmed the comic book. "You're a funny kid, Emile. You really believe you've got clues to your father's disappearance?"

"Maybe."

"That sounds awfully farfetched, don't you think? Like something you'd find in this Tintin book."

"So?" I wished my voice didn't sound so defensive.

"Okay, fine. Tell me what happened to your father."

"No, never mind."

She rolled her sleepy eyes. "Have it your way." Then she added, "Will you tell me someday?"

I shrugged.

"Because if it's true—well, it could be a really interesting story. Think of the headline." She spread her hands out to either side as if she were holding a newspaper, and said in a perfect reporter's voice, "*French Résistant Kidnapped Twenty Years After War.* A Frenchman involved in the Resistance as a teen mysteriously disappeared from his château in Lyon last Wednesday. His son reports that his father possessed information from the Second World War that is still being sought after today."

I allowed one side of my mouth to turn up—a half grin. She grinned back.

We were sitting there, happy and comfortable, so comfortable in fact that I finally got up the nerve to ask Eternity a question that had been bothering me since I'd met her. "So why did your parents name you Eternity?"

"My momma said that her labor with me lasted an eternity, and my pa thought that was the funniest thing he'd ever heard—which tells you a lot about the sensitivity of my father. He started calling me Eternity right there at the hospital, and it stuck."

"Oh, so it's not because they're religious or anything."

She narrowed her eyes so that they seemed like one long black slit drawn across her face. "You've never met my parents, Emile. If you had, you wouldn't even bother asking."

seven

I did get to meet Eternity's mother that very afternoon, but not because Eternity invited me to her house. The bell rang, announcing the end of the last class; I had survived three days of American school. Griffin and I were walking toward our lockers when I stopped short. Farther down the hall I saw Ace and Teddy and Billy and three or four other boys from our grade laughing at Eternity, shaking copies of the school newspaper in her face.

"Nigger lover!"

"Civil rights, my foot! Civil idiot!"

"White trash! That's what you are. So quit acting so high and mighty, Miss E-ternity."

I could see the humiliation spreading out across her cheeks like spilled red wine seeping onto a white linen tablecloth. I wanted to rescue her from their cruel words. But Eternity didn't need rescuing.

She slammed her locker door shut and whirled around, intentionally bumping into Teddy. She was carrying her books tight against her chest, and she suddenly thrust her weight, books and all, on the already unstable Teddy, and he fell to the ground. Then she strode down the hallway.

I ran to catch up with her. "Don't worry about them, Eternity.

They're just rednecks." I had learned this Southern expression from Griffin. "No-good rednecks."

She wheeled around and seethed, "Don't you feel sorry for me, Emile! And what do you know about those boys, anyway? Don't you try to protect me! You're no better than I am, Emile de Bonnery, no matter if you came from French nobility! Don't you dare use a condescending tone with me!"

I stood there, just watching her walk off, as Griffin caught up with me.

He shook his head. "Strange girl."

Ace called to us from down the hall. "You like that Eternity girl, don't you, A-Meal? Well, she ain't no one you should hang around. She's real low."

I wanted to defend Eternity, but I didn't dare open my mouth and give them another opportunity to laugh at my accent.

"She's white trash, I tell you. She lives in a trailer, next to a bunch of Negroes. Go see for yourself."

"You think he's telling the truth?" Griffin whispered as we hurried out.

"Of course not! He's just a bully. Anyway, it doesn't matter what he says, she's my friend."

Griffin's dark eyes lit up, ready for mischief. "I'm going to find out."

"You can't."

"Of course I can, and you'll come with me."

"No, I won't." But just in case, I asked, "How?"

He gave me his most winning smile. "It's easy, *amigo*. We'll ride the bus to her house."

"You mean get on the same bus that she's on? She'd kill me."

He patted my back, like one of those older cowboys in the John Wayne movies I watched with Mama in French. "Don't worry. She won't even *see* you."

I shouldn't have done it, but I liked Griffin. And he was the one boy who had shown an interest in befriending me. So I trotted after him, offering, "A teacher from the elementary school brings Eternity's sister and brother here after school, and they wait for her in Mrs. Harrington's office."

"Perfect, *Emilio*. We'll get on first, go to the back, and she won't even know we're there."

A thirteen-year-old boy moves on instinct, the prospect of adventure, and the power of peer pressure. I did not stop to think about how I would return from this trip to an unknown part of town. All I was thinking about were the words *culture* and *white trash*, wondering how they fit together. In truth, I didn't even know what *white trash* meant, but from the sound of it, it wasn't a compliment.

Before I could change my mind, bus number 5 pulled up, and Griffin and I got on and hurried to the very back. I did get a little twittering in my stomach when my bus, number 7, pulled up behind us, but I sat perfectly still. Five minutes later, Eternity appeared with Jake and Blithe. They obediently climbed up the steps and took seats at the front. Eternity never looked around, didn't speak to anyone, just stared straight ahead. I could see her long black braid and Blithe's fluffy blond head resting on Eternity's shoulder. Jake sat ramrod straight across the aisle. Watching them up there, so stiff and alone amidst the noise and confusion of the bus, I felt like a traitor and a spy.

Ten minutes into the ride, after we'd passed fancy houses with neat yards and a synagogue and more houses, the bus turned onto a road that was lined not with houses but apartment buildings, some well kept, some not in good shape. Then we wound past factories for cars and electricity and wood. This did not look like a residential neighborhood at all. But in the midst of these factories, the bus pulled to a stop beside a small white building with a sign in front: *Chattahoochee Mobile Village*.

A dozen kids stood up and made their way to the front of the bus. Eternity, Jake, and Blithe were the first to exit. I saw no houses with nice, neat front yards or sidewalks shaded by tall trees with rustling leaves—just an industrial looking area on a road with cracked pavement and a hot burning sun in a cloudless sky.

I didn't budge until Griffin elbowed me and whispered, "Hurry up! Before the bus leaves."

"She's going to see us!" I said, too loud.

"Shh, stupid! Just wait a sec!"

We rushed to the front of the bus, watching through the window as Eternity and Jake and Blithe and the rest of the students disappeared down a side road that curved around and out of sight. We hopped off the bus and followed at a distance.

"Would you look at that!" Griffin said as we rounded a curve in the road.

Before us opened a narrow road crowded with mobile homes on either side, dozens and dozens of trailers—white and blue and green, some with little porches built out front, some with flowers in pots. The trailers on the first street seemed to be well cared for, but as we followed the Jones kids through the village and onto other small roads, the trailers became older and dirtier.

The three Jones children never turned around. They just kept walking until we could barely make out Eternity and her siblings disappearing off to the left of the paved road. By the time we got to where they'd turned, we saw that the road twisted around a few turns. It felt like we kept walking for an hour, because I was sure that at any moment Eternity would spin around and see us.

Finally, sitting at the very end of a dead-end road was a clearing. No grass, no flowers, just a patch of dusty clay and a light blue trailer, the color faded by the sun, looking like it might topple over or split in two. An old car, hopelessly beyond use, sat off to the left, and Griffin and I ducked behind it as Eternity opened the trailer door and they all went inside.

At that moment, I figured that Eternity really did have a disease, and the name of it was insanity. My idea of culture—symphonies and operas and five-hour meals with eight courses and four different wines—was as foreign to this place Eternity called home as my stiff French accent.

"Would ya look at that," Griffin said softly. "Sure enough, she lives in a shanty."

"What's a shanty?" I asked.

"Just means some no-good ol' place to live—worse than a cabin, something thrown together, just to give poor folks a roof over their heads."

The trailer reminded me of where a gypsy family might live in France, with lots of other *caravans* around, a whole commune of them.

As Griffin and I crouched there, a feeling of despair settled down on me. I could taste it in the afternoon dust, could feel it buzzing around my head with the mosquitoes. But I didn't have time to consider that gloomy mood, because right then a woman came out of the trailer. She was taller than Eternity, but she wasn't thin like Eternity. She was enormous. She had thick, tangled brown hair. The flesh on her face was grayish white with brown splotches, and everything about her body hung down—her face, her chins, her arms, her breasts.

I had never seen someone as fat as this woman. People in France were not obese. This woman's flesh was spilling out all over her, and I was repulsed. She had deep sunken eyes, and she looked disgusted, or maybe intoxicated. She sat down with difficulty in a rusted metal type of rocking chair, something you'd find discarded by the side of the road, and she called out, "'Ternity, git out here and git ta work!'"

"Wouldja look at that," Griffin said, whistling low. "You think that's her mother?"

I shook my head no, but I knew it was, and I felt sick to my stomach.

"We should go," Griffin said. But it was too late. A mangy dog, big, with a head like a German shepherd but all tan and skinny, had come out of the trailer with the woman and was now barking furiously, coming our way.

"Let's get outta here!" Griffin said, grabbing my arm. "Come on, Emilio."

But I couldn't move. I felt trapped by Eternity's life.

"Go on. I'll come later."

"How you gonna get home?"

"I'll figure it out."

"You're crazy!" he said before dashing off into the trees.

But I was drawn to this spot, to Eternity, and once again I felt like a spy. When the big shepherd, baring his teeth and howling like a wolf, found me, I stepped out into the open, cooing in my best animal-placating French, *"Du calme, le chien, du calme."* I thought I might wet my pants right then.

"What's that varmint up to now?" the big woman was calling.

Eternity came out of the trailer, with Jake and Blithe following. She saw me standing there and narrowed her eyes, daring me to move.

"Bonjour" was all I could think to say, and that weakly.

"Who's that?" the woman slurred.

Eternity paid no attention to her, but walked past, leaving Jake and Blithe cowering on the porch and all the while motioning to me with her eyes to come forward. The big varmint wasn't about to let me move, and I gave her a helpless look. For some reason, that made Eternity break into a rare smile. She came over to me, grabbed the dog by the scruff of its neck, and said, "That's enough, Demon." Then, to me, "What are you doing here?"

"I . . . I don't know. I mean, I rode the bus—your bus. I wanted to see . . ."

"Oh, I get it," she said, disgusted. "You wanted to see for yourself if I was really white trash like Ace said. Satisfied?"

I couldn't even look at her. "Sorry," I mumbled, feeling the sweat on my brow.

She just kept staring at me, enjoying my humiliation.

"I guess I'll go," I choked out, my throat dry.

Finally she shrugged. "Nah, you're here now. You might as well come in."

I followed her, as if on a leash, like Jake and Blithe and Demon, to the trailer.

Eternity said, "Ma, this is Emile. He's a friend from school," and she walked past her.

"Hello, ma'am," I said in my best American accent.

"Drunk, as usual," Eternity whispered. When we were safe inside, Demon still yelping furiously, she snipped at me, "Don't stand there looking so horrified. This is my life, okay? Don't feel sorry for me, or I'll never speak to you again, you hear me?"

I just nodded, but I thought to myself, *I hear you, Eternity. I hear you loud and clear.*

The trailer was one continuous path of filth: empty Coke bottles, old magazines, dirty clothes, a hamper of what might have been unfolded clean clothes, plates of food with crusts and crumbs and flies swarming over them, left as if by accident throughout the two rooms I assumed were the kitchen and living room. And there was a terrible stench. We walked past what I supposed was a bedroom, though the bed was virtually hidden under stacks of old newspapers. Several old TVs, or parts of them, sat on the floor.

Eternity stopped in front of a closed door, which I assumed was the bathroom. She produced a key, unlocked the door, and commanded, "Come on," opening the door just wide enough for me to slip in behind her, then slammed it shut, shooing her little brother and sister off and locking the door from the inside.

I was astounded. It was a bedroom, her bedroom. Or perhaps I should say their bedroom, because a single bed was pushed against one wall and covered with a beautiful old quilt and a worn pillow, and on the other wall were bunk beds, recycled or reconstructed from some junk store. They, too, had pillows and quilts on them.

Eternity lives in here, I thought to myself. *She shelters her siblings and herself in one little room of security.* The room was immaculate, the linoleum flooring, though worn, scrubbed to a shine, the walls a strange greenish-yellow color, bright and clean. It made me think of *Chartreuse,* a liqueur Mamie Madeleine liked, made by the Carthusian monks of Grenoble only an hour's drive from my home in Lyon. The walls were decorated with posters as bright and cheery as the color itself—a field of tulips with windmills in the background, surely taken in Holland, and a poster of a young girl in a gingham dress, her hair in pigtails, a smile on her face and the advertisement reading, in French, *Cacao pour le petit dejeuner.*

The room even smelled fresh and sweet, like the *chèvrefeuille*—which I would learn was called honeysuckle—that peeked over the ancient stone walls into Mamie's garden.

"Quit gawking, Emile!" she hissed. "So this is where I live, and maybe it is strange, but you lived in a run-down castle." She let her arms circle the room and said, "This is home. And *only* this. Not that, not out there. Not her. This is where *we* live, Jake and Blithe and I. Jake calls it our safe room."

She lifted the bottom of the quilt, which was just touching the floor, so that she could reach under her bed with her other arm. She pulled out an old wooden crate crammed with books, let the quilt fall back down, and said, "This is my culture, and no one can take it away. This and two other crates."

She took out the top book. It was a worn volume of the Encyclopedia Britannica, the letter P. I opened it and found that on the inside cover was a small piece of stiff paper stamped *Atlanta Public Library*.

"I collect books that libraries are getting rid of. That's how I got all these." She frowned impatiently. "I said to quit gawking, Emile! I promise I didn't steal them, so don't get all worried, okay?"

I nodded, leafing absently through the encyclopedia while a hundred questions collided in my brain. Finally I asked, "What about your father?"

She shrugged. "He took off right after he named me Eternity."

"And Blithe and Jake?"

"Different men my ma picked up somewhere or other. Never stayed around for long."

"I'm so sorry." I knew I shouldn't have said it, but it just escaped from my mouth, like a hiccup.

She ignored the comment. "Mrs. Harrington's the only one at school who knows about us . . ." Her face turned red. "Well, maybe a couple of other people do, too, but you better swear to me on your mother's liver that you won't ever breathe a word about it to anyone. You swear?"

She had stood up and was towering over me, scowling, her lethargic eyes somehow haughty in spite of the droopiness.

"I swear. I swear I won't say a word. But how does Mrs. Harrington know?"

"She found out from a teacher at the elementary school. Blithe came to school one day with a black eye, and then Jake showed up with a broken wrist. The authorities wanted to split us up—send us to foster homes. But I told Mrs. Harrington I could take care of us if she'd just help me get a few things. She got me the beds and the quilts and the posters and some clothes. Came one day when Ma was too drunk to spit straight and helped me clean this room. We used up a whole big bottle of bleach. I found the paint buckets out by the city trash—mixed some colors together and came up with this.

"Mrs. Harrington got me a lock and a key, and that's how I keep Ma out. And it's working out okay now, Emile, so don't you dare say a word and don't you dare feel sorry for us or I'll spit in your face in front of the whole school, I swear I will."

I wondered if Eternity's fear of Ma and determination to protect her siblings was why the elementary schoolteacher brought Jake and Blithe to Northside every day to wait on Eternity after school. I realized then that, in spite of the anger and the tragedy and the injustice of her life, Eternity was a survivor.

"So you've never even seen your father, Eternity? Not even a picture of him?"

"I don't even know his name. If Ma has to refer to him, she just says 'yore pa' . . . or 'that bastard.'"

I swallowed hard, not sure what to say. Was this another taboo subject that would get me in big trouble if I continued, or did Eternity really want to talk about her father?

She plopped on the floor beside me, pulled out a copy of *Gulliver's Travels*, and asked, "Which do you think is worse, Emile? To have some contact with your dad, even if he's lousy and good-for-nothing, or to never know your father at all?"

I took a deep breath, tried to think of something to say, and was immediately interrupted before I could begin.

"Because I've thought about it a lot. I've thought that surely it would be good to know your father, to meet him and talk to him. Surely there would be good and bad mixed in together, once I got to know him, and surely he would have been thinking of me and would like me, even love me. I've thought even that maybe he was a fine man, with a respectable job, and that maybe he tried to take care of Ma but he just couldn't deal with the drinking, or maybe she threatened him like she does us kids and it just drove him away."

She was in another world, not listening for any kind of response.

"But the only part that doesn't fit is that surely he would want to come see me, and then want to rescue me from this life, and since he's such a fine man, he would naturally want to rescue Jake and Blithe, too, even if they aren't his kids. And he'd want to get Ma into some kind of sanitarium." She mashed her lips tightly together and frowned. "That's the part I can't quite figure out. Why he hasn't come back."

There was a huge knot in my stomach. Eternity became in that moment just another silly thirteen-year-old girl, hoping for a fairy-tale ending to her thus-far tragic life. Even I could see that her father was some no-good tramp, and he'd left as soon as she was born and never taken one look back. Maybe he didn't even know that his cruel remark had given Eternity her name.

The room felt muggy, hot, and all I could think to do was to keep turning the pages of the encyclopedia, past *pewter* and *peyote*.

"I need to go home," I said finally.

"Well, now you know about me."

"I won't say a thing to anyone, Eternity. I swear I won't." I wanted to grab her hand and squeeze it tight between my fingers, but I refrained. "And I like your room. I like it a lot. And all the books and everything."

She barely acknowledged my comment, but asked, "How do you plan to get home?"

I shrugged. "I guess I could call my mother." But even as I said it, I realized I hadn't yet memorized my grandmother's number.

"We don't have a phone."

"Oh."

"You sure are dumb, Emile. Coming over here without one notion of how you'll get back home."

I thought of Griffin and wished he had stayed. Together we could discover the road back to where we wanted to be, even if we had to walk half the night. I could feel my face going scarlet.

"Well, come on. Let's go see Mr. Leroy Davis."

"Who?"

"Our neighbor. He has a phone."

"I don't know my phone number," I admitted.

"Idiot! Well, maybe he can give you a ride."

Jake and Blithe were waiting right outside the door. I thought their eyes looked hungry. "You have a really nice room," I told them.

Blithe grinned, and Jake stuttered, "H-h-he gonna stay for d-d-dinner?"

"No, Emile's going home now. C'mon, kids. We'll walk him over to Mr. Davis's house."

"Mista Davis ain't gonna like it, Eternity. No sir, he's gonna git as mad as a hornet. I ain't goin' over there," Jake said.

"Okay then." Eternity sounded irritated. "Just go in the room and lock the door." Jake nodded, his big brown eyes empty, expressionless.

"I'm staying with Jake," Blithe piped up.

Eternity knelt down in front of them and said, "That's fine, then. But you lock the door, you hear? Go on in. I want to hear it click." She patted them along. "I'll fix dinner when I get back."

When we left the trailer, Ma was still sitting in the metal rocking chair, a dark bottle in her hand.

"Good-bye. Nice to meet you, ma'am," I said, but I don't think she heard me.

Eternity led me back onto one of the main roads in the trailer village. I wondered what time it was and if Mama was worried about me. After a few minutes' walk, we came to a well-kept yellow trailer. A man was out in front working on a pickup truck. I could only see him from the back: tight black hair with strands of gray wound in it, worn blue overalls—and black skin.

"Mr. Davis. Excuse me, Mr. Davis." Even Eternity sounded a bit meek as she pronounced his name.

Mr. Davis pulled his head out from where he'd been inspecting the engine and looked around. He was thick and muscular, scary looking. I'd have preferred dealing with Demon.

"I'm sorry to disturb you, but I have a favor to ask. This is my friend Emile, and he needs a ride home. I was wondering if you'd be kind enough to oblige us."

He examined me carefully. My curls had never felt blonder. I fleetingly wondered if he had a shotgun under the seat of the pickup.

"Need a ride, huh?"

I nodded.

"He rode the bus home with me, and now he needs a ride home."

"What you doin' invitin' boys ovah to yore house, Miss Eternity?

You ain't got enuf trouble ovah there?" He said it gruffly, in almost a fatherly way.

"It's not like that, sir. He just came over to help me with homework. We're just friends."

"Well, lemme see. If I can git this thing workin', I guess I kin take ya home."

"Thank you, Mr. Davis."

"Where d'ya live, son?"

I froze. No matter that I had no idea *how* to get home, suddenly I couldn't even remember the name of the street Grandma lived on.

"Is this boy normal, Miss Eternity? Can he speak?"

Mr. Davis had walked right up to me. He smelled of tobacco and gasoline and sweat.

"He's just shy. He's new around here. Just got to America all the way from France."

Mr. Davis lifted an eyebrow and showed his yellow teeth. "France? You from France? Whereabouts, son?"

I glanced at Eternity for help with his accent. "Where are you from," she translated.

"I'm from Lyon."

"I know Lyon. I been ta France. Fought ovah there at them Normandy beaches."

Eternity and I stared at each other, eyes wide.

"Well, I'll be," he said, and with that, Mr. Davis got in the truck and turned the ignition. It sputtered twice, then roared to life.

I felt relieved and terrified at the same time.

"Well, climb on in, son, and tell me where you live now."

"I can't remember right now," I admitted, miserably.

"Well, how in tarnation am I sposed ta git you home if ya don't know where you live?" Mr. Davis shook his head and said to Eternity, "This here is a strange boy."

Right then, the unusual street name came to me. "Anjaco!" I announced, almost giddy with relief. "My grandmother said the street was named for the man who developed the neighborhood: Andrew Jackson Collier. An-ja-co," I pronounced carefully. I was immensely pleased with myself.

"Well, I'll be," Mr. Davis said, shaking his head and mumbling to himself. "Glad he remembered. Never met a boy who didn't know where he lived." Then he said to me, "Yeah, I know Anjaco Road. One of my girls used to work over in that part of town."

I climbed into the pickup with a fearful glance back, wondering if Mr. Davis hated white people as much as the whites seemed to hate the Negroes. And if he did, what would be my fate?

"Bye," I said to Eternity.

"Bye, yourself, you idiot." But she was almost smiling.

The pickup truck jostled and bounced its way to the road, spitting dust behind it. I watched the hard ripples in Mr. Davis's arms as he held the wheel. He asked me, "So you bin to Normandy, son?"

"Yessir."

And before I knew it, we were talking about Arromanches and Ste Mère Eglise and the way his unit waded onto the Normandy beach as if the Germans were using them for target practice.

I was thinking to myself, *According to Papa, this man is a hero. So why does he live in a trailer on the bad side of town?*

We drove for no more than ten minutes, going by the time on Papa's watch. It was five-thirty. The adventure had lasted almost two hours. The sun was still high, the air heavy. I felt myself loosen up when we drove past a gas station that I recognized. Five minutes later, Mr. Davis pulled the truck into the parking lot of a red-brick apartment building on the corner of Anjaco.

"I know where I am now, sir. Thank you for the ride. I can pay you for the gas. I'll give the money to Eternity tomorrow."

"Never mind, son. You go on and git outta here before one of them white fellas sees ya driving around with me and I git in a heap a trouble."

For the rest of my life, I would never forget the way it felt walking down the wide sidewalk with the lazy sun on my back and the noise of Mr. Davis's pickup coughing its way out of sight. But before I reached my grandma's front yard, my mother, sunglasses in place, came running up the street toward me. She grabbed me so tightly and started crying— or continued, because her face was already splotchy red.

"Oh, Emile! Thank God! Where have you been? Oh, my dear. I've been so worried! I'm sorry I pushed you to go to school. I'm sorry I brought us to America, but I swear we'll get through it. I swear."

When she finally let me go, I explained. "Mama, it's okay. I didn't run away. I went to a friend's house. That's all."

"A friend's house? But you said you don't have friends. Oh, Emile, we were so worried. We called the school and the police, and some folks were getting ready to go out looking for you. . . ."

"I'm sorry, Mama," I said, ashamed.

We'd reached Grandma's house. I stared at the mailbox with the address *1861 Anjaco Road* on it, and I knew I would never forget it again either.

Grandma was standing in the driveway and talking to people—neighbors, I presumed—and then she came and hugged me and whispered, "Thank you, Lord. I do thank you that this child is okay."

Standing there, smashed tight against Grandma Bridgeman with a view over her shoulder of her house, I had a fleeting thought. *Get used to it, Emile. This is home.*

Late that night I was lying in bed, remembering the afternoon and all that I had seen. It seemed stranger than any story Papa had told me about the Resistance—the truth of Eternity's life. Now when I pictured her in my mind, all I could see was that filthy trailer and her obese, drunken mother. Then I thought about the secret room, heard her instructing Jake and Blithe to lock its door, thought how it kept all the awful things in her life away. I imagined then what my "safe room" would be like. It would be in a little corner of the attic in Mamie's château. I'd have to climb up a ladder to get to it and duck down low not to bump my head on the ancient wooden scaffolding. I'd lie on my stomach on a worn, comfortable old mattress and I'd read my Tintin comic books with a little flashlight, and I would hear the rain pattering on the roof and I'd be cozy and warm underneath a blanket.

And there would be a wisp of smoke curling up in the corner and the hazy outline of the only other thing I wanted in the room. My father.

| *eight* |

It's true what they say about news traveling fast. When I arrived at school the next morning—Friday—I'd been transformed from the misfit French boy into the French boy who had tried to run away from home.

Mrs. Harrington called me into her office. "Emile," she began. Mrs. Harrington was well suited to her position—tall, serious, with a deep voice. Her hair was pulled back tight in a bun so that her face looked almost stretched, free of wrinkles. "Please, have a seat."

I sat.

"I know this has been a very hard week for you, Emile—the sudden change of cultures, languages, a new school. It can't be easy. We want to help you get adjusted."

"I didn't run away, ma'am." I pronounced every word slowly.

"You didn't? Do you mind telling me where you were for nearly two hours yesterday?"

I stared at my shoes, concluding the scuffs on the black leather seriously needed polishing. I did not want to answer her question, but Eternity had said that Mrs. Harrington already knew about her home.

"I was at Eternity Jones's house, ma'am."

Mrs. Harrington set down her pen and crossed her hands on her desk. "Eternity Jones's *house*, you said?"

"Yes, ma'am. The trailer where she lives."

"Why did you go there?"

"She's my friend." That, after all, was the simplest explanation.

"She invited you to her house?"

"No, I just went. But then she invited me in, and I saw her safe room—I saw the room you helped her clean up."

I finally looked up from my shoes and caught the guidance counselor's eye, then looked back down. The glance was enough to confirm to me that she was surprised.

"I promised Eternity I wouldn't tell anyone, but since you already know, well, I think it's all right."

Mrs. Harrington had obviously been caught off guard. "Then you were not trying to run away?"

"No, ma'am. I don't like this country or this city or this school, but I'm not planning on running away. At least not yet."

She almost smiled. "Well, I certainly hope not. You gave your mother and grandmother quite a scare." She stood. "And, Emile, if there's any way we can help you—someone to tutor you, extra time for homework—you'll let me know?"

"Yes, ma'am." I got up, but before I left her office, I said, "I think what you did for Eternity and her brother and sister was very nice."

It wasn't the right word. It never was. But she nodded, and I think she understood perfectly well.

Griffin found me in the hall before homeroom. "Boy, am I glad to see you! It's all over the school that you were trying to go back to France!" His coffee eyes were smiling, making his copper skin look all the warmer. He thought this news was better than football. "How'd you get home?"

I related my story, without giving the details of the inside of the trailer or the color of Mr. Davis's skin. Then Griffin told a tale of hitchhiking and getting picked up by a Negro and almost refusing to get in the car but changing his mind and praying all the way home. I thought that our stories had similar endings, but I didn't tell him.

"Griffin, Eternity doesn't know you were there. So can you promise not to say anything to anyone? I swore I wouldn't tell."

"Kids know anyway. You heard it yourself from Ace."

"I know, but for her. Don't let it come from us, okay?"

He grinned. "For you, amigo." Then, eyes dancing, he added, "Can you believe the size of that woman—her ma? Now that's something to talk about!"

I frowned, and his eager expression softened.

". . . But I won't. Hey, you coming to the football game tonight?"

"Maybe—but I don't know where it is."

"We play all our home games at Grady High School's football field—since we don't have one here. I'm sure your mother and grandmother know where that is—across from Piedmont Park."

"What time?"

"Seven-thirty—game starts at eight. Meet me by the concession stand, okay?" He gave me a friendly slap on the back and a wink. "I'll introduce you to some of my friends—girlfriends."

"Sure," I said, "I'll be there," hoping he didn't notice how red my face had turned when he mentioned girlfriends. It was only after he was long out of sight that I realized I had no idea what a concession stand was.

I couldn't meet Eternity's eyes when she walked into English later that morning—our first class of the day together.

She chose a seat on the other side of the room. But after class, she came by. "I'm glad you made it home all right, Emile."

"Yes, thanks. I told Mr. Davis I'd pay for gas." I pulled several dollar bills from my pocket. "Will you make sure he gets this?"

"He won't take charity."

"It's not charity. It's paying for a service."

"Anything that comes from white hands is charity to Mr. Davis. Keep your money."

I tagged after her to the lunchroom and sat down at the same table, but I couldn't think of anything to say. The silence felt like failure, like a condemnation of my childish behavior the day before.

I'm sorry about yesterday, is what I wanted to say, but the words stayed lodged in my throat along with a piece of tough beef. I swallowed, getting up my nerve, but as usual, Eternity beat me to it.

"What are you thinking about right now?"

"Nothing," I lied.

"That's impossible. You have to be thinking about something."

"I'm not."

"I say that's impossible. You can't just force your brain to stop working."

"I don't have to force it. It just stops. I can sit here for a long, long time and not think about anything in particular."

"That must be awful. Sad. Scary."

"Not at all. It's very peaceful, actually. You should try it sometime. Just sit and be. Enjoy. No planning, no worrying, no schedule."

She looked almost wistful. "I envy you, Emile. I wish I could stop thinking for a while. I wish I could erase all the things inside my head." She made a face, chewed slowly, and said, "This beef tastes like leather," then reached across the table for the salt and pepper shakers.

It was then that I saw the bruises—just barely. Her sleeve slid up her right arm about three inches, exposing her wrist and forearm, covered in deep purple with an angry red slash across the wrist. In the next instant, she'd pulled her sleeve down, oblivious to my gaze, sprinkled salt and pepper on her meat, and was saying, "I'll bet you have better cafeteria food in France."

So we talked about things that didn't matter, and didn't say a word about my visit to her trailer or the safe room or the deep ugly bruises on her wrist. But I couldn't help wondering for the rest of the afternoon if somehow those bruises were my fault.

I turned the corner from the bus stop to Anjaco Road, relishing the sun on my back once again, happy it was Friday afternoon and school was over. Then I saw the police car parked in Grandma Bridgeman's driveway. I almost turned back around.

"Oh, Emile! You're home already. This is Officer Dodge." Mama had a fake smile plastered on her face, the sunglasses were in place, and she was talking in a nervous, agitated way. "He came by to check on things here—I told you that we'd reported you as missing yesterday afternoon."

The officer, wearing a blue uniform and crisp white shirt, was an angular sort of man with sharp features—his nose, his chin, his greased-back brown hair that almost rose to a point, and especially his glare—eerily authoritative as he stared at me through frosted blue eyes. He was young and self-assured and towered over Mama and me.

"Hello," I said, and offered my hand, which he took and shook forcefully.

"Do you mind if I ask you a few questions, son?"

"Okay."

"Where did you go yesterday afternoon?"

"I've told everyone. I went to a friend's house. I rode the bus there."

"Would you mind telling me the name of your friend?"

"Yes, I do mind. It's not your business."

Mama looked startled.

"You're not in trouble, son. This is routine procedure."

"Why does it matter?"

"Did you go to this house of your own accord?"

"Yes."

"And was anyone else with you?"

"No—just my friend and her family."

"*Her* family? A girlfriend?" Mama asked.

"Just a friend from school, Mama."

"And no one forced you to go or followed you to this house?" the officer asked.

"No, I don't think so."

The officer wrote something on a notepad, looked at my mother, and shrugged. "That'll be all. Good day, Mrs. de Bonnery, young man."

When he'd driven away, I confronted my mother in French. "Why are you trying to ruin my life? I haven't done anything wrong."

"Emile, it's not like that. It's routine—questioning after a report is made."

"He's a bit late, isn't he?" I left her in the yard, ran up the flagstone steps, and let the screen door slam shut after me. I stayed in my room until it was time for the football game.

On the way out to the car, I managed to say to Mama, "I'm sorry I got mad at you."

She gave my hand a squeeze and said, "Things will get better, Emile. I promise."

Mama knew exactly where the Grady football stadium was and even showed interest in staying for the game, but I simply said, "If you stay, I won't." She reminisced all the way to the stadium about attending games there "eons ago."

She pecked me on the cheek and explained that the concession stand was where food was served. "I'll pick you up here at ten o'clock. You wait for me here, okay?"

I nodded and headed toward the stadium with its perfectly green football field and the concrete stands rising on either side and the stadium floodlights sticking way up in the air.

I found American football violent as I watched my first game, perched on the concrete bleachers with Griffin explaining each play. Grunts, bodies clashing, helmets hitting, people cheering—many people—not just the high school kids, but parents and grandparents and other adults. And cheerleaders! This was unbelievable—girls all dressed alike in short skirts, jumping and chanting and encouraging the spectators to yell and cheer.

"The quarterback is a guy named Mitch McClary—he's Ace's big brother, a senior and a real good player. Already has three colleges after him for next year."

"After him?"

"For football scholarships."

"Oh," I said as if I understood perfectly. "Where's Ace?"

"He's over on the bench. Freshmen don't get much varsity playing time. He might get to play in the fourth quarter if we keep our lead. He's a defensive linebacker. He's nothing like his brother. He's all beef and no smarts, but he's gotten some pretty good tackles in the last two games."

Halftime came, and the score was 17–10, our team leading by a touchdown. I tagged along with Griffin, who despite his size was not afraid to speak with girls a head taller. He had a smooth, slow laugh and eyes that were always exploding with mischief.

"This is my friend, *Emilio*," he introduced me. "*Emilio*, this is Mary Jane and this is Sally."

My face was burning. "Hi," I said, figuring maybe a one-syllable response was safe.

But it wasn't. Sally giggled, and Mary Jane said, "Say something else. Your accent is cute."

I wished in that instant that the ground would open up and swallow me. I could feel sweat running down my back, my heart pumping fast as I stared at Mary Jane's round, freckled face and the way her shoulder-length brown hair flipped out just perfectly on the ends. I wondered if she'd used some kind of hair spray to get it to stay like that.

"Poor *Emilio*. Don't put him on the spot," Griffin crooned happily.

All I could think to say was, "I think I'll get a Coke."

As I walked away, I heard Mary Jane cooing, "Oh, how ro-maaan-tic! Did you hear how he said that? *I zinc I'll geet a Coke.*"

I went to the concession stand and bought a Coke and some French fries.

Griffin followed me. "Relax, buddy. Wanna come with us and have a smoke in the park?"

"No. No thanks. I'm going back to the stands."

"Whatever you want, amigo."

Sure enough, with Northside leading in the fourth quarter, Ace came onto the field, an impressive sight, all six feet of him, his already hefty frame padded with all the football attire. After one particularly violent play, a heavyset man sitting further over to my left in the bleachers shouted, "Come on, Ace! Let 'em have it!" And when a penalty was called—for some kind of foul I didn't catch—the man yelled, "C'mon, ref! Are you blind? The offense was offside."

Griffin shrugged, "That's Mitch and Ace's dad. He tends to get worked up."

Northside won the game easily. I said good-night to Griffin,

Mary Jane, and Sally and was walking with my head down, sipping my Coke through the straw in the bottle, when I caught sight of Ace with his father.

". . . Can't believe you missed that tackle! You're almost on probation because of grades. If you don't focus, you'll ride the pine all year!"

Mr. McClary obviously did not have a "library voice" in his vocabulary.

Ace was cradling his helmet under one arm. His cropped blond hair was wet with perspiration, and he almost looked small beside his father. The man was several inches taller than Ace, with a protruding belly, a square face that looked angry and tight, and muscular arms the size of tree trunks. His face was just inches from Ace's, and with every word his father pronounced, Ace's eyes turned further down.

Finally he said, "Look, Dad, I gotta get to the locker room."

His dad grabbed his shirt and pulled his head up. "Don't ever let them see you hanging your head, you hear? You are not going to embarrass us! I expect you to do better next week, you understand?"

"I know, Dad. I know that."

I walked out of the stadium, thinking that even the biggest bully could be bullied by someone else.

————

Mama let me sleep in on Saturday morning. I was finally over jet lag, and I didn't wake up once until the sun was bright and bold and the clock said 9:45. In Lyon I'd have been out on my bike riding by the Saône River with my friends. We'd trade stories of the time we dived off the dock into the river at midnight—something that was strictly forbidden. Then I'd be getting ready for a football match—our kind of football. Mama would come to watch, so would Mamie Madeleine. And Papa. When he was in town, Papa would be there too.

I tried to imagine something that sounded fun in this place, but nothing came to mind. So I got out my collection and arranged the items in the order in which my father had given them to me across the desk in the dormer window. First there were the two newspapers—which had been concealed and smuggled inside an old log back in the Resistance—then the thumbtack tin, then the fountain pen, then *The*

Black Island, then the oilcan, the bicycle pump, the hairbrush, and finally Papa's wristwatch, which I was wearing every day, as if its untold secrets would seep through my skin and travel up to my brain and enlighten me.

I read the dates from the newspapers: June 1941 and May 1943. *Jean Moulin Caught!* proclaimed the headline on the second one. Immediately I was transported back to a night when I was around ten and Papa was telling me another story.

"Papa! Jean Moulin is the name of my school!"

"Yes, Emile. And now you will learn why. Jean Moulin was a brilliant, brave, and honest man who helped save the lives of many Jews and soldiers. He knew everything about the Resistance—which put him in great danger. Do you know why?"

I thought. "A bad guy could catch him and try to make him reveal secret information!" This was always happening to Tintin, so I reasoned it probably had happened to Jean Moulin as well.

"Exactly! If the Nazis ever caught Jean Moulin, they knew they could find out information about many, many other people and the plans of the French Resistance."

Papa had reached over to my shelf and taken down an old rusty tin, no bigger than a man's wallet. The faded label on the outside advertised its contents: thumbtacks—his birthday present to me when I was no more than five or six. I had opened the tin enough times to know it was empty.

"This held a radio."

I screwed up my face and protested, "How could a radio fit in there?"

"It was a homemade radio. That's how my parents and I secretly listened to the news coming in from England and elsewhere. That's how we first heard General de Gaulle calling us to resist the occupation.

"We got coded news over the radio, Emile. Every night they would make announcements about things that made no sense to anyone else. 'Three packs of beans for Cary,' 'a dog wandered in the street in

Neuville,'—phrases that meant nothing on the surface."

"Secret messages, Papa?"

"Exactly.

"The *résistants* would huddle around the tin-can radio and listen to see if there was a signal—to tell us the coast was clear—so they could blow up a train track or deliver a message or a hundred other things.

"One night, Mamie Madeleine and Papy Pierre and I were waiting for the news when three taps came on the door. Then silence, followed by six more taps." Papa imitated the sound on the wooden frame of my bed. "It was our signal, and we opened the door to find a panting Jean-Paul in front of us—one of my friends who also worked in the Resistance.

"'They've captured him! They've got Jean Moulin!'

"We were shocked . . . and afraid. We knew the Gestapo tortured *résistants* to get information. If Moulin talked, my parents and I and hundreds of others would be in danger for our lives."

"Oh, Papa! Did he talk? What happened to poor Monsieur Moulin?"

"He was taken to Montluc prison in Lyon, and he was tortured, Emile. He was beaten and tortured by the Gestapo in the most horrific ways possible. Poor Monsieur Moulin died in the Montluc prison."

I swallowed hard, shivering with chills.

"But Jean Moulin revealed nothing of what he knew about the French Resistance to the Germans before he died." Papa's eyes shone with pride. He patted my hand and touched me softly under the chin.

My lips were tight, and I felt that thick ball in my throat. As I looked up at Papa, I realized that maybe his eyes weren't shining with pride. Maybe they were shining with tears.

Besides the two newspapers, I had clippings in one of my Tintin books, *Tintin in America*. Every time I read that comic book, the four pieces of newspaper would float to the ground when I got to the page about the Indians. And I would stick them back in, a talisman and a bookmark.

Now I took them out. Papa had marked the clippings in his almost illegible handwriting with a red pen. One said, *Le Monde, 25 Novembre 1954.* The headline read, *Butcher of Lyon Condemned to Death in Absentia.*

Klaus Barbie, the infamous "Butcher of Lyon," was sentenced to death in absentia by French courts for active complicity in the killing of 11,600 French Jews. He was responsible for the torture unto death of Jean Moulin, the man who united the different factions of the Resistance. Barbie has not been seen since his disappearance from Lyon in the summer of 1944—he is believed to have escaped to Germany soon after the Normandy invasion.

As I sat at the desk, holding the clipping about Klaus Barbie, I remembered another of Papa's stories.

Papa was in his office—a small, clammy room in the far end of the château. I was not allowed inside. But I was curious, and one day I sat outside on the cold stone floor until I finally got up the nerve to go in. I was eight or nine, ten at most. There were newspapers on his desk, and a thin trail of smoke ascending from the cigarette in the ashtray. This newspaper, the one with the headline about Klaus Barbie, was on top.

"Why are you reading this, Papa?"

"It is of no interest to you."

"Did you ever see the Butcher of Lyon, Papa?"

He didn't look at me. His face was grim and determined. He shuffled the newspapers under other papers and books. "Emile, would you like to go for a walk with me?"

Time with Papa was always scarce, so I agreed. As we walked by the Saône, I asked him, "Papa, are you a spy?"

He laughed. "Me, Emile? A spy? Why do you ask?"

"Because you were a spy. A very good spy."

"I worked for the Resistance, like many other Frenchmen. That isn't exactly the same thing."

"Sometimes it was, though."

"Well, yes. Sometimes."

"I want to be a spy like you someday, Papa."

"Shh, Emile. Let's not talk about spies anymore."

Why should I not ask about spies? Why would he tell me the stories if he didn't want me to ask questions? Papa knew I loved Tintin and mysteries. Why wouldn't he tell me more?

———

On that morning in early October in Atlanta, this was my conclusion: My father, a spy, was after Klaus Barbie. My father had discovered something, and now the Butcher of Lyon, the man who had escaped justice twice when condemned to death, the man who had inflicted such horrible pain on Jean Moulin and countless others—this man had captured my father, and perhaps even as I sat here reading these newspaper articles, he was inflicting pain on Papa.

Grandma and Mama and Eternity pitied me for my silly juvenile ideas of espionage and murder. It didn't matter. I would not give up until my father was free and back home with us.

———

Sunday morning meant church, again; it meant Second-Ponce de Leon Baptist Church. It was a strange name for a church—the result of Second Baptist Church merging with Ponce de Leon Baptist Church, Grandma had explained—but I liked the name because the Atlantans didn't know how to pronounce it. Instead of saying *Ponce de Léon* as any Frenchman would, they said a nasally "Pawns der Leee-on," and that made me smile.

And Second-Ponce de Leon Baptist Church meant another sermon on the wages of sin and the promise of eternal damnation if we did not accept Jesus into our hearts, another hour of watching the pastor's face turn all red, another time of eating a tiny square part of Jesus' body and drinking His grape-juice blood. And it meant Sunday school with those unfriendly kids and the bullies Ace McClary and Billy Moharty. One good thing, Mama had bought me a jacket and pants that actually fit. She had also bought me brown penny loafers that looked exactly like what every other boy at church was wearing.

It turned out we did not eat wafers this Sunday, and the regular pastor was back. The rampaging man from last week had been a guest. The real pastor, Dr. Swilley, was a middle-aged man with a deep, smooth voice. It had a calming effect, but it didn't lull me to sleep. I liked this pastor. I liked his sermon about the prodigal son and his kind eyes and friendly assurance. So I survived my second Sunday at church.

Later, after a dinner of roast beef and green beans and mashed potatoes smothered in delicious Southern gravy, Grandma asked if I wanted to take a walk with her around the block. I agreed out of boredom. According to Grandma, Sunday was a day of rest, and that meant no gardening, no homework, no housework.

While Mama took a nap, I followed my grandma outside. Sunday afternoon walks were something I was used to. Every French family took a walk after Sunday lunch. I was actually pleased that Grandma had the same tradition.

"How was Sunday school, Emile?"

"Okay."

"Just okay? What did you study?"

"The Ten Commandments."

"Ah."

"Grandma, I guess your church is fine, but can I ask you a question?"

"Certainly, Emile."

"Do you think it's worse to drink a glass of wine or to hate a black person?"

I could tell my question surprised her.

"Well, Emile, what do you mean by that?"

"In Sunday school class we talked about all the things we weren't supposed to do if we were Christians. And the teacher talked about how dangerous alcohol is and asked if any of us had ever 'been tempted' to drink it. Well, nobody else was saying anything, so I raised my hand and said, 'I've had wine before. Lots of times my dad lets me have a little wine at dinner.'

"Everyone got real quiet, and the teacher looked embarrassed and gave me a strange look, like I had said something wrong. Some of the

kids laughed, and a couple of them said it was a big sin to drink alcohol and their parents would never put a wine bottle on the table at
dinner."

Grandma shook her head. "I'm sorry, Emile. I hadn't thought—"

"But that's not the problem, Grandma," I interrupted. "I don't
care if they laugh. But they were saying all these things about not
drinking wine, and then after class we were walking down the hall,
and the same boys opened a closet and let some brooms and mops
spill out. One of them said, 'Let the nigger man clean it up. He'll be
here tomorrow,' and the others just laughed."

Grandma gave a heavy sigh.

"So that's what I mean. In America, is it not a sin to hate a person,
but it is a sin to have a glass of wine?"

For some reason, Grandma suddenly put her head back and
laughed. "Emile de Bonnery, you have hit the nail on the head! Do
you mind if I share your story with some friends?"

I shrugged and said, "I don't mind, Grandma."

I guess we talked about other things before we had gone all the way
around the block. I don't remember anything else, except for the way
the sidewalk was all uneven with moss and little weeds pushing in the
cracked spots and the way the breeze was soft and warm and the way I
kept wondering how in the world I was going to get used to America.

| *nine* |

On Monday morning I rode the bus to school, then waited at the stop for Eternity to get off her bus with Jake and Blithe. Then the four of us walked to Mrs. Harrington's office, where another woman was waiting to take the children to E. Rivers Elementary.

As we walked, Blithe slowly reached out and took my hand, smiling up at me shyly and saying, "You're nice, Emile. You have hair like mine and you're little and I can tell you wouldn't hurt anyone. I like you a lot, even if you do talk funny."

"Your hair is a lot nicer than mine, Blithe," was all I could think to reply.

Jake didn't say a word, but I could tell that something inside that oversized head was working, ticking away like a clock.

"Do you like your teacher?" This seemed like an appropriate question to ask Blithe as she clutched my hand.

"Oh, yes. Miss Robinson is really, really nice, and she never gets mad at us. One time she let me help her erase the whole blackboard, and another time I got to be first in line for recess. And another time, I saw Jake at recess, just across the way. But the big kids never talk to the little ones and he pretended he didn't see me."

"I didn't pretend! I just didn't see you! I was playing with my friends."

"No, you weren't, Jake. I saw you standing all alone by the slide, and you looked sad. Like always."

Eternity gave Blithe a cross look and said, "Hush up, you two."

I waited as Eternity pecked Blithe and then Jake on the cheek and said, "You wait for Miz Mavis after school, and she'll bring you right to this office. I'll be back to get you as soon as my classes are done. You wait here for me, you promise?"

And each one nodded solemnly.

"Why do you always say the same thing to them?" I asked, sitting across the table from her at lunch. Twice the week before, I had heard her repeat the exact same phrase. "Are you afraid they're going to run away? It's not like the teachers would let them leave school without you."

"Repetition makes it stick. I want it to stick."

"And why does that lady meet them here in the mornings and bring them back after school? Can't they ride their own bus home sometimes?"

Eternity turned on me, her eyes flashing anger. "This bus doesn't go to E. Rivers, but they have permission to ride with me to and from school, and Miss Mavis takes them back and forth. It's for protection, Emile. They can never, ever ride a bus home by themselves. Never. You've seen Ma."

"Okay. Sorry. It was just a question."

"Nothing is just a question, Emile. Everything has a consequence, and you just can't understand. Don't even try."

But I did understand. I knew what Eternity was doing.

"You're not their mother, you know. I don't quite see how you think you can be their mother and sister and a student and a cook and their protector. I don't see how you can do all that. Or maybe I mean I don't know if you should do all that."

"What else can I do? You want me to leave them to fend for themselves? I didn't ask to grow up this fast, Emile. Some things you don't ask for. You just get them."

I felt my face get hot. I wished I hadn't said a word. There was no way I'd ever be right when talking to Eternity.

It was time to change the subject, so I asked, "Are you going to make another planet?"

"Of course not. No inspiration today. You know, I don't play with my food just for fun. I do it for Jake. He's always making things with his food, and I just try to understand how he looks at life. That's all." She lifted a forkful of some sort of mashed potato to her mouth, inspected it, then set the fork down without taking a bite. "You've noticed how different Jake is. He was born premature and he's a little slow."

"Retarded?" I'd heard Griffin use this word.

Eternity frowned. "Yeah. Mentally slow. But he also has another problem. Sometimes he can't breathe well and chokes and spits up blood. That's why I want to be a journalist."

"You do?"

"Of course, dummy. That's why I write for the school paper—to get experience. I want to interview doctors, visit hospitals, ask questions. I couldn't be a doctor—I don't love science that much—but I love to read and research and write. I could raise questions and maybe give them firsthand reports of what it's like to live with Jake. Somehow I could help the doctors find out what no one has been able to tell us yet—how to make him better." She looked down at her plate. "It may not happen soon enough to help Jake. He's not supposed to live past ten or twelve."

I couldn't believe the matter-of-fact way she said it.

"But I hope I'll be able to help someone else, so that other kids won't have to suffer so much, so their families won't either."

I was growing used to the way Jake rarely spoke, how he looked at me with big, blank eyes, how everything he did seemed to take extra long. I hadn't known Eternity long enough to ask her why, but there she went again, surprising me with what was inside her mind. I had secretly hoped the food creations were signs of her great creativity, but even this had some altruistic purpose I could not comprehend; I simply could not identify with Eternity Jones.

Out of the blue she looked at me, took a bite of broccoli, and said, "I named Blithe, Emile."

"You named her?"

"I named my little sister Blithe because I wanted her to be everything I was not: carefree and glad and cheerful. I thought if I gave her a good name, she might just become what she was called. I missed a whole year of school to take care of her. I gave her bottles in the middle of the night and changed her diapers. But I didn't mind. She's worth it."

She was giving me too much information to digest at once. I blurted out, "So your ma doesn't do anything around the house? She's never taken care of any of you?"

"My ma spends all her welfare check on bottles of booze. Then she sits in a chair all day and drinks herself into oblivion."

"Oh," I murmured, and my face betrayed me: pity, the one thing Eternity could not stand.

She stabbed a piece of meat, leaned forward, and hissed, "Stop looking at me like that, Emile! Don't you feel sorry for me! I've told you before!" Then she asked, "You know why we're friends, Emile? You want to know? It's because we're the same. You think we're so different, but deep down we're the same. We've both been abandoned by our fathers. We're both way out of the culture that these kids know about. We talk different, we look different, we act different. We don't fit in, and we never will. And we don't want to either."

I was about to protest, but she wasn't finished.

"You and I are a whole lot alike, Emile. We both have just got to learn how to survive."

No, no, no, I wanted to say. *No, Eternity, you've got it all wrong. You never really had a dad—he never loved you, never thought about you. He just disappeared. But my dad was around for thirteen years. He was part of my life. I know he left me, but I'm sure there's a reason. There has to be a reason.*

She settled back in her chair, put down her fork, and relaxed a little. "I shouldn't have said that, Emile."

"Never mind."

"I hate it when people feel sorry for me."

"I know." I got up to take my tray to the shelf at the back of the lunchroom, even though my stomach growled in protest. There was nothing else to say, and I had suddenly lost my appetite.

Ace was waiting for me outside the lunchroom. He looked even more intimidating than in his football attire or his Sunday suit—the way he leaned over me, a mass of muscles, his over-padded rib cage precisely at my eye level.

"See you outside, Frenchy. We already know Frenchies like to drink wine. Now we'll see if Frenchy fries can fight." He slapped me on the back of the head before sauntering off with Teddy and Billy.

"Don't pay any attention to him, Emile," Eternity said, coming up behind me.

"That's easy for you to say. He's not hitting you on the head all the time. I think I'll just stay inside today."

"No, you don't, Emile. Don't you dare let them think they've scared you."

"They do scare me," I protested.

But Eternity had cupped her hand under my elbow and was steering me in the direction of the glass doors leading outside into the blinding October sun.

"Wouldja looky here," Ace said. "A-Meal is hanging out with the only white trash in the school. A faggot and a slut."

He grabbed me by the sleeve and shoved me backward while Teddy and Billy blocked Eternity. I stumbled and fell, and the three bullies howled with delight. Then Ace knelt down, jerked me to my feet, and pulled me out of sight behind the hedge, with Billy and Teddy right beside him.

"This is for being a skinny, wine-drinkin' sinner," Ace said, his fist ready to slam into my nose.

I kicked him in the shin as hard as I could. His fist missed my nose and skimmed my ear. He cursed while I pulled myself up, but short, stocky Teddy put his head down and tackled me, sending me sprawling on the ground again.

I picked myself up, shaking my head clear when I heard Eternity yelling at me, "Fight! Fight, Emile! Don't you dare let them get the best of you or it'll be all over. Fight!"

She bent down toward the ground, scooped something up in her hand, and flung a fistful of dirt into Ace's eyes. He cursed again and said, "You know better than to do this, girl! Git her, Teddy! Go after him, Billy!"

Teddy was gearing up to grab Eternity by the collar when, seizing on Eternity's bright idea, I threw a handful of dirt in his eyes. He started cursing along with Ace, furiously rubbing his eyes. "You low-minded trash!"

Fury pulsed in my ears, and I wished I could have taken Papa's switchblade and stabbed it right into Ace's fat belly.

"Emile, watch out!" Eternity screamed, and I ducked, just barely missing Billy's fist. With an image of me holding the switchblade, I knocked into him full force.

We tumbled to the ground, and as I scrambled back up, I saw Mrs. Chalkin, the English teacher, coming out of the building.

"Come on, Emile. Let's get out of here," Eternity said, grabbing my hand. She flipped her long braid over her shoulder and spat to the bullies, "Y'all are a bunch of redneck Klanners with nothing in your heads but a bunch of horse crap, and you'd better stay away!"

Their eyes shot out fire, but they didn't say a word.

Mrs. Chalkin walked over to them and asked, "What's going on here, boys?"

We didn't stay around to hear their answer.

"Where'd you learn to fight like that?" I asked in awe.

"Self-preservation, Emile. That's all it is," she said. "I learned it a long time ago, and you better learn it too if you want to survive around here. Anyway, I gotta go."

I watched her leave, and couldn't help the grin on my face.

I thought about that incident with the bullies for the rest of the afternoon. In spite of our apparent victory, I knew my trouble wasn't over. But by the end of the day I had a plan.

I found Ace alone by his locker. Hands stuffed in my pockets so he couldn't see how hard they were shaking, I said, "I know you're having a hard time in French. I think I can make sure you get a C if you'll promise to leave me alone."

One side of his mouth turned up and he snarled, "Whadda I care about French, Frenchy Fry?"

"I doubt you care anything about French, but I think you care a lot about football. And if you want to stay on the team, your French grade needs to . . . to get better." I tried to control my breathing, but I couldn't, the way Ace towered over me, one thick hand locking on my shirt collar. "B-b-but if you're not interested—well, never mind."

"Whaddaya know about my grades in French?" He gave my collar a jerk, and it tightened on my throat.

"Mrs. Harrington told me that athletes have to maintain a C average," I squeaked. "And, and I heard your father say—"

He picked me up off the ground, literally, and I guessed I was going to be lynched all right, even if the noose was only the collar of my shirt. I squirmed, gasping for breath. Ace let go, and I landed hard, falling to my knees.

He bent down and said, "Don't you ever listen to a private conversation between my father and me again, you hear?" His greased-back hair glistened, its spikes only inches from my nose. I thought he was going to flatten me. Instead, he whispered, "Just how do you plan to get my French grade up?"

Relief flooded through me. "Oh, I can help you, Ace. I promise. It won't be hard. I can start today."

"I got football practice, Frenchy."

"Well, I can help you anytime. You tell me when."

Ace didn't answer. He just slammed his locker door shut and walked off.

I slowly got back on my feet and turned to see Eternity standing behind me.

"How did you know he was failing French?" she asked.

I filled her in, and the hint of a smile moved across her face.

"Not bad for a French fry," she said. "See ya tomorrow."

I think what enticed me into Grandma's garden each day after school was simply Grandma—plus my desire to avoid conversation with Mama, as it seemed often to turn into an argument. But maybe it was the garden itself that lured me.

On the day of the fight, I came home and quickly ate a peanut

butter and jelly sandwich, then went outside and found my grandmother on her hands and knees. She was twisting a thin wire around
the bottom of a lattice that ran up the side of the garage, intent on
attaching an unruly, thorny rose shoot to the wooden fence.

"School okay?" she asked.

"I guess. I hope I survive." The confession escaped, unplanned,
from my lips.

She looked over her shoulder at me, shielding her eyes from the
sun. "Another hard day?"

"They keep getting worse."

"I'm sorry to hear that."

"You know, Grandma, in France I was funny and smart and had
lots of friends. Nothing comes out right in this school. Every time I
open my mouth, kids laugh."

"Dear Emile. It's not easy to be different at your age. But you're
going to survive. More than that—you'll blossom! You'll see."

With one snip of her garden shears, she cut a bright yellow rose
whose edges were tinted with orange.

"See, this one is still blooming, straight through the spring and
summer and into the fall. I'll have roses right up till Christmas."

She handed the thorny stem to me. It pricked my fingers, and she
could tell by my expression that I was unconvinced.

"What would you like to plant today, Emile? Look at all these
bulbs I got at the nursery. Tulips, jonquils, hyacinths, crocuses, narcis-
suses."

I answered, "Let's do tulips," mainly because I was sure of what
they looked like.

We walked over to an empty flower bed and knelt down. With a
trowel, Grandma began removing dirt, making a narrow hole in the
soil, and then placing a fat brown bulb into it.

"Do you ever wonder how this hard, dry bulb can months later
start to poke its shoots out of the frozen ground? Do you ever wonder
how it survives?"

I shrugged. I'd never thought about it.

"It's a natural process, but very slow. The bulb has to spend time
in the dark earth, brooding, growing roots, preparing to push through

the ground. You know what the Lord Jesus said?"

I shook my head no.

"'Unless a grain of wheat falls into the earth and dies, it remains alone; but if it dies, it bears much fruit.'"

"Oh." I nodded as if this explained everything.

"Trust me, it will happen. Then the days will speed by faster than you can imagine, and you'll only wish you could slow them down again. God cares for us. Do your part, just like the bulb. He'll do His. I guarantee."

I was using an old green trowel and had just stuck my first bulb in the wet ground. I thought about Grandma's riddles and said, "But what am I supposed to do?"

"'Whatever your hand finds to do, do it with all your might.' Your job is to go to school, do the work, make friends, love your mother, pray for your father."

"Oh," I said again, wondering about this grandmother who intertwined Bible verses with gardening and somehow made it relate to me. I brushed aside a few brittle leaves, dug another shallow hole, and dropped in a bulb.

Grandma hummed as she worked, and I planted quietly for a time. Then my curiosity overrode my silence. "Grandma, what did you do when Mama left? Did you try to stop her?"

She laid down the trowel, sat back on her heels, and said, "No. She was already 'gone' in her heart, and I guess I just knew she needed to get away. I let her go."

"That's all?"

"For a while. I watched her go, and I didn't do anything else."

"What about your husband?"

"Miserable. Furious with me. Blamed me for chasing away his little girl. I think he would have strangled me, except he was afraid of tarnishing his reputation."

She sighed heavily, and I felt bad for making her remember.

"We lived through an awful six months with Clyde—your grandfather—calling the authorities, contacting Janie, begging her to come home . . . yelling at me."

I slapped the trowel over the soil, flattening it down. "Then what did you do?"

"I buried myself in activity. I tried to keep going."

"And you never went after her? Never tried to find her?"

"We knew where she was after a while. Clyde paid for her college. He went to see her a few times at school. She didn't want to see me. Then she met your father and left for France. And you were born there."

"And that was okay?"

"No, of course not. I was brokenhearted. So was her father. We struggled along. I honestly thought Clyde was going to divorce me. Instead, he had his heart attack, and things all of a sudden got clearer for me. We moved to this house. And that's when I finally started dealing with all that was locked up inside."

"How did you do that?"

"In this garden. I went out and pulled up all the weeds. It was all grown up and a mess, and I just spent all my energy and tears in the garden. I'd yank weeds and yell at God and whoever else I could blame and just tell Him how furious I was that my life wasn't working out at all as it was supposed to." She chuckled. "At least how I thought it should."

I couldn't imagine Grandma cursing God and mankind at the top of her lungs. "Then what happened?"

"Not much, for a long time. But at least I expressed some of my anger and my grief—because, Emile, I really was devastated, but too proud to show it. And then a strange thing happened. Spring came around. It actually started in February. Daffodils started popping up all over the yard. I had no idea, you see. We had bought the house in early fall. I didn't know if there was much of anything planted here." She made a wide circle with her arms. "But this yard was full of surprises. I guess you might say that nature taught me a Bible lesson. The garden got reborn, and somewhere inside of me, I did too."

I had run out of questions. Grandma started humming again, and before I knew it all the tulip bulbs were nestled safe in the damp earth, waiting for spring.

There was something else that preoccupied me besides Papa's absence and surviving at school and Eternity. I could not exactly put a name on it, *it* being one more thing that didn't make sense. This was what I wondered: How could Mama have completely ignored Grandma for all those years? Why did Grandma, who obviously liked to travel to faraway places, never once just come to Lyon and find us— find me?

And this was the big question: Why did they seem to like each other so much now?

There's always *le revers de la médaille*, Mamie Madeleine used to say—the other side of the coin. Grandma Bridgeman had given me her version in little bits and pieces, so I decided to ask my mother. I thought that maybe if I went about it the right way, without making her defensive, this was one secret she would reveal. She was driving me to the A & P when I launched into my question.

"Mama, how could you not talk to your parents for so many years? That seems so mean, so cruel." Obviously I had not picked the right words, even in French.

But Mama didn't shrink into herself. She just said matter-of-factly, "I hated them. I especially hated your grandmother. I was furious with her—confused. It was wrong, Emile. I know it now. But"—and she said this with a hint of unbelief in her voice—"you've got to understand something, Emile. The woman you see out there in the garden, the woman who is peaceful and calm and kind, that's not the woman I grew up with. Your grandmother is so different from how I remember her. Sometimes it's as if I walked into the wrong house. Everything is different—the way she is, the way she lives, everything."

"She used to be mean?"

"Not exactly mean. Controlling. And I was bursting at the seams to try on life, no matter how it fit. She kept pulling me back, and I kept pushing forward."

She was staring straight ahead, and I noticed the way her knuckles got a bit white as she gripped the steering wheel harder. I think she was about to cry, but her sunglasses hid it.

"I would have stayed if I'd known she was going to become someone different, someone better." She gave a stilted laugh. "I know that sounds ridiculous. Now I just feel bad about all the lost time. I wish she'd seen you as a baby. I wish so many things. . . ."

"Never mind, Mama," I consoled her in French.

When we returned from the grocery store, I unloaded the car for Mama, and she, amazingly, put on a pair of blue jeans and a man's old button-down shirt. She took Grandma's garden gloves and a rake and said, "I'll be back in a little while, Emile," and disappeared into the backyard.

I watched her out the kitchen window as I took beans and peas and peanut butter and eggs and milk and a dozen other things out of the strange brown grocery bags—in France, women loaded up big straw baskets with their daily purchases from the *marché*.

Mama raked the leaves as if she were racing with the wind to get them all in piles before it blew more to the ground. She didn't look peaceful or calm. She raked the grass with determination, the dried leaves crackling and curling, a few frittering away in the breeze like naughty children at recess. She went after the stray leaves, raked them back into the piles. Eventually she slowed down. She got the wheelbarrow from the garage, loaded it with leaves, and drove it up the little path out of view behind the garage. I'd done this yesterday with Grandma—dumped the dead leaves on her compost pile.

At least Mama likes being here now.

I made myself another peanut butter and jelly sandwich and chewed on it by the window. That's when I decided that what Eternity Jones needed was some time in my grandmother's garden. She needed to see living things, pretty things, nature and growth. Blithe and Jake needed to snuggle up in the comfort of Grandma's hospitality. It seemed to me the perfect solution to their misery and secrecy. I could hardly wait to go to school the next day and invite them.

| *ten* |

Despite my deal with Ace, I was terrified to see him the next morning.

When I joined Eternity, Blithe, and Jake at the bus stop, she merely said, "Remember what happened yesterday, Emile. We won. Don't let them intimidate you today, understand?"

I nodded mutely. The matter was settled in Eternity's mind, but mine was filled with grim possibilities. Thankfully any immediate confrontation was avoided, because Griffin came up and shook my hand as soon as I stepped into the hallway.

He looked me straight in the eyes and cooed with a strong Mexican accent, "Well, amigo, you did not tell me you knew how to fight. I'm proud of you."

"I just hope I survive homeroom."

"No worries about that, *Emilio*. You've earned the respect of all the students. Ace won't dare take you out in front of the whole class."

"Oh, great. You mean he'll corner me in some dark alley instead?"

"Relax." He patted me on the back as Ace and Teddy walked into homeroom without giving me a single glance. "You see?"

I met Eternity in the school library at ten-thirty—our study hall hour on Tuesdays. The whole ninth-grade class was whispering about us, but she made no comment. Instead she surprised me by saying, "So tell me another story, Emile, about your dad. Got any more ideas about what happened to him?"

I was fiddling with my watch, and without thinking I grumbled, "Sure, I've got other ideas. Just ask my mom. She says he ran off with another woman."

"She does?" This had Eternity's immediate interest. "Well, did he?"

I shrugged.

"Does she have proof?"

"I don't know if she does, but I do."

"You do?"

Miserably I related the story of my wristwatch, the way it had been an early birthday present, the visit to Vieux Lyon, seeing my father at the café with the other woman.

With every detail, the creases on Eternity's brow became deeper, more pronounced. At last she said, "Well, then, that's it. That's the whole thing. He's having an affair."

I gave her a disgusted stare. "That is *not* it! My father would not do that to us, I tell you. It's just some type of cover-up or misunderstanding. That's why I have to discover the truth. I know it's tearing Mama up to think he's off with someone else. She loves him."

She rolled her eyes at me. "Emile, really. Quit pretending."

I fumed as she opened her math book, furious with myself for having said anything. "The only reason I told you is so you could understand the complexity of the situation. I need your help to figure it out. See, I want to go to the library—not this one—a big public library. Could you get me into the library you go to?"

She was working on a math problem and turned her head halfway to look at me, her eyes sleepy and bored. "Anybody can go to the public library, stupid. You don't need me."

I shot her an annoyed look, and she softened. "Sure I can. Why?"

"Well, it's that I need to get information about Klaus Barbie."

"Who's he?"

"This awful Nazi from the Second World War. They called him the Butcher of Lyon. I want to see what happened to him after all."

"What do you mean, after all?"

"He was condemned to death twice in absentia in France. So I want to find out where he was hiding out and where he is now—if he's still alive. Maybe that would help me with my dad."

"And what does Klaus Barbie have to do with your dad?"

I wanted to act cross and tell her it was none of her business. But then again, I wanted her to care about my business, so I said, "He tortured lots of people in the Resistance; he was responsible for the murder of one of France's biggest heroes. And my father saved newspaper clippings about him. If he was *obsédé* with Klaus Barbie, there must be a reason why."

"*Obsédé?*"

"It's the same in English. You know . . . obsed . . ."

"Obsessed?"

"That's it."

She chewed on the end of her braid, deep in thought, probably pleased at the information she had gleaned from me. "We always go to the library on Wednesday afternoons for story hour. Jake and Blithe love it, and I have plenty of time to wander around the stacks." She got a mischievous gleam in her eye and added, "And if you happen to remember your street address, you can even sign up for your own library card."

"So how do you get there?"

"Mr. Davis takes us, almost every week."

"Does he really?"

"Yes. Is that a problem?"

"No. I mean, yes. I thought you were scared of him."

"Did I ever say I was scared of him?" Her eyes were defiant.

"No," I admitted. *But you sure looked scared.*

"He likes to drive us around in his pickup. He takes us to the library, drops us off, and comes back two hours later. Anyway, if you want, you can ride the bus home with us, and then he'll get us there. Your grandma could pick you up afterwards—around five."

This sounded feasible to me, something Grandma would agree to. "I'd like to."

"Then come." My problem solved, she nonchalantly slid a piece of paper in front of me, asking, "Can I show you the article I've been working on for the next edition of the school paper?"

And suddenly we were far away from Klaus Barbie and Lyon and right back in the middle of the civil rights movement.

A History Lesson for All of Us

I have a black friend who says you have to be taught to hate. I believe him. If we were all thrown into a room together, blacks and whites and Mexicans and whoever, and we had no preconceived ideas about each other, would we hate each other? Would we say, "Because your skin is different than mine, I'm better"? My friend fought in the Second World War, in France. Everyone was treated the same way over there. They cared about each other. It wasn't until he came back to America that he was considered a "lower class of humanity."

"You're talking about Mr. Davis, aren't you?"

"Yep. I decided to interview him. It was really interesting."

"It's good, Eternity," I said carefully. "But do you think these students care what a middle-aged black man thinks? Maybe you should interview someone white who is favorable to the civil rights movement. Someone from this school. Is there anyone like that? Someone well respected?"

"Well, Mrs. Harrington is. She does a lot of volunteer work to help what she calls 'the underprivileged.'"

"Yeah, that would be good. Interview Mrs. Harrington," I said. But what I was thinking was, *Maybe I can talk to Mr. Davis tomorrow. Maybe he'll tell me some more things about the war. It can't hurt to ask.*

Ace decided that I could help him with French that afternoon, right after school, which meant I'd miss the bus. I didn't dare argue, though. I was so relieved that he and his friends were actually leaving me alone that I felt almost excited to oblige him. I'd been paying attention to the streets the bus used to get to school, and I figured if I had to, I could walk home. It might take an hour or more, but I'd rather face Mama's worried expression, and even Officer Dodge's interrogation, than Ace's meaty hand lifting me to the gallows any old day.

I spent an hour with him, teaching him how to conjugate the two most frequently used verbs in French: *avoir* and *être*. And I discovered something. Ace wasn't as stupid as he looked. He actually caught on pretty quickly, once his buddies left him alone. When we'd finished the homework for the week—I'd even gotten a few extra worksheets from Mrs. Smith, who was delighted to see me helping Ace—he asked, "How ya gettin' home, Frenchy?"

"I thought I'd walk."

"Where'd ya live?"

"Anjaco Road."

"That's over by the hospital. It'll take you half the afternoon. We can give you a ride."

"Okay. Thanks," I said, relieved to think of Ace's mother picking us up.

But it wasn't his mother who showed up; it was the big, bulky man from the football game.

"Hey, Dad, can we give this kid a ride home? He's the one helping me with French."

I saw then how much Ace resembled his father. Up close they both had the same square face that curved only at the jaw, the thick blond hair cut in a crew, massive shoulders and forearms, and eyes that got lost in their full cheeks, especially when they attempted to smile.

At the moment Mr. McClary wasn't smiling. He was measuring every inch of me, and looking pretty disappointed. "You the new French kid?"

"Yessir."

"Ace says you're Maggie Bridgeman's grandson."

"Yessir."

"Well, that's fine. You staying at her place on Anjaco Road?"

"Yessir."

"Hop in then."

Mr. McClary pumped me with questions the whole way to Grandma Bridgeman's house. When he dropped me off in front of her house, I said, "Thank you, sir."

"You're welcome, boy."

Ace grunted, "G'bye." But he didn't whack me on the side of the head. Surely this was progress.

Grandma was not out in the garden, nor in the kitchen, and her car was gone. Maybe she and Mama were out together, I reasoned. The door was unlocked, so I went in and set my books on the kitchen table. I heard a feeble sound coming from my grandmother's bedroom and went to investigate.

The room was almost pitch-black, the shutters closed, the air heavy and strong. Once my eyes got used to the dark, I saw that my grandmother was in bed, lying on her back, perfectly still, the rise and fall of the covers the only sign of movement. She had a wet towel lying over her entire face.

"Grandma," I whispered.

She turned her head slightly and said, "Oh, Emile. Hello, darling. Home from school. I was just thinking of you."

"What's the matter, Grandma? Do you need me to get you something?"

"Shh, no dear. Don't worry. Just a nasty migraine."

"Migraine?"

"Bad headache. Only thing that helps is darkness. I get them often."

"How long does it last?"

"A day, sometimes two. Don't worry. I lie in bed and pray for everyone I know."

"Does it hurt really bad?"

"Pretty bad, Emile."

"I'm sorry," I whispered. "I'll let you rest, Grandma." I tiptoed out of the room, closing the door behind me, made myself a peanut butter and jelly sandwich, and went outside.

I was kicking a soccer ball that Mama had bought me against the garage wall when Mama drove the Chevrolet into the driveway.

"Hello, Mama," I greeted her optimistically.

"Well, hello, Emile. Where's Grandma?"

"Migraine. She's lying down in her room."

Mama considered the news with a frown. "She has always been prone to those headaches."

I nodded, not really paying attention, my mind on the library outing planned for tomorrow. I had learned a lesson from following

Griffin to Eternity's house, so I decided to be forthright this time. "Mama, do you know where the public library is?"

"Why, of course, Emile. That is, if it's still in the same place as fifteen years ago."

I handed her a paper with the street address on it and she said, "Ida Williams Library. Yep, it's the same."

"Could you pick me up there tomorrow afternoon around five? A friend and I are going there after school to do a research project."

"How nice—I knew life would get better. Yes, of course. I'll be there."

On Wednesday, Eternity and I were by our lockers after school when Blithe and Mrs. Harrington came down the hall toward us.

"Jake's real poorly, Eternity," Blithe said. "We prob'ly have to take him to the emergency room. He's all blue and pitiful."

Mrs. Harrington broke in. "He's waiting in my office, Eternity. I think he'll be okay. He just had a bad coughing fit. He's lying down."

Eternity followed Mrs. Harrington to her office while Blithe confided in me. "He's almost died a bunch of times. It's so scary. He gets blue and then can't breathe and then Ma starts screaming for help and Eternity has ta git Mr. Davis. I just try to make him feel better, but I can't do much. The doctor said Jake won't live past ten years old, and he's almost eight now—I wasn't s'posed to hear it, but I did, and it worries Eternity awful much."

She wore the saddest expression on her cream white face, but somehow it seemed she liked telling her story. "One time Mr. Davis wasn't home, so I had to heat the water and Eternity kept putting compresses on Jake's chest and then she squeezed him around the middle, him sitting on her lap and that would loosen up the phlegm and he'd spit it out into the toilet—all thick and green and putrid. Eternity is always saving his life. And I help."

By this time, Eternity and Jake were out in the hall.

"Hush up, Blithe," Eternity said, putting an end to her sister's recital of Jake's near demises. "Jake'll be just fine. He just needs some rest. Now hurry up, or we'll miss the bus."

"I'd better just go on home," I said.

"Why, Emile?" Blithe whined.

"Well, you won't be going to the library now."

"Oh, can't you and me go together? Eternity can stay with Jake. Please? I don't want to miss story hour."

When she looked up at me, pleading with her big blue eyes, I couldn't resist her request. So I rode the bus with them, Blithe sitting smushed up against me with her little blond head on my shoulder. Eternity didn't say a word; her face was expressionless as was Jake's, but I could tell she was nervous.

We arrived at the bus stop by the trailer village and got off, Eternity holding Jake around his waist as we began walking to their trailer. Jake was wheezing loudly, head bobbing awkwardly as he held on to Eternity, almost yanking her off-balance. The sight was so distressing that I began to feel a tightness in my chest and a need to take in deep gulps of air.

When Jake suddenly doubled up and starting choking, Eternity said, "Emile, can you take Blithe and go to Mr. Davis's house? Tell him we need him to bring the pickup. Hurry!"

So we ran, Blithe holding fiercely to my hand, whimpering, "I told you it was bad, mighty bad."

We arrived at the little yellow trailer, both of us bent over and gasping as I rapped on the screen door. Instead of being afraid, I felt like hugging Mr. Leroy Davis when he came to the door.

"Jake's in trouble. He's sick. Eternity told me to get you, sir." I was speaking fast and stumbling over my words in English.

Mr. Davis wore a perplexed expression, and I thought he couldn't understand me. I repeated myself.

"I heard you, son. Where 'bouts are they?"

"Up the hill by the bus stop," Blithe offered.

He retrieved the keys to the pickup and took off. I wanted to follow, but Blithe was crying, "Don't leave me!"

We waited impatiently, sitting on Mr. Davis's step, taking turns throwing small pebbles into the sand, trying to hit an empty watering tin that sat a few feet away. I purposely missed the tin several times, until Blithe succeeded in landing her pebble with a *ping* right on the rim. Her smile spread across her cheeks and up to her eyes.

"You want me to help you aim, Emile?"

"Yes, please."

Eventually we heard the truck coming down the dirt lane.

"He's all right, now," Eternity explained, hopping out. "He had a bad spell, but he got all the stuff out. I'm going to take him to his room. Thank you kindly, Mr. Davis."

"I'll help you," I said.

"No need. Do you mind staying here with Blithe?"

I shrugged.

"It's 'cause Jake's spittin' up blood, and 'Ternity doesn't want me to see it," Blithe assured me. "She says it'll give me the heebie jeebies. But it won't. I've seen it lots of times, and I never have bad dreams. Not about Jake, at least."

So I spent another half hour sitting on Mr. Davis's porch while Blithe played with a scrawny kitten and Mr. Davis worked on his truck.

I wandered over to the truck and asked, "Do you help them a lot?"

"We help each other. Miz Jones helped me back when my missus was so poorly. Saw me through some real rough times after my wife died."

"How long have you known them?"

"Lived here just down the street from them for seventeen years. Knew Miz Jones 'fore Eternity was born."

"That long ago?"

"Yeah. Poor Miz Jones. She was a right perty lady—girl, really, back then. Big-boned and tall, but not like she is now. Lived in that trailer with her own mother—two of 'em tryin' to survive. Her mother took in men for money—till one of 'em refused to pay, and when the mother screamed at him, he just shot her down dead. So there she was, Miz Jones, all by herself.

"When her little Eternity was born, she tried her best to care for her. Jus' didn't have much luck, that's all. She didn't get all big like she is now till after Jake was born. Guess it was worry. Worry and . . . some rotten luck and . . . now you see what she is today."

The more Mr. Davis talked, the less scary he seemed. Just a man probably around fifty with black skin and tight grayish-black hair and sagging skin under his eyes—eyes that were yellow where they should have been white. His faded overalls were stained with oil from the truck, and his fingernails were all black and chipped. But he no longer scared me.

"You said you fought in the war. At Normandy. That makes you a hero. My dad says you were all a bunch of heroes—the ones who lived and the ones who died."

"That what he says?" He laughed.

"Yessir."

"Well, he's right about one thing. Lot of boys died. Saw it myself. I shoulda been one of 'em, but I guess I got lucky. Just shot through the knee. Got me a medal for it."

"My dad fought in the war too, Mr. Davis."

"You don't say?"

"He was only a teenager, but he was a *résistant*. Have you heard of the Resistance in France?"

He looked at me with suspicion. "Do I look dumb, son?"

"No, sir."

"Well, you're right. I ain't dumb. Some of them folks in the Resistance saved our lives." He threw down an old greasy rag. "One time they was down by the railroad, in the dark, laying out some kind of explosives. We wouldn't have had enough troops to take out the Germans. But those boys and girls—and they was nothin' more than boys and girls, I tell you—they knew what they was doing. They blew up that train track, derailed the train, and we got away jus' fine."

I was listening to Mr. Davis, but I was remembering one of Papa's stories at the same time.

———

Papa picked up an old-fashioned oilcan, black metal with a long, narrow snout. "This was the type of can we used to hide the plastic explosives," he explained.

"What do you mean?"

"The explosives had the consistency of dough, like when Mama makes bread. And we molded these homemade bombs to fit in whatever container we chose to use. As little as two kilos of the stuff could blast a hole big enough to sink a ship."

"Wow. Did you sink any ships, Papa?"

"No, son. But I helped derail a dozen trains."

"With bombs hidden in oilcans?"

"With bombs hidden in all kinds of things—an oilcan, a birdhouse, a bottle of varnish. We were very clever."

"Did you come up with the ideas, Papa?"

"No, not usually. I was too young. I just carried out plans. I was small and could shimmy into spaces that the men couldn't."

"Did you ever kill anyone, Papa?" I was nine, and I figured I was old enough to ask this question.

I remember the look on his face, the way the smile faded and his eyes became somber. I remember his hesitation.

"Yes, son, I did. I killed men. With these plastic explosives—when they exploded on the train, sometimes people died. And other times, I . . ." He didn't finish his sentence.

"How old were you, Papa?"

"I was sixteen."

———

"You listenin' to me, boy?"

I jumped and looked up at Mr. Davis. "Yessir. I mean, no, sir. I mean, I was thinking about something my papa told me."

"Mmm, hmm. I imagine you do all right listenin' to him, boy. He can tell you the truth—more truth than you gonna hear on the news." He gave a grunt, slammed the hood of the truck shut, and brushed his filthy hands back and forth. "That's enough for today. Yessir, I probably wouldn't be alive today if it weren't for people like your father. We were there for each other, fighting for our country and yours. We were fighting hate and cruelty and evil.

"And then I got back home and I found out what I'd known all along. Hate and cruelty and evil lived right across town here—just as real as on the beaches of Normandy."

And I had nothing at all to say to that.

It was almost four o'clock by the time Eternity came back to Mr. Davis's trailer. I was surprised to see Jake with her, head tucked down but breathing fine.

"If we hurry, we can still make most of story hour," Eternity said, looking as determined as ever.

So we all got into the pickup, Jake and Blithe sitting up close to Mr. Davis while Eternity and I rode in the back. I couldn't hear what he was saying, but through the window of the cab, I saw his gray head turning to the side as he talked to the children. Once in a while he reached over and patted Jake gently on the back.

"I see why you're not afraid of Mr. Davis," I said to Eternity as the wind whipped my hair in my face.

"If you don't understand that," she said derisively, "you don't understand much of anything."

I didn't answer—I don't think Eternity meant to make me feel stupid. I think she just had the same disease as my Mamie Madeleine and lots of other women—she had to have the last word.

Well, let her, then, I thought. *Might as well give her some small pleasure for all she's been through.*

Mr. Davis let us off at the Ida Williams Public Library, saying, "I'll be back for you at five-thirty, Miz Eternity."

"Thank you, Mr. Davis."

We went into a red-brick building with pretty white columns on the outside. As soon as the lady at the reception desk saw the Jones children, she smiled and whispered, "Story hour just started about five minutes ago." Eternity took Jake and Blithe downstairs to the children's area, then came back to the front desk.

"I've got a surprise for you, Eternity," the librarian said. She held out a big hardback book, very used and covered with clear plastic. "We've just received a new copy, so I saved this one for you."

Eternity took the book and cradled it as if it were a baby. I thought she was going to burst into tears.

"Thank you," she whispered, almost reverently. Then she showed me the worn book, the spine crumbling off, several of the pages almost loose. "Look, Emile. It's *Immortal Poems of the English Language.* I've always loved this book!"

The librarian, who introduced herself as Mrs. Stevenson, began talking to me. "Eternity tells me you are French."

"Yes. My father is French, my mother American. I've always lived in France until a few weeks ago."

"What a rich experience. This must be very different. Strange, even."

She said it as if she knew, and I noticed that her accent was different from the other Southerners I'd met.

"I came here from Boston many years ago. I love the South. Most of the time. People aren't always what they seem, though. So friendly and soft on the outside. Now tell me, Emile, what is it you'd like to research?"

"The Second World War," I said. Then I added, "Especially anything you might have about the Resistance in France and Klaus Barbie, the Nazi war criminal. I want to know if he's still alive."

"Well, let's look at the card catalogue and see what we can come up with."

Before long I was sitting at a round table with a tall stack of books about World War II.

Although the numbers are unknown, France has no doubt produced its share of Nazi hunters. Even though most of the French were more than happy to return to a semblance of normality after the war, there were those avowed to avenge their families' deaths, determined to find the Nazi war criminals. Their goal is simple: find these men and extradite them to Europe to stand trial. . . .

Mrs. Stevenson came toward me with something in her hand. "Did you find anything interesting, Emile?"

I nodded, while the words *Nazi hunters* echoed in my mind.

"Well, you can come back anytime you want, now that you have your library card." She handed the card to me.

Eternity, Jake, and Blithe had already gone home by the time Mama arrived. She found me sitting on the front steps, lost in thought about Nazi hunters and my father hiding plastic explosives on trains. But of course, when she asked me, "How'd the research go, Emile?" all I said was, *"Très bien, Maman."*

| eleven |

Grandma seemed in fine shape Thursday morning, so I decided it was the perfect time to bring up the subject that had been on my mind the past few days.

"Could I invite a friend over to the house tomorrow?"

"Why, I think that would be lovely. Don't you, Janie?"

"Who is it, Emile?"

"A girl in my class, and her little brother and sister—"

"A girl?" Mama repeated, and began tugging on an eyebrow. "The same girl whose house you went to last week when—"

"Yes," I interrupted her. "And we're just friends, so don't get worried."

"I'm not worried," Mama replied defensively.

"We'll be delighted to meet your friend and her siblings," Grandma said, with a sweet look at Mama.

All I had to do was mention the idea in front of Jake and Blithe to be assured of my plan's success. Blithe begged and begged till finally Eternity said to me—a scowl on her face—"If your grandma can get us back to the bus stop on Chattahoochee Avenue by five-thirty, I guess we can come over."

"She can take you all the way home, if you like."

"No. Gotta pick up some stuff at the store for supper." And that was settled.

So after school on Friday, the four of us rode the bus to Anjaco Road. When we walked up the driveway to the gray-shingled house, Grandma opened the door as if she'd been waiting right there for us to arrive.

"You have a nice place," Eternity told my grandmother before Grandma had even had the chance to say hello. "I like it."

"Well, thank you, young lady." Grandma was beaming. "And what is your name?"

"Eternity. Eternity Jones."

Grandma took in the name with a slight crease in her brow, but her smile was as warm as ever. "Very nice to meet you, Eternity Jones. I'm Mrs. Bridgeman."

"Nice to meet you, Mrs. Bridgeman. This is my brother, Jake, and my sister, Blithe." She pushed them both forward, and they stood silently looking up at my grandmother.

"Well, come on in! Let's get you children a snack. You must be starving. Your mother is out at another job interview this afternoon, Emile. She'll be back in a little while."

Grandma hummed happily in the kitchen as she made us peanut butter and jelly sandwiches, which Jake and Blithe devoured, leaving their faces stained with purple jelly. After Eternity had washed them up, we all climbed the stairs to my room. Grandma had laid a box of Lincoln Logs on the floor, and Jake and Blithe immediately began to build a cabin.

Eternity walked slowly around my room, examining each print and photograph and all of my books. Then she leaned her hands on the desk and stared out the dormer window. "Nice room. Nice view."

Jake and Blithe had barely gotten the first layer of Lincoln Logs fitted together when Grandma called up the stairs to us, "Anyone want to help me in the garden?"

With a squeal, Blithe said, "Oh, I do!" Then she turned for permission from her sister. "Can I, Terni? Please."

Eternity nodded. "If you promise to help and not just get in the way."

"I promise!" And she hopped up and ran down the stairs with Jake calling after her, "Wait up, Sissy! Wait up."

Eternity stooped down and examined every one of my books, finally choosing one and taking it from the shelf. She plopped down on my bed, opened the book, and began leafing through it. After a few minutes she asked, "Where all have you been, Emile? Have you seen this place?" The book she had chosen was in fact one of those coffee table sorts with all kinds of pictures of Tunisia.

"Yes, I've been there with my parents. We vacationed at Hammamet—it's a city on the Mediterranean, and the water is so clear you can see ten different shades of blue in the sea." I stopped abruptly, thinking of Eternity's old trailer and obese mother. "Have you ever . . . gone on vacation?"

She just shrugged. "I can go on vacation every day of my life if I like. I just close the door to my room and I'm on vacation. My imagination and me."

I didn't know if I'd ever get a straight answer from Eternity Jones. She stretched her legs and hopped off the bed, and said, "So let me see all your 'treasures'."

"Sure!" I opened the little door to the attic space, slid out the suitcase, and lifted up the lid. "I've put them in the order he gave them to me, to see if maybe this will give me a clue about my father."

Eternity glanced at me, back at my collection, and then at me again, smiling in that annoying, condescending way of hers. I almost wished I'd never said a word to her about my father's gifts.

"What?" I asked, impatiently.

"Nothing."

"You're lying. Just tell me what you're thinking."

"You're a funny kid, Emile. Sometimes you seem really old for your age, and other times you act like such a little boy."

"Why do you say that?"

"Well, this whole Tintin thing, for instance. And the secret hunt for your dad." She swept one arm across the suitcase, indicating the collection.

"You don't believe he's a spy?"

Her face went from disbelief to pity to annoyance, and then

Eternity's stare was back. "Okay, sure, he's a spy."

"No, I'm serious. You don't believe it?"

"No."

"You think he ran off with another woman. That's what you think, isn't it?"

Disbelief registered on her face again. "Of course that's what I think, Emile! And I think it because that's what happened."

"You have no idea!"

"You told me yourself! You saw her! And your dad goes away all the time. It's obvious."

"You're wrong. He wouldn't run off with another woman."

"Yes, he would. It's what men do best. Oh, Emile, you are impossibly naïve. All men have affairs."

Her remarks made me furious. "Quit saying that! How do you know? You act as though you're a real adult! You always have to make things tragic and ugly!"

"Fine, forget I said anything. Let's keep looking for your dad."

"No, never mind," I said, trying to calm down.

"Look, Emile, I'm sorry. You know why I act like an adult? Because they stole my childhood! I didn't *give* it away, you know. They stole it. Men stole it." Her Cleopatra eyes went dull.

Neither of us spoke for several minutes.

Finally she said, "I'd better check on Jake and Blithe. No telling what kind of mischief they're getting into," and then headed downstairs.

In fact, they were happily picking the very last tomatoes from a vine in Grandma's vegetable garden. Eternity and I stood on the little flagstone terrace outside the kitchen, side by side, watching Grandma with the two children. The sun on my back melted my anger.

"She seems like a nice lady, your grandma."

"She is. She's really swell. A little old-fashioned, but swell." Then for some reason, I started telling Eternity about the Baptist church and my experience at Sunday school.

"Do you think it's a sin to drink wine, Eternity?"

"I don't know about sin. But I know it can make life hell."

I was disappointed. I was hoping that Eternity, with her goal of being "cultured," would have a different view. "Did you learn that at church?"

"Learn what?" She looked confused. "Why'd you think I'd go to church? I've already told you my family isn't religious."

"I thought maybe that's where you learned that drinking alcohol is so bad for you. That's what the people at my grandma's church say."

Her eyes were cold. "All you'd have to do is live with Ma for a little while, Emile, and you'd figure it out all by yourself. You don't need a Bible to tell you."

What could I say to that?

I had wanted Eternity to enjoy being at Grandma's house and to feel peaceful in the garden, but all I'd done was get mad at her and make her think about how miserable her life was. I made a final attempt to make peace.

"Eternity, why don't you bring Jake and Blithe to the football game tonight?"

"I hate football."

"Well, I don't like it very much either, but the kids might. And, well, you wouldn't have to go home to Ma quite yet."

"Don't try to fix my life, Emile," she snapped.

But then Blithe came running over to us, her hands all brown with damp soil. "Terni, come help us! We're planting bulbs, and there is a beee-u-tiful orange and black butterfly just flitting around. Miz Bridgeman says it's called a monarch! You have to come see!"

Eternity could not resist her angelic little sister any more than I could. So for the rest of the afternoon we all worked in the garden, and when Eternity asked Blithe and Jake if they wanted to go to the football game, I didn't even crack a smile. But inside, I felt as warm and happy as my "amigo," Griffin.

Mama drove us to Grady Stadium after we'd eaten some of Grandma's leftover fried chicken. Blithe was bouncing up and down in the back seat, chanting, "We're going to a football game. Oh, thank you, Eternity! Thank you, Emile!" Even Jake seemed excited in his somber way.

"I'll be back to pick you all up at ten, you hear," Mama said as we got out of the car.

We walked over to the home team side of the stadium. Griffin and his friends—Sally, Mary Jane, and a few other boys—were laughing and joking off to the side of the concession stand. I liked the way Mary Jane looked at me.

"Come on over, Eternity," I coaxed, but she just frowned and shook her head no and hugged the kids nearer. I had an idea. "Here, Jake and Blithe. Would you like to get a Coke?" I handed them a quarter.

Wide-eyed, Blithe grinned and nodded and, taking Jake's hand, trotted over to the long line that had formed in front of the stand.

"You be careful, now," Eternity warned them. Then she reprimanded me. "Don't just hand out money to them!"

"Come on, Eternity. Let them enjoy it."

I had caught Griffin's eye, and he wandered over with the rest of his followers. "Hey there, Emile, Eternity."

When Eternity wanted to look like an ice princess, she did a great imitation. She didn't say a word, just stood there with an expression cold enough to freeze us all. An awkward silence hovered over the group, until finally Mary Jane said, "Well, I'm going up in the stands. I don't want to miss the kickoff."

"Why can't you be a little friendlier?" I complained to Eternity when they'd left.

"I don't feel like being friendly to a bunch of hypocrites. I can tell by one look in their eyes what they're thinking. They're calling me white trash. And when they hear about your father, you'll be no better than I am!"

She had done it again, compared my father with hers, and that same rage started boiling inside me. I grabbed Eternity by the front of her shirt and lifted my arm back. I was a hair's breadth from pushing my fist right into her face when I stopped. I couldn't hit a girl. I couldn't hit my best friend.

I let her go, the anger still pounding in my ears, my face hot and sweaty. I finally managed to say, "Sorry."

She was breathing hard, looking scared, but it soon turned to indignation and anger. "You're just like every other man, Emile. You get mad, you know I'm right, and you wanna hit me. Well, go ahead. I'm not afraid of you! I've been hit before. Ma's boyfriends all liked to hit me. Hit me or do other things. I didn't think you'd be the same."

I shook my head. "I'm sorry! It's just . . . you made me so mad! Quit saying my father is like your pa and all the other awful men you've known. Just quit saying it! You can think it, if you want. I can't stop the way you think. But please stop saying it."

We stared at each other in silence for probably two minutes. At least it seemed like a really long time for Eternity to say nothing. Finally, I did the only thing I could think of. I went over and stood beside her and gave her a very awkward hug. I would've felt better if I could have just kissed her on each cheek like we did in France, but I knew better. So I hugged her, very stiffly, off to the side, putting my arm around her waist because I couldn't reach her shoulders.

"I'm sorry," I mumbled again.

But Eternity wasn't afraid of my hug. She grabbed me fiercely and pressed me to her chest. "I'm sorry too, Emile. I won't say it again. I wanted you to feel the hurt. I, I thought if we shared it, maybe it would make me feel a little better."

Then she let me go, flipped her long braid over her shoulder, and said, "I've gotta go find Jake and Blithe anyway. The game's about to begin."

I didn't go sit with them for the first quarter of the football game. Instead I walked very slowly up toward the school buildings, glad it was twilight. I kept feeling the anger in my body, saw myself lifting my fist to hit Eternity, saw myself barely able to get control. Then I felt myself smushed up against her, confused by those other thoughts that jumped into my head.

Eternity will never be normal, I thought. *Not in her whole life. She'll never get over what those men did to her.*

I didn't know all the details of her past, but I knew she was way too complicated for me. Yet I couldn't help hoping that sometime soon I'd find another reason to hug her.

———

I thought that maybe I'd lost Eternity's friendship after that Friday night, but I hadn't. In some odd way, I had gained another ounce of her confidence. In fact, she came back to Grandma's house on Monday, with Jake and Blithe. The children headed straight out to the garden after having a snack, and Eternity's expression as she watched them tag along after Grandma was tender. She observed them from the kitchen window for a few minutes. Then, rather suddenly, she left the kitchen, went through the hall and up the stairs, a girl with a purpose. Of course I followed.

She walked right over to the little door by the dormer window, opened it, retrieved the suitcase, and after examining each item inside, picked up the hairbrush. "I don't know about this one. What was it used for?"

I eyed her suspiciously. "What do you care, anyway?"

"Look, Emile. I may not believe your father is a spy *now*, but I do find it fascinating to hear about his life back then, in the Resistance."

I tried to look angry and aloof, but failed miserably. "Before my father and his parents were caught by Klaus Barbie, my father left home for a year and joined the *maquis*."

"The what?"

"The *maquis*. Groups of men who hid out in the mountains and fought the Germans."

I opened one of my Tintin books and pulled out a leaflet. "Papa gave this to me—it was how they recruited the *maquisards*—that's what they called the individuals."

I read it to Eternity, translating from the French. "'Men who come to fight live badly, in precarious fashion, with food hard to find. They will be absolutely cut off from their families for the duration; the enemy does not apply the rules of war to them, they cannot be assured any pay, all correspondence is forbidden.'"

Eternity took the leaflet from my hand. "Wow. Who would want to be a *maquisard*?"

"Lots of young men, even boys. Especially since the Germans had ordered all men over twenty to report for work in German factories. Thousands of Frenchmen headed for the mountains instead."

I took the hairbrush with the black boar's bristles and flat, oval wooden handle from Eternity's hand. "They used this brush for directions. See?" I removed the wooden top of the brush to reveal a hidden compass.

Eternity lifted one eyebrow and for a brief second looked impressed.

"One time the Germans and the French traitors—they were called the *Milice*—decided to starve the *maquis* out of one of their hideouts. There were only about four hundred and fifty *maquisards*, and over four thousand Germans and *Milice* surrounding them. But the *maquisards* refused to surrender. When the Germans finally attacked, the fighting was terrible.

"In the end, when the *maquis* leaders realized they couldn't hold the plateau, they ordered their men to fight their way out. Forty-two of them were killed fighting and another eighty *maquis* were captured and executed or tortured to death. But the Germans and the *Milice* lost many more men—over eight hundred in all."

"And your father?" Eternity asked.

"My father killed seven Germans and saved the life of two of his fellow *maquisards*—he dragged them to safety and stayed with them until finally help came. Then he returned to Lyon for three days, and that's when he and his parents were caught."

Eternity sat on the floor by the bookcase with her knees hugged up against her chest. "So your father really was a hero, Emile. He saved lives."

"Yes," I agreed, sitting beside her, the hairbrush still in my hand. I felt a kind of smug satisfaction that at last Eternity had admitted the obvious truth. Now there would be no more comparisons between my father and hers.

"I used to dream about my father, Emile," she said, as if she were whispering a secret to a priest in the confessional. "When I was still a little girl, before Jake and Blithe were born. It was just Ma and me—and all the other men. But sometimes it was just the two of us. Ma was still pretty back then."

I couldn't imagine Eternity's mother as anything remotely resembling "pretty." Then I remembered that Mr. Davis had said the same thing.

"She didn't get fat until later, until after that man . . ."

Her face twisted into such a grimace of disgust that I thought she would surely forget the story she was going to tell me. But eventually she continued.

"I used to sit outside our trailer and pretend we lived in Alabama, down by the Gulf. I'd close my eyes and imagine the salt air washing over me, and then I'd imagine my daddy coming to me from across the ocean. He was a sailor, a very famous sailor, the captain of a ship, maybe, who went out to save lost souls at sea. He almost never came back to land. He had a long black beard and kind eyes and wrinkles everywhere."

She sounded like an adult telling a story to a roomful of six-year-olds. My Eternity was suddenly nowhere in sight.

"It was a hard, sad job he had. But he did it for his country, and he was a proud, good man, and that's why he couldn't come home very often—or ever, really. That's what I told myself as I pretended to sit in the sand and stare at the ocean. It was only a matter of time until he would come back for me. He loved me very much, Emile, that's what I'd tell myself. He loved me so much that he called me Eternity— because he wanted me to be with him forever. That's what I told myself to help me get through all the hard times with Ma and the other men."

She unfolded herself and stood up, staring out the dormer window, her back to me. "When I turned seven, I stopped believing my father would come back."

"Why?" I said, and immediately wished I hadn't.

"Because when cruel things happen to you as a child and keep happening and happening and no one tries to help you, something dies inside. Ma was busy with Jake—he was a sickly baby. She always thought he was going to choke to death—I don't know how many times she had to rush out of the trailer with him in that old beat-up car, wondering if she'd make it to the hospital in time. I used to go with her and hold little blue Jake, thinking he was gonna die in my lap and trying to get the mucus out of his lungs like the doctor had showed us. You grow up quick when it's up to you to save your brother's life a few times.

"Eventually Jake got a little stronger. Ma still had to rush him to the emergency room a lot, but she didn't need me to come along. And so there I was, alone in the house with Marvin."

"Marvin?"

She turned around and looked at me. "Ma's boyfriend."

"Jake's father?"

"Oh, no. I don't even think Ma is sure who Jake's father is."

"Oh."

"Marvin came along after Jake was born, and he taught Ma how to drink whole gallons of alcohol. Said it would make her feel better when she kept thinking Jake would die. Before Marvin she was a whore, but not an alcoholic. Pretty soon, she couldn't feel all the fear of Jake's sickness. She just got kinda numb. And she didn't even care when Marvin would slip out of her bed and into mine."

Eternity was telling me this story without emotion, as if she were recalling a particularly boring picnic she was forced to attend. But I hated her story. It scared me. I felt my face turning red and hot when she talked about Marvin getting into her bed.

"My father never came to rescue me, even though I screamed out for him to help me night after night after night. And I finally admitted that he wasn't ever going to come. That no one on earth cared what happened to me.

"Marvin finally left us, but by that time, Ma's thyroid had started acting up, and then she kept getting bigger and bigger and no men wanted her anymore, so she didn't have any money and we didn't have anything to eat. Sometimes she got jobs cleaning houses. That's how she got pregnant again. Cleaned the Herndons' house on Monday mornings when Mrs. Herndon was out shopping and Mr. Herndon was home. She had Blithe, and I would stay home from school to care for both of the kids. To protect them from our crazy drunk mother."

I don't think Eternity had ever revealed these things to another human, and even as she talked, I kept watching her change from a wounded little girl to a bitter woman, back and forth, back and forth—innocence, hatred, confusion. I wanted her to stop the story. I wasn't even sure she was telling me the truth. Maybe Eternity just needed to invent a story sadder than mine. But one look at her face and I knew it was true. It was a determined, hardened face that belonged on someone five times her age. That belonged on no one.

Then it changed again, and she looked fragile and afraid.

"I'll help you, Eternity," I blurted. "I'll help you take care of Jake and Blithe. So will Mama and Grandma. All of this is too much for you to handle alone. But you'll see. It'll be okay."

"Oh, Emile." She wiped her hand across her face. "You're so sweet. Such a good friend. But you're naïve."

When she said that, she touched my face with her hand, softly brushing it across my cheek. I wanted to grab her hand and squeeze it tight and then hold her against me and let her cry for all she was worth, if that was what she needed.

"You can't always be older than you really are, Eternity. It's not fair, what happened. You're just a kid."

"I'm head of the family, Emile. No one else can live my life for me. I know you want to help, but there's really nothing you can do." Practical Eternity the survivor was talking again.

"You could let me try. And my grandmother too. And Mrs. Harrington. There are people who want to help."

She shrugged, her head down, her long black braid falling over one shoulder. "I don't trust anyone anymore."

I didn't have any idea what to say to that. I didn't know how you taught a person to trust, especially if everything that had happened to her before taught her not to.

But then she leaned over and threw her arms around me, and she started sobbing. So I just naturally closed my arms around her and held her there, awkwardly, terrified and yet also satisfied. Somewhere down deep, Eternity Jones trusted me after all.

I wasn't sure she'd ever stop crying, but when she did, her nose was all red, and I thought the heat from her tears was warming the freckled planets that moved in orbit around her face.

"Just stay up here awhile, Eternity. Lie down on my bed. I'll take care of Jake and Blithe."

She climbed onto my bed, and before I left I whispered, "I'm sorry about everything that happened." Then I closed the door and let her sleep.

| *twelve* |

I wanted to go back to the library on Wednesday, so I rode the bus with Eternity, Jake, and Blithe and walked with them to the trailer. Demon greeted us first, wagging his tail at them and then, seeing me, bracing his legs out and barking furiously until Eternity whacked him on the backside and said, "Hush up, stupid dog." Ma was there, sitting in the rusted metal rocking chair in front of the trailer.

It made me nervous just seeing her, and I figured we'd walk right on by without her noticing, but she called out while we were still in the yard, "Who've you got there, 'Ternity?"

"This is Emile, a friend from school. You've met him before."

She grunted and tried to sit up straighter in the chair. "Hello, Emile. That's a different name."

"He's from France, Ma."

She leaned forward as if trying to get me into focus. I was within a few feet of the porch and could see every brown splotch on her face, every roll of flesh not covered by her dress.

"Well, what's a scrawny French boy doing in Atlanta?"

Eternity didn't want me to talk to Ma, that was clear. She quickly ushered me into the trailer, shooed Jake and Blithe out to play, then led me down the narrow hallway to the safe room.

I was once again struck by how spotlessly clean it was. The beds were made without a wrinkle, the shoes were lined up neatly under each bed, and there wasn't one piece of clothing on the scrubbed and shiny linoleum floor.

I sat down on her bed. "Do you hate your mother?" I asked.

Eternity thought for a moment. "I hate what she's become."

"She seems like she can be nice."

"Oh, sure, she can be nice—when she's not drunk. Anybody can be nice every once in a while. Let's leave it alone, okay?"

"Okay."

She slid the boxes of books out from under her bed, and we sat down beside them. Right on top was the book of English poetry she'd received the week before.

"Did Mrs. Stevenson give you all of these?"

"Not just Mrs. Stevenson. Lots of other librarians too. I have the whole Encyclopedia Britannica and Webster's dictionary and a thesaurus and lots of history books." She began to take them out, one by one, and hand them to me.

I had flipped through three or four books on art and European history when Blithe's voice came from outside, "Let us in, Eternity!"

"Go away, will you?"

"But we'll be late if we don't leave for the library in five minutes. Mr. Davis says so."

"We're coming! Quit being a pest!" Eternity quickly placed the books back into their boxes, slid them under the bed and stood up. "Okay, time to go."

She locked the door behind her, and we traipsed down the hall and out onto the "porch" where Ma still sat in the metal rocker.

"Good-bye, ma'am," I said as we left and got into Mr. Davis's truck.

"Good-bye, French boy," she called after me.

Once she'd delivered Jake and Blithe to story hour, Eternity headed for the card catalogue. "I'm doing research for another article," she said.

"What are you going to write about?"

"The Ku Klux Klan."

I gave her a blank stare.

"Oh, come on, Emile. You surely know about the men in long white robes and pointy white caps who terrorize Jews and Negroes?"

I shrugged.

"Well, they used to meet in the old cotton factory on Peachtree Street, but I want to see what else I can find out about them."

Eternity was a born reporter, and she went straight about her business. Meanwhile, I took out books on the Second World War and laid them on one of the long wooden tables. I looked in each index for references to the Resistance, to Nazis in Lyon, to Klaus Barbie. I jotted down on little note cards anything that seemed remotely pertinent.

One book was filled with pictures of Lyon, and seeing the way the light was playing on the Saône River and the Fourvière Basilica on the hill above it, seeing the statue of Louis XIV on the huge open Place Bellecour, I suddenly felt a physical pain of longing in my gut. I closed the book, my enthusiasm gone. After an hour of research, I left the table feeling tired and sad.

But Eternity was elated. Without asking if I'd wanted to hear it, she started reading me her article: "You don't have to wear a long white robe and a pointed cap covering your head to be part of the Ku Klux Klan. All you have to do is turn your head the other way when you see injustice occurring at the expense of a Negro. Maybe some of your parents are part of the Klan. I pray it isn't so. Have you read anything printed by them lately? Or do you say that the Klan doesn't exist anymore? Well, I have proof that it does. Come and ask me, and I'll show you. In the meantime, vote *yes* for the integration of Northside and show the school leaders that we as a student body are open-minded and non-prejudiced, that we recognize, as the Declaration of Independence states, 'the certain unalienable rights' of every citizen."

I couldn't even muster up a "Good job, Eternity." My thoughts were thousands of miles away.

I was lighting a candle for my grandfather in Fourvière while Mamie Madeleine stood beside me, reciting a prayer. . . . Then I was in a crowd of people standing in front of a tall stone monument. It was the eighth of

May, and we had come along with many others to honor those who died
in the world wars. . . . Then I was with Papa, looking at a small stone
marker that proclaimed this to be the exact spot where two Resistance
fighters were shot down by the Nazis.

"Emile! Hey, Emile, what's the problem?"

"Nothing," I replied, still lost in thought.

"Liar."

"I guess I'm just homesick," I admitted, mortified at the way my
voice cracked as I pronounced those words.

"Oh." Eternity actually looked a little embarrassed for me.

Jake and Blithe were looking through books in the children's section, and we sat down at one of the small tables with the miniature
chairs. Eternity looked comical sitting there with her skinny knees
almost touching her chin. She glanced at her siblings, then back at
me.

"What's it like to feel homesick, Emile?"

"I don't know. . . ." My face got hot, and I cleared my throat to
keep my voice from squeaking. "You've never been homesick?"

"How can you be homesick for something you've never left? I've
always lived right there in the trailer."

"True, that's true. . . ."

"Anyway, I think homesickness is about missing something you
love. There's nothing about Ma and the trailer that I'd miss."

"Well, I guess you're right." I tried again. "Actually, homesickness
just kind of surprises you. It can come from a smell that suddenly
reminds you of home, or a picture, or something someone says. And
it hurts. It physically hurts, like a pinching in your chest or a squeezing."

"It must be nice to feel homesick."

I looked at Eternity as if she were crazy. There was nothing nice
about what I was trying to explain, this feeling that kept me on the
brink of tears.

"I just mean, it sounds like a good thing, to miss someone or
something that much."

"Hmmm."

"But I know it must be really hard—the missing and not knowing when you'll get to see that place or those people again."

"And you're just expected to fit in right away in a new place, and people think you are weird if you can't."

"I've never felt homesick for a place I've known . . . but sometimes I feel homesick for something I'll know in the future. Sometimes I can almost see it or feel it. A place where children are happy and grown-ups get along and there is respect and order and sunshine and I'll never run out of books to read!"

It was a new idea, being homesick for the future, but I understood and smiled. "Like a gigantic safe room."

"Yes, that's it, Emile. A gigantic safe room."

Mr. Davis arrived at the library at precisely five-thirty. I watched the Jones kids squeeze into the cab of his old pickup, watched Blithe wave enthusiastically at me through the cab window as the truck drove away. I sat on the steps trying to make this ambush of strange feelings go away.

I missed Lyon, missed Mamie Madeleine, missed the narrow cob-bled streets of Vieux Lyon with their sidewalk cafés. I longed for a taste of Camembert cheese, for a walk by the river with my friends. I even longed to hear harsh words between Mamie and Mama and to have Papa walk into the room and quiet the fight. It hurt, how much I missed it all.

But there was something else gnawing at my insides, like the feel-ing of knowing without a doubt you are not going to get what you'd asked for at Christmas. Yet at the same time my insides were twisting with excitement—like maybe you were wrong after all, and the longed-for present was there somewhere under the tree.

Part of me longed to get on a plane and fly straight back to Lyon. But the other part of me ached for Eternity Jones and her family. And I wondered how it could hurt so much to be thinking about people I had known for less than three weeks. . . .

Mama arrived a few minutes later. When I slid into the seat of the Chevrolet, she said, "You look sad, Emile."

"Just *fatigué*. It's nothing."

"I'm worried, Emile. I know it's not easy for you, and I haven't been very available. I've been busy trying to make things work, to find a job, to fit back in. But I have a surprise for you."

Mama reminded me of a little girl, all excited with her idea. I couldn't imagine that her "surprise" would be anything I needed. We got on the interstate and drove past the Varsity and Georgia Tech and onto streets with names of Piedmont and Courtland and Baker and Ivy and Spring. Finally she pulled into a parking lot and in front of a restaurant with the name *Chez Tatie*.

"I found this place yesterday when I was on my way to an interview. Come on."

"Are we eating here?"

"You bet!"

As soon as I walked in the door, I felt as if I were stepping off the streets of Vieux Lyon into one of the many *bouchons* in that part of town. There were bright framed prints on the walls, which themselves were almost a fire red, and cozy booths. Something about the look, the feel, and the smell took me back to my city.

I don't think the restaurant was actually open for business at that hour, but Mama walked in as if she'd been patronizing the place for years. When a young woman came to greet us, Mama said, "We'd like to see Jérome."

The young woman nodded and walked off, and Mama whispered to me, all excited, "Jérome's the chef. He's from Lyon!"

A young man with jet-black hair, slight in build and draped in a white apron, came out a few minutes later, a big smile on his face. "Mme de Bonnery! *Quel plaisir!* And this is Emile? *Enchanté.* Have a seat, please," he said, indicating a table.

He sat down with us, and when we began to talk, it was as if the dam had burst and my mouth was the water rushing swiftly, delightedly into the river. French! Words, with no thought of how they sounded or what they meant.

I almost forgot that Mama was sitting at the table with us, as Jérome and I talked for thirty minutes, talked about food and *real* football, of school and rivers and vacations in the Cevennes mountains and skiing in the Alps. No explanations, no wrinkling of the brow because he couldn't understand my accent. This, I decided, must be the other side of homesickness . . . home found-ness?

Finally Jérome announced that we must be hungry, and he began to serve us, himself, starting with the *aperitif*, a glass of Muscat for Mama and a Coke for me. The restaurant didn't really open for another half hour, so he brought us our food and then sat with us as we ate, an eager expression on his face, awaiting our approval of his cooking. Every bite melted in my mouth, the *paté* served on thin slices of dried toast, the fresh green salad with vinaigrette dressing, then the salmon and the pasta and on and on. When customers began to arrive, he left us, and Mama and I continued our meal.

"Thank you for finding this, Mama," I said in between the cheese course and dessert. "It's perfect."

She was pleased with my reaction. I could tell that she too felt at home, even at peace. For that evening she became the best of the mother I knew. She flirted with the waiter, who was also French and was charmed by her American accent. She leaned across the table and insisted I taste her grilled salmon. She let me sip her wine and then giggled, "Goodness, I hope no one from Grandma's church comes in."

It tickled us so that we couldn't stop laughing, and as I watched my mother's happy, flushed face, I realized just how much she loved me. In fact, I got the feeling she'd been looking for a restaurant like this to bring me to ever since we had landed in Atlanta.

———

The day was warm, the windows thrown open to welcome the last traces of early autumn. The sun's dusty rays settled on Eternity's bent head, highlighting her black hair as she sat in front of the dormer window looking at my book on Tunisia. Then she jerked up her head, put her hand to her mouth, and said, "Shh!" She listened intently, then she stood up and ran for the stairs, taking them two at a time.

"What is it?" I asked, on her heels, breathless.

"Jake."

Jake! Had she heard his heavy breathing, his rasping for air, from up in my room? I hadn't heard a thing.

We were by the back door in the kitchen when she stopped, peering through the screen.

I heard sounds now also—although not rasping. Far out in the backyard, Grandma, Blithe, and Jake were bent on their knees, looking at something on the ground—and Jake was laughing.

"Do you hear it?" Eternity asked. She stepped outside, then turned back to me with a look of wonder in her eyes and said, "Jake never laughs."

Blithe saw us then, and ran down to greet us, blue eyes bright. "First there was a lizard and then a squirrel and then a bluebird! We saw them all, Eternity! Every single one! I wish we could stay here forever."

The children's laughter was contagious. I offered to take them for a walk around the block, and Eternity shrugged. "If they'd like to go, that's fine."

"Oh, yes! Ye-es!" Blithe was dancing around my legs.

Eternity gave her little sister a pat on the head. "I think I'll stay here. You two go along and have fun with Emile."

For half an hour we examined lizards sunning on rocks and bees buzzing by flowers. We stopped to talk to two dogs on leashes, a cocker spaniel and a black and white mutt.

Once, as the sidewalk became uneven, Jake grabbed my arm and said, "Watch out!"

When I looked at him, Blithe explained, "You're about to step on a crack."

"So?"

"Don't you know 'step on a crack, break your momma's back'?"

"No, I've never heard of that."

Blithe looked crestfallen. "Well, just be sure not to step on the cracks, okay?"

I grinned. "I'll try. I'll try really hard."

When we'd been all the way around the block and were once again in front of Grandma's house, I said, "Let's get a snack."

I wandered out to the screened-in porch and found Eternity sitting there, sipping a glass of iced tea and talking with my grandmother.

"Can I get the kids something to drink and eat?"

Grandma smiled. "Of course, Emile, you don't have to ask," she said, and went right back to her conversation.

I was pretty sure that Eternity had been crying. Her nose was reddish, and her eyes looked all liquid and red too. What on earth was Eternity Jones telling my grandmother?

There was a tiny sting in my chest, and suddenly I didn't want to be with Jake and Blithe. But it was very obvious that whatever Grandma and Eternity were discussing was not intended to include me.

Reluctantly I fixed the children snacks and talked to them about frogs and lizards. I even helped them build a cabin with Lincoln Logs. But the happy feeling I'd had on our walk had vanished.

Grandma was no dummy. After she had driven the Jones kids back to their trailer, she called me onto the porch. "Emile, dear. I just wanted to thank you for introducing me to Eternity."

I shrugged.

"She's a lovely girl. Lonely and bruised, and smart as a whip. And she thinks you hung the moon. Thank you for giving us time to talk. She doesn't seem to be able to talk with her mother, and she has so many questions about life."

I shrugged again and fidgeted with some coins in my pocket.

"Why don't you sit down, Emile? I haven't heard how things are going with the bullies these days."

I couldn't hide my surprise. "The bullies?" I didn't remember telling her about them.

"Eternity mentioned that you'd been doing a very good job of handling them."

Now Eternity was betraying secrets! But I couldn't stay angry at Grandma, and before I knew it, I had told her about Ace and his father and the way I was helping him with French.

I felt safe on the porch with Grandma. But after we'd talked about school for a while, I brought up another question I'd been pondering for several days.

"Grandma, wasn't it awful waiting for Mama and never knowing if she was going to come back?"

"Yes, Emile, it was, just as you say."

"But you never gave up hope? You always knew she'd come back?"

"In my heart I held on to hope. You know the kind I'm talking about, don't you, the kind that's a sure thing, even if you can't see it yet? That's what I was holding on to."

"For fifteen years! Didn't it ever seem too long?"

"Of course it did, Emile. After I'd cried all my tears and waited and waited, I just went back and held on to hope."

"It seems to me that waiting for someone you love to come back, and never knowing if he will, well, that seems like the hardest thing a person would ever have to do."

"It was the hardest thing," she agreed. "The very hardest thing."

Grandma stood up then and said, "Come with me, Emile," and we walked into the backyard and up on the little slope where all the flower beds were.

"I used to walk around the garden and look at the plants and think how each one has its proper season. The pansies and the primroses poke their heads through the snow, and the daffodils show up in early spring, but so many others have to wait for plenty of sun, wait for spring to come completely before they show their heads. And I'd think to myself that wherever Janie was, it must still be winter. But some-time soon, she'd warm up to spring and she'd come on home."

"And she finally did."

"Yes, Emile. And she brought with her something more wonderful than all the roses in my garden blooming at once." She put an arm around my shoulder. "She brought you."

| *thirteen* |

We were in the middle of French class on Friday morning and I was having a hard time sitting still. Griffin called this "having ants in your pants." I slipped Eternity a note: *Want to hear a story about the fountain pen my father gave me?*

She turned around in her seat and gave me an uncomprehending stare and mouthed, "What?"

I replied with another note. *You asked me about it the other day, so I thought I'd tell you.*

She had just scribbled, *Tell me about it later, idiot. Pay attention!* when Mrs. Smith asked in French, "Emile, can you come up to the blackboard and help me?"

I stuffed the note in my pocket and replied, *"Oui, Madame,"* and went to the front of the classroom. We were doing verb conjugations, and I'd volunteered to help with the pronunciations.

That was one of the good things about French class—when the kids couldn't understand what I said, they didn't make fun of me. Instead they had a look of awe on their faces. It felt really good, especially when that adoring look was on the face of Mary Jane.

Mrs. Smith spoke French very well, in spite of her strong accent, so that we truly engaged in a conversation. I also liked it when she complimented me, saying, "What I just love about French kids is that you are so well informed about things. So much more aware of what's going on in the world."

But one thing was obvious. Mrs. Smith would not be with us for much longer. I was no expert on babies, but by the looks of her rounded stomach, hers was due pretty soon. As I stood at the blackboard, pronouncing the *imparfait* conjugation of the verb *voir*, I thought about how I would miss this teacher and the snatches of conversation in my native tongue.

When I met Eternity at lunch and we'd taken our seats, I said, "Remember when you were looking at the fountain pen the other day?"

"Yes, I remember, stupid. And you were being stubborn and wouldn't show me what it was used for. But why in the world you'd decide to tell me the story in the middle of French class . . ."

"I was bored. You get bored sometimes in class, don't you, Miss Know-It-All?"

She gave a half grin. "Fair enough. What's the secret about the fountain pen?"

"It held poison. A tiny vial of poison that the Resistant carried with him in case he was caught. It looks like a tiny glass test tube with a cork stopper."

"So that he could poison the *boches*?"

"No, not at all. It was for the Resistant to take."

Eternity made a face. "He was supposed to poison himself?"

"Yeah. Awful, *n'est-ce pas*? If he couldn't stand the torture—if he was going to reveal important information and be a threat to The Cause—he, well, he had to choose to die."

Eternity digested this news with a frown on her face. "Will you show me the vial next time I'm at your house?"

"Sure, but there's no poison in it now."

"Well, maybe that means somebody used it."

"Yeah, maybe . . ."

His back was to me, the smoke from his cigarette making a halo around his profusion of black hair. I held the writing pen in my hands. Papa cleared his throat again and again. I could almost swear he was crying. Right in the middle of his story about the poison vial, he had stopped and walked abruptly to the window in my room. It must have been my question that bothered him.

"If the vial is empty, Papa, does that mean someone had to use it?"

He turned back around and ruffled my hair, taking the pen from me. "No, son. I emptied the poison myself. I thought you would like to see how we carried it."

"Why didn't Mr. Moulin carry a pen like this? That way he wouldn't have been tortured; he could have simply died quickly."

"Mr. Moulin was an incredible man. He didn't need the poison, didn't want it. He knew how to keep quiet, no matter what."

"And Papy? Did Papy ever carry the pen?"

He put his arm around my shoulder and I smelled the sweet scent of tobacco and aftershave. I relished the nearness of my father. "Someday, son, I will tell you Papy's story."

But he never did.

"Okay, now tell me about the bicycle pump. What was it used for?"

Once again Eternity was yanking me back from the past. I wanted to resist. I felt I could almost reach out and touch my father, could almost feel the cigarette smoke making my eyes itch.

"It transformed into a single-shot gun." I felt that aching inside again. It was one of the rare occasions that I wanted Eternity to stop talking, to leave.

"Has your mother seen all of your collection?" Eternity asked me.

"Well, she's seen the newspapers and the thumbtack tin and fountain pen and *The Black Island*. When I was little, Papa used to give me my special birthday gift each year in front of the family. But on my ninth birthday, Mama caught Papa explaining the story of the oil-can and the explosives to me, and she got really mad. So from then on, she didn't see the other gifts. And she doesn't know I've brought them with me—except for *The Black Island.*"

"Look, Emile, you've got to ask her about Klaus Barbie. She must know a lot more than she's telling you."

"She'll have a fit if I start talking about Papa and the Resistance."

"Can't you just try?"

Eternity had made her blob of applesauce into a perfect moon and was in the process of placing peas, seven at a time, into little star shapes around it. Her rectangle of fried fish, cut lengthwise into three narrow strips placed side by side, had become the beach beneath the moon and stars. A wad of jiggling blue Jell-O became the ocean.

"The beach at night," she said, smirking.

Relieved to change the topic of conversation, I reached over and with the tines of my fork pierced the Jell-O. It wriggled apart.

"That is so, so gross," I said, using my most newly acquired American slang. "No French person would ever put that sugary congealed blob in his mouth. It's made from horse hooves, you know." This piece of information had come from Griffin.

She grinned at me. "I don't care what you think about Jell-O. It makes a great ocean." She narrowed her eyes, blinked, and said, "But before you do anything else today, when you get home, ask your mother about Klaus Barbie. Okay?"

I didn't answer, just shrugged, but that was good enough for Eternity Jones.

"Mama, um, I came across some old newspaper articles, and I was wondering if you knew anything about them."

"Hmmm?" She was tasting her spaghetti sauce, leaning over the steaming pot. "Newspaper articles. What are they about?"

"They're about Klaus Barbie. Do you know what ever happened to him?"

"Klaus Barbie? The Butcher of Lyon?" She set down the spatula and gave me a perplexed stare.

"Yes."

"Why in the world do you want to know about that madman?"

"I just thought . . ."

She caught on. "Oh, it's about your father, isn't it? Look, Emile. I told you to stop. Stop it!"

"But why did Papa keep articles about Klaus Barbie being sentenced to death twice? Why did he care? Maybe it has something to do with why Papa left."

"Emile! Of course your father would keep articles about the madman who killed his own father!" She said it so quickly it took her a minute to realize what she'd done. Then her face turned red, she closed her eyes and let out a sigh.

"Klaus Barbie killed my grandfather? Why didn't Papa ever tell me?"

"It's not that simple." Her thumb and forefinger tugged on her eyebrow. "He didn't kill him with his own hands. He had him sent to the concentration camps, and Papy died there."

"I know that. Mamie and Papa were there too for a while."

"Yes, yes. It was a horrible time. But leave it all alone, Emile. It has nothing to do with your father right now. Leave it alone."

So I did, but I had found another piece of the puzzle. My father held Klaus Barbie responsible for killing my grandfather. I would have to find out more from either Mamie or Mama. In the meantime, a little word flashed into my mind and would not leave. Now when I thought about Papa and Nazi war criminals, that word appeared in neon colors: *Revenge.*

Griffin and I were at the football game that night, sitting high up in the stands with Sally next to Griffin and Mary Jane in between Sally and me, gradually edging herself in my direction so that her arm was touching mine. She was trying to make conversation, which was slightly annoying since I really wanted to watch the game. But every time her skin brushed against mine, I felt my hands grow sweaty and my stomach start to twitter. As halftime approached, I offered to buy her a Coke and felt this was true bravado.

I was heading for the concession stand when I stopped short. Jake and Blithe were standing in line. They saw me and ran over to me, losing their place in line.

"Hey, kids! What are you doing here? Eternity said you couldn't make it to the game tonight."

"She changed her mind," Blithe volunteered happily, but Jake nudged her with his elbow. "Somebody else brought us."

"Sissy! You're not 'spose to tell."

"It's just Emile. He won't tell anyone."

Eternity was nowhere in sight. "Where's your sister?" I asked.

"I dunno. She gave us some money and said get a Coke and she'd be right back."

This sounded like a strange thing for overprotective Eternity to say. I knelt down beside Blithe. "Wait here, okay? Get your Coke and then just wait here."

Blithe nodded, her blue eyes solemn. Jake looked miserable.

I left the concession stand and looked around, behind the bleachers. No Eternity. I headed in the opposite direction, toward 10th Street. I crossed the street and there, at the corner of Piedmont Park and Monroe Drive, was Eternity, talking to a man, a grown man—tall, husky, and blond. His back was to me. From the expression on her face, I could tell she knew him. He was holding her arm, gripping it tightly. Eternity wore a belligerent look, but she also was wincing, as if in pain.

"Leave me alone!" she said, wriggling free of his grasp. "It's none of your business."

He moved closer and said, "*You* are my business, Eternity. Let me see!"

She gave him a hateful look and jerked away from him. "No. Never mind! I've got to get Jake and Blithe." She spun around, ran back across the street, and marched toward the concession stand.

The man turned around and crossed the street after her, and I shrank into the shadows. It was Ace's father—all six-feet-five of him! He hesitated as if he was going to go after her, but then the crowd cheered for some good play, and he headed back inside the stadium.

"Eternity!" I called softly. "Eternity!"

She wheeled around. "Emile! You scared me!" Then she recovered. "What are you doing here?"

"How do you know him? How do you know Ace's father?"

"Never mind. It doesn't matter."

"It does matter. You said you weren't coming tonight, and then I find Jake and Blithe alone and see Mr. McClary wringing your arm. What's going on?"

She ignored me, waved to Jake and Blithe, and trotted over to meet them. With one arm around each child's shoulder, she said, "Let's go watch the rest of the game. See ya later, Emile."

I'd been dismissed.

That's when I got a creepy feeling ... the same feeling I'd had when I saw the bruises on her arm two weeks before.

My fourth Sunday at Second-Ponce de Leon Baptist Church held a new intrigue. Ace's father. Of course it made sense that Ace's parents would attend the same church that he did, but I hadn't noticed them there before, or given it any thought. So when I sat down on the left side of the sanctuary and saw Mr. McClary's unmistakable large form sitting three rows up on the right, I got those goose bumps again. In fact, I thought I might throw up. Without even asking permission, I slipped out of the pew and hurried to the back of the church and ran down the steps. Somewhere downstairs there was sure to be a restroom. I made it just in time.

As I was washing my hands in the sink, I got a glimpse of my ashen face in the mirror. I told myself that Mr. McClary was not a child molester, was not using Eternity in some sadistic way. But the story of Marvin and the memory of disgust and fear I'd seen on Eternity's face as she described those years of abuse flashed before me, and my insides twisted again. I stayed in the bathroom for a while.

When I got back to the sanctuary, the congregation was standing up, singing a hymn, so I slipped in virtually unnoticed. Except for Grandma Bridgeman and Mama, of course, who both gave me quizzical glances.

I sang for all I was worth, " 'When I survey the wondrous cross on which the Prince of glory died . . .' " but my mind was thinking, *Do men who go to church also treat their sons and teenage girls with cruelty?*

Another question to ask Grandma.

Mama acted almost giddy at dinner on Monday night. She laughed a lot, and her eyes were brighter and her cheeks pink. Watching her, I had a moment's hope that she'd heard from Papa. I willed her to tell us this. So when she said, "I have some good news," I was prepared.

Then she added, "At least I hope you'll see it as good news, Emile."

I gave her a puzzled look, and she hurried on, "I've found a job."

"Oh, Janie. Wonderful! I knew it wouldn't take you long."

"What is it?" I asked.

"Well, I've been hired at Northside."

"*My* Northside? Northside High School?"

"Yes, *your* Northside," she answered, laughing.

"To do what?" But before she told me, I had guessed.

"I'm going to replace Mrs. Smith. I'll be the new French teacher. Provisionally, that is."

"What does that mean?"

"Well, until Mrs. Smith decides if she will come back—you know, after the baby is older."

I had suddenly lost my appetite.

"What a wonderful thing! It's a great opportunity!" Grandma said.

"Yes, isn't it? I'll start at the beginning of December."

I couldn't find anything to say. Life had been going pretty well with me only seeing Mama a few hours a day. The thought of her invading my school life sent a surge of anger through me. And to be honest, I didn't really know why.

Eternity was not at school on Tuesday. I went to Mrs. Harrington's office after school and learned that Jake and Blithe had not shown up either. All I could think about was Ace's father and his humongous hand squeezing Eternity's thin wrist. Instead of riding my school bus home, I got on their bus and rode out to the trailer.

It looked deserted. No Ma sitting in the rusted rocking chair, no children playing in the dust. The door was propped open, and I went in. Ma was sprawled out on the battered sofa, her dress wadded up under her so that I could see her tremendous thighs. I tiptoed past her to the safe room and rapped softly on the door.

"Eternity? Eternity, are you in there?"

No answer.

"Jake? Blithe? It's me, Emile."

"I keep the key on top of the kitchen cabinet by the stove. Mama's too fat to fit in there and reach up and get it," I remembered Eternity explaining. I tiptoed back out into the kitchen, found the key, opened the door to the safe room, and walked in. My heart was beating hard.

The room was empty and spotless, as always. The beds had been made. There was no sign of stress or hurry. I bent down to look under Eternity's bed. The boxes were in place.

Too late, I heard a muffled sound in the hallway. Too late, I realized my mistake. I had not locked the safe room door behind me. I rushed to it and pushed it closed, started to turn the lock, when Ma burst in, knocking me to the floor.

I guess I had never really seen someone who was stone drunk and raving mad at the same time.

"Wha're ya doin' in here?" she demanded, yanking me up by my arm. "What'd ya do with the children?"

I was standing, backing up; she shoved me with such force that I banged my nose and forehead hard against the wall. I felt dizzy and sank to the ground. I tried to slide under the bed to get away and felt blood running from my nose.

Then she wiped her fat arm clumsily across the top of the chest of drawers, and a lamp crashed to the floor. She yanked at the chest and threw one of the drawers on the floor. I heard the wood splinter. With a grunt and a curse, she yanked the quilt up off the bed where I hid. She pulled out the boxes that held Eternity's precious books and began tossing them around.

I wanted to scream for her to stop, but no sound would come from my dry mouth. I imagined her grabbing the bed and holding it high with one hand, kind of like King Kong, while swatting me like a pesky fly as I crouched below. *What a strange way to die, I thought, beaten to death by a drunken whore.*

She pushed the bed away from the wall, and I jumped up, fueled by fear, and darted past her. I flew out of the trailer and ran as fast as I could to Mr. Davis's place. I banged on the door and yelled, "Help! Mr. Davis. She's gone mad, and she's destroying everything!"

The door opened at once, but it was not Mr. Davis's dark face and tight grayish hair that stared back at me. It was Blithe, her blue eyes wide and her blond hair curling around her face. She took one look at me and started screaming, "Emile! You're bleeding! You're hurt!"

Her face went pasty white, and I thought she might faint. I grabbed her as she leaned out the door toward me, and we both went back inside to the bathroom. I leaned over the sink and said as calmly as possible, "I'm okay, Blithe. I promise. Could you just get me a washcloth?"

She nodded silently and opened the little closet door beside her. I had turned on the spigot and was splashing water on my face. When Blithe handed me the cloth, I began blotting the wounds on my nose and cheek.

"Does it hurt real bad?"

"No, no. It doesn't hurt at all," I lied. "It just looks bad."

"What happened, Emile?"

I had no idea what to tell her, so I just said, "I fell down coming to your house. Where is Mr. Davis?"

"Jake got real sick. He was spittin' up blood, and Mr. Davis took Eternity with him to the emergency room. He made me promise to stay here. Ma's all drunk."

It took a while to stop the nosebleed, and I knew that tomorrow I'd have some nasty bruises to explain. But for the moment I just lay down on Mr. Davis's couch, put the cool wet washcloth across my brow, and said to Blithe, "I'm going to close my eyes, but you stay right here and wake me as soon as Mr. Davis gets back."

As I lay there with my eyes closed, all I could think was that it was my fault. Ma had destroyed the safe room, and it was all my fault.

We stood in the wreck of the safe room—Mr. Davis, Eternity, and. . . . Ma was asleep on the couch, and Jake and Blithe were resting at Mr. Davis's house.

"Lawd, have mercy," was all Mr. Davis could say. He and I tried to put the furniture back in place, but one of the feet on the bunk bed had broken off, so that it sat crooked on the floor.

I thought Eternity might burst into tears, the way she picked up ripped-out pages from her books and lovingly put them back in the right place.

"I'm so sorry," was all I managed to say over and over.

And though she acknowledged my confession, she never said anything like, "It's okay, Emile. You had no idea what Ma can be like." In fact, she didn't say anything at all. But she went to work cleaning. She gathered up the clothes strewn across the floor, folded them neatly, and put them back in the dresser, which Mr. Davis had helped me to set right. Then she swept up the broken pieces of wood and glass and paper. She placed each book back in its box. After an hour of cleaning, the room was once again "safe."

"She can't stay here," I said to Mr. Davis. "The children's bed is broken. I should get my mother to come out. They can spend the night at our house."

"You've got no right to do that, boy. Miz Jones is real protective of her children."

"Protective! She tried to kill me, and I'll bet she does the same thing to them when she's drunk."

But Mr. Davis shook his head as if I didn't understand. "I can fix this bed for 'em so as it'll be fine for tonight. Now I'd best get you home. Put some ice on that face, you hear? And I don't know about that nose of yours. I hope it ain't broken, but I don't know."

So I left Eternity and Jake and Blithe at the trailer. Ma was still fast asleep, and Mr. Davis assured me that she'd wake up meek as a lamb. I protested again, but he paid no attention. As we walked away, I could hear Jake's raspy breathing, and I could see the strain on Eternity's face.

"I'm sorry," I said again. "I was just worried about you."

She just shrugged, and they all waved good-bye. I could hear Blithe asking her sister, "Why is he sorry? He's the one who got hurt."

In French society, and in my family's circle of friends, wine was a necessary accompaniment to a fine meal. It was sought after and appreciated. Of course there were people who abused it, but no one I knew. The wine at our house made Mama laugh gaily and Papa slap his long arm around her shoulder and kiss her playfully on the cheek.

I had never seen the link between alcohol and abuse until that day when Ma came after me. But I would never forget it. Eternity was right. Alcoholism could make life hell. I was terrified of Ma from that day on.

And Mr. Davis was right. I had a lot of explaining to do when I got home. Mama and Grandma were a flutter of emotion, Mama exclaiming, "You will *never* go there again, Emile! You understand?" and Grandma wringing her hands and assuring me the children could come to her house whenever they wanted.

Later, after I'd showered and Mama had cared for my wounds and insisted I hold an ice pack on my nose for what seemed like hours, I came back downstairs. Grandma was saying something to Mama about "checking with the authorities" and "getting the children in foster care." I didn't know what she meant, but there was that creepy feeling again.

———

The Jones kids spent more and more time at Grandma's house. I didn't mean to be jealous of Eternity and Grandma, but it got to be their habit to sit out on the porch and talk while I entertained Jake and Blithe. I didn't mind; I liked the little ones. Still, I just couldn't understand what those two had to talk about. Eternity was my friend, and if she needed to share some big secret, well, she should share it with me, not with my grandmother!

But it wasn't like that for her. As the weeks passed, I think Eternity looked forward to coming to the house more to see Grandma than to be with me.

"There're just some things that girls need to talk about with other girls," Grandma told me one day.

I was unimpressed, but what could I do? The only choice I had was to share Eternity with Grandma.

"With a name like Eternity, you must start understanding things about heaven," Grandma said to her one day.

"I don't believe in heaven."

"Not yet," Grandma corrected. "Remember those bulbs we planted, how they die underground and will come to life in spring? Those dry brown bulbs will become bright, happy tulips—yellow and red. And you can become someone bright and happy too."

I thought Eternity would laugh and snort at this remark. Or at least secretly mock Grandma's words. But she simply listened, even seemed intrigued by my grandmother's analogy.

"It's very simple theology, displayed for us every year, over and over. Birth and death and rebirth."

Grandma repeated these lessons from nature again and again, every time they were at my house. I thought surely they would get tired of hearing it. But it didn't work that way. For as often as Eternity could look cross or bored or condescending to me, when she was talking to Grandma, or more often listening to her, Eternity's sleepy eyes were wide open and alert and filled with something like the wonder I saw in Blithe's eyes when she was chasing a butterfly.

I didn't know what to call it in Eternity. Fascination, intrigue. Or maybe it was exactly what I'd wanted her to find all along. Hope.

———

Three times in late October I had called Mamie early in the morning, unbeknownst to Mama and Grandma. Each time I'd whisper in hurried French, "Why haven't you written me? What's the matter? I miss France!"

And each time I heard her voice with her beautiful Lyonnais accent, I got that deep ache in my chest. "You know I'm not much for writing letters, dear. I'm sorry. I miss you, too. I say a prayer for you each day. I even say a prayer for your mother."

I could tell she was trying to make me smile.

"Why can't I come home? I want to come back."

Her voice got stiff, as if she were repeating something she'd memorized. "Emile, *mon cheri*, it's wiser for you to stay in America for now."

"Why?"

"You must put all your energy into getting acclimated."

"That's crazy. I don't want to! I want to come home."

"I understand. But tell me about your life there."

So I would. And then, near the end of our conversation, I'd get up the nerve to ask, "Have you heard from Papa?"

A pause. "No."

The falling sensation would come again in the pit of my stomach, and eventually I'd mumble *"Au revoir, Mamie."*

By the end of each conversation, I became more convinced that Mama and Mamie were isolating me. It didn't make sense. Or it only made sense if something really was the matter with Papa. I felt a type of panic inching up on me. I felt as if I were being poisoned—not by swallowing a vial of liquid, but little by little, poisoned by lies told by the people I loved most.

And so the leaves turned yellow and red and pumpkin orange and then floated to the ground and they were covered in frost in the mornings and we started wearing coats to school. Griffin and I went to every football game and sat with Sally and Mary Jane. Sometimes Eternity brought Blithe and Jake, but she remained cold and aloof and she never sat with us. I tutored Ace at least twice a week, and he got better in French and only smacked me on the head every other day. And I got better in English so that by mid-November my strong accent had diminished somewhat and I was actually starting to use American slang correctly.

I made a B+ on my first English paper—an essay on *1984* by George Orwell—and Mrs. Chalkin wrote all kinds of encouraging notes in the margin of the paper. She didn't take off any points for the nine misspelled words, and she commented twice about how absolutely beautiful my penmanship was and how neatly the whole paper was presented. All of these compliments were so very un-French that I didn't know how to take them. I wondered if perhaps she had let down her guard a little too much.

My class went to a play at the Fox Theatre, and we ate lunch once at the Varsity, and Mrs. Smith asked me to help her with a skit for the

French class to perform right before she planned to stop teaching. In history we studied the Civil Rights Act, which President Johnson had passed earlier in the summer, and we talked about sit-ins and bus boy-cotts and Malcolm X, and then at night we watched some of those very things happening on our television screens.

Every day when I got home from school, before going to make a peanut butter and jelly sandwich, I'd look through the mail. I was sure that sometime before my birthday, which was only two weeks away, my father would write me and explain the mystery of the wristwatch and why he'd left and not given me another sign of life for five long weeks.

Grandma did less gardening and more baking, and it seemed to me there was always a neighbor or church member sitting at the kitchen table drinking hot tea with her when I'd return from school.

And on many days, Eternity and Jake and Blithe would ride the bus home with me.

So all in all, in spite of my protests, Mama's prediction was coming true. I was getting used to life in America.

| *fourteen* |

It had rained the night before, and the sky was still gray and cloudy—angry looking—with brief moments of the sun slipping through. The weather couldn't make up its mind, and I thought it matched the rumblings and confusion I felt inside on my fourteenth birthday. I had built it up in my mind, had been so sure I would finally hear from Papa. For all his other shortcomings, he never forgot my birthday.

The day dawned without a word from abroad.

I looked at myself in the bathroom mirror. Nothing had changed—I was still a skinny kid with curly blond hair, several inches shy of normal height. I suppose even if I had miraculously sprouted like a bean plant overnight, my mood would not have altered.

"What's the matter, Emile? You look awful," Eternity greeted me at the bus stop.

"It's my birthday."

"And that makes you sad? Your mother forgot?"

"No, she didn't forget. She and Grandma are taking me to a fancy French restaurant for dinner tonight."

"The one with the chef who is from Lyon?"

"Yeah."

"So what's the matter?"

"I was sure I'd hear from my father. He always makes it home for my birthday."

"At least he gave you that birthday gift early," she said, pointing to the wristwatch. "So probably he knew he wouldn't be with you today."

"I know, I know. But I was sure he'd write or call me." I looked at her miserably. "Even if he left us for another woman, he could at least wish me happy birthday."

"My dad has never once called me on my birthday."

"Well, thanks. That's encouraging." We sat in silence. "And I thought he'd tell me something about the watch—since he never even explained it to me."

Suddenly she grabbed my wrist, pulling me close to her, and my heart gave a little lurch.

"That's true. He gave it to you right before he disappeared, right?"

"September 22. He said he needed to give it to me early, then he got called away to the phone. And the next day I saw him in town with that woman."

Eternity let go of my wrist and hit me hard on the back. "Well, there's no doubt there must be something special about it. All the other gifts are more than what they seem to be."

"I haven't been able to figure it out. Maybe it's just a wristwatch."

"But if he just wanted to give you a watch, Emile, wouldn't it be a nicer one? Surely it was used for something else—messages, I'll bet."

Then I remembered something. "He did say it still tells time as well as it did back in 1943."

"Ah ha! Let me see it," she ordered, and obediently I unhooked the watchband and handed the watch to her. She turned it over in her hands. "Maybe you could have it inspected by a, I don't know, a watchmaker. He'd know what to look for if you explained it to him."

I felt a tinge of embarrassment that I had not even considered this idea.

"It doesn't make sense," she said. "Your dad gives you this watch two months before your birthday and then disappears. There's definitely something fishy going on here."

I stared at her. "You are the strangest girl I've ever met."

"Why do you say that?"

"You don't believe my dad is a spy, and now, suddenly, you want to help me find out clues about what he's up to. What in the world makes you go back and forth all the time?"

She smiled and said, "Nancy Drew."

"Who?"

"Nancy Drew is a girl detective—there's a whole series of books written about her. When I was younger I read them all—kinda like you and Tintin. Anyway, I still think your dad is having an affair, but I also think we need to check out the watch. Find out what it was used for. Unless . . ." She thought for a moment. "Unless he just gave it to you for sentimental reasons, because he knew he was going to run off with this woman and wanted you to have it." She chewed her braid.

"Thanks, Eternity. That's really encouraging."

"I'm not trying to be encouraging. It isn't in my nature. I'm just trying to help you figure out your life."

"Okay, then, I'll find a watchmaker and take it to him. But you have to come along."

"Well, of course I'll come along. We're in this together, remember."

Eternity slipped me a piece of paper during English class the next day. She'd scribbled on it: *Joseph Epstein, Watchmaker, 239 Lindbergh Dr. Office hours 9–5.*

"After school," she mouthed when Mrs. Chalkin wasn't looking. "It's not that far away."

So it was decided. I think we were both secretly excited, but neither of us wanted to admit it. We rode the school bus to a stop that met up with a city bus. Jake and Blithe complained about not getting home on time, but Eternity hushed them up with a bag of Sugar Babies she'd bought in a vending machine.

It was the first time I'd taken public transportation. Even though we'd just studied the Busing Act, which allowed blacks to sit anywhere they wanted on a public bus, there were five black women seated in the back and no one else on the bus.

"Maids," Eternity whispered.

"Maids? You mean 'maidens'?"

She burst out laughing. "Maids are black ladies who do the cooking and cleaning and minding the kids in the white people's houses. They're just getting off work."

"Are all maids black?"

"As far as I know."

"We could go back there and sit with them."

"Oh, sure. That would be nice and condescending."

I thought to myself, *You always have to have the last word, Eternity,* but I kept quiet until we arrived at Lindbergh Drive.

Mr. Epstein looked over his single eyepiece at me, then squinted back at the watch. "You say your father worked for the French Resistance, eh? And you think this watch is actually concealing something else?"

"That's right," Eternity stated matter-of-factly, before I could even get a word out. "We are absolutely positive that this cannot be a simple watch. There must be some sort of message attached."

I thought I saw a trace of amusement in the watchmaker's face as he opened the watch and continued to study its interior. We waited quietly for five minutes, not daring to disturb his concentration, Jake and Blithe wiggling like tied-up puppies.

Finally he handed the watch back to me. "Well, son, I'm sorry to say there is nothing very secretive about the interior of this watch. It's a classic model from 1943."

He couldn't help but see the disappointment that registered on my face or the look of total disbelief on Eternity's.

"What about the wristband?" I asked hopefully.

"Just a plain leather wristband that has seen better days."

I mumbled, "Thank you for your trouble, sir. How much do I owe you?"

He chuckled good-naturedly. "Not a thing, son. Not a thing."

Eternity, impatient and angry with her siblings, was already marching them toward the door. I could imagine her insisting that Mr.

Epstein was old and incompetent and we should try someone else.

I offered him my hand, and Mr. Epstein shook it firmly. Then he looked me straight in the eye, and I saw that his were twinkling.

"You might want to take this with you to the science lab at your school." He handed the watch back to me.

"What do you mean, sir?"

"It's true there's nothing out of the ordinary in the interior of your watch. However . . ."

My heart started beating faster.

". . . I noticed something unusual about the glass crystal covering the watch, and sure enough I found a microdot."

I stared at him dumbly.

"You can read it if you put the watch crystal under a microscope."

"What is a microdot?"

"Ah, it was a very ingenious piece of technology developed during World War II. It is a photograph reduced to the size of a printed period, no bigger than ⅟₃₂ of an inch, and it has been fastened to the crystal of the watch. During the war, messages were hidden in that way and later enlarged to reveal secret information. No one would ever think to look for it unless they knew about it. I'm pretty sure that if you use a microscope, you'll find some sort of message encoded on it."

"Oh, thank you, sir! Thank you!" I pumped his hand up and down, up and down.

I hurried out the door, practically pushing Eternity in front of me. "Did you hear?" I asked.

She grabbed me in a hug and said, "Yes, I heard! I'll talk to Mrs. Hunt as soon as we get to school tomorrow. I'm sure she'll let us use a microscope!"

———

I could barely sit through school the next day, terrified that somehow the microdot would disappear before we had a chance to get to the science lab. When I explained our quest to Mrs. Hunt, she seemed very interested and took the microscope out of the cabinet and placed it on one of the black-topped tables in the science lab.

"Here you go, Emile."

I took a seat at the table and made sure there were no suspicious-looking men lurking in the shadows, then looked through the eyepiece and enlarged the dot until I could read the words. Eternity hovered at my elbow.

"I want to read it alone first," I told her.

She actually looked a bit disappointed and took a seat at a different table.

Dear Emile, my son,

I had hoped to give this to you on your fourteenth birthday, so appropriate. That was when my father presented this watch to me. I cannot tell you the story now, only give you the watch in hopes that your wonderfully curious mind will discover this dot.

There are problems. Big problems. Your mother knows a little, but it is not safe for her to know more, not safe for any of you. I trust you will find this—you have always been clever—you knew my tricks before I showed them to you.

I must hide for a time. I cannot say how long.

I know this sounds strange, that you will be confused. You will like America, son. I know you will. Please cooperate with your mother, Emile, and take care of her. It is a hard burden to place on you, but you are ready. When I can, I will come back. I will find you both. You have my word.

Your loving father

I swallowed repeatedly, wiped the beads of perspiration from my brow, copied the message onto a piece of paper in my spiral notebook, and finally allowed Eternity to read it for herself.

"Wow, Emile," she said with due respect. "Wow, Emile. You were right after all."

I flew home on the energy of our discovery. I was right! I had been right all along! My father was in trouble, and he would come back.

"Mama! Mama!" I was out of breath from having run home. "Mama, he didn't abandon us! He had to leave. There's not another woman. He'll come back! He was planning to explain it all to me that night when he gave me the watch. This watch here."

I pulled it out of my pocket. "See, he gave it to me and then he got the phone call and then he disappeared and you told me about another woman. But it's not true. Papa's a real spy and he will come back." My words tumbled out in French.

I could not read Mama's expression at first. Numbly, she reached for the watch and held it in her hands, turning it over and over.

"It was a microdot, Mama. That's where the note was hidden."

But she was no longer listening. She was actually shaking, her hands trembling, her arms too, and then she was crying, sobbing.

My heart leapt—she was crying with relief; she was overjoyed.

She murmured, almost to herself, "Oh, Jean-Baptiste, what have you done?" Then she grabbed me by the shoulders and began to shake me. "Quit it, Emile. Quit it! You must stop now! Do you understand? You must stop this now." She looked both angry and afraid.

"But, Mama—it's good news!"

"Good news, Emile? Good news? You have no idea what you're saying! For heaven's sake, this isn't Tintin! Tintin is make-believe. It works out in the end. He gets the bad guys. He always wins. Emile"— she kept her grip on my shoulders—"this is real life, and it is dangerous, and way too often you don't even know who the good guys are. Your father isn't in a game, Emile. He's in a war, and for all we know, he may not win. I told him! I told Jean-Baptiste he was just feeding your already overactive imagination with these gifts. I told him it was a mistake."

"You knew all along that he is a spy! You've been lying to me!"

"Lying? And what was I supposed to do, Emile? Tell you what he's up to when even I hardly understand? 'Laugh and say, 'Guess what, sweetie, you're right. Daddy's a spy. Oooh, isn't this sooo exciting?' Are you crazy? Do you know what he goes through, Emile? Don't you see? We had to leave."

Then she took the spiral notebook from me, collapsed on the couch in the den, drew her legs under her, and read the microdot message. She said nothing for the longest time, reading and rereading what I had scribbled on the page.

Finally she patted the couch, and I came and sat beside her.

"He told you the truth, Emile. He was afraid for us. I've only seen your father afraid twice. Not when the CIA came to our door in America with rifles in their hands. Not any of the times he packed hastily in the middle of the night. He knew we were safe with Mamie. Bless her heart, your Mamie. She loved us and protected us, for all the ways she drove me crazy.

"The first time your father was afraid was when you almost died of rubella when you were three years old. He was beside himself, and there was nothing he could do but wait. And the second time was the night he gave you the watch. He sent us away because he was afraid for us. Do you understand? We can't know. We don't want to know. He said we had to leave. Immediately."

"But why?" I could barely get the words out, seeing my mother all white and trembling and terrified.

"They had found him out. He was disappearing, and we had to also."

"*Who* found him out, Mama?"

She ran her hands through her hair, tears running down her cheeks. "Please, Emile! I don't know!"

"Mamie Madeleine? Is she in danger?"

"Mamie Madeleine knows what danger is, and she is not afraid." Mama said this with a whimper, and I found my palms sweaty, my head throbbing. She grabbed me in a fierce hug. "I'm sorry, Emile. I wish you didn't know. I'm sorry. He shouldn't have told you."

My father was a spy. My father was in trouble. I had been right. But the thrill was gone, replaced by fear, replaced by images of Mama trembling, feeling it as I held her, replaced by her words: *"Your father isn't in a game, Emile. He's in a war, and for all we know, he may not win."*

I lay on my bed, holding the page I'd ripped from the spiral notebook and reading for the tenth time Papa's message. I had wadded it up in anger, then straightened it back out, and now was staring at it, trying hard to decipher its meaning. Papa had known about leaving early enough to fix a microdot and attach it to this watch. So to some extent, his disappearance had been planned.

A knock came at my door.

"May I come in?" It was Mama's voice.

She came into my room, rubbing her swollen eyes and then running a finger along her pencil-thin eyebrows. She sat on the bed beside me and reached for my hand. "Would you like to hear what I know?"

I nodded.

She gently took the paper from me and read the note again. "Jean-Baptiste loved to tell his stories of action and adventure and danger. He liked for the odds to be stacked against him."

It scared me, the way she talked about Papa in the past. I watched her carefully. She no longer looked strong and stubborn, just small and young.

"The Resistance was a cause filled with action and excitement and plenty of danger. Your father was only twelve when his parents were first involved. He craved adventure. He thought it was only natural to follow his parents into the Underground. But then they were caught, all three of them, and taken to the Montluc Prison in Lyon. I don't know what happened in that prison. Awful things, I suppose."

"Things that Klaus Barbie did to them?"

"Perhaps. They were sent from Lyon to a concentration camp in Germany, and your grandfather died there. The way Papa told it, his mother was so strong and courageous beside her husband. But when your grandfather died, something in her died too. She gave up wanting to live." It was the first time I'd heard Mama's voice soften as she spoke of my French grandmother.

"But your father . . . your father told her, 'Mama, we're going to survive. I want you to promise me you'll try. I don't want to go through life alone—without either of you. Please, please survive.' And she did. They both did."

My eyes were burning and itching, and I needed to blow my nose. Instead I wiped it across my sleeve.

"You know, Emile, after the war, most people in France chose to forget the horror. They chose to pretend it had not been so terrible. And the hundreds and thousands who had been Resistants were suddenly out of a job. All of their daring and risking of their lives was never acknowledged or publicly appreciated. They felt cheated, unappreciated. They crawled back into the woodwork and became anonymous.

"But in their hearts, they could never quite be normal again. And your father was like that. The adrenaline kept pumping. He could not stop thinking about the war and all he had lived through. He needed the danger, the adventure, the risk. He was addicted to it, like a drug."

"And was Mamie Madeleine like that too?"

"Perhaps."

"She's a brave woman, isn't she?"

"Yes, Emile, very brave. Very brave indeed."

"A good woman, then?"

"Yes."

"But you don't like her, Mama! You hate her!"

"Ah, Emile. *Hate* is too strong. Deep inside I greatly respect Mamie Madeleine. Perhaps we would even have liked each other, if only she hadn't been my mother-in-law. She was smart and gifted with organization. Maybe she got bored after the war and needed another cause. She became very controlling—of her life, her son's life. Wounds were always there, just below the surface. The mother-son bond became stronger, dangerously strong. So when I was added to the picture, she resented me for stealing him away. She wasn't a bad woman. She was an injured woman protecting the only thing in life that mattered to her—her son."

"She must have hated it when he moved to America."

"Yes. She used to call him every day. It must have cost a fortune. I think it drove him crazy."

"Did he come to America to get away from Mamie?"

"Perhaps, to an extent—we were both running away from controlling mothers. But he also was studying—he had gotten a scholarship for a year to study in the States. He was looking for yet another adventure.

"And then we met in school, and I fell in love with him, Emile. I fell in love with his daring, his courage, his refusal to fit into society, his French-ness. I was willing to drop everything to follow him. As I look back, I think he tried to warn me what kind of life I might have with him. Of course, he was in love too."

She said that last sentence almost defensively, as if she were trying to convince herself, and it made me squirm inside.

"But he told me a few of his stories, and he let me know he was motivated by risk and revenge. I guess I knew there was a part of the Resistance that would always be there with him. It sounded exotic and exciting at the time."

"And so he asked you to marry him?"

"Yes." She hesitated. "Well, not exactly. I might as well tell you the whole truth. I was pregnant with you. He married me because I was pregnant."

I tried to hide my surprise. "Papa wouldn't have married you otherwise?"

"Let's just say it complicated things."

"Secret things."

"Yes. Your father was gifted in espionage. He continued this work in America. I never knew who he was working for—the French police or the CIA or the CIC—that was the equivalent of the American CIA in Germany. He was always seeking justice—he could not live with himself if the Nazis went unpunished. I think he felt very lonely most of the time—so much of what he did had to be kept secret from everyone. I honestly don't know how he kept it all straight."

"And having a wife and a baby was . . . was . . ." I searched for the word that I had heard Papa use when describing the expense of owning the old château. "A liability?"

"Sort of. Yes." She kept swallowing hard, and tears were in her eyes, which she brushed away. "This is sounding all wrong, Emile. Please understand. He loved us. If your father could have cut out his heart and been attached to no one, he would have preferred it. His biggest fear in life was that, because of his clandestine activities, someday you might have to live through the horror of what he had seen as a teen. He swore he would never allow you and me to experience the things he did. He was determined to protect us."

"And so he disappeared to protect us, Mama? Is that what he did?" I felt a rush of relief go through me.

"Yes, yes, that's what he did. . . ."

But I could see questions and doubts written across her face.

"He was determined to protect us."

I wished she wouldn't keep saying that.

"And so he left. He cared, dear. He always loved us and cared."

"You don't sound convinced!" I blurted.

She took my hands and looked me straight in the eyes. "Emile, I know you want your father to be a hero. You imagine him either as a hero or a traitor. You want to know which. But suppose he was just an ordinary man, some good, some bad. Brave, daring, smart, but also vain and careless. Suppose he wanted to do the right thing, but suppose he was motivated by hate and revenge, and it was too strong—"

"Why do you keep talking as if he's dead?"

She gave one of those deep sighs and lay down on the bed beside me, massaging her temples and looking like something was crushing her on the inside. "I'm sorry, Emile. All of it *is* in the past. Now we just have to keep living in the present."

I stared at her. "So we just forget Papa? We give up?"

"No, of course not." But she was sounding exasperated. "Look, Emile, I'm sorry I can't tell you anything about where your father is. I don't know. I don't know if he is dead or alive. I have no idea."

Bile burned my throat. "You lived with him for fifteen years! You must know something about his other life!"

She started talking again, like that little girl, lying on my bed and talking to the wall, talking to herself. "I guess I just got used to all his traveling. I knew it wasn't really with his business. I knew it was secret, underground. But I was thinking of you and me, and not what kind of pressure he was under. I have thought of it a hundred times in the past weeks. I have no idea who that man was—the one who called him the night before he left us."

"But you know some things, Mama! I heard you crying the night before he left; I heard Papa telling you things."

"You heard him telling me to leave. He was so tense and worried that it scared me."

It was Mama who looked tense and worried at that moment. So I didn't say, *I saw him with another woman, Mama. I saw him holding her hand. The very next day. He hadn't left. He was sitting at a café with a pretty woman and holding her hand.*

| *fifteen* |

Perhaps the story should have been over with Mama's tearful confession. Papa was a spy, Papa had disappeared, and we didn't know when, or if, we would see Papa again. The truth, plain and stark. I should have accepted it as that—I had been right all along—and felt some sort of relief. Now that I had Mama's side of the story, I should have believed that he had *not* been having an affair with a pretty young woman. That was what I had wanted to believe all along.

So why did I keep seeing his face, carefree, laughing, why did I keep remembering the way his hand was on top of hers and the happy smile on his face?

In any case, I just couldn't accept that there was nothing more to be done. *Curiosity killed the cat*—this was an expression I'd heard Grandma use. And it applied to me. I was just plain curious. I sat in my room and tried to reason with myself. *Emile, you have your collection, you have Papa's stories, you have Mama's too, you have many, many memories. Perhaps you won't have Papa yet—or ever—but there's absolutely nothing you can do about it. Anyway, America is waiting to be discovered. So lay it to rest.*

Unfortunately, I just couldn't.

Gardening was over for the year. Most of the leaves had been raked, and the trees were naked and spindly. I worried that Grandma might get bored without flowers and plants to tend to. Instead she moved into her winter mode and pronounced one word over and over. *Thanksgiving.*

"How wonderful to have you and Janie this year for Thanksgiving."

"I always invite several neighbors for Thanksgiving."

"We'll need a great big turkey this year for Thanksgiving."

And the one I liked best, "Don't you think we should invite Eternity and her family for Thanksgiving?"

Grandma's cheeks were flushed, almost like Mama's got—the same childlike excitement—when she mentioned the holiday. That's when I first started noticing how much Mama did look like Grandma. One day I picked up that photograph of Grandma as a young woman—the one where she looked beautiful—and carried it up to Mama's room, setting it beside the picture of Mama and Papa on the bedside table.

In both pictures the women's heads were turned a little to the right, and I marveled at the resemblance, the turn of the nose, the slant of the eyes, the same slightly mocking look. *I wish I'd gotten to know Grandma sooner,* I thought. *I wish I knew the "before and after" picture of Grandma. I wish I could see the difference like Mama can.*

The longer I thought about it, the angrier I felt—mad at Mama and Mamie and Grandma herself for having kept her presence hidden from me for almost fourteen years. I had only vague memories of Mama even mentioning Grandma Bridgeman, and it was never with much more affection than when she talked about Mamie Madeleine.

There I went missing Papa again, but this time for a different reason. I was tired of being surrounded by women. For all of my life, right smack-dab up until the present, women were controlling me. Where were the men? Why did they die or leave or disappear? I needed them. I didn't know if I was supposed to be a Frenchman or an American, if I was supposed to live in a château in the Beaujolais region of France and host elaborate dinner parties and choose the right wines from the *cave* and attend Mass, or if I was supposed to buy a house in the suburbs of Atlanta and work for Coca-Cola and watch football games on the weekend and be a deacon in the Baptist church and take my kids to Sunday school.

How would I find out? Who could help me sort out the confusing thoughts? My grandmother, for all her hard-earned wisdom, could not teach me how to be a man.

I found Grandma in the kitchen, slaving over a pumpkin pie, her hair gathered up off her neck and sticking out like a wispy web around her head, which was bent down as she rolled out dough on the kitchen counter.

"Why didn't you ever come to see me, Grandma?" I almost shouted, coming up from behind.

She turned around, looking startled, her hands white with flour. "Goodness, Emile! I had no idea you were there. You gave me a fright!"

"Sorry," I mumbled. "But why? You had plenty of money, and you told me you liked to travel. And even if you couldn't come for a visit, you could've at least written me and told me about your life."

Grandma's eyes went all watery and sad. "I knew you'd ask me that sooner or later, Emile. It's a good question, a fair question." She set down the rolling pin and dusted her hands on her apron. "I guess you could almost say I wasn't allowed to come to visit. I wasn't welcome."

"Why?"

"Lots of complicated reasons that probably don't mean anything. Things I said, things your mother said, things your Grandmother Madeleine said. It all got way too serious and complicated. So I backed down."

"You couldn't even write to me? Acknowledge my presence on the planet Earth?"

She reached toward me with one floury hand, but I backed away, crossing my arms over my chest and squeezing them tight. Finally I blurted, "You couldn't visit me because Papa was a spy! It was too dangerous. That's it, isn't it?"

She brushed one hand through a few wisps of hair and placed the other on my shoulder. "Emile, listen to me. I didn't know anything about what your father did. I only knew I wasn't welcome. Janie wrote me letters once in a while, sent me a few pictures of you. I'd made such a mess of her childhood that I decided I wouldn't intrude on yours when your mother begged me not to."

"Didn't you miss me? Didn't you want to know me?"

"Oh, Emile. You're my only grandchild. Of course I wanted to know you. It broke my heart." She grabbed me then in a strong hug, and I didn't really mind the bits of dough and flour that stuck to my shirt. I let her hold me there in the kitchen, tightly, holding on for dear life, holding me to make up for all the years when her arms were empty.

At last she let go, and all I could say was, "Can I help you get something ready for Thanksgiving?"

"I'd be delighted to have some help. Have you ever made corn bread?"

I hadn't, of course, but she put a recipe in front of me and told me what to do. In the midst of stirring the eggs into the cornmeal, I said. "You see, Mama's admitted the truth—and I was right all along. Papa *was* a spy, and we had to come here because life was dangerous in France. And·I'm sure that's why she never wanted you to visit us there."

I had pushed my luck too far; Grandma was getting exasperated with me.

"Dear, dear Emile. I guess you have a mind like your father's, a mind that wants to figure everything out. But you can't. So many things that happen in life we can't understand. We won't understand this side of eternity."

Her words caught me off guard. "Eternity?"

"Heaven."

"Oh."

Grandma finished chopping an onion and tossed it into the bowl with the celery and dry bread crumbs. "Emile, you know there is more to life than looking for answers. Some answers you will never find— some you will. As long as the most important question is answered, the 'not knowing' of the others doesn't seem so unbearable."

"And what *is* the most important question?"

"Eternity," she repeated.

"Oh."

The day before school got out for Thanksgiving, the elementary school performed a skit, and lots of parents came to see it. The students from Northside who had siblings in the skit were allowed to attend as well. I begged Mrs. Harrington to let me go with Eternity, and she agreed. We sat near the back of the auditorium, waiting for Mr. Davis to arrive.

"Ma never shows up for this kind of thing, but Mr. Davis wouldn't miss it for the world. He says we're his second family."

I noticed several other black people peppered throughout the auditorium. "What are they doing here?" I asked.

"Maids," she said confidently, and then waved to Mr. Davis, who had just stepped through the doors and removed his hat.

He came and sat beside us and shook my hand. "Nice to see you, Emile."

Jake was a pilgrim and looked funny in his tall black hat that sat askew on his big head. Blithe was a grain of wheat that had survived the harsh winter of 1621 and become a beautiful stalk. I thought the role fit her perfectly with her silky blond hair and her light yellow shirt and pants.

By the end of the skit I'd gotten up my nerve, and I asked Mr. Davis, "Will you come to our house tomorrow for Thanksgiving dinner? My grandmother is fixing a feast, and Eternity and all her family are coming."

He pretended to be caught off guard, and looked as if he was going to refuse. Then he broke into a big grin and said, "I thought you weren't ever gonna ask, son. It's all Blithe and Jake have been talkin' about for the past week. They kept sayin', 'Well, of course you're invited, Mr. Davis.'"

"Well, they're right. My mother and grandmother would be happy to have you."

"Well, I'd be happy to come."

Thanksgiving Day before our guests arrived, Mama was helping baste the turkey. She and Grandma looked so content together, scurrying around like those little gray squirrels I saw everywhere in Atlanta and had never once seen in Lyon.

"What did you do to celebrate Thanksgiving in Lyon, dear?" Grandma asked, just making conversation.

"I'm afraid we didn't celebrate, Mother. You can't get a turkey in France in November. They only fatten them up for Christmas."

"That's too bad."

"I tried once. Ordered it from my butcher three weeks ahead of time. Scrawniest thing you ever saw when it came, complete with its head and feet. Jean-Baptiste made fun of me, and the meat tasted awful, and Mamie . . . well, you know Mamie."

I remembered the scene well, though I was only five or six. Mama wanted us to experience Thanksgiving. She had told me about the pilgrims as she spent what seemed like days baking strange American goodies while I followed her around. I helped her decorate the dining room table with turkey-shaped nametags I'd made by tracing my hand on construction paper and adding a "gobbler" to my thumb.

Mama proudly set the golden turkey, scrawny though it was, and five or six other yummy-smelling dishes on the table and called Mamie Madeleine and Papa into the room.

Mamie took one look at the table. "You mean we're supposed to eat all of this at once?" she asked. "Unthinkable."

Mama frowned, and Papa tried to come to her rescue. "It's the way they do it in America. Just try it, Mama."

"I will not mix savory food with this, this sweet stuff. What is it, anyway?"

"Congealed orange salad," Mama stated.

Mamie Madeleine gave a little shudder. But my mother paid her no attention and proceeded to load her own plate with every single item on the table. I'd never seen a plate so full.

Then Mama proclaimed happily, "Now let's all take a moment to say what we're thankful for."

Mamie muttered, "I'm thankful I don't have to eat this way ever again."

Then we all just sat there in silence and no one talked about being thankful for anything. I waited for Mama to burst into tears. Instead she loaded up my plate too. Papa winked at me, but the tension at the table was thicker than the gravy Mama had made.

Mamie refused to put more than one type of food at a time on her plate. One by one, she tasted Mama's dishes, commenting on it being bland and inedible and lukewarm, and grimaced as she chewed each bite. I wanted to yell at her to be nice to my mother who had worked so hard to make this a special Thanksgiving. But of course I said nothing.

Papa made an effort to try everything. "This is good, Janie," he offered once, and I could still see the cold, harsh stare Mamie Madeline gave him and remember how it silenced him.

I wanted Papa to tell my grandmother she was being mean, to hug my mother and say she had worked so hard and it was all delicious. But Papa sat there in between Mama and Mamie and said nothing more. I felt sick to my stomach and couldn't eat another bite. I worried that Mama might think it was because I didn't like her food.

My mother ate slowly, silently, chewing like some relentless machine, and finished every last morsel on her plate. Long after everyone else was busy elsewhere in the house, she stayed in the kitchen, cleaning up from her disastrous Thanksgiving meal.

Surely Thanksgiving at Grandma Bridgeman's would be the exact opposite. I got a comfortable feeling inside my stomach when Mama got out her mother's fine china and silver and hummed softly as she spread a white tablecloth on the table and began setting it. Grandma brought in pretty white napkins, and they giggled together like the silly girls in my class as they got ready for their guests. This was going to be a good Thanksgiving.

Mr. Davis and the Joneses arrived at noon, the kids all windblown and shivering from riding in the back of the pickup. I watched the gentle way Mr. Davis helped Ma from the car, his hand under her elbow, supporting her as she waddled to the house.

Blithe ran up to me carrying something covered with a red-and-white-checked kitchen towel. "Look, Emile! It's a pie, an apple pie, and I helped Ma bake it!" She danced around and around the kitchen and the den, blond hair floating softly up and down, singing, "We're celebrating Thanksgiving! I am soooo happy!" which of course made everyone smile.

Another great thing was that Ma seemed perfectly sober. "Thank you kindly, Miz Bridgeman, for invitin' us," she said, and her voice sounded low and smooth and not frightening.

"You're most welcome, Mrs. Jones. We're so happy everyone can be here."

I wondered if the four other neighbors were going to worry about having Thanksgiving with a Negro and an obese alcoholic, but I guess Grandma had briefed them on the situation. Twelve of us crowded around the table, and we all held hands as Grandma said grace. That's what she called praying before dinner—*grace*. I thought it was a soft, peaceful word.

Then Grandma asked each of us to mention something we were thankful for, and when it was Ma's turn, she said she was thankful for her three children. Eternity said she was thankful for civil rights and Dr. King, and Blithe said she was thankful for lots of food to eat, and Jake didn't say anything. When it was my turn, I said I was glad for my first Thanksgiving in America and a big fat turkey, and everybody laughed at that.

Mr. Davis said he was thankful for freedom in this country and progress, and the way he said it made me get a little choked up, and I was afraid the piece of turkey I was chewing on might get stuck, but finally I swallowed it down.

Near the end of the meal, Grandma got out her little camera and took a picture of all of us around the table. I loved that snapshot—I kept it with my collection, inside one of my Tintin books. I thought we all just blended in together like a watercolor painting.

I wish I'd savored the peace and calm of that afternoon as much as I savored the food we ate. But voices do not warn you from heaven—they hadn't on that bumpy airplane flight to America, and they didn't on that chilly afternoon in November with the aroma of plenty and the buzz of happy conversation in the air.

Northside lost the last football game of the season, and everyone was in a foul mood afterward. Except for Griffin. As usual, he was still smiling. He whispered to me as the girls walked in front of us, complaining about the way our team had played.

"Hey, amigo. What would you say to a little adventure with Sally and Mary Jane?"

"What did you have in mind?"

"Emilio, sometimes you are the slowest kid I've ever met. She's waiting on you to make a pass, dummy. At least hold her hand."

And just like that, Griffin had his arm sloped comfortably over Sally's shoulder, and she was giggling with Mary Jane. Griffin and Sally crossed 10th Street and went into Piedmont Park. My face caught on fire when Mary Jane grabbed my hand. I was so startled that I almost jerked it away. But she held on tight and squeezed my hand and gave me that adoring smile.

Just then, Eternity appeared with Blithe and Jake. She gave us her ice princess look, then narrowed her eyes and focused on Mary Jane's hand in mine. Her expression said, *You are the biggest jerk in the whole wide world.*

I could tell Mary Jane was enjoying Eternity's humiliation, but she kept her mouth closed in a sweet little smirk. "Come on, Emile," she chirped and pulled me after Griffin and Sally.

"You go on," I mumbled. "I'll be there in a sec."

She looked annoyed but let go of my hand. I went after Eternity, who was stomping off with Blithe and Jake on each side. I could hear Blithe whining, "Why is he holding Mary Jane's hand, 'Terni, when he loves you?"

"Eternity!"

She kept walking.

"Eternity, can I please talk to you for a second?"

She left Blithe and Jake and walked over to me, the expression on her face making me shiver.

"Why are you so mad at me?"

"I'm not."

"Are you jealous?"

"Of Mary Jane Willis? No."

"Then why are you mad?"

"I thought we were friends."

"We are friends, idiot."

She shrugged and threw her long braid over her shoulder. "I've got to be getting home."

"Look, Eternity, I don't like Mary Jane or anything. She's just a silly girl—someone I hang around with at the football games with Griffin and Sally—"

"Someone you hold hands with!" she accused.

"Let me explain . . ." I started, but she walked off without another word.

My stomach did a flip-flop as I tried to decide whether to follow Eternity or head across the street. In the end, I headed into the park after Mary Jane, but she was nowhere in sight. In fact, I couldn't see anyone around in the darkness. I walked ahead until I heard some whispering, and was just about to say, "Hey, wait for me!" when I realized this group was not Griffin and the girls.

". . . just a no-good nigger is all," I heard.

Five shadows stood in a circle around a much darker shadow. As my eyes adjusted to the darkness I made out Ace, Teddy, Billy, and two other football players from Northside. Standing in their midst was a young Negro boy—he was smaller, or perhaps he had simply shrunk from fear, crouching down and holding a hand over his eye.

"We'll teach you once and for all, you hear? You don't ever speak to a white boy unless we ask to be spoken to." Ace had grabbed him by the collar. "What'll we do with him, fellas?"

For an answer, the biggest player grabbed the boy's arm and twisted it until I heard a sickening crack. The Negro said nothing. The terror in the whites of his eyes was the only thing lighting the scene. I stood there, knees weak, unable to move. I moaned with vicarious pain.

Ace turned and spotted me. "Well, looky who's here! Frenchy's spying on us! Come on, French Fry. Help us teach this boy a lesson. He shouldn't fool with football players."

Still holding the boy by the collar, he started walking toward me.

I'd never seen any boy look so afraid, and I met his eyes, terrified myself.

"Slug him, Frenchy."

I swallowed hard. "I gotta go. You should too."

"What did you say, Frenchy?" Billy came up and shoved me hard and would have slugged me, but Ace must have remembered his vow not to harm me.

"Leave the faggot alone. He's too much of a sissy to do anything, anyway. He can just watch." So Teddy and Billy held me as the other three turned on the Negro boy. I watched them beat him black and blue. He never said a word, never screamed in pain, never attempted to fight back. I tried to wriggle free of Teddy and Billy, and I had to squeeze my eyes shut when the Negro's nose started squirting blood. They were going to kill him.

"Stop it!" I finally screamed, but it came out more like a whimper. "Stop it, Ace!" This time my voice splintered into the darkness.

Ace let go of the Negro, who slumped to the ground, and then turned on me full force. He shoved me to the ground without effort, and I prepared myself for death, reciting some vague prayer to whatever saint was supposed to protect battered kids.

I had closed my eyes, anticipating the clenched fist smashing into my face, when I heard Mary Jane's high-pitched voice calling impatiently, "Emile, are you coming or not?"

In the second it took me to open my eyes, the football players had fled farther into the park. I rolled onto my stomach and pulled myself over beside the boy, who lay unconscious on the ground.

Mary Jane walked into the clearing and saw me kneeling by the Negro. "What are you doing?" she asked. Then she came closer and said, "What have you done?" She let out a cry and started to run, but I grabbed her arm and said, "He's hurt bad, Mary Jane. He needs help."

I called for Griffin, and he and Sally came running, and we all just stood there looking at the boy.

"Is he dead?" Sally asked.

"No, but they knocked him unconscious."

"Who?"

"Ace and Teddy and some others."

Griffin knelt down and righted the boy to a sitting position, saying, "Hey, hey you! You okay?" but the boy made no response. "Go call the police, Sally," Griffin ordered.

The girls just stood there, holding on to each other, until Griffin yelled again, "Did you hear me? Get help!"

As the girls darted back across the street toward the stadium, Griffin and I half dragged, half carried the unconscious boy outside the park, where we laid him on the ground and waited.

"What in the world have you gotten into, Émile?" Griffin asked. "This isn't good at all."

I didn't like the way Griffin seemed to place the blame on me for being at the wrong place at the wrong time.

An ambulance came and took the Negro away on a stretcher. Mama had arrived and was standing near the concession stand, talking to some other parents and twisting an eyebrow. A group of students were hanging about too. A policeman came over to where Griffin, Sally, Mary Jane, and I had been instructed to stay put.

"All right, young'uns. Mind telling me what's been going on here?"

The girls quickly said, "We didn't see anything."

In shaky English, I explained what I'd witnessed in the park.

"Would you recognize those boys?" the policeman asked, putting his frowning, round face within inches of my own. I hesitated for an instant, and he continued, "We've had a lot o' trouble with them niggers beating each other up. Looks like it's happening again. Isn't that right, son?"

The way he stared at me, like he was forcing his idea into my mind, made me cringe.

"I said, isn't that right?"

"Maybe." Then I imagined Blithe's angelic face looking up at me and I heard Eternity saying around the Thanksgiving table how she was thankful for civil rights and I saw Mr. Davis happily chewing his food and I blurted, "No. No! That's not right! It was some of the football players from Northside's team. They're the ones who did this. I know them. I can pick them out!"

He shook his head. "You sure about that, son?"

"Yessir."

As the policeman left, he muttered, "Lousy foreigners don't know when to keep their mouths shut."

I had a sinking feeling he was right.

They wanted only me to come to the police station. Sally and Mary Jane disappeared into the safety of their parents' cars. Griffin offered to stay with me, but his mother whisked him away before I could accept.

The policeman explained to Mama that they needed to take me, the only eyewitness, down to the station to ask a few routine questions. I thought Mama would burst into tears, but when he added, "You can come too, ma'am," she relaxed a little.

She gave me a hug and I muttered, "I'm sorry, Mama," and then I was escorted to the back of the black and white police car, its red light blazing into the still of the school campus.

The officer who questioned me at the police station was none other than Officer Dodge, the man who had been to our house the day after I'd supposedly run away. I could tell he considered me a scrawny troublemaker. While Mama waited at the front desk, he led me down a dark hall and into a room with a single table and two chairs.

He flipped on the light and said, "Have a seat. I'll be right back."

He showed me all kinds of photos, what he called mug shots, of kids, most of whom were Negroes. I turned page after page, each time assuring the officer, "No. It's none of these boys. I can show you who they are. Just get me a yearbook from Northside."

After ten minutes, I realized this policeman wasn't about to let me name the real attackers. I had no idea why. Then I thought about Mr. McClary. Maybe Ace's father ran the whole town. Maybe he wrote this man's paycheck.

After half an hour of leafing through every page of "possible suspects," I was allowed to go home. Mama hugged me tightly in the waiting room, and I started trembling. She hurried me out of the police station, and I made it to the car before I broke down, my voice cracking as I explained in French, "It was the second-string football players, Mama, who did it. They did it just to be cruel. Why won't Officer Dodge let me identify them?"

"I don't know, Emile."

But one glance at her face, and I understood that she did know, she knew as well as I did. A fine white boy couldn't be accused of a crime against a Negro.

"You need a good night's sleep," she said. "We'll set things straight in the morning." Then she glanced over at me and said, "I'm proud of you for what you did, Emile. Don't you ever forget, you hear me?"

I nodded, brushing away my tears. But I was still trembling inside.

sixteen

The next morning, at the bottom of the front page of the *Atlanta Journal*, was an article revealing the Negro's name. He was Edward Hasty, an eighth grader from a black middle school. He lay in critical condition at Grady Hospital after a "grisly beating by yet undisclosed assailants," said the paper that was spread out on the kitchen table.

I felt so sick to my stomach when I read those words that I ran up to my room, my breakfast uneaten. My mind kept replaying the awful images of the sweaty, shining faces of the football players gaining real pleasure from torturing Edward Hasty. Torture! The word surprised me. Ace McClary and his buddies were on the road to Nazism. That's what I thought as I sat in my room that Saturday morning, pretending to do homework.

Every time the phone rang, I flinched. Griffin called midmorning and cursed softly when I explained that the police didn't pay attention to my accusations.

Grandma brought me hot chocolate with a piece of toast smothered in grape jelly, which went against her principles that breakfast was meant to be eaten in the kitchen. I guess some principles could be overruled in emergency situations.

Throughout the rest of the morning, I sat on the stairs, nibbling my toast and listening when Mama answered the phone. One call seemed particularly promising.

"So they did call him in for questioning? . . . Good. He's down there now? . . . Yes, yes, thank you."

But my relief evaporated at eleven when the doorbell rang. Grandma opened it to find a police officer standing there, hat in hand.

"I'm sorry for disturbing you, ma'am, but it seems we have a discrepancy in stories. I'm afraid I'll have to take your grandson back down to the station."

Peering through the railing into the hall, I recognized first the voice and then the intense, angular face of Officer Dodge. I saw a flicker of anger in Grandma's eyes.

"Officer, my grandson did not beat up that young man. I'm ashamed of you for insinuating such a thing!"

Officer Dodge dropped his head a few inches. "I'm sorry, ma'am. I'm just doing my job."

"Well, I'll be coming to the station with him."

This she said as a threat, and I think Officer Dodge was actually intimidated by this usually meek but suddenly fierce grandmother.

"Janie, come on!" she commanded, and I caught a glimpse of a once domineering personality.

I was totally unprepared to find Ace McClary and his father at the police station. I shrank a little behind my grandmother, never meeting the eyes of either of them.

Ace had perfected his story overnight. I guess he figured I'd rat on him. Now he repeated it belligerently, pointing a finger my way, eyes ablaze.

"Who'd Mary Jane Willis find standing over that black boy? Emile de Bonnery's the guilty one. He's mad about having to leave France, and he's jealous of me for some reason. He tried to pick a fight with me and my buddies at school. Lotsa kids saw him. He's a shrimp, but he's mean.

"I think that poor Negro kid got in his way, is all. De Bonnery was going into Piedmont Park to make out with Mary Jane Willis— you just ask her. She screamed, and the Negro came to help, and

Emile just beat him up, beat him to a pulp. I'll bet you anything that's what happened!"

Mr. McClary winced a little as Ace's temper flared. He placed his hand on his son's shoulder and seemed physically to will him to calm down. And Ace, as if he suddenly remembered his role, added, "But, as I've told you before, I wasn't anywhere near the park. I was in the locker room with the whole football team."

The story was so outrageous that I was sure no one would believe it. Surely the whole football team wouldn't vouch for him! Plus, the thought of me pummeling another boy about my size to near death was unfathomable, almost laughable. Still, I found my face turning purple when he mentioned I was going to "make out" with Mary Jane, and I wished that Mama and Grandma had not been sitting right beside me.

When I was allowed to explain my version, my voice was so shaky that the policeman had to ask me at least four times to repeat certain sentences because he couldn't understand me. His tactics, intentional or not, made me feel like what Griffin called a "moron." The way my voice quavered and my accent grew so pronounced did nothing to lend credibility to my version of the events.

Officer Dodge said, nodding over at Ace, "Mr. McClary has an airtight alibi. The whole football team has sworn he was with them in the locker room. Do you have an alibi, young man?"

I realized with a desperate, hollow feeling that my only alibi was Edward Hasty.

But I told them again about being with Griffin and Sally and Mary Jane, and talking with Eternity, so they were brought to the police station and questioned about what had happened.

Griffin told me later that he had vouched for me. He told them he heard several voices coming from that part of the park, but Officer Dodge kept coming back to the fact that he hadn't *seen* the football players, even though he supposedly walked through the park nearby only a few minutes before. Griffin said that Sally quickly cleared herself of any involvement. Mary Jane didn't exactly lie, but she certainly didn't sway things in my favor. She told the police she had "gotten away from me" and then come back when she heard a "ruckus." That's when she found me on the ground beside the Negro.

Traitor! I thought when Griffin told me this. Never again would I give a thought to her adoring gaze.

When Eternity was escorted from the room, she glanced over her shoulder at me and said, "He's innocent, Officer. I am absolutely positive that he's innocent." Then she looked the policeman in the eyes and said, "And I'll prove it. I guarantee you, I'll prove it."

She was waiting for me when they let me go. "I know what you did to help the Negro," Eternity said. "I'm sorry my testimony wasn't helpful. But you'll see. It'll be all right."

"Oh, come on, Eternity. Quit trying to fix things. The fact is I'm in a mess." Then I let out a string of curse words in French.

That made Eternity smile, and for some odd reason, seeing her grinning at me, I mocked the police officer in my best Southern drawl, saying, "Lousy four-een-er."

"I'm not mad at you anymore, Emile."

"I don't like Mary Jane."

"I know."

I couldn't bring myself to say, "But I do like you." She probably knew that too. At least Blithe seemed to think so.

"It's gonna be okay, Emile." Eternity wrapped her skinny arm through mine and leaned against me so that I got all nervous and hot, and she whispered, "Let's go find your mama. Don't worry."

But I *was* worried. I didn't think anyone really believed Ace, but unless Edward Hasty woke up real soon, it looked like I was going to get blamed for beating up—and possibly killing—a Negro.

I didn't come downstairs for breakfast on Sunday, and Grandma and Mama didn't ask questions. I guess they knew there was no way I was going to show my face in church.

Grandma simply called out, "We're leaving now, Emile. We'll be back shortly after noon."

They were probably relieved to have me stay home, especially since the story continued in the Sunday paper: *Negro Remains in Coma after Grisly Beating.* It said there was "strong evidence that Edward Hasty had more than one attacker." Surely that was good news.

Still, I was terrified. Would they lock me in jail for assault and battery or even homicide? Griffin explained these terms to me in graphic detail when he called right after Grandma and Mama had left.

"Anything's possible, Emile. Sure wish that Edward Hasty would wake up and clear your name. Otherwise, you might be a goner."

"A what?"

"Let's just say you'll need a lawyer." Then he had another thought. "Maybe we could smuggle you back to France."

"Great idea, Griff," I said. I wasn't about to tell him that, according to my mother, going back to France was even more dangerous than remaining in Atlanta. For some reason I got a smug feeling of importance, like Tintin in the midst of his troubles, when I admitted to myself that either way, I was a marked man.

Mama and Grandma left me in my room most of the day, where I read Tintin, tried in vain to do some math, and dozed off and on, dreaming once that Officer Dodge came in the middle of the night and took me to jail where I'd be locked up forever. Late in the afternoon, with the sky dark and the wind whipping outside, Mama came in and settled herself on my bed.

"Your grandmother and I have been talking, Emile. We think the best thing to do is to get a lawyer—she knows several good ones—and for you to stay home from school for a day or two, until everything is settled."

"Do you think I'm guilty, Mama?" I asked her in French.

"Of course not, Emile."

"But won't it seem like I'm guilty if I stay home and hide?"

"Well, I don't know . . . I just thought maybe you wouldn't want all that attention."

"I can go to school."

She rose to leave, so I added quickly, "Mama, I'm sorry for causing so much trouble. About Papa and now this."

She sat back down on the bed and took my hands in hers. "Emile de Bonnery, I am so proud of you, I don't even know what to say. You're willing to stand up for the less fortunate. Maybe it seems like you're causing trouble, but the truth is . . . the truth is we'd all be a lot better off if more people would cause trouble the way you do."

She hugged me tightly so that I could feel what seemed like two months of pent-up emotion seeping out of her.

After she left the room, I sat at the desk by the dormer window and slid my wristwatch off and turned it over and over in my hands. Maybe all the bad things that had happened to me lately were worth it just to hear Mama say that she was proud of me. It was as if she and I had been standing on either side of the wide Saône River glaring at each other for a very long time, and all of a sudden I was running across that old suspension bridge that had been there for centuries, running to Mama and she was running to me and we met in the middle of the bridge and hugged and knew that from then on, whichever side we went to, we would stay together.

Later that night, before going to bed, I went into Grandma's bedroom to give her a good-night kiss. It had become our ritual in the past weeks. Only I did it the French way—a kiss on each cheek—and then she would hug me close. She was usually sitting in her green armchair that overlooked the backyard, reading her Bible, which otherwise sat on the little table by the chair. She read it in the mornings and at night and then she prayed. On that same table she kept a pretty red clothbound notebook where she recorded "prayer requests." Once I dared to open it and read a few pages.

She dated each request on the left side of the page, then next to the date she wrote a brief description—things like *Janie's job* or *Emile's adjustment at school*—and sometimes she'd even get real personal and add, *Please, Lord, let him make a good friend. Just one.* Beside that request on the right of the page she had written in *Eternity Jones* with the date of the first time Eternity had come over.

Other requests I'd glimpsed on that page were *Jake's health* and *Blithe's security* and *Leroy Davis needs a job.* There was one that made me get prickles on the back of my neck for some reason: *Lord, let me talk to Eternity again about You. Salvation.*

I felt guilty, reading these secret notes of an old woman. It looked like she actually believed that God heard her prayers and answered them. But instead of making me think she was senile, I actually felt sort of secure, protected by what I considered my grandmother's superstitious habit. I was often tempted to sneak another peek, just to see if her prayers for me were going in the way she wanted.

So this night, I came up beside her while she was reading, leaned against the chair and, summoning up my courage, asked, "Grandma, do you think you could pray for me?" And before she could say anything, I added, "Whatever you think is best will be okay, but could you mention something about school tomorrow and seeing Ace and the others?"

My heart was beating harder than when Eternity hugged me. In fact, asking that question took a lot more courage than hunting for my father or screaming for Ace to stop pummeling Edward Hasty, but I had no idea why. I turned to leave, having registered my request, but Grandma took my hand.

"Sit down, Emile, and I'll pray for you right now," she said.

"With me here?"

"Of course."

"Don't you think you should talk to God alone? I mean, it's kind of private. I don't want to interfere or anything."

She chuckled and said, "I assure you that you will not be interfering."

I obediently perched on the side of her bed. Then she bent her head and closed her eyes and reached for my hand and started having this very personal conversation with God.

She said things like, "Dear Heavenly Father, thank You for being the one who is in charge of every detail of our lives," and "Thank You for Emile's courage standing up to those boys," and "Lord, we know that You can take things that seem so evil and use them for good. I don't know how You do that, but thank You. Use this situation for Your good and protect Emile."

She prayed for what seemed to be a long time, but I didn't mind. When she finally said, "Amen," I waited a few seconds before opening my eyes.

She kissed me and said, "Good night, Emile. I love you."

"Thank you, Grandma."

Back in my room, I felt cozy and peaceful and unafraid. She had put into words what I was fervently wishing—that all the difficult circumstances of late could end up producing something positive. But whereas my reasoning was based on luck or fate or coincidence, my grandmother had attributed the working out of these things to God.

This was all very strange to me. On the day that I didn't even go to church and was being falsely accused of beating a Negro, God suddenly felt very, very close, as if He had floated in through the dormer window and was sitting in the chair watching me as I lay in bed and drifted off to a dreamless sleep.

God did a good job of answering Grandma's prayer for me on Monday at school. The whole football team was absent for three days. Rumor had it they'd all been suspended for drinking beer.

I had three whole days of freedom from Ace, and I celebrated by playing a pickup game of soccer with Griffin at recess. Before long, several other ninth graders had joined us, and a small group of kids stood watching on the sidelines of our homemade soccer field. Occasionally I heard someone say, "Wow! Griffin and Emile are really good!" and "You can tell he played on a team back in France," and "Maybe Northside should think of starting a soccer team."

It all went straight to my head. I didn't mind the hypocrisy of a school full of prejudiced kids suddenly considering me a hero for saving a Negro and getting the bullies—normally the most popular guys at school—in trouble. I devoured their praise as if I were eating a Varsity chili dog. Not that I gained more friends. I simply gained a little respect. And it felt good.

Then the next day, Tuesday morning, as Edward still lay in a coma, the *Journal* proclaimed that new evidence had been found and the previous suspect—me—was now cleared of all charges. Officer Dodge had called from the precinct late the day before and explained to Grandma—who answered the phone—that I was cleared. I had no idea what the new evidence was or who had supplied it.

A week later, Edward Hasty woke up from his coma. He never identified his assailants—claiming, so the paper said, that he had been beaten so badly he'd never gotten a good look at them—but he had identified me as the one who begged them to stop and who had screamed for help. As far as I could tell, the football players were never punished for their cruelty—only for their drinking—but by the time they came back to school, I was well on my way to being accepted, and I felt pretty sure that Ace wouldn't bother me again.

———————

Mama started teaching French at Northside the day after Edward woke up, which made things a whole lot easier for her. She was immediately promoted to the status of "mother of the hero," which reminded me vaguely of the Virgin Mary being called the Mother of God. Like I said, my new popularity had gone straight to my head.

Since Mama and I were back on the same side of the river, I really didn't mind that much when she asked me to help her conjugate verbs in class that first day or discuss ways to help the students that night. I had suddenly gained a whole new confidence in my life, and I felt willing to share this hard-earned position with my mother. I hadn't forgotten my father, hadn't forgotten Mamie Madeleine and my friends in Lyon. Not exactly. But the awful aching, the desperate longing to be somewhere else gradually evaporated, and it was as if my former life in France were a million miles away.

It was Eternity who kept bringing me back to the reality of my father's disappearance. She believed in causes—in civil rights, in research about Jake's illness, in a hundred other things. She seemed convinced she could save the world, or at least a part of it, if she tried hard enough. Almost every week she assured me, "I'll find out what happened to your father. It may take a while, but I'll find out."

The same day that Mama started teaching, posters went up for the spring play auditions. Eternity was standing beside me when I saw the poster by the water fountain. *Friday, December 11, 3:00 p.m., tryouts for the spring play: Hamlet.* Our English class had studied *Hamlet* during the first semester of school. Now the theater club would perform it.

In an unusual display of enthusiasm, I said, "You should try out, Eternity. You'd be great!"

She gave me her best droopy-eyed Cleopatra look. "Practices are after school three afternoons a week. What would I do with Jake and Blithe?"

I seized upon her faulty reasoning immediately. "They can come to Grandma's house with me on the days you have rehearsal after school. Please, Eternity. You're a natural. You'd be a really, really good actress." I was imagining her as Elizabeth Taylor in *National Velvet*, young and innocent and beautiful.

For one second Eternity hesitated, but it was enough for me to notice the flicker of interest in her eyes. "I'm signing you up," I announced, and amazingly she did nothing to stop me.

———————

She got the part of Ophelia, as I had known she would. One look at Eternity—pale, tall, profound—and anyone could see that Shakespeare's tragic heroine fit her like a glove. I even thought secretly to myself that I could imagine her floating dead in a brook, a victim of her own hand, if ever anything happened to Jake and Blithe.

I had attended plenty of plays with Mamie Madeleine, who loved the theater. But French schools generally didn't have extracurricular activities offered on campus, so I didn't know much about school plays. I didn't know that most high school theater groups did not perform *Hamlet*.

I secretly congratulated myself on having convinced Eternity to try out. My intentions were pure and simple—let her enjoy something in life and have a break from the responsibility of caring for her younger siblings. My whole family would be happy to help.

Twice that same day, the last Tuesday before Christmas break, I caught sight of Mama in the hallway talking with Mr. Jeffers, the ninth-grade history teacher. When I saw she was eating at the same table with him in the lunchroom, I became alarmed.

I met her in the hall outside the lunchroom and asked, "Why are you always spending time with Mr. Jeffers?"

"I beg your pardon?" Two red splotches formed on her cheeks.

"I think he likes you, Mama."

"For heaven's sake, don't be silly. We're colleagues."

"Maybe he thinks you're divorced."

"Emile! For heaven's sake," she repeated, although this time she sounded more nervous than incredulous.

"Well, you're not wearing your wedding ring, you know," I accused, and she looked satisfyingly guilty. "I hear the rumors, you know. People say that Papa ran off with another woman and left us to fend for ourselves, so we had to move back to America."

"Is that what you've told them?"

"I've never said anything." Then I remembered my conversations with Eternity. But I knew she hadn't repeated my confidence. "It's just that people talk, that's all."

"Emile, we've already discussed why he left. You know it wasn't really another woman." She was running her right fingers around the base of her left finger where her wedding band used to be. "Your father wanted me to take off my ring—it was . . . it was another precaution. Please believe me, Emile. I'm not interested in anyone else."

"Are you thinking of divorcing Papa?"

"No! Of course not! I promise you, I am not interested in Mr. Jeffers." Then she tugged on an eyebrow and added, "But speaking of precautions . . . I am also applying to get you an American passport."

"I don't care how long we'll be here, I don't want an American passport!"

"Well, it's nothing to get worried about. It's just a precaution, that's all. It's a necessary precaution."

A precaution against what? I thought to myself.

"I'll meet you out at the car after school," Mama added.

"I've got to go to class," I said in French, and I stomped off, wondering why every time I thought things were getting better with Mama, something else came along to mess it all up.

That same day, Eternity practically danced up to me after school, beaming in a most un-Eternity way. "We won! We won! I can't believe it, Emile! We really won!"

"You deserved the part, Eternity. You *earned* it," I countered, assuming she was still riding high on the posting of the cast list.

She gave me her best *you are truly the biggest idiot on the face of this earth* look and said, "Emile, what planet are you living on?"

I didn't ask, *Okay, then, what did we win?* I had learned the way to goad Eternity was through silence and feigned disinterest.

She shoved the *Atlanta Journal* in front of my face and pointed to the headline: *District Court Rules Heart of Atlanta Motel at Fault.*

"Read it!" she ordered.

I had not yet gained quite enough confidence to disobey Eternity Jones. I took the newspaper from her, plopped down by my locker, and read.

> The District Court held that Congress acted well within its jurisdiction of the Interstate Commerce clause in passing the Civil Rights Act of 1964, thereby upholding the act's Title II in question.... Having observed that 75 percent of the Heart of Atlanta Motel's clientele comes from out of state, and that it is strategically located near Interstates 75 and 85 ... the Court found that the business clearly affects interstate commerce. As such, it therefore upheld the permanent injunction issued by the District Court and required the Heart of Atlanta Motel to receive business from clientele of all races.

"Great," I said without enthusiasm.

"You didn't even read my article in *Tiger Tales* in October, did you?"

"Sure I did." And I had, I was sure, but at the moment I couldn't remember what it was about.

She produced a copy and pointed to her article, which I glanced at. Now I remembered.

> The Civil Rights Act banned racial discrimination in public places and particularly in places offering public accommodation. The Heart of Atlanta Motel, by refusing to rent rooms to black patrons, was in direct violation of the terms. The owner of the motel had argued that his rights were being violated, and the case went to trial in October.

"Now do you understand, dummy?"

"Yeah—a victory for civil rights."

"Exactly. Negroes can now stay in that hotel and any other hotel they choose. Isn't that fabulous?"

On a "fabulous scale" of one to ten, a hotel being forced to admit Negroes did not rank very high for me. *Fabulous* was reserved for finding out news about Papa, or getting one of Eternity's rare hugs, or learning I was no longer accused of beating Edward Hasty to near death. I cared about individuals, not causes.

But for Eternity's sake I said, "Yep, that's really, really swell."

I should have expected the outcome. That night, Eternity and Mama and Grandma and Mr. Davis and Jake and Blithe and I all piled into the green Chevrolet and drove to the Heart of Atlanta Motel. With a great big smile on his face, Mr. Leroy Davis went up to the reception desk and reserved a room—paid for by Grandma Bridgeman, at her insistence.

We all rode the elevator to the third floor, where we crowded into the room and celebrated by drinking Coca-Colas and eating Lay's potato chips. Eternity raised her bottle of Coke into the air and led us in an off-key rendition of "We Shall Overcome."

To my surprise, the feeling of shared excitement and triumph stayed with me long after we left the motel where Mr. Davis spent the night watching the news on the TV in his room.

seventeen

For the last three afternoons of our last week of school before Christmas break, Jake and Blithe came home with me after school while Eternity stayed for play rehearsal.

That first day when Blithe walked into Grandma's house, she let out a soft, high-pitched squeal. "I've died and gone to heaven!" She ran into the den and stood entranced before Grandma's Christmas tree. "It's real, Jake! Real! Come here and smell it!"

I had always viewed Blithe as otherworldly and angelic, but on that dusky afternoon, with the Christmas tree lights blinking off and on, she glowed, a feather-weight cherub. "We never had a Christmas tree! Not a real one. Only once we had an old plastic tree. Remember that one, Jake?"

He nodded solemnly and, in a rare moment of speech, said, "It had bugs so Ma threw it in the trash."

"Mr. Davis had a Christmas tree one year, 'member that, Jake?"

He nodded again. "He had a good job at the filling station, and he bought that tree. He bought it 'cause you wanted one so bad, Sissy."

"Did not."

"Did too."

"Wasn't just me, Jake. You asked him to get a tree too."

They argued back and forth, all the while walking around the tree and examining the dozens of ornaments hanging on the spruce limbs. Grandma and Mama had placed them there two days ago while songs like "Rudolph the Red-Nosed Reindeer" and "Frosty the Snowman" and a bunch of other American Christmas tunes I'd never heard of played on the record player.

Christmas seemed to have cast a spell on Mama, pushing her back into her childhood, before the stormy teen years stole away so much. She and Grandma giggled as they decorated the tree and the house.

I had helped—stringing lights, unwrapping ornaments, hanging tinsel. Mamie Madeleine did not celebrate Christmas with trees and lights. No gaudy decorations, no baking of cookies. Christmas was a solemn family affair—first the midnight Mass and then the feast that lasted straight through the night. In France, Christmas was all about food, the best food money could buy. After the family had spent hours at the table, in the wee hours of the morn, the children would receive one gift before they tumbled into bed and slept.

But in America, Christmas seemed to be about *everything*—real trees and ornaments and Nativity scenes and parties with friends and Christmas carols and baking yummy treats and lots of presents wrapped in shiny paper and placed under the tree weeks before Christmas.

After Blithe and Jake had inspected the tree, Grandma invited them into the kitchen to help bake cookies. Mama, who was busy planning her French lessons for the week, came downstairs and put a record on the hi-fi, and soon the house was filled with the aroma of sugar cookies and the sound of Bing Crosby crooning about a white Christmas.

Grandma, Jake, Blithe, and I picked up Eternity after her rehearsal, and we drove across town to the trailer. Ma was sitting in her rocking chair on the porch with Demon by her side, in spite of the fact it was only fifty degrees outside and nearly pitch-black.

Grandma walked the children to the door and greeted Ma as if she were her next-door neighbor. Ma was drunk, no doubt about it, but Grandma didn't seem one bit fazed. I saw her nose wrinkle just the slightest bit when she smelled the bourbon on Ma's breath, but then Grandma thrust out her hand, shook the startled Ma's pudgy wrist, and said, "Hello, Mrs. Jones. Maggie Bridgeman. Nice to see you again. I certainly have enjoyed getting to know your children. Thank you for allowing them to come to my house. They are fine children. You must be awfully proud of them."

Ma's face registered slight understanding, then suspicion.

"We baked some cookies for you, Ma!" Blithe said and handed her mother a bright red paper plate stacked with a dozen decorated cookies.

Ma looked from the plate to Grandma to Blithe and then to the plate again. I guess the fog in her brain began to lift, because she said, "Thank you kindly, Miz Bridgeman. Would you care to come inside?"

Eternity and I stole disbelieving glances at each other, but I wasn't surprised when Grandma said, "Well, I'd love to. I can only stay a minute, though. I've got dinner in the oven."

Ma motioned to Eternity, who grabbed the screen door and held it open while Ma slowly lifted her enormous body out of the chair, swayed for a precarious second till she caught her balance, then trudged back into the trailer, tossing clothes and dirty plates and trash and even a cat I'd never seen before onto the floor.

"Have a seat, Miz Bridgeman," Ma slurred, settling on the couch with a grunt.

Despite the overwhelming stench of rancid milk and cat's urine and several other disgusting odors, Grandma sat down as if she had been invited into Windsor Castle for tea with the queen. Seeing there was not any space for the rest of us, Eternity said, "Ma, we're going into our room for a minute."

I said to Grandma, "Just call me when you're ready to go."

I never did meet anyone who didn't like my Grandma Bridgeman. She was gentle and quiet in a good way. Strong, sure of herself, compassionate, with no fear of standing up for things she knew were right—like my innocence in the beating of Edward Hasty. But the way she accomplished those things was different from other women, certainly different from Mamie Madeleine and Mama. I had no doubt that she'd work her special brand of magic on Ma.

Meanwhile, Eternity unlocked the safe room and the four of us crowded inside. For the next thirty minutes, we decorated that room with leftover tinsel and ribbons and old Christmas cards we'd brought from Grandma's house—and a few boughs of spruce we'd cut from the bottom of our tree. We'd even brought an old strand of Christmas lights, and these we rigged to go around the doorpost and across the side of the bunk bed.

Jake and I mostly watched. Seeing Eternity make that room become Christmas convinced me of her vast creative genius. Something inside her knew exactly how the room should look, and she accomplished this with a pair of scissors, a roll of Scotch tape, and a bunch of leftover ribbons and ornaments.

When everything was in place, Eternity turned out the overhead lights and plugged in the strand of Christmas lights. Blithe whispered, "Magic!"

And it was.

The lights twinkled and we could smell the fresh scent of spruce. The little silver-ball ornaments Eternity had taped to the sides of the bed gleamed and glimmered when the lights flashed on and off. It was peaceful, and almost holy.

Using for a stable the little brown box in which we'd carried the ornaments, and for hay the shredded paper that had protected the ornaments, Blithe had busied herself constructing a little Nativity. The small figurines were cheap plastic ones Grandma had found in the attic space and given to the children—but to Blithe, it was as if Jesus were right there in the room with us. She kneeled on the floor beside the scene and whispered to the baby in the manger, "Sleep in heavenly peace."

The next afternoon we repeated our visit to the trailer. This time the weather was almost muggy, nearly seventy degrees—not so unusual for Atlanta in December, others said. Grandma pulled up a chair on that filthy old porch and sat down beside Ma, stuck in the rusted rocker, and they talked as if they'd been good friends and neighbors for years. They talked about the children, about school, about cooking, and even about Christmas. That last subject made me nervous because, besides our secret decorating of the safe room, the trailer bore no sign of the holiday except for one faded Christmas card with Santa Claus on the front that sat by a dirty plate on the kitchen counter.

Grandma told Ma how bright Eternity was, and how gifted Jake seemed to be with his hands—how the little seedlings he'd planted at her house had survived and were becoming plants—and how Blithe seemed to have a natural ear for music. As she talked, Ma chuckled and nodded, and a strange peacefulness descended on that old trailer.

While Eternity was fixing dinner, Blithe took my hand, put her finger over her mouth, and whispered, "Follow me." Almost on tiptoe, she led me down the narrow hall to the safe room. She produced the key, and when I shot her a questioning glance, she whispered, "Eternity gave it to me so I could show you."

She unlocked the door, and we stepped inside. The overhead light was off, and in the dusk the little strand of Christmas lights twinkled off and on, off and on. I breathed in the scent of fresh pine. I smiled at Blithe and sat down on the bottom bunk.

"It's really nice."

"Do you see what's different, Emile? Can you tell what I added?"

I looked around the small, spotless room with its mishmash of ornaments hanging from the bed railing, the chairs, and the little plywood desk where the Nativity scene sat. I was about to admit I didn't see any difference from the night before when I glimpsed a shadow moving across the Nativity. I looked up. Dangling from the ceiling on long strings of colorful thread were dozens of white paper stars, five-pronged but uneven, cut no doubt by Blithe's own hand.

"Stars!" I exclaimed, and she let out a high-pitched yelp. I thought I'd never seen her eyes dance quite as they did then.

"I made 'em, every one, and then Jake stood on the chair and we got some thread from Eternity's sewing box and taped it to the backs of the stars. And then Jake, standing on his tippy toes, could tape the thread to the ceiling. See!"

"Oh, and look at this one," I said, reaching up and touching the big yellow star that hung lower than the rest right over the plastic Nativity.

"It's the one the Wise Men followed to find Baby Jesus! See, it's bigger and brighter than all the rest, and it led them right to the stable in Bethlehem. See! See, Emile. I made it! I made every one."

She threw her arms around my waist, and I awkwardly placed one arm around her and found myself breathing in deeply, breathing in Blithe's innocence and the scent of Christmas and the way this room, tucked inside a rusted old trailer, seemed filled to the brim with something pure and holy and good.

Around six o'clock, Mr. Davis came over and sat on the steps and tossed rocks with Jake while he listened to Ma and Grandma talk. Eternity was in the little kitchen peeling carrots and slicing them into little round coins. I was perched on the steps with Blithe, reading her the story of Christmas from a thick storybook with beautiful illustrations that Grandma had brought over.

Somewhere out of the blue, it seemed to me, Mr. Davis asked, "Y'all wanna come to my house for dinner, Miz Bridgeman?"

Grandma looked startled for only half of a second. She glanced at her watch and said, "Oh, my! The time has slipped away!"

I could tell she was about to decline, saying something about how Mama might worry if we didn't show up. But then I guess she saw the way Blithe bounced up and down with excitement and Mr. Davis smiled solemnly, as if he were offering us his most treasured possession, because she astounded me by saying, "Well, we'd be delighted to stay for dinner, Mr. Davis, if you're sure you have enough."

"Oh, yeah, I got plenty. I always fix dinner for the Jones family on Thursday nights. I got some chitlin and black-eyed peas with hog's chow and some corn bread and a Jell-O pudding. And Eternity's making us a salad."

"I'll just need to let Janie know."

"You kin use my phone," Mr. Davis said.

Just like that, Grandma and I were crowded around a small table in Mr. Davis's house, sharing his food with Eternity and Jake and Blithe, and with Ma, who didn't say a word the whole meal, but who managed to eat two helpings of everything. Blithe kept prattling on about Christmas until Eternity frowned at her, and she remembered her manners and sat quietly. Mr. Davis reminisced about the war and launched into a story about Normandy and about being terrified as he hid in a foxhole with the Germans close by. Then he told us about picking cotton in South Georgia when he was a kid and about the influenza virus that nearly killed him way back in the 1920s and about when Ma first arrived with her own mother as his neighbors. I listened to him, spellbound, and wanted life in America to go on like this for a long time.

Eventually the conversation drifted to religion. At least it seemed to drift, just floating this way and that on the air, but I think somehow Grandma was steering it, or maybe blowing it, in that direction.

They began to talk about how Baby Jesus came to be the Savior of all mankind, and I was astonished to hear Eternity say, "So many people just go to church without ever grasping the Gospel's message of grace." She glanced at my grandmother as if checking out her story. "They still believe in good works as the way to get to heaven. If that were true, there'd be no point in Jesus becoming human and dying for our sins."

She sounded like a preacher, and I wondered where she'd gotten all of her theology, since she never went to church. But the conversation just hummed along and others expressed their opinions. I didn't have one thing to say.

Near the end of the meal, Grandma said, "Well, we would certainly enjoy having you share Christmas dinner with us this year, Mrs. Jones, Mr. Davis, kids."

Blithe's head popped up, eyes sparkling.

Grandma continued as if assuming they would naturally accept her invitation. "I generally just ask each guest to bring one thing—a vegetable or a salad or a dessert—and I supply the honey-baked ham. You are all certainly welcome."

Ma came out of her stupor enough to grunt, "Thank you kindly. That would be nice. I have a right nice chess pie I like to make, and Eternity makes a good green pea and broccoli casserole."

"And Mr. Davis can bring some of this corn bread!" Blithe piped up. "It's deeelicious, ain't it?"

"Isn't it," Eternity corrected, but she seemed pleased with the prospect of another holiday meal at Grandma's.

"I'll be delighted to come to yore house and make as much corn bread as you like," Mr. Davis said.

Grandma made it sound as if she had a houseful of guests every Christmas, but I knew for a fact that ever since her husband had died, she had either been invited to the home of her friends who lived on

Blackland Road or had flown out to Chicago where her only brother lived with his wife and kids. Having a houseful of family and friends at Christmas was Grandma's resurrected dream, and it looked to me like she intended to make it the best celebration yet.

Back at home that evening, Mama and I sat on the couch in the den, sipping hot chocolate she'd made for us, even though the weather was still muggy. I told her all about our meal at Mr. Davis's house and Grandma's dinner invitation for Christmas.

"Well, it doesn't surprise me that Mother would plan a big party," Mama said, taking a long sip of hot chocolate. "When I was a girl, we dressed up all fancy and went to party after party at friends' houses for the whole month of December.

"Mother threw a party for Daddy's office every year—she was the perfect hostess, and it was always an elaborate affair. That's when they lived in the big house on Blackland Road. Your grandfather would have a special gift for each employee. He was a harsh businessman and ran his company like a drill sergeant, but Christmas brought out the good in him. I loved those parties, the fancy little hors d'oeuvres, the way the Negro at the bar served eggnog spiked with bourbon and punch loaded with alcohol so that by nine o'clock everyone was laughing and in fine humor." She looked at me and winked. "That was before Grandma started going to church.

"But then, when I got to be a teenager, I saw all the parties as pretense—a way to impress others with who had the biggest tree and the prettiest ornaments. Everything had to be perfect, and I just wanted to escape. . . . Funny how much I missed those parties when I got to France."

Mama cleared her throat and leaned back on the couch, watching the Christmas tree lights blinking on and off. Then she wrapped her arms around me and rested her head on mine and we just sat there for a while.

"But we never had the poor into our homes for Christmas, Emile. This is going to be a very special holiday. I tell you, Mother has changed."

Once school was out, Eternity, Jake, and Blithe spent several days at our house before Christmas. I was reading John Steinbeck's *Of Mice and Men* without enthusiasm, an assignment for English that needed to be completed before school started back in January. Blithe was busy with Grandma rolling out dough for yet another batch of Christmas cut-outs. She had flour all down the front of her dress and looked like a very messy white angel, giggling, sneaking pieces of the dough and popping them into her mouth.

"This is the most depressing book," I commented to Grandma.

"At first glance." She handed Blithe the rolling pin and set a tray of unbaked cookies in the oven.

"What do you mean?"

"Well, when you first read it, it just seems depressing. But once you study the novel, you can see a great story of friendship. Steinbeck speaks of one central theme, time and again: caring for each other." Then out of the blue she said, in a voice full of nostalgia, "'Because I got you to look after me and you got me to look after you and that's why!'"

I stared at her in disbelief. "How do you know that line?"

"I memorized lots of literature in my day. I always loved the way Lenny said that. Caring about each other is a theme as old as the world. If we would try, think of the changes it would make. Remember who said 'Love your neighbor as yourself.'"

"Grandma, why do you always talk in riddles?"

"She's like Jesus," Blithe offered, brushing her hands on her apron. Her little tinkling voice startled me.

"She tells stories, and she only wants the ones who are really interested to be able to understand."

When Blithe said that, I was absolutely convinced she was a messenger from God. He sent her to earth to explain things to dim-witted people like me.

———

All through the week before Christmas, Grandma continued her habit of spending an hour or so talking with Ma when she dropped the children off back at the trailer.

On the way home from one of these encounters I blurted out, "Do you *like* talking with Ma?"

"I do."

"Really? Half the time she's drunk, you know."

"I know that. But half the time she's not, and I figure I can learn a lot about her and her children either way. You know, Emile, it's a lot harder to hate a whole race of people, like the Negroes, or a type of person, like alcoholics, when you start getting to know individuals. Prejudice likes to make generalizations and stay far away. I wanted to get to know Ma before I judged her too harshly."

"So what do you think now?"

"I think she has had a real hard life, and who knows what I would have done in her situation."

"You feel sorry for her, is that what you mean?"

"Maybe," Grandma admitted. "But I hope it's not perceived as pity. I hope she can tell that I really care about her and her kids. I just feel like that's important."

I knew Grandma meant it—that for her there truly was nothing more important than taking time to be with this strange family. There were a lot of other things she could be doing, but she chose to spend time with Ma. That was the question I wanted to ask my grandmother: How did she know when something was worth doing and when it wasn't?

She'd told me about Mama leaving and my grandfather's heart attack and the decision to slow down. She'd even told me about getting "reborn," like the flowers in her garden every spring. But *how* did she know these things? How was I going to know what was worth my while?

I couldn't flat-out ask the real question: *How can you be sure I should just leave alone everything that has to do with my father? How do you know that is the right thing to do?* But if I could phrase the question correctly and ask it at the right time, maybe I'd get another clue.

As soon as we knew the Jones family would be spending Christmas with us, Grandma, Mama, and I kind of collectively had the idea of buying gifts for them. We spent two afternoons shopping at a place called Lenox Square. I left Mama and Grandma and went to Rich's, a very popular department store. In my wallet I had twelve crisp dollar bills, one given to me each week by Grandma. With this money I carefully selected my gifts.

When gift after gift appeared under the tree labeled for Blithe or Jake or Eternity, I began to worry. "Grandma, won't they see this as charity? Won't it make Ma mad—like a slap in the face that she couldn't provide for her own kids and so we had to do it? She can be really awful when she's mad, you know."

Grandma and Mama waved my apprehension away, and I later realized that Grandma had talked with Ma about the extent of the Christmas celebration planned at the Bridgeman house. As the day approached, I found myself alternating between excitement, anticipation, and fear. For Jake, but especially for Blithe, I wanted this to be the best Christmas ever. I was pretty sure it would be Grandma's favorite Christmas in many years. But for us, for Mama and me, I secretly hoped that amidst all the colorfully wrapped gifts there would be a simple envelope with a letter from Papa, saying how much he missed and loved us.

So many things about Christmas in America were vastly different from Noël in France. But one thing was the same: we went to church on Christmas Eve. In Lyon, it was midnight Mass, in Atlanta it was the Christmas Eve service at Second-Ponce de Leon Baptist Church. We invited the Jones family to the service, but Ma, in one of her more verbal moments, had said, "Thank you kindly, but the children have to get to bed early, it bein' Christmas Eve and all. And I got stuff to do," she added, as if she would be wrapping presents all night long, which I doubted.

Grandma and Mama and I sat up near the front. I could have almost reached out and touched the handbells and the red poinsettias. The church was dimly lit with a reverent feel about it. I looked around me in wonder, thinking this was indeed an appropriate place to be on Christmas Eve. The choir sang, and the bells rang out some joyful Christmas hymn, and then Dr. Swilley got up and spoke in his warm, kind voice that echoed throughout the sanctuary.

I could easily imagine Blithe sitting in Dr. Swilley's lap, innocence shining in her eyes as he told her about a Savior come to earth to redeem mankind. In fact, the way he spoke, so real, so sincere, I wished I could climb into his lap and believe.

At the very end of the service, all the lights were turned out in the sanctuary. Some men in dark suits came down the aisles, holding small white candles with their flames flickering. Slowly, from person to person and row to row, we passed that flame along, lighting the candle each of us had received when we'd first entered the sanctuary. Soon the whole room was ablaze in a heavenly light. We sang "Silent Night, Holy Night," softly, reverently, and I was gazing up in the balcony and all around me when I suddenly felt the warmth drain right out of my body. Several rows in front of us on the left sat Mr. McClary and Ace and his brother, Mitch.

In that brief glance two things registered in my mind. First, I was scared, embarrassed, and humiliated. I wanted to hide from them, pretend I'd never stepped into Piedmont Park at the end of November. But second, I suddenly realized I'd never seen a Mrs. McClary. There they sat, one oversized man with his two sons. And I felt sad. I had no idea why, but I felt very sorry for them that night with bells ringing and the choir singing and Christmas come down to us from above.

After the service was over, Grandma and Mama visited with friends. I had to go, so I hurried downstairs to the restroom. I was just zipping up when a voice said, "Hey, Frenchy Fry, don't you look handsome tonight."

Ace McClary was the only other person in the bathroom. For all I knew, he was the only other person downstairs.

"You're sure proud of yourself for getting us in trouble over that nigger, aren't ya, boy?"

He walked slowly toward me, and I could feel myself shrinking into the tiles.

Please don't kill me on Christmas Eve! Don't ruin Christmas for Mama and Grandma. Wait for another time.

"You're gonna pay for what you did, Frenchy. I swear to you you're gonna pay." His hand went to my throat and he whispered, "And what you saw us do to that Negro is only a tiny beginning of what we're gonna do to you. Not tonight, Frenchy. Not tomorrow. But someday, when you're not thinking about it, when you're not being careful and on your guard, we'll get you. We'll make you sorry you ever came to this country. You understand me?" Then he snickered and said, *"Tu comprends?"*

I must have nodded, and he left me there, quivering like the flame on my candle before I'd blown it out and watched the faint spiral of smoke disappear into the air. Every holy and reverent thought went straight out of my head, and I raced up the steps to the foyer where I stood, my spirit extinguished, between Grandma and Mama.

———————

Whereas Thanksgiving had been a roaring success, the beginning of the Christmas Day meal at Grandma's bordered on disaster. Ma arrived drunk and cursing with no pie and Blithe in tears. Mr. Davis had burnt the corn bread, and Eternity was in a foul humor.

"Here," she said, thrusting her broccoli and pea casserole into my hands.

"We didn't get any presents," Blithe whined.

Eternity rolled her eyes, and I was thankful that half a dozen of the packages under our tree were for Blithe.

In the end, the meal was delicious and Ma sobered up a little, but my mood remained glum. Terror from Ace's threat combined with homesickness slipped up on me, and once again I was hungry for France—for the meal Mamie Madeleine had planned for weeks, and shopping with her for fresh oysters and smoked salmon and the best *foie gras* in the region and stuffed roasted duck and a sip of Papa's champagne and laughter and a table filled with guests, a meal that began at midnight and ran into the wee hours of the morning.

Most of all, though, I missed the presence of my father around the table, with his loosened tie and the cigarette hanging from his lips and the way he had a story about each different bottle of wine he opened and why he was serving it with this specific course.

"This one came from Sauterne, Emile. You know where that is? It is the perfect wine to drink with the goose liver that Mamie purchased from her cousin's neighbor. . . ."

His presence, or rather, the memory of that presence, hovered over me during the Christmas meal so that the merry conversation between Grandma and Mama and the Joneses and Mr. Davis and the two widows from down the street and the old bachelor from around the corner blended into a pleasant clattering of background sound in which I could not participate. I watched Mama's flushed cheeks as she told happy stories of long ago, and I could tell she was relishing every aspect of Christmas in America, which she had missed for so long. But for me, the meal was a blur of bland tastes heaped together and eaten too quickly. Even Blithe's squeals punctuating the conversation every so often couldn't keep me from my wandering memories of life in Lyon.

But after the meal, when we went into the den and I knelt down beside the Christmas tree and retrieved the presents Grandma and Mama and I had so carefully wrapped for the Joneses and Mr. Davis, I began to feel a thrill for this Christmas. Jake and Blithe laughed and exclaimed as they unwrapped their presents, and Mr. Davis sat back in his chair and chuckled when he opened a new wrench and said, "Would ya look at that!" Even Ma's swollen face wore a smile each time she unwrapped a small gift intended for her.

Then Grandma handed one more gift to each of the Jones kids. Jake and Blithe each opened a beautifully illustrated children's Bible.

"Oh, it's beautiful! Thank you so, so much!" Blithe said, giving Grandma a hug around the waist. She nudged Jake until he murmured, "Thanks a lot" without looking up. Then they both sat down on the rug with all the wrapping paper littered around and began leafing through the books.

Blithe gave a commentary on the pictures, saying, "See, Jake, that's when Abraham had to sacrifice his son, Isaac. 'Cept for God stopped him and gave them a ram instead, and that ram's like Jesus. And see here, that's Moses leading the poor Israelites across the Red Sea and God opens up the waters and then when the mean Gypsies come, He closes the water over them."

I wasn't sure where Blithe had learned these stories, but I suspected Grandma had been indoctrinating her while they planted bulbs in the garden.

Eternity opened her gift from Grandma, and it was a white leather Bible. I thought I saw tears in Eternity's eyes when she opened it and read Grandma's inscription. She touched the fine thin pages edged in gold, then flipped almost automatically to the back of the Bible. I watched her look for something specific as if she'd been reading the Bible all her life.

"It's a red-letter version," she confirmed to herself.

I knew this meant all of the words that Jesus said were printed in red, instead of black. Grandma had explained this to me when she'd given me my Bible on my birthday. But how did Eternity know this term?

"Oh, thank you, Mrs. Bridgeman. Thank you very much." She too gave Grandma a hug, and even in the midst of the warmth and beauty of Christmas, that little sting of jealousy came again.

"Oh, Jake! Here's Jesus! Just look! Jesus with the little children!" Blithe again, squealing with happiness. Then, as if it were the most natural thing in the world, she began singing: "'Jesus loves the little children, all the children of the world, red and yellow, black and white, they are precious in His sight, Jesus loves the little children of the world.'"

How did she know that song—the one the children in Sunday school sang just about every week?

Perhaps I should have left the Jones children enraptured with their Bibles. But they hadn't opened their gifts from me yet, and I wanted to see their reactions to my carefully chosen presents. To be honest, I wanted them to like the gifts as much as—no, even more than—the Bibles from Grandma.

And I wasn't disappointed. Blithe squealed again when she unwrapped the doll I'd picked out for her, which was almost half her size, and Jake grinned bashfully when he got the latest thing for little boys: a G. I. Joe complete with accessories.

Then I watched carefully, feeling a knot in my stomach, as Eternity opened my gift to her—a fancy pen and pencil set. *For Eternity, so you can write forever,* I'd written on the card, hoping she'd like my pun. *From Emile.*

She grinned, raised an eyebrow, and said, "Thanks, Emile. I really, really like it."

Then Blithe handed me an envelope with my name written on it in crayoned capital letters. "It's from Jake and me," she said.

Two sheets of construction paper fell out. Jake had drawn a picture of Grandma's garden, a precise rendition with the rows of vegetables and the different flowers and a rabbit nibbling on a carrot. Blithe had drawn a page full of stars and colored them in a rainbow of colors. At the bottom, in her childish print, she had written, *Mary Chrismus, Emile.*

From Grandma I received a journal sort of like the one she kept. Mine looked masculine, though, with a leather cover and fine, crisp gold-rimmed pages that made me feel like I had nothing to say that was worthy of this book. And yet I was drawn to it, wanting to find something rich and profound to put in its pages.

Then Eternity handed me a gift wrapped in some of the leftover paper in which we'd brought the old Christmas ornaments to her trailer. "Merry Christmas!"

"Thanks," I murmured, embarrassed and surprised. I slowly unwrapped the gift and found inside three small paperback novels, obviously used, which had probably been given to Eternity by some benevolent librarian. *H.M.S. Ulysses, South by Java Head,* and *Ice Station Zebra,* all by an author named Alistair MacLean.

"They're spy novels," she said matter-of-factly. "I think your English is good enough. If you can read Shakespeare, you can read Alistair MacLean."

"Thanks," I said again.

"They're really good. You can't put them down. *H.M.S. Ulysses* is best—it's set during World War II, so I thought you'd like it."

"I'm sure I will," I said, my face burning, and the two of us just standing there, me clutching my books and Eternity holding on to her Bible and pens, grinning at each other like the giddy, self-conscious teenagers we were.

| *eighteen* |

I spent the next two days after Christmas alone in my room reading about spies and boats and Germans and Allies, devouring *H.M.S. Ulysses* like a leftover piece of Grandma's chocolate pound cake that she'd baked "for Jesus' birthday." Eternity didn't mean to put fuel on the fire—at least I don't think she did. But with every page I turned, I was seeing Papa and remembering yet another of his stories from his days in the Resistance.

———

Papa took the small log and placed it on my bed. Then he and I sat on the bed, our backs against the wall, our legs dangling out front, mine barely reaching the side of the bed, his hanging off the edge. I could smell a mixture of the sweet scent of his aftershave, the sweaty odor of his long workday, the cigarette smoke on his breath. I was perfectly content to be sitting so close to him, my shoulder touching his arm, his hands brushing mine as he used them to talk.

His white cotton dress shirt was unbuttoned at the top, his tie removed, the sleeves rolled up. He took the small carton from his shirt pocket and tapped the underside with his fingers until one cigarette protruded. He placed the small white cylinder in his mouth, removed the lighter from his pocket. Mesmerized, I watched the quick flame appear, watched him bring it to the cigarette and inhale while lighting, watched the end of the cylinder flicker into a small red circle, watched as he blew the first puff of smoke.

Papa picked up the piece of wood. "This looks like an ordinary log that's been chopped for firewood, doesn't it? But this log was much more." He gave a quick tug, and it opened up into two parts with hinges holding the parts together. The inside had been carved out and was stuffed with yellowed newspapers.

"I was twelve when Mamie and Papy started an Underground newspaper," Papa said. "It was near the end of 1940. Paris was occupied, and the first groups of *résistants* were forming—just ordinary French citizens who were determined to do something about the humiliating situation of being under Nazi rule.

"I carried the logs to different neighbors and people in town, delivered them in the winter along with a truck full of real logs. We passed along national and foreign news—some we got illegally from the BBC broadcasts."

"You put secret information in the newspapers, to help the good guys and make the bad guys mad. Is that right, Papa?"

He chuckled happily. "That is exactly right, Emile. We set up in temporary offices, and in the event of a Gestapo raid, we could hide the printing plates and typewriters and other things in secret cupboards—within seconds. But the trickiest part was to get these newspapers distributed to the subscribers. We had to do it right under the Germans' fat noses."

He made a face and blew a ring of smoke up into the air. I sat silent for a moment, in awe of my father, in awe of his story.

"Often the papers were carried around by women who hid copies in their purses or shopping bags. Or in false-bottomed suitcases or in the clothing of their children."

"Or in logs!" I exclaimed.

"Yes, of course. In logs, just like this one."

"And what was your newspaper about, Papa?"

"Well, at first it was just something a local group of *résistants* wrote up and distributed. But eventually we became involved with a news-paper called *The Christian Witness*. Mamie and Papy were helping a very well-known and respected priest named Père Chaillet. He was the first priest in Lyon to join the Resistance, and the main force behind starting this newspaper."

Papa handed me the yellowed pages that had been stored inside the log. "Père Chaillet worked with other Catholics and Protestants to hide Jewish children and to help get Jews from France to Switzerland. French *résistants* would take the refugees to the boat on one side of Lac de Genève, and they'd be picked up by Swiss *résistants* on the other side.

"In January 1943, Père Chaillet was arrested with four other *résistants*. He was carrying some very important papers with him, and he knew it would be terrible if the Nazis found those papers.

"All of the prisoners were forced to stand with their noses against the wall and their hands behind their backs for hours and hours. For-tunately, Père Chaillet had on a very big coat with large shoulders and long sleeves, and somehow he got those papers out of his pocket, tore them into little pieces, and then slowly ate them."

"He ate them! He ate the papers?" I couldn't imagine it, and I wanted more details.

"Shh, now, Emile. That's tonight's story." Papa put the newspapers back in the log and closed it, then put it back under the bed. "We don't want Mama to find our secret treasures, do we, son?" He winked at me.

"Thank you for the story, Papa. It was very exciting."

"Good night, Emile." He left the room, leaving only a faint trail of smoke and the odor of his long day of work.

I went to sleep that night dreaming of funny, carved-out logs. But before I drifted off to sleep, I tore a small piece of paper from a page of schoolwork and put it in my mouth. I chewed and chewed and chewed until at last, like Père Chaillet, I could swallow it down, and nobody ever knew.

The closer it got to the time for school to start, the louder Ace's threats echoed in my mind, so that by the time I stepped into the halls of Northside in early January, I was indeed on my guard. I had told no one about our encounter. I did not run into Ace or Teddy or Billy that first day back, but I imagined Ace with his smug smile, knowing I would be trembling inside, waiting.

I was occupied with these thoughts that Monday afternoon as I walked with Eternity to the bus stop. Play rehearsal didn't start up again until Wednesday, so she and the children were taking their bus back to the trailer park. I usually rode home with Mama, now that she was teaching at school. But on this day she had left early.

"Shoot!" I said to Eternity. "I forgot my math book. I'll be right back."

She smiled at me. "Hey, you're sounding more like a Southerner every day!"

I grinned back and then dashed into the building toward my locker.

I don't know what made me suspicious first—their dark suits, their forced smiles, their shifting eyes, back and forth, back and forth. Two men, walking straight toward me as I retrieved my math book from my locker. They looked like the bad guys in Tintin or the thugs I'd read about in Alistair MacLean's novels or perhaps some undercover spies who were following Père Chaillet around and reporting his every move to the Nazis.

I shut my locker and walked back down the long hall, glancing over my shoulder every few steps. Sure enough, those men were following me. My heart raced.

I walked faster.

The two men came beside me, one on each side. "Follow us out to the car, Emile."

"Leave me alone. I'll call the police."

"No, you won't, son. If you want to see your father alive, you'll get in the car."

Papa! I didn't know what to do. Was it a trap? Of course it was a trap! It always worked that way—intimidation, a promise of seeing the lost person, and then death after the information is gathered.

"I don't know what you want or what you are talking about. My

father is dead!" I burst into tears as I pronounced the words. "He died a long time ago, so leave me alone."

"I'm sorry to hear it, son."

"Leave me alone."

"We know you're lying. We know your father has given you certain information. He's betrayed you, Emile. He's hiding and afraid, and he's told us that you have the information. So don't try to hide the truth."

I was scared witless, just as Mr. Davis had been in that foxhole in northern France. I wished I had the vial of poison with me. I imagined these two spies threatening to make me talk, imagined them pulling back my fingernails, as Klaus Barbie had done to poor Mr. Jean Moulin. Every gruesome scene I'd read or been told about the war flashed through my mind.

One thing was sure. If they were after information about my father, I would not give it to them. They could beat me until I was like a piece of rare beef, but I would say nothing.

Then the other man began to yell at me in French, "We can make you show us the information, or you can give it to us nicely. Either way, we will get what we need."

"Stop talking to me in another language! I don't understand you and I can't know anything about my father because he died when I was young and he didn't leave me anything! He just woke up one day, had a heart attack, and died."

"Have it your way, son."

As they turned to leave, one of them called after me, "Emile, tu aime le chocolat?"

It took every ounce of discipline that I had to keep my mouth shut, refusing to answer the familiar French that flowed almost effortlessly from this man's mouth. But I didn't turn around, didn't react at all. I was glad for Tintin's example of an amateur sleuth, of MacLean's savvy hero who was trained to never give away his nationality by replying in that native tongue.

My heart was pumping wildly. Perhaps now they would leave me alone.

But no! One of the men pulled something out of his pocket. He gave me an evil smile, pushed a button on the shiny silver object, and the *switchblade appeared. "We have ways of making you talk." He took me by the shoulder—*

I felt the hand tighten on my shoulder, and I jumped with a start.

"Hello, son," one of the men said to me. "Didn't mean to startle you." He gave me a fake kind of grin and reached toward his pocket.

I shook myself free of him and prepared to dash down the hall, when he said, "We were looking for the principal's office." He studied a piece of paper. "We have an appointment with him."

Mortified, I pointed and said, my voice cracking, "It's right down that hall and to the left."

"Thanks, son."

They walked away, but I heard one of them say, "Did you see how scared that kid looked? You'd think we were selling rifles instead of encyclopedias. . . ."

Fortunately for me, no one else was around to witness my total stupidity. After my heart had slowed down and my hands stopped sweating, I actually let out a nervous little laugh. *Emile,* I said to myself, *you have got to quit reading those spy novels!*

When the bus let me off at the corner of Anjaco Road, I felt an immediate sense of relief. The street looked calm. Children were riding their bikes on the sidewalks, a man was trimming tree limbs, and cars were parked by the side of the road. No spies, no agents. My street was safe.

I went into the house and fixed a peanut butter and jelly sandwich. I heard Mama talking on the phone in the hall. She seemed to be arguing, although she gave me a smile when I came and stood beside her.

"You mean that by applying for the American passport, my son has to forfeit his French passport? Are you sure?"

Her face was flushed as she listened to the reply. "Really. I didn't realize that."

She smiled sympathetically at me and motioned with her eyes for me to go into the other room.

My appetite was suddenly gone. I tossed the rest of my sandwich in the trash can and waited in the kitchen. Mama hung up the phone and met me there. She was holding a manila envelope and several official-looking papers.

"That was the consulate on the phone. Apparently the American government doesn't allow a citizen to hold a passport from another country and an American passport as well."

"So?" I said. "I won't get an American passport. Who cares?"

"Don't get worked up, Emile. We'll figure something out. But the fact is, you need an American passport."

"Why?"

"You just have to have one," she replied firmly.

"But why? Can't you give me a reason why?"

"Emile, let's not argue about everything. Just trust me."

"I don't want to talk about this!" I said and went out the front door, letting the screen door slam behind me.

"Emile! Emile!"

I heard her calling after me, but I didn't turn around.

I had not taken a coat, and it was near freezing outside, but I didn't care. I walked as fast as I could, walked down every sidewalk on every street in the whole neighborhood. I walked until the sun went down and my fingers were numb and my ears were so cold they felt as if they'd been pricked with hundreds of little needles.

By the time I returned to the house, the cold, crisp darkness of January had sliced through the neighborhood, leaving it frigid and gloomy. In spite of the promise of a new year and new beginnings, January seemed like a month to be endured, without any hint of renewal or spring. I shivered all the way home.

The light on the screened porch was shining out, as well as the one in the lamppost, but I felt no welcome as I walked up the driveway of 1861 Anjaco Road. I came around the back of the house and quietly let myself in the kitchen. I could hear Mama and Grandma talking.

Actually, Mama was doing all the talking, talking and giving little heaving sighs in between sentences and blowing her nose and talking again. I crept close enough to hear her.

". . . and he always did the same thing, disappearing like this, over and over."

"I don't know how you stood it all these years, Janie."

I guess Grandma gave Mama a hug or something, because there was a slight sound of movement. Then Mama said, "I loved him, I really thought I loved him, but now look what he's done. He's forced me to chase away Emile. I hate that man. I tell you, I hate him!" She was sobbing so hard her voice came in tiny puffs of exclamation.

Grandma's soothing voice said, "Honey, show Emile the list. He deserves to know. He'll understand."

"What if it's too late? What if I've driven him away in his heart just like . . ."

"Just like I did to you all those years ago?"

She sniffed. "I'm sorry. I shouldn't have said it."

"It's okay, dear. Just don't go projecting the past onto the future." Then Grandma must have left the room, because all I could hear were periodic sniffs coming from Mama.

When I finally walked into the den, it was dark, except for the red glow of the dying fire in the fireplace. Mama, sitting on the couch, had her knees hugged to her chest, her arms wrapped around her legs, her lips mashed together. When she saw me, she leapt to her feet and said, "Emile! Oh, Emile! I'm sorry! I'm sorry!" She grabbed me in a fierce hug, trembling and crying.

Once again, as when I'd shown her the microdot note, my mother seemed tiny and fragile to me, as if even scrawny me could break her in two.

I pulled myself away from her, walking behind the winged arm-chair as if I could use it for protection.

"I'm sorry about the passport. We'll figure something out." She stood in the middle of the den, wiping her eyes and gesturing to the chair. "Sit down, sweetie. Will you please sit down? I'll explain it to you."

Something in the way she was crying melted me, and I sat.

She covered her face and kept crying. At last she handed me a crumpled piece of paper. I took it and smoothed it out. Papa's pen-manship filled the page.

No contact with Mamie Madeleine
No phone calls to France
No mail forwarded to American address
No wedding ring
Get a post office box address
Get an American passport for Emile as soon as possible
Change your name to Bridgeman on all important documents

"It was Papa's idea?"

"Yes." She sat down lightly on the couch, as if she was suddenly afraid it wouldn't hold her. "These are the instructions he left me the night before he disappeared. I promise, Emile, I wouldn't have asked you to get an American passport if I had known you would have to give up your French one. I wouldn't. Do you believe me?"

I gave a stiff nod.

"Oh, Emile. It's such a mess. I'm so sorry—for everything."

Grandma came into the room. "Child. Janie, come now. Calm down." She wrapped her arms around her daughter, her voice warm and even cracking a little with emotion. "Dear boy, your lips are blue."

I began shaking so violently that Mama got up, left the room, grabbed the quilt from Grandma's bed, and smothered me in it while Grandma hurried to heat up milk for hot chocolate.

I began to understood then a tiny bit of what this move from France to America was costing my mother. She was afraid for me, she worried every day for my safety, and probably every time I was late coming home, she wanted to call Officer Dodge.

I looked down at Papa's scribbled words and felt the bile rise in my throat. Mama was afraid she was going to lose me. She was afraid I would leave her—that I, with a temper a lot like the one she had displayed at my age—would get up one day and run away.

"It's okay, Mama," I said. "Don't worry. I know you are just trying to do the right thing."

We stood huddled together in the den, our arms around each other like a tiny, misfit football team. Then Grandma brought me the hot chocolate and Mama put another log on the dying fire and I lay down on the sofa with the quilt on top of me.

Lying there thawing out, surrounded by the love and warmth of these two women, I had the strangest thought flash through my mind. *This is what eternity will feel like—a big safe room. Yes, safe at last.*

| *nineteen* |

Late that night, I took out the leather-bound journal that Grandma gave me for Christmas and began to write in French.

January 4, 1965

America seems to me like one big chain of embarrassing situations. My life wasn't like this in Lyon. I got along okay. Here it's one blunder after another. My latest bit of idiotic behavior was with two men at school who were selling encyclopedias—I was sure they were spies! But I guess I should be glad I was the only person who knew how foolish I'd been.

Sometimes I wonder if I will ever get it right. If I will ever blend in. But other times, like after school today when Eternity complimented me for my Southern accent, I'm scared to death that everything that makes me French is just slipping quietly away.

And speaking of Eternity—I especially feel confused about her. Sometimes I think I will be able to forget about Papa, given time. But I don't think I will ever get Eternity Jones out of my mind, even if Mama came home and said we could go back to France tomorrow.

Here's another thing—in a funny way, I'm jealous of Grandma. Not jealous, maybe, but she is just so good and wise, and everybody loves her. I know she made some big mistakes when she was younger, but now she just seems so sure about life, so peaceful. I guess I'm just tired of being confused. Peaceful, I am not!

There, I had done it—gotten my jumbled thoughts onto paper. I closed the journal and stashed it in the attic space inside the suitcase that still held my collection.

When I climbed into bed, the weight of all of my thoughts had left me, transferred to the pages of my journal. I fell into a dreamless sleep.

————

At study hall the next day, I explained to Eternity about the passport papers and how I might have to give up my French citizenship and how mad I'd gotten and how hard Mama had cried.

"So you think your mother is scared for you?" Eternity asked.

"Yeah, I think so. She showed me this awful list of things Papa told her to do so that we would be safe. He wants her to change our names and stop wearing her wedding ring and never call France and get me an American passport. He really is trying to protect us."

"Or protect himself."

I looked at her blankly. "You think he's just trying to get rid of us?"

"I don't know. It's all too weird for me. Maybe he's been living a double life all this time, and he's tired of doing it, so he's getting rid of you all."

"All spies live a double life," I said, irritated.

"Yeah, I know. Look, the way I see it, you're never gonna figure this out, so why keep trying? Maybe your dad was a traitor all along and is hiding somewhere in Argentina with a bunch of Nazi criminals, or maybe he really did run off with another woman and is happy on some foreign beach, or maybe he's dead—they kidnapped him and tortured and killed him and well, who wants to know that? You'll never really know, Emile, so you might as well leave it alone. I don't think there is any way this story is going to have a happy ending."

"I never thought I'd hear you saying that."

She tossed her pigtail over her shoulder and said, "I'm not promising that *I'll* leave it alone."

I thought I saw the trace of a grin on her lips—something almost
playful. "I just think *you* should. For now at least."

I shrugged. "Maybe you're right. Grandma says the same thing."

I didn't plan on following the advice of either Eternity or
Grandma, but at that moment I wanted to sound agreeable to Eternity. I didn't mean for it to happen, the way my palms grew a little
sweaty when I talked to her or the way I suddenly felt the thumping
of my heart when she sat next to me. Liking Eternity in that way, I
knew, was probably not a good idea.

And yet, sometimes it seemed she liked me back.

Griffin had even commented on it one day. "You better watch out
for Eternity, amigo—she's got the hots for you!"

"The hots?" I'd asked, bewildered.

"Oh, come on, Emilio. Can't you see she's crazy about you?"

I didn't have much experience in trying to figure out a girl's mind,
but I liked the thought that Eternity cared, that she was on my side,
that perhaps she liked me more than just as a friend. It was getting to
where not thinking about Eternity was just as hard as not thinking
about my father.

————————

I was never certain how it came about that Eternity and Jake and
Blithe began attending church with us. I guess Grandma's gifts of
Bibles at Christmas started it. Maybe it was Eternity's idea, or maybe
it was Blithe who begged, but at any rate, Ma agreed. So on the second
Sunday in January, Grandma and Mama and I drove out to the trailer
park to pick up the Jones kids.

By now I was familiar with this route and had memorized the
names of the roads. We drove up Anjaco, turned onto Collier Road,
and crossed Howell Mill Road. We passed apartment buildings, a dry
cleaner, gas station, Chinese restaurant, and the industrial neighborhood until finally we turned onto Chattahoochee Avenue. Soon I recognized the little white house on the right side of the street with the
sign *Chattahoochee Mobile Village* in front of it. Eternity and Blithe

and Jake were waiting right there for us, huddled together and shivering in the frosty January air.

Jake had on a button-down shirt and a jacket and a tie, and his hair was all slicked back and his loafers polished. Both girls were wearing white gloves and holding their Bibles. Blithe was wearing a frilly pink dress and a white sweater that looked like it was meant for summer and shiny black patent-leather shoes, and her blond hair was worn loose except for a few strands that she had pulled back from either side of her face and fastened with bobby pins. Eternity wore a long-sleeved blue dress with sparkly things around the neck and the bottom, a dress that seemed to me to belong on a full-grown woman. She didn't quite fill it out, but it made her look older and sophisticated and womanly.

When I looked at her, my stomach started fluttering again. We had to squish tight to fit into the back seat, and Eternity's arm was touching mine and that made all kinds of things happen inside me that didn't have much to do with church.

We arrived at Second-Ponce de Leon Baptist Church at 9:25, just in time for Sunday school. I was happy to see the tall white steeple and the carpet of green grass and everything looking pure and inviting. This was my church, and I was pleased to bring my friends along.

We entered by what was called the North Bridge and immediately took the stairs down to where the Sunday school rooms for children were located.

On the way down the long hall, Blithe declared, "I need Jake in Sunday school with me. I'm afraid to go alone." Of course I didn't argue with her, and deposited them in the kindergarten class, introducing them to the teacher. But as I walked away with Eternity, I realized that Blithe wasn't taking care of herself; she was taking care of her brother, her big brother with the slow mind and the disease that seemed to have condemned him to an early death.

I dreaded seeing Ace in Sunday school, but if Eternity was there with me—even though she knew nothing about his threat—at least there would be two of us against him. We had already beaten him once. I had hardly glimpsed him the whole week at Northside. He'd made a B- in French for the first trimester, and I was no longer tutoring him. But I knew there was no way to miss him at church.

But Ace was not there.

Eternity participated in the discussion of the first chapter of the book of Daniel, where Daniel refused to eat meat, and only ate vegetables. She came up with the comparison from his culture to ours and how "God-believers"—that was her term—should look different in society. Once again I was surprised and a little irritated with her knowledge of biblical things.

Jake and Blithe loved Sunday school. On the way into the sanctuary, Blithe grabbed my hand and said, "Our teacher was so nice! She told us Bible stories and showed us pretty pictures of Jesus healing the leper and the blind man and the pary—the parlay—"

"The pair-a-*lit*-tic, Sissy," Jake said.

"Yeah, that's it!"

By then we were in the sanctuary, and she squealed, "Oh, it's so big and pretty! And the organ! Listen to the organ music!"

The church service began, and every once in a while, as the choir sang or as Dr. Swilley preached or when we all stood and recited the Lord's Prayer or sang the Doxology, Blithe would look at me with adoring eyes, as if this were heaven, right here and now. Once Eternity reached over and gave her a loving pat on the hand, and Blithe squeezed her sister's gloved hand in return, and I knew without a doubt that the Jones family would be returning to church with us the next Sunday.

———

Ace did not make good on his threat in January. In fact, he barely acknowledged my presence at school, giving only a small grunt when we passed in the hall. He never touched me, never slapped my back or called me French Fry. Once, when I was standing with Griffin by the lockers, he even came up and said, "Hey, guys," and left.

I knew what he was doing, of course. He was trying to get me to let down my guard, to assume he'd forgotten his threat or decided it wasn't worth it. But I wasn't fooled. Someday when I least suspected it, he and his troops would come at me from behind and that would be the end.

It took great effort to be constantly on the lookout for him. In fact, I began reciting to myself a Bible verse that Dr. Swilley had used in a sermon: *"Be of sober spirit, be on the alert. Your adversary, the devil, prowls around like a roaring lion, seeking someone to devour. But resist him. . . ."*

This was my defense against Ace—a Bible verse about the devil. Surely God would understand. In the Old Testament stories I heard at church, God was always promising terrible deaths to the wicked. Surely Ace McClary ranked among them.

So chilly January turned into gray, frosty February with Blithe and Jake at our house every Monday, Wednesday, and Friday while Eternity rehearsed at school for *Hamlet*. I'd ride in the front seat of the Chevrolet as Mama or Grandma drove them all back home.

Sometimes on those rides Eternity would recite her lines. She loved to goad me by singing songs sung by beautiful, mad Ophelia. "He is dead and gone, lady, He is dead and gone; At his head a grass-green turf, At his heels a stone." Or she would wag her finger at me and quote from Ophelia's speech to Laertes before she became deranged:

> "I shall the effect of this good lesson keep,
> As watchman to my heart. But, good my brother,
> Do not, as some ungracious pastors do,
> Show me the steep and thorny way to heaven;
> Whiles, like a puff'd and reckless libertine,
> Himself the primrose path of dalliance treads,
> And recks not his own rede."

And when I complained that I was still struggling with American English and it wasn't fair to expect me to understand Elizabethan, she just laughed.

"Ophelia's just chiding her brother for being a hypocrite—as all men are."

As Griffin would say, I was not about to touch that with a ten-foot pole.

One Sunday in February—maybe the fourth or fifth time the Jones children attended church, Dr. Swilley gave his frequent invitation to come forward and accept Jesus. This always made me nervous. I felt sorry for him when no one responded, but he didn't seem to mind. Actually his voice was so smooth and inviting that I wondered how anyone could resist running down that aisle, even if they'd done it a hundred times before. It seemed like the most comforting, reassuring thing—to come to the Good Shepherd and be accepted into the fold with the other sheep.

Of course, I resisted. I wasn't about to walk down that long aisle to the front of the church with everyone's eyes on me—especially Ace McClary's. But sometimes I thought about it. I thought about what Dr. Swilley was saying, about God's grace and being saved from my sins. It didn't sound a thing like what I heard when I attended Mass in Lyon three times a year.

On this Sunday, as the whole congregation sang verse after verse of the now-familiar-to-me hymn, "Just As I Am," Blithe slipped out of the pew. She looked back at Jake who said, "Wait for me, Sissy. I'm coming too," and they walked to the front of the church, hand in hand.

Mama looked startled, and Eternity's face was a puzzle I could not figure out, but Grandma had her eyes shut, her face turned toward heaven, and her hands clasped across her chest. She was whispering, "Thank you, Jesus," over and over again.

They stayed after the service and talked with Dr. Swilley. Well, Blithe talked and Jake stared straight ahead, nodding occasionally when a question was directed at him.

"Yes, I believe in Jesus," Blithe stated emphatically. "Yes, I know I'm a sinner and I need to be forgiven of my sins, and when Jesus died on the cross He made it possible for this to happen."

The whole time they were talking, I wanted to interrupt and say, *Wait a minute! You've got it all wrong! I'm a sinner, and you're a sinner, but not Blithe. Blithe is an angel. She's a real live angel who floated down from heaven to make me happy and bring goodness to the earth, and there's no way she needs saving because she is perfect, and anyway, she's just repeating what the pastor says. She doesn't really understand.*

But I didn't say a thing, and Blithe just looked as happy as could be at the prospect of being a saved sinner. "And I want to be baptized," she added.

I'd never thought much about this. In France, most everyone was baptized as an infant. Then after you'd attended years and years of catechism and done your First Communion, you were confirmed. As far as I could tell, the main point of confirmation had nothing to do with faith and everything to do with your parents throwing a big party in your honor and you receiving lots of great gifts.

But Blithe had never been baptized as an infant, and when she insisted that she wanted to be baptized, Jake added, of course, "Me too."

"Are you happy that Jake and Blithe are getting baptized?" I asked Eternity the next day while we were walking from Mrs. Chalkin's English class to the library for study hall.

"Yes, of course. Aren't you?"

"Sure, why not? I guess it's about time. In France, everyone is baptized as a baby."

"That's because you're all Catholics over there. I think the way they do it in the Baptist church makes more sense. You aren't baptized until you decide you want to follow Jesus. It's a symbol of your faith. Like Mrs. Bridgeman says, 'You can't inherit faith in Christ. You have to accept His grace for yourself.'"

It irritated me when Eternity spouted off Bible stuff as if she knew it better than I did, when she'd only been attending church for a month. I guess she'd been paying more attention to Dr. Swilley—and, I thought grumpily, to Grandma, who was probably indoctrinating her into the faith while they sat on the screened porch.

Almost as a dare, I asked her, "Eternity, do you believe in the God that Dr. Swilley talks about?"

She swung her pigtail over her shoulder. "I haven't come to any definite conclusion yet. Have you?"

I struggled for an answer, but as usual, Eternity beat me to it.

"I do think there is something big out there—a spirit or a god or a type of energy—something that can move people's lives around. I used to believe God was just a strict, distant judge who didn't care about me but demanded obedience. And who allowed awful things to happen to people.

"But after talking to your grandmother and coming to church and reading the Bible, well, I'm beginning to think that maybe there is a God who loves us. Maybe He loves me so much that He plopped you and your mom in Atlanta and sent you to Northside just so I could meet you and come to your house and get to know your family, so things in our life wouldn't be so sad anymore.

"Things have been a lot more interesting since you came into my life, Emile. And I think that God did it. I'm not sure about it yet— but I'm thinking."

I just nodded, swallowing the lump in my throat over and over again. She hadn't exactly said she *liked* me, but she had certainly implied it, and with Eternity, every word and look and gesture counted. I didn't care one thing about her theology. What mattered was what she had just admitted: *"Things have been a lot more interesting since you came into my life, Emile."*

Later, after school, I thought some more about what Eternity had said. I had considered many details of the past four months to be complete disasters. How in the world could Eternity see things so differently? I decided it was Grandma's influence—the way she had of being contagious, so convincing about her faith, of "practicing what she preached." That expression I had learned from Eternity, and it certainly applied to Grandma.

But I was afraid that Eternity would be disappointed. She was going to embrace this church and Grandma's beliefs, and then wake up one day and see that nothing had changed. She still had an alcoholic mother who spent her welfare check on liquor and was prone to violence. And Eternity would be more disappointed and disillusioned than before.

I didn't want that to happen. I didn't want her to become mad Ophelia, picking rose petals as her clothes gradually weighted her down in the brook and she drowned.

———

A few days later, Grandma was out in the backyard pruning the rosebushes, trimming the low hanging limbs on the trees, getting ready for spring.

"Can I ask you something, Grandma?"

"Of course, Emile."

"Do you believe that God picks people up from one place where they are living, minding their own business, and then just plops them down somewhere else on earth so that they can help another person in that new place?"

She didn't answer for a moment, her brow furrowed, so I added, "That's what Eternity believes."

"Ah. Does she now?"

I saw a little gleam in Grandma's eyes.

"I believe in a God who is so big that I will never be able to figure Him out—nor do I want to. He's a great big God who can do anything, Emile. He made the whole universe and all the things in the world, and yet He knows all about every one of us. The Bible says He causes all things to work for the good to those who love Him. It says the hard things we go through are temporary, and that we'll live forever with Him."

I was about to point out that she hadn't answered my question, but then she kept going.

"And yes, I believe God can 'plop someone down,' as you say, to help others. That's what He's done with you and Janie. He's given me my family back. And He's added a new family to it, the Joneses. It's a wonderful blessing."

"Well, not for me! He yanked me away from everything I liked!" I hadn't meant to say this out loud.

Grandma was unperturbed. "Sometimes the way God helps us grow involves a lot of yanking, Emile. Sometimes it hurts. But that doesn't mean God isn't part of it, and it doesn't mean it is wrong, or that He made a mistake."

"I guess it means *we* made a mistake?" My voice was filled with sarcasm.

"Sometimes. But it always means He knows better than we do. In my case with your mother, I was wrong—controlling, manipulative—and she left. The leaving was in great part my fault, but God used it to get my attention. It was very painful, but it turned out to be a redemptive experience."

I wondered as I got my peanut butter and jelly sandwich if someday I'd look back on everything that had happened this year as a "painful but redemptive experience."

————————

Blithe and Jake were baptized on the last Sunday in February. Miraculously, Mr. Davis had convinced Ma to come along. We were quite a sight, the enormous white woman and the dignified black gentleman sitting side by side in the front pew right next to Grandma and Mama and Eternity and me. While the choir was singing an anthem, Dr. Swilley left the pulpit and went to the baptistery located behind the choir. He'd put on a flowing black robe over his suit, and when the choir finished singing, he stood behind the baptistery and, one at a time, the new converts came to him—five of them in all. He dunked Blithe first, dressed in her white robe and looking even more cherubic than usual, and she came up from the water all shiny and breathless and beaming.

She was supposed to walk out on the opposite side of the baptistery, but instead she turned back and held out her hand to Jake. He stepped into the water and gave a low moan and made a face and gripped Blithe's hand fiercely until finally Dr. Swilley persuaded him to take his hand and let Blithe escape. Jake grabbed his nose and held it, took a big breath, and Dr. Swilley laid him back into the water. Jake came up sputtering and flailing, but I guess that didn't matter much to God.

Was baptism Blithe's way of finding protection for herself and her brother? Did she see it as a way of securing a "safe room" in heaven, a permanent safe room? I've wondered about that many times since. But on that Sunday morning, baptism seemed like a happy affair, and Grandma took everyone out to lunch at Kentucky Fried Chicken afterward. We laughed and jabbered, and Ma ate six pieces of chicken—two breasts, three thighs, and a wing. The rest of us ate just one each, even Mr. Davis, but no one seemed to mind.

It was while Jake and Blithe were at my house later that week, and

Eternity at play rehearsal, that Blithe saw it.

"Emile! Emile! Miz Bridgeman! Look!"

We rushed into the yard, where Blithe was jumping up and down and hollering.

"It's just like you said, Miz Bridgeman! The flowers are blooming in the winter. Look here." She pointed to two clumps of purple crocuses that had sprung from out of the ground overnight. "And looky here! The daffodils that Jake planted are coming up too!"

In truth there was only the tiniest hint of green pushing through the ground where Jake had carefully planted his bulbs, but it struck me just the same—that whole thing Grandma had explained about a grain dying and being reborn. I knelt down and felt the almost frozen February earth. How in the world did that bulb germinate and push its way up through this hard ground? And if nature was supposed to be teaching me a Bible lesson, what did that mean?

After sipping a cup of hot chocolate, which painted her top lip a rich, frothy brown, Blithe took my hand. "Can we take a walk around the block, Emile?"

"Sure."

"Make sure you bundle up, young lady," Grandma said. "It may be almost March, but it's near freezing out there."

As we left, just the two of us, Blithe looked back at Jake.

"Go on, Sissy, and ask him," Jake said.

We'd made it halfway down Anjaco, successfully avoiding stepping on cracks and breaking our mothers' backs, when Blithe grabbed my hand, looked up at me with those pastel blue eyes, and asked, "Do you like my sister, Emile?"

"Of course I do. She's my best friend."

"Do you like her enough to marry her, Emile?"

"*What?*"

"To marry her! I hope you do, 'cause then we'd be practically related, and you'd be with us all the time."

"I'm kind of young, Blithe, to be thinking about marrying somebody," I answered.

She considered this, then persisted. "Yeah, but if you were ever thinking about marrying someone, would it be my sister? Would it be Eternity?"

"Why are you asking me that, silly girl?"

" 'Cause I want to know. 'Cause I think you should marry Eternity, and we should come live with you and Miz Bridgeman and your mama, and that would be so good."

"But your mother would be lonely. And Mr. Davis, too."

Then Blithe's eyes got all serious, and she answered in the softest voice I'd ever heard her use, "But maybe Ma would be nicer if we left for a while. Maybe she wouldn't hurt us then. I know I'm a bad girl, and I'm always sorry to make Ma mad. I wish we could live with you for a while until Ma felt better, and I learned to be nicer. I'd grow Ma flowers and make her pretty bouquets and then things would work out okay. And I know Mr. Davis would still go see her every day, and he'd probably come see us too and take us to the library."

We were at the top of Anjaco, and the back entrance to Piedmont Hospital sat right in front of us. Hearing her confide those horrible thoughts, so innocently, like the angel she was, I wanted to run with her across the street and find the best doctor in all of Piedmont Hospital and beg him to take care of Blithe, to cover her with some kind of protective sheet so that nothing could hurt her again.

My family did what they could. Mr. Davis, Mrs. Harrington, and Miss Robinson were all looking out for the Jones children. And Eternity was fighting tooth and nail, as Griffin said, for her family. But I realized then what Mama and Grandma had known for a while: Nothing was enough. There was no real "safe room" as long as they were all there together in the dilapidated trailer with their mother, one minute sprawled out in a drunken stupor, and the next crouching like a crazed tiger, ready to kill her own.

| *twenty* |

With all my heart, I was so thankful that Blithe got to see the first daffodil poke its head out of the soil in Grandma's garden on the first day in March.

"Spring is comin', Miz Bridgeman! Spring is comin'! I just know it is!" she chanted as if she had just made an amazing scientific discovery.

"Yes, indeed," said Grandma, bending down beside the lone yellow flower. "It's certainly on the way, and spring in Atlanta is always splendid. First it's the daffodils, then the yellow forsythia, and then the tulips and the dogwoods and the azaleas. And before long," she added, nodding to Jake, "you'll get to see your asparagus plants in bloom, and the strawberries too."

The snapshot I can still see in my mind is of Jake Jones bending down in the strawberry patch later that month, his big head disappearing for a while; when he finally stood back up, the pinkish stain around his mouth betrayed his secret.

All that month of March, Blithe and Jake got to see rebirth or renewal or resurrection, whatever you wanted to call it. They saw the lesson of nature that Grandma had been trying to teach us. I saw it too, of course, as did Eternity, but I think it meant the most to Blithe.

I was helping carry Mama's books to the car after school and watching Jake and Blithe follow Eternity to the bus stop, feeling disappointed they weren't coming to our house that afternoon. "Mama, did you ever wish you had a brother or sister?"

"Sure I did. I used to dream of what it'd be like to have a little sister, someone I could play with every day. I wanted that."

"Me too."

"Yes, I'm sorry your father and I never had another child. You enjoy playing with Jake and Blithe, don't you?"

"Yeah. When they're at our house I just think of all the things I want to show them and teach them and how I want to help them. I want Jake to learn to shoot baskets and kick a soccer ball, and I want to help teach Blithe to read and buy her beautiful books about animals and flowers."

"I've always thought you'd be a teacher someday."

"You have?"

I remembered then a note Mrs. Chalkin had written at the bottom of my last essay. *You have a way of explaining things, Emile. I see a teacher's heart in you.*

And a few weeks earlier, Griffin and I had been playing a game of soccer at recess with some of his friends. Several other boys from our grade had wanted to play, but the first group wasn't very enthusiastic about letting them in.

"They don't know anything about dribbling. All they know is rough and tough American football."

"I'll teach them the rules," I'd volunteered. I'd actually enjoyed standing off to the side of the field and drawing in the red clay, explaining soccer to these kids.

Griffin subbed out during the second quarter and came over to see what I was doing. "You're a natural coach, Emilio." And he'd grinned and patted me on the back.

Maybe there was something to Mama's prediction.

One week before *Hamlet* was to be performed, Eternity asked me, "Can the kids come to your house today, Emile?"

"Of course, like always."

"Only I won't need you to pick me up after school. Your grandmother can take Jake and Blithe home a little after six. I'll be there by then."

"Where are you going?"

"Nowhere. I just need to stay later at school. I've got a ride."

"With who?"

"What does it matter, Emile?"

Her behavior seemed odd to me, a little defensive.

When we got to the trailer it was dusk, and there was a biting chill in the air. Lights shone from inside the trailer, and a car was parked out front. Demon began barking furiously, then wagged his tail when he realized it was us.

I walked the children to the trailer door, and they burst inside, calling out, "Eternity! We've got strawberries! Lots of Jake's strawberries. And Emile's here!"

Eternity came almost immediately. "Oh, hi, Emile." Her voice was pinched, uncomfortable. "You're early."

"It's five after six."

"Oh."

"Can I come in?"

"Um, well, I just got home, and I've got to fix dinner."

Ma's voice called out, "Who's there?"

"Just Emile, Ma."

Then a man's voice boomed out, "Eternity, come on back here now."

"Gotta go," she stammered, and closed the door.

I hesitated for only a second, the time it took for me to recognize the man's voice. I had heard it before, several times. Mr. McClary.

Without another thought, without explaining a thing to Mama who was sitting in the car, I took off running down the street to Mr. Davis's trailer, arriving out of breath and banging on his door. "You gotta come quickly! That awful man is after Eternity and the kids!"

Mr. Davis was drying his hands on a dish towel when he opened the door. "What in the world is the matter, son?"

"Mr. McClary's at the trailer! He's going to hurt her. He's done it before!"

"What?"

"That big blond man who treated her so badly."

"I know Mr. McClary. He is big, sure 'nuf, but he ain't mean. He's been helpin' this family for years."

I let the screen door slam closed. *"Comment?"* In moments of great surprise, my French returned. "Helping them! What are you saying?"

"Yeah. He comes over 'least twice a month."

"But—but he hurts Eternity. I saw him."

He narrowed his eyes. "You saw him hurt Eternity?"

Quickly I explained the scene at the football game with his hand on Eternity's wrist.

Mr. Davis shook his head. "Eternity doesn't like him much, but he's good to them all. Ain't Mr. McClary who hurts Eternity, son. He checks on 'em, though. To make sure Ma isn't beating them."

"How do you know?"

"I see things, son. And I know things."

He could tell I didn't believe him, so he stepped outside and put both hands on my shoulders. "Mr. McClary is Ma's uncle—*her* mother's baby brother."

I was dumbstruck.

"I told you I've lived here a long time. Miz Jones's mother was a hard lady herself. She and Mr. McClary grew up with all kinds of abuse. When his sister died, he started checking up on Ma and the kids."

"But lots of men have hurt Eternity! He's no different."

"He's a good man, Emile. Strict, that's for sure. And he doesn't mind telling Eternity when she's out of line—when she's takin' too much on herself. He got the social services out here several times, tried to shake Ma up. If it weren't for him, the children would have been split up and sent to foster homes a long time ago."

"But he's prejudiced, and he cusses. And he looks mean," I said, as if this would seal my case.

"He ain't all that prejudiced—not like most white folks. And as for cussing and looking mean, well, so do I."

I laughed in spite of myself. Grandma's car stopped in front of the trailer just then, and Mama called out, "Well, there you are, Emile. I didn't know where you'd gone, scooting off like a jack rabbit."

"Good evenin', Miz Bridgeman," Mr. Davis said with the nod of his head.

"Hello, Leroy. Nice to see you. You all right? Sorry to have Emile bothering you."

"I'm fine. And this boy ain't no bother."

I got in the car and rode home in silence. Before dinner, I got out the journal and scribbled one sentence: *Just one more time when I got it all wrong.*

――――――――

The first performance of *Hamlet* was on Thursday night. The cast and crew stayed after school to get everything in place—the props, the costumes, the makeup, the last-minute revisions. Some of the mothers were bringing dinner for them.

Blithe and Jake ate dinner at our house, and we left early for the play to get good seats. Mr. Davis met us at school, and by the time the play began, Northside auditorium was packed.

From the moment she stepped onstage in scene three of the first act, Eternity stole the show—at least in my opinion. Even when she had few lines, she played Ophelia so convincingly that all eyes were on her.

I could not imagine that Jake and Blithe understood the plot, but I was always underestimating them. Jake seemed very upset by the ghost of Hamlet's father until Blithe reached over, took his hand, and whispered, "It's not real, Jake. It's just pretend. Everything will be all right."

When Ophelia became obviously mentally disturbed, Blithe again reassured him. "Sissy's fine. She's just pretending."

We gave them a standing ovation—the whole auditorium rising to their feet in a burst of enthusiastic applause. Eternity stood hand in hand with the other actors across the stage, and her face, so pale and serious, broke into the smile that set her freckles in orbit.

I will always remember that too. The way she smiled, the way she glowed on the stage, as if standing right there in that very spot was where she belonged in the deepest part of herself.

———

Ma had agreed to come with Mr. Davis to Friday night's performance. On Friday afternoon, Mama and I went to pick up Jake and Blithe at the grade school, just as we'd arranged with the principal. But when I got to their classroom, it was empty, and Blithe's teacher was nowhere in sight. I began looking in the other classrooms—all empty. At last Miss Robinson came around the corner, her arms piled high with books.

"Oh, hello, Emile. What are you doing here?"

"I came to get Jake and Blithe."

A brief look of concern passed over her face. "They've already gone."

"I was supposed to pick them up—Eternity's in the play and couldn't come."

"Yes, I know. I'm going to the performance tonight." But she wasn't really paying attention to me. "Your mother didn't get the message?"

"What message?"

"I left it with the secretary at Northside. Jake was having trouble breathing, and Mr. Davis came and took him to the hospital. Blithe went too."

"Is he okay now?"

"Yes, he's much better. I talked to a nurse a little while ago, and he'd already been discharged."

"Thank you, Miss Robinson."

"Of course, Emile. Sorry about the mix-up. See you at the play tonight."

"Yes, ma'am," I said, calmly enough. But inside I felt afraid. I wasn't sure why. I ran out to the car and explained to Mama about Jake.

"I never got a message," she said.

"I think we should go check on them at the trailer."

Mama took the news with a slight frown, pulled on an eyebrow, and said, "Yes, I think that's a good idea. But let's not worry. It sounds as though Jake is fine now."

We found Blithe sitting in the rusted rocking chair. She looked rumpled, a fallen angel, her eyes hollow and empty. Mama stopped the car, and I jumped out and ran to Blithe. She was bruised and bleeding. There was an ugly gash on her scalp, and her fluffy blond hair was matted with blood on one side.

Mama was right behind me; she grabbed Blithe and pulled her into a close hug. "Blithe, oh sweetie! What happened?"

"Mr. Davis and I told the nurse at the hospital that Jake should stay there longer, but they said we could go. So Mr. Davis brought us back home—and Ma was all drunk and mad. Mr. Davis stayed with us and tried to calm her down. But Jake wasn't any better and he couldn't breathe, and so Mr. Davis said he'd better call the ambulance this time." She tried to take a gulp of air, shivering.

"And so he had to go to his house to call the ambulance and he told us to hide in the safe room and lock it and we did, just like Eternity always showed us how. And then—" Blithe caught her breath before the next words tumbled out—"she, she was all drunk and she broke down the door and started hitting me and said I couldn't go to no play. And Jake tried to pull her off me, and then she started hitting him and then Mr. Davis came running in . . ."

Inside the trailer, Mr. Davis was holding on to Ma, who was rocking back and forth, wailing. He looked up at me, and the expression on his face told me something awful had happened. The trailer was in a shambles, and Jake was nowhere in sight.

Mama took Blithe to the kitchen sink and started dabbing her head with a cloth.

"Where's Jake?" I managed.

"Ambulance here yet?" Mr. Davis asked, as though he hadn't even heard me, and then we heard the sharp, piercing siren coming our way.

I hurried toward the safe room.

Mr. Davis called after me, "Emile, ain't gonna do no good now. I tell ya."

The safe room door had been smashed in, ripped off its hinges, the key hanging helplessly in the lock. There was blood on the floor where Jake lay crumpled and still. I sank to the floor beside him and cried.

When the police and ambulance workers came in, Mama was rocking Blithe in her arms, and Mr. Davis and I were in the safe room beside Ma, her obese body sprawled on the floor, her arms cradling the lifeless form of her son. Ma was crying and saying over and over, "They always said he wouldn't live past his tenth birthday. That's what they always said."

The trailer park was lit up with police cars, their red lights flashing news of tragedy to the whole neighborhood. The ambulance had sped away with Jake. The families in the trailer park were huddled in little groups, talking in whispers. A policeman led Ma, in handcuffs, from the trailer.

Mama and I rode in another ambulance with Blithe to Piedmont Hospital, and Mr. Davis drove his truck over to get Grandma. I kept seeing Jake's face, stained with strawberries and a half smile, and then his crumpled body and the blood on the floor.

The nurses washed Blithe's cuts and spoke gently to her, but I don't think she heard them. Her eyes were vacant. She didn't even whimper when they gave her a shot of anesthesia. A doctor at the emergency room stitched up the gash in her head and put a cast on her broken wrist. Mama stayed by her bed, holding her hand.

When Mr. Davis arrived and came by her bed, Blithe whispered, "Where's Jake, Mr. Davis? I need to see Jake. He needs me."

Mr. Davis had tears running down his cheeks. "Shh now, honey," he said. "You need to rest."

The doctor showed us out into the waiting room and assured us that Blithe would sleep through the night, with the medicine she'd been given.

"Does Eternity know?" I asked Mama, and before she could answer, I begged, "Please don't tell her yet. Let her have one last moment when she is happy."

We left Blithe at the hospital with Mr. Davis, who insisted that he'd stay by her bed all through the night.

Grandma and Mama and I got to the school in time for the opening scene. We huddled near the back of the auditorium in the last available seats, miserable and stunned, and watched Eternity play Ophelia. When the queen announced that Ophelia had been found floating in the brook, fiction and reality collided in my mind, and I burst into tears again. Grandma and Mama circled their arms around me, and when I looked up at them, they were crying too.

After the play, after the standing ovation and the bowing and the presentation of flowers, Mrs. Harrington asked Eternity to come with her to the office. Miss Robinson and Mama and Grandma and I all came too. Grandma was the one who told Eternity the news.

I watched the flush of excitement on Eternity's face change to concern and then to total shock and grief. Tears started pouring out of her eyes without her making a sound. She just sat there, with all of us standing around her, and cried.

We drove her to the hospital to see Blithe, who was sound asleep with Mr. Davis sitting by the bed and holding her hand, himself sleeping.

Right then and there, Grandma and Mama decided that Eternity—and Blithe when she was released from Piedmont Hospital—would stay with us. None of us said a word during the brief drive from the hospital to Anjaco Road. When we got inside, Grandma fixed us some hot chocolate, which we didn't drink, and Mama helped Eternity get all the makeup off her face and lent her a robe and pajamas. After a while of not knowing what to do or say, I finally went upstairs to bed, mumbling "I'm so sorry" and "See you tomorrow morning" to Eternity.

I woke up twice in the night, and when I went to the bathroom, I saw light coming from under the closed door in Mama's bedroom where Eternity was staying. I was pretty sure I heard Grandma's soft voice offering some kind of hope behind that shut door.

It was the wrong day for a funeral, the sun so bright and the air fresh and clean and the birds making up one song after another outside the dormer window.

"We've got to go, Emile," Grandma called up to me, her voice heavy.

I slipped on the dark jacket Mama had laid across my bed and came downstairs in slow motion. I went through the kitchen and out the back door into the yard and gathered up every strawberry and tulip I could find.

The funeral was in the chapel at Second-Ponce de Leon. Many of those who attended were church members who didn't even know the Jones family, but felt a kinship simply because they had watched Jake being baptized by Dr. Swilley here only weeks before.

Eternity sat rigid beside Blithe. From the back she looked like a witch, tall and skinny and all clad in black, and Blithe like a wood nymph, tiny and pale. Mr. Davis sat on the other side of Blithe. Ma was there beside them, a policeman hovering behind. The charge against her was involuntary manslaughter.

Ace and his brother, Mitch, and Mr. McClary were sitting near the front. When they first came in, I saw Mr. McClary stoop down beside Ma and whisper something to her.

Eternity looked like she would snap in two, and I wished she could just cry and cry so that all the tension and pain would come pouring out. I knew what she was thinking: she had failed in her mission of saving her family.

"He's in heaven now," Blithe stated with a sob, and I was glad she believed that with all her heart.

Dr. Swilley's voice had often calmed me on a Sunday morning, but I decided it was even better suited for a funeral. His voice rose in a strong, comforting rhythm that made you think the God of the universe was concerned about poor Jake Jones and his family.

"'The Lord is my Shepherd,' the psalmist wrote. My friends, He is. He is able to lead us through the valley of the shadow of death. He is able to comfort . . ."

Blithe held on to every word. Eternity blew her nose twice and would not look at me. Ma, sober, sat in a stricken silence, perhaps for the first time in years completely aware of what was going on around her. And Mr. Leroy Davis kept vigil with them.

They buried Jake near the trailer park at Crest Lawn Cemetery. When the graveside service was over, the casket was lowered down into the ground and people threw dirt on it. I tossed little ripe strawberries in and handed Blithe the tulips.

She threw them onto the casket. The day before, she had said to me, "It's my fault, Emile. I made Mama mad and then she killed Jake."

Without a thought, I had grabbed little Blithe and held her tight against my chest and said, "No. No, Blithe, you're wrong. It's not your fault. You saved Jake. You made him smile. It wasn't your fault."

I wished I could have been more convincing.

Now Eternity gave me a stiff smile and took Blithe's hand and led her to where the cars were parked. A few of us were going to Mr. Davis's trailer afterwards.

"I'll walk there in a few minutes," I told Mama. It was only a half mile away.

She didn't argue.

I stood by Jake's grave as the cemetery emptied out, turned my eyes to the sky, and said, "Why, God?"

Suddenly Ace appeared out of nowhere, looking to me like an enraged bull. My pulse accelerated, and I was preparing for a fight when he said, "Hello, French Fry."

I backed away.

"I'm not gonna hurt you." He didn't sound convincing.

I figured he'd toss me into the grave with Jake. I knew Eternity would yell at me not to give up, but I had nothing with which to defend myself. I braced myself for his first blow, but then Mr. Mc-Clary came forward and extended his hand.

"Hello, Emile."

I nodded.

"Ace is right," Mr. McClary said. "We aren't here to hurt you. You've been a big support to Eternity, and I want to thank you. She's my great-niece, you know. I've tried to watch after the children for several years now. This tragic thing . . ." He motioned to Jake's grave. Then he cleared his throat and looked at Ace. "Well, tell him."

Ace would not meet my eyes. "It was Eternity who talked to the other football players and got them to admit the truth about Edward Hasty. My father worked it out with the police so they didn't put my name in the paper. But I spent three nights in jail." He looked down at his feet. "And I'm doing community service. It's not fun, but it's keeping me out of the detention center. So don't worry." He was still staring at the ground. "I won't hurt you."

Every word he said sounded as if it had been rehearsed, as if he had learned it just as surely as the theater troupe had learned their lines for *Hamlet.* I heard no conviction or sorrow in his voice—or repentance.

I looked at Mr. McClary. "How . . . how are you going to help them now?"

"I'm not sure," he said, for once looking unsure of himself. "Eternity has always resented what she considered my interference—she was always afraid I'd split the family up. Send the kids to foster care. I'll be meeting with social services next week."

"I see," I said, and they were gone.

———————

Eternity and Blithe spent the first week after Jake's death with us. Mama stayed downstairs with Grandma, and Eternity and Blithe took Mama's bedroom. I know it was supposed to be a horrible time of grieving, but really that week was like a sort of pause in all of our lives. For a brief amount of time I had two sisters, and Mama had three children, and Eternity and Blithe had a real family. We played Monopoly and ate all kinds of cookies and Grandma fixed us pancakes three times for breakfast.

We went to the Varsity once for dinner—Mr. Davis joined us—and we watched *The Sound of Music* at the Fox Theater, and when people from Second-Ponce found out the girls were staying with us, they brought food to the house.

And of course, we all worked in the garden.

I was clipping the grass around the daffodils and Eternity was pruning a rosebush when Grandma brought us peanut butter and jelly sandwiches.

Blithe, who had been examining a long slimy worm, took her sandwich. She thanked Grandma and then she asked, "What will heaven be like, Miz Bridgeman?"

The wrinkles on Grandma's face seemed to be more prominent, a whole road map of lines crossing and intersecting. She didn't answer right away. She walked over to where she kept her garden tools, slipped on the old gloves, picked up the clippers, and cut a rose from the trellis by the garage.

"Heaven will be like my garden," she said. "Sometimes I walk out and see the flowers just beginning to bud, and I think, *This is the most beautiful thing I have ever seen.* And then I come back later that day or the next, and things have changed, and I think, *No, this is the most beautiful time ever. This is even better than what I saw before.*

"You see, Blithe, in heaven it will only get better and better. From glory to glory. God lets us have a little taste of it here now on this imperfect earth, but we can't really imagine how wonderful it will be."

"So Jake is okay now? You really believe that?"

Grandma set down the clippers, took off her gardening gloves, handed the rose to Blithe, and hugged her. "Yes, Blithe. I really believe he is okay now."

But the week came to an end.

Despite our plea to let the girls live with us, the social services made another decision. On a Monday after school, Mrs. Hall, the social worker, Mrs. Harrington, Mama, and Grandma sat together in the den, along with a young couple dressed in suits, plus Mr. McClary. Eternity, Blithe, and I had brought in chairs from the kitchen, and all of us were listening intently to the social worker.

When we realized the couple was going to be Blithe's foster parents, Eternity pulled me back into the kitchen. "Oh, Emile!" She threw her arms around me and sobbed. "I never should have gone out for the play. It was too complicated. Now Jake is dead and they're taking Blithe away! I'll never forgive myself. Never in my whole life."

She clung to me. "Tell them, Emile. Tell them I can take care of my sister. Tell them we can survive. We'll be fine here with you! Tell them. Don't let them take Blithe away from me!"

Mrs. Hall had followed us into the kitchen. She placed a hand on

Eternity's shoulder. "Eternity," she said calmly, as if she were used to talking to inconsolable teens, "what has happened is a terrible tragedy. You cannot be expected to protect your little sister for years on end. It is too heavy a charge. You can visit her anytime you want."

Mama and Grandma were "not qualified" to be official foster parents, Mrs. Hall explained to us. If they weren't qualified, I couldn't imagine who was, but apparently there were a lot of rules and regulations and paperwork involved.

And so the sentence fell. Blithe would go to live with this couple and attend an elementary school near their house, clear on the other side of Atlanta. Eternity would be sent to a girls' home south of the city until a suitable foster home could be found for her.

Blithe did not cry when the couple gathered up her belongings and led the way to their car. She walked obediently behind them, the Bible from Grandma tucked under her good arm.

Eternity followed, and I watched the two sisters embrace.

"I love you, Blithe," Eternity said, her voice cracking.

"I know, 'Terni. I know it."

"Mrs. Harrington will bring me to see you on Saturday, okay?"

Then Blithe hugged Grandma and Mama, and finally she threw her arms around me. "I hope you'll marry Eternity. And when you do, I'll come live with you and it will be okay."

The young man opened the back door to the car and smiled and held out a hand to Blithe to help her inside. She started to climb in, then at the last second she turned and ran back to Eternity. "When my flowers bloom in Miz Bridgeman's garden, will you pick them? Will you pick them and put them on Jake's grave?"

The next day it was Eternity's turn. I carried her boxes of books to the car, and Mama helped with her clothes.

Grandma took Eternity in her arms and held her tightly. "Don't you forget what we've talked about, you understand? It was not your fault. This is not the end. It can be a new beginning, and nothing is too hard; remember that, Eternity. Nothing."

Eternity's face was paler than I had ever seen it, and her lip quivered. "I won't forget it, Mrs. Bridgeman. I promise I won't." She threw her arms around my grandmother's waist as if she were Blithe, and held on for dear life.

Then, wiping her eyes, she turned to me. "Well, Emile. I guess I need to say good-bye. We won't be seeing each other much now."

I wanted to cry or scream or hit something or someone with all my might. My best friend in the world was being ripped out of my life. I wanted to grab her and hug her and hold her and even tell her that I might care about her more than anyone else on earth. I might care about her more than my father. But I couldn't bring myself to do a thing besides stare blankly at the way she was crying.

"Aren't you going to say something, Emile?"

"I can't get it out."

"Me either." Then she handed me a book, the one about immortal poems that she had gotten from Mrs. Stevenson at the Ida Williams Library. "I thought you might like this. I'll miss you."

I nodded and could not even choke out the words *Me too*. If I opened my mouth one little bit, a gigantic sob would erupt like a volcano, and I had no idea if I'd ever be able to stop it. So I blinked about a hundred times and waved good-bye, and I felt that agonizing, empty sensation, that falling and helplessness, that utter terror.

The car pulled out, and Mrs. Hall drove away with Eternity.

Back in my room I opened the book of poetry. Eternity had slipped a note inside, written on a page torn from her spiral notebook.

Dear Emile,

I can't believe I have to leave. I know we'll see each other some, and I'll write you when I can. And you better write me and call me. Please know that 1861 Anjaco Road was a beautiful slice of heaven for me, I swear it was. I'll never forget you, Emile. I'll remember every second of the six months, two weeks, and three days since we met, and I'll never stop thinking of you. I promise I won't.

Eternity

I stood in my room, holding the torn sheet of lined paper, staring at the frayed edges that curled where they had been ripped out of the notebook. I tried to swallow, but the lump was still there. I squeezed my eyes shut, squeezed the tears back behind the lids.

She was gone.

| *twenty-one* |

If the first six months had at times been a scream of agony and at times a shout of joy, without Eternity at school April and May and June seemed like a low, whining cry.

Mama, Grandma and I went to visit Blithe at her foster home every Friday after school, and sometimes her foster parents would invite us to stay for dinner. On our first visit, Blithe greeted us with tears and clung to me and begged us not to leave; the second time she was a little more reserved.

By the third visit I could tell she had gotten used to her new home and felt safe there. She didn't seem to need us quite so much—which Mama said was normal and good. She missed Eternity and Jake terribly, and it hurt to see her blue eyes so serious, her expression so sad.

Grandma and I went to see Eternity two days after she arrived at the girls' home. It took us almost an hour to get there, and the visit passed way too quickly. It felt a little awkward with the three of us together sitting on a bench out in the park behind the big old house. It depressed me to see her surroundings, and I ached for her even worse after that visit.

She wrote to me every day, as if I were her personal journal.

Dear Emile,

I hate this place! You saw it! It's awful. I have nothing to do. I miss the trailer. I miss Blithe and Jake. I start to make a planet with my food and then I remember that it doesn't matter anymore.

I think I will go crazy. I miss you and your grandmother and your mom, and I miss the house and the garden and keep thinking it is probably really magnificent now, everything in bloom. . . .

Dear Emile,

No one at the home likes me much. The other two girls my age have both been arrested twice. Mrs. Hall says she thinks they've found a foster family for me. . . .

Dear Emile,

Thank you so much for coming to see me again. I know it was weird and all, but it meant the whole world to me.

I guess you've heard that Ma is in the psychiatric ward of the women's correctional institute. I think she's doing a treatment program for alcoholics. I don't know how long she'll be in there. Mr. Davis wants to take Blithe and me to visit her. I don't want to go. . . .

Dear Emile,

I met my foster parents, Mr. and Mrs. Land. I think that sounds funny: Eternity Land. Kinda like the Promised Land. Of course it's not my last name, really, but I thought that might make you smile. Do you smile anymore? I don't. Not yet.

The Lands seem nice enough, and I can't wait to leave the girls home and get back to school. They say the little public school near where they live is good (they live in the boonies—ask Griffin to explain "the boonies" to you).

Dear Emile,

Well, I live on the other side of the world, it seems. It takes us forty-five minutes to go visit Blithe in Roswell. But I like this place. I like this family—a lot better than the home. My school is small and I write for the paper and the Lands go to church every Sunday. They *really* go to church—I mean, it's like with your grandmother. It means something to them.

I saw Blithe yesterday, and she cried the whole time. I am going crazy not seeing her. I was calling her on the phone every afternoon, but her foster mother says it makes her so sad afterwards that maybe I shouldn't call quite so often.

Her hair is grown out and you can't see the scar.

I'm in honors math and honors English and I'm taking third-year French. *L'état c'est moi!* Guess who said that? Too bad the school year is almost over.

Dear Emile,

Ma wants Blithe and me to come back with her once she gets out. There is no way we are going back to the trailer, even if it meant we'd be together again. I think Blithe and I are much better off in these families. I can't believe I'm saying that, can you?

———————

At the end of April, Blithe and Eternity spent a whole weekend at Grandma's house. Once again, we enclosed ourselves in a dream world for two full days. We took walks and ate lunch at the Varsity. Eternity and I spent Saturday afternoon with all my collection spread out on the bed and rehashed every story I could remember from Papa. That night, we had Mr. Davis over for dinner. We went to church together on Sunday, and Blithe and Eternity got to talk to Dr. Swilley, which seemed to mean a lot to them.

On Sunday evening Grandma spent two hours in the car driving Eternity and Blithe back to their foster homes, and of course I rode along. When each girl got out of the car, Grandma grabbed her hands and said, "We're going to do this every month—I've already worked it out with your foster parents."

I loved the way Blithe beamed at that, and Eternity's face held a soft look of—what was it I read in her eyes—gratitude. That was it. Extreme gratitude.

Grandma kept her word, so all through May and June and July we celebrated—that's what it felt like, a celebration—once a month.

But then life would come to a screeching halt again on the Monday morning when I'd walk into Northside High School without Eternity.

She kept on writing to me.

I answered her letters as best I could, told her about Northside and church and the garden. But after a while I didn't have anything else to say, and every time I looked at her letters, I'd get an awful aching inside, worse than any ache I'd ever felt for my father or for France. I sat on my bed and wondered if there would ever be one second of one day when I didn't think of her and miss her and wonder what she was doing.

In late May, when school got out, Griffin and I started spending most of our time together. We'd find pickup soccer games in his neighborhood, and one day I left my latest letter from Eternity, unopened, at the soccer field. When I realized what I'd done, I hurried back to find it and couldn't. I felt terrible, and yet relieved. I had forgotten her for a half hour.

One day I woke up and realized that just as I had gotten used to America and being away from France and my father's absence, I had also gotten used to life without Eternity. By the fall of 1965, when school started back up at Northside, I sounded like a regular American. No one teased me, no one called me French Fry. At lunch I sat at a table with a lot of boys, and no one made the universe out of the cafeteria food.

Grandma and Mama and I kept up our regular visits to see Eternity and Blithe, and they still came to our house pretty often. But something was different between Eternity and me. I no longer shared secrets with her, and the stomach-cramping urgency I used to feel before I would see her had become just a soft ache. Eventually I even felt a little bit awkward around her, though I never would have admitted it. Our lives had been forced in two separate directions. It wasn't fair, but there was nothing we could do about it.

There was one important thing that happened to me, though, just before school started that fall. I went to a youth camp with twenty-five other kids from Second-Ponce de Leon. I only signed up to make Grandma happy, and when I found out that Ace was also going, I tried to think of a way to get out of it.

The camp was located about two hours north of Atlanta in the mountains. The cabins had dusty mattresses, and the bathrooms smelled like Lysol and, well, like bathrooms. Mosquitoes were everywhere.

A young preacher from a nearby church was the speaker. His voice was nothing like Dr. Swilley's, not soothing and kind. He liked to say things to shock us and challenge us. He warned us about compromise and told us over and over again that now was the time to commit our lives to Jesus.

I was getting tired of his messages, especially the "night talks" when we sat outside by a campfire with woods all around. In spite of Ace's reassurance after the funeral that he wouldn't hurt me—what I considered an obligatory confession forced on him by his father—I just knew that one evening he was going to grab me from behind and haul me through the woods and beat me to a fine pulp and leave me to be devoured by wolves. It was hard to pay attention.

But on the last night, Ace was sitting directly across from me. I could see him plain and clear by the campfire light, so I knew I was safe. The preacher started telling the story of his life. It was much more interesting than the other messages he'd told so far. In fact, I wondered why he hadn't told us about himself the first night—we might have paid more attention all week.

But he knew what he was doing.

"My father left us when I was ten," he told us. "I used to sit on my bed at night and wait, wait to hear his footsteps in the hall. I was sure he would come back someday. But he never did. And I hated God for that.

"When I was finally eaten up by hate and bitterness, and nothing was going my way, I went to a camp not so different from this one and sat by a fire like this. I met my Father—my heavenly Father—at that camp. I learned He loved me—oh, I had heard that before—but I *felt* it that night. Felt His love . . .

"And maybe you're like me, looking for love, waiting for someone to come home and make things right. I want you to know, you can come home to your Father this very night."

His story kept going, and the fire was dwindling down, dying into bright orange embers, and I was saying in my mind, *I don't want to hear this anymore! Stop talking about fathers! Stop it!* And then all of a sudden I was on my knees by the campfire and begging for forgiveness and love from this other Father and fighting back tears, vaguely aware that a lot of other kids were doing the same thing—without having consulted each other.

It was a holy moment that was going to change us forever. It was kind of foggy to me, and yet crystal clear at the same time. This was what I wanted to do. I closed my eyes and prayed with that pastor, and some other kids did it too.

When I opened my eyes, the first thing I felt was a kind of warmth and love. The second thing I felt was total shock. Ace McClary was on his knees right beside me, tears running down his big, round face.

PART II

*A Time for War and a
Time for Peace . . .*

| *twenty-two* |

Nashville, Tennessee, 1972

I went down the steps from Rand Cafeteria to the mail room below, on the campus of Vanderbilt University. The stairwell was plastered with ads for baby-sitting jobs and pleas for rides home to Atlanta and Memphis and Knoxville for the weekend. Rows and rows of small gray mailboxes lined the walls and cubicles of the mail room. I dialed the combination and opened my box. It was empty except for a small sheet of paper announcing I had a package to claim.

Grandma's cookies. She faithfully sent them each month. They arrived in pieces, which my hungry suite mates and I devoured within minutes every time.

I went to the window and handed the lady the slip of paper. She brought me the package from my grandmother, but it wasn't cookies this time. Just a large, flat manila envelope. I walked back upstairs, bought a Coke and fries, and took a seat. I ripped the envelope open and found a letter from Grandma on her monogrammed stationery with some other papers folded inside. I read the letter first.

October 15, 1972
Dear Emile,

I hope college is treating you well. I've been trimming the rosebushes, and I picked our last tomato this morning. Fall is in the air.

This letter came to me a few days ago, along with the newspaper clipping. I thought you would certainly want to see it. We always said Eternity would become a journalist. Well, there you have it.

Looking forward to seeing you at Thanksgiving,

All my love,

Grandma

I opened the folded newspaper clipping and found another envelope with Eternity's studied cursive across it: *Mrs. Maggie Bridgeman, 1861 Anjaco Road, Atlanta, Georgia 30309*. I turned the envelope over and read the return address: *Eternity Jones, PO Box 2194, University of North Carolina, Chapel Hill, N.C. 27599*. I pulled out the letter.

Dear Mrs. Bridgeman,

Thank you for your letter this summer. I'm sorry it has taken me a while to respond. I've been working two jobs as well as attending school. It is paying off, though. I'll get my degree in journalism in May, and I am already writing for the town paper—mostly small stuff, but I did get my first editorial column and thought you would like to see it.

I've been wondering how Emile is doing. It's been years since we've communicated, but you said he's at Vanderbilt studying literature. I'd like to write him. I have a good friend who goes to Vanderbilt, and she has invited me to visit.

With love and thankfulness,

Eternity

Dozens of images paraded across my mind in the course of a few brief seconds—Eternity at the bus stop with Jake and Blithe, Eternity at the trailer with Ma, Eternity in the safe room, Eternity whispering to me in the library at Northside, Eternity looking at my "collection," Eternity writing articles for *Tiger Tales*, Eternity as Ophelia, Eternity at Jake's funeral.

I headed back to the Towers and took the elevator to the seventh floor. The suite was empty. I walked into my room, knelt down on the floor, and slid an old suitcase out from under the bed. I still kept my father's gifts in the same suitcase I'd used at Grandma's house. Eternity's letters were there as well, and the one and only picture I had of her, taken at the Thanksgiving meal in 1964. In the photograph, Eternity was turned so that all you could see was her profile—a tall girl with a long black braid—and she was obviously in the middle of explaining something to me because I was leaning toward her across the table.

I remembered exactly what she was telling me when the light bulb flashed. She was swearing up and down that she had seen Ace bullying a black teen at the grocery store the day before. I was arguing that she was nuts, that Ace didn't live anywhere near her and would never be shopping at the Winn Dixie in her part of town. And then at the next football game, Ace had beaten up Edward Hasty.

I set down the picture, went to my desk, and reached for the volume of poetry that stood sandwiched between my Webster's dictionary, my thesaurus, my French-English dictionary, and my two anthologies of English literature. *Immortal Poems of the English Language*—the book Eternity had given me on the day she moved away. I had read it so often over the past seven years that the book's spine had completely detached from the pages, and I'd had it rebound during my first year at Vanderbilt.

The book fell open to page 121, "God's Grandeur" by Gerard Manley Hopkins. In the margin Eternity had written, *This is my favorite poem of all time!* I had grown to love it too. I read the first stanza:

> The world is charged with the grandeur of God.
> It will flame out, like shining from shook foil;
> It gathers to a greatness, like the ooze of oil
> Crushed. Why do men then now not reck his rod?

Beside the word *reck* she had written *regard.*

I shut the book; I knew the poem by heart. It was this book that had introduced me to the beauty of the English language in poetry. It was because of Eternity that I had decided to major in French *and* English literature.

I went to class, but I couldn't get Eternity out of my mind. I wanted, needed, to see her again. But writing her back proved to be ten times harder than the comparative lit paper I was presently working on. What to say? How to say it? I stayed awake half the night composing the letter in my mind.

Hey, Eternity! Long time, no see!

Dear Eternity, Grandma forwarded me your letter, which I read with great interest. . . .

Eternity, boy, have I been a poor correspondent. But it was great to get some of your news from Grandma and hear that you plan on coming to Vanderbilt. It would be wonderful to see you again, so let me know the dates. . . .

Each rough draft I mentally ripped to shreds. The next morning I drank three cups of coffee and dug around in my bottom desk drawer until I found a packet of unopened note cards Grandma had given me years ago. They were reprints of paintings of famous places in Atlanta: The Swan House, The Varsity, The Wren's Nest, Martin Luther King Jr.'s birthplace. The cards were rather feminine, I'd thought, so I'd never used them. But they seemed appropriate for Eternity.

I took the one of King's birthplace and began to write.

Dear Eternity,
    Please don't faint. A note from your long-lost French friend. Grandma sent me your last letter. It'd be great to get together if you come to Nashville. Let me know the date, and we'll set up a time to meet. Then we can talk about old times and catch up. No way could I do justice to my incredibly interesting life in a letter.
                                    Bye and au revoir,
                                    Emile

I included my address and the phone number for my suite. Then, in what I suppose is typical male fashion, I pushed the whole possibility as far back into the recesses of the neurological spot reserved for emotions as I could.

Her reply came the next week.

Hey Emile,

Thanks for writing. I'm coming for my friend's fall party in her sorority, November 12–14. You can imagine how excited I am about attending this thing, but it evidently means a lot to her. I'll explain later. Would you be my date? I hate being set up. I'm afraid it's a rather formal affair—black tie—you know. If you don't mind, you can just call my friend and let her know. Debbie Dixon: Campus Tel. # 8314.

If that doesn't work for you, I'm cool with something else.

See you soon,

Eternity

A date with Eternity! This made me laugh out loud. I rarely had a date. I had not joined a fraternity, finding my niche in the Creative Writing Club and the French Club. In spite of all the women who had surrounded me in my formative years, I was not at ease around females my own age. In my three years at Vanderbilt, I had never attended a sorority party, and never in my life had I been to a "black tie affair."

But right away, I knew I'd do this for Eternity Jones.

————

We met on Rand Terrace on that Saturday afternoon in November. It was a chilly, sunny day, and there were plenty of other Vanderbilt students congregated on the terrace. She was right on time, of course. She had on bell-bottom jeans, worn down low, and a snug-fitting short leather coat. Her black hair was long and loose, and her brown Cleopatra eyes were sparkling. She waved at me, smiling broadly when she was still a ways off, and broke into a run.

I'd rehearsed a dozen times in my mind how to greet her. A handshake, a stiff hug? I needn't have worried. Eternity grabbed me by the shoulders and gave me a kiss on each cheek. I felt inebriated, drinking in her familiar scent.

Then she stood back, held me at arm's length, and said, "You've changed. You're taller."

"You've changed too," I said stupidly, because she hadn't gotten any taller, but she'd changed all right. She had filled out with beautiful, womanly curves.

"Stop gawking," she hissed good-naturedly, and I wanted to crawl under the terrace.

Then she slipped her arm through mine and asked, "So, Professor Emile, how are the studies going?" She reached over and gave a playful tug on my hair, which almost reached my shoulders.

"Okay," I said, with a hundred other words on the tip of my tongue. "Fine. Doin' fine."

"Hey, you are a real Southerner, Emile. Not a trace of that beautiful French accent. *Dommage, mon amour.*"

When she cooed at me in French, I was so taken aback I was speechless.

"I've kept up my French, silly. Don't look so astonished. I did it for you."

"For me?"

"Hey, I have a promise to keep to you, remember?"

Honestly, I couldn't remember a thing. I felt a dizzying thrill and could barely concentrate on her words. My hands were dug deep in my pockets, and all I could do was stare.

"Are we gonna stand here all day with the rest of Vanderbilt, or could we maybe go somewhere and sit down?" Good ole Eternity was enjoying my embarrassment.

"No, um, no. Would you like to get something to drink? There's a pub downstairs. It opens at five." I looked at my watch. It was three-thirty.

She laughed. "I don't drink, remember? Living with an alcoholic made me vow to stay sober—perpetually."

"Well, I don't drink much either, really. I guess Grandma's Baptist church got to me." This was not at all how I had wanted to start our encounter. My whole brain, every piece of gray matter, had turned to mush. I kept swallowing and thinking, *You big fat jerk, get yourself together.*

"Maybe we could get a Coke? Anywhere to do that?"

"Yes. That we can do. Right inside at the cafeteria. That we can do."

We sat at one of the cafeteria tables, sipping our Cokes in silence.

Finally I thought of something to say. "So you're graduating in May. Journalism major?"

"Yeah." Her face broke into a grin. The freckles were still there, still orbiting on her face, her lovely, feminine face. "Looks like it."

I couldn't quit staring at her, this woman-child from my past, my closest friend for six short months, now miraculously sitting across from me and chattering as if this meeting were the most normal thing in the world.

"Tell me about your life . . . I don't even know where to begin." Finally I said, "Ma?"

"She died—liver gave out."

"I'm sorry."

"Your mother and grandmother went to the funeral last year—didn't they tell you?"

My face got hot. I had no memory of this news.

"Don't worry. You've been busy."

"Blithe?"

"She's doing pretty well. She loves her foster family—you know—you met them all those years ago. She's in eighth grade, growing up fast. I go and hang out with her family on holidays. It's pretty cool. Mr. Davis goes too. I think she's happy, but you can never quite tell with Blithe."

I thought about how Blithe had always seemed enchanted with life—before Jake's accident—but I said nothing.

"Did you ever hear anything from your father?"

"No." I said it too fast, slammed the book on that subject closed before it could be opened.

Eternity took it in stride. "Let's see, I know your grandma is doing fine—still gardening and telling everyone about Jesus." This she said softly, almost reverently. "And your mom is still teaching at Northside, and the kids like her."

I nodded.

"Oh, come on, Emile. Say something."

"Sorry. I'm just . . . I'm so glad you're here, and I'm remembering so many things. . . ."

"Me too." She pronounced those two words in the same tone of voice as she had used when describing Grandma still telling others about Jesus. "There's a reason I looked you up, Emile. I mean, my friend has been begging me for two years to come visit her. But I chose now because I've found a scoop."

"A scoop?"

"I've got some information about Klaus Barbie."

She could have slapped me across the face. I felt the jolt. "About my dad?"

"I don't know. Maybe. It's sketchy, but it's something."

"Well, go on."

"I've met some people who are hunting for Barbie."

"There are people hunting for Klaus Barbie, and you've *met* them?"

Her laughter tinkled brightly, almost like Blithe's all those years ago.

"I'm sorry, Emile. I've shocked you, completely overwhelmed you. It's just that I've kept looking for information about your father for all these years. I shouldn't be just throwing it at you like this."

"No, no, it's okay. It's fine. I want to hear. But you're right. I haven't thought about any of this for so long."

She sat back in the cafeteria chair. "I guess I need to give you some background. First of all, I spent last year in Italy—an exchange program. And I got to France a few times, and I even did some snooping around in Lyon one day—"

"You went to Lyon?"

"Yeah. Just really briefly. I wished you were there with me." Her voice faltered for a second. "Anyway, I found out some things about Nazi war criminals."

Of course I wanted to hear this, but part of me just wanted to drink in Eternity Jones. "You're stunning," I whispered.

"What?" she asked, annoyed. "Are you even paying attention to anything I'm saying?"

"I'm trying to, Eternity. Honest. But all I can see is you—my tall, skinny, strange, freckled friend. You've grown up. You're beautiful."

She rolled her eyes.

"No, I mean it." Instinctively I reached over and took her hand in the protective, brotherly way I'd done with Jake and Blithe all those years ago. "I can't say it right. It's just . . . I'm so proud of you. I'm a moron and a geek and a nerd and whatever else, so forgive me. But it's just blowing me away to see you again."

She had no idea what to say to that.

"I've been waiting for this day for a long time, Eternity."

"You have?" She cocked her head, skeptical. "I thought you said you hadn't thought of me or any of this other stuff for years."

I grinned, feeling a little bit more comfortable, perhaps because she suddenly seemed so ill at ease. "Well, of course I *thought* about all those things. I just never acted on those thoughts."

She shrugged and let out a long breath. "Well, if the truth be known, I was embarrassed to contact you, too. You stopped answering my letters years ago, and I didn't have any more information to give you about your father, and I figured if you wanted to get in touch, you could always ask your grandmother for my address."

"What can I say? I was a jerk. But I always wanted to see you again."

Our eyes met for just one brief moment, then we both stared at our empty Coke bottles.

"You want to look around the campus?"

"Sure. Why not?"

It was the perfect fall day to walk around Vanderbilt. The campus sat in the middle of Nashville, but you would never know it unless you ventured past the red-brick buildings and numerous trees and green lawns, which created an atmosphere of erudition and tranquility. On this day, most of the trees were half bare of their leaves, but the ones that still clung tenaciously to the limbs were vibrant in color. The air smelled crisp and exciting. I was in no hurry, enjoying Eternity's presence beside me as we walked past the library and the divinity school, where several of my literature courses were held. Conversation finally began to come more easily as we compared notes on classes we'd taken, books we'd read, college life in general.

We walked through Furman Hall, the only gray stone building on the whole campus, where all my French lit classes were held.

"This is the perfect place for you, Emile. This building, this campus—I could see you teaching here someday."

"I don't know about that. But it's true, I really like the atmosphere of university life."

We wandered along the streets with the fraternity and sorority houses until we came to The Towers, four tall brick apartment buildings that were considered top student housing.

"Wanna come up to my suite?"

"Sure."

"I don't know who'll be there," I warned her as we rode the elevator up. "A few of my suite mates are a bit off the wall."

"I'm not afraid." She laughed in a carefree way that again reminded me of Blithe.

The suite was in fact empty.

"This is a pretty cool place. How many guys live here?"

"Six of us. Come with me—I want to show you something."

She followed me into my room, and I pulled the suitcase out from under my bed. We could have been fourteen again and sitting on the floor in the yellow bedroom in Grandma's house, the little attic door beside the dormer window opened, the suitcase between us.

She opened it up. "Oh, Emile."

I thought she might throw her arms around my neck and kiss me, so loving was her look.

"Is the watch here?"

"Of course." I rifled through the items and located it. "And Tintin . . ."

"Oh, Tintin! I haven't thought of that old comic book in ages." She held it lovingly and opened it, running her hand through the cut pages. "I always thought of you as my little Tintin, Emile, my little detective." She closed the book and touched the hard cover. "Tintin and his trusty dog, Milou, to the rescue. Like you, Emile. You tried to save us—Jake and Blithe and me."

I could not think of one thing to say.

Eternity touched every one of the treasures—the newspapers, the thumbtack tin, the pen, the hairbrush. Then she saw the letters.

"You kept my letters?"

"Of course. Remember, I told you once I kept all the things that were important to me." I felt my face go red as if I were once again an awkward fourteen-year-old.

She flipped through the envelopes addressed in her penmanship, then she spotted the picture of all of us at Thanksgiving. She picked it up and studied it. "I was telling you about Ace, wasn't I?"

I nodded, unable to say the thought pumping into my brain. *We remember, we remember it all, all of those exciting, scary, cruel days in 1964.*

She brushed her fingers over the old playbill of *Hamlet.* "I've never been in another play."

"You were so good."

"It was always too painful."

I wanted to veer the conversation back to something safe, but Eternity was not afraid to broach the subject.

"Sometimes I still have nightmares about Jake. Sometimes I still think it was my fault."

"You're wrong."

"I know." She frowned. "But I wonder if Blithe knows. She won't ever talk about him. It scares me—it's as if she erases her past as soon as it happens. She forces herself to live in the present."

Now her face wore such an expression of grief that I was sure she would burst into tears.

"Except she does mention you every once in a while. Out of the blue, she'll ask if I've heard from you." Eternity rested her head on her hand and looked off into the distance. "I've wondered if you might visit her with me sometime. Maybe she'd like that—I mean, if you wouldn't mind. I figure you go to Atlanta fairly often?"

"Yes," I said, but I was still processing *Hamlet.* "Yes, that might work."

She stood up and leaned on my desk. "Hey, look! My old poetry book. I barely recognize it—you've had it rebound."

"Yeah. I used it so much it completely fell apart."

She flipped through the pages, looking at her scribbled notes in the margins, then looking back at me. "It's amazing how close we got in just six months. I've never had that happen to me since. Have you?"

"Never." I went to open a window, glad for the rush of biting air. "What time is your party?"

"Seven." She glanced at her watch. "Oh, my, it's five-thirty. I guess I better get back to Debbie's. She'll wonder what's happened to me." She got up to leave, then said, "Emile, I almost forgot. Here's what I've been wanting to show you—from my gallivanting in Europe."

She fished several newspaper clippings out of her jeans pocket and handed them to me. "I came across these while doing some research for an article on France. I thought you'd like to see them." Her fingers touched mine. "I'm assuming you still read French?"

Her eyes were teasing, and I stuck out my tongue and made a face. In that moment, I *was* fourteen again and Eternity was my enigmatic and slightly condescending new friend.

"Thanks. I'll come by Mayfield to pick you up a little before seven. I want you to know, this is the first time I've ever worn a tux."

"Really? Oh, Emile, you are going to look absolutely smashing"— this she said with an exaggerated British accent—"in a tux."

She was looking at me in a way that made me want to grab her and kiss her for all I was worth.

"See you in a little while, Eternity."

"You bet, Southerner! I'll find my way down."

My head was pounding, my heart beating, my hands sweaty—I was having the same reaction to Eternity Jones as I did seven years ago. No wonder I'd stopped writing, tried not to think about her.

I grabbed a four-day-old slice of pizza out of the fridge and sat down to read the articles. Two were clipped from the French newspaper *Le Monde*, and another from *Le Figaro*.

October 1972

BARBIE DOSSIER REOPENED

Following the revelation of new information, Munich's Public Prosecutor has annulled the mistrial pronounced for Klaus Barbie this past June, which stated that Barbie was not guilty of war crimes because he did not know the Jews would be exterminated in the concentration camps. . . .

BARBIE SEEN IN PERU

A German citizen living in Lima, Peru, recognized a photo of Klaus Barbie that appeared in the newspaper, and notified authorities that Barbie was living in Peru under the assumed name of Klaus Altman.

Upon learning that his identity had been uncovered, Barbie fled from Lima to Bolivia. . . .

"BUTCHER OF LYON" LOCATED IN PERU

Klaus Barbie, the head of the Gestapo in Lyon from 1942 to 1944 and the man responsible for Jean Moulin's torture and death, was spotted yesterday in Lima, Peru.

Barbie was responsible for over 4,000 assassinations and 8,000 deportations as well as the torture and death of more than 26,000 people. . . .

It was true I had not heard any news of my father during the past seven years. I had accepted it as a bitter pill capable of producing a whole range of emotions inside. But maybe he really had a reason. If Barbie could disappear for twenty years in South America, protected by crazy dictators, I was pretty certain my father could have disappeared too—and not of his own accord.

All of a sudden the feelings from years ago came rushing back. I almost picked up the phone to call Mama in Atlanta.

No, not yet. Instead I held the Tintin book in my hands and said out loud, "Papa, please. Please. What were you trying to tell me all those years ago? I'm sorry I ever doubted you. I'm old enough now. I can come and find you. Tell me, Papa. Please."

I got no answer, of course, but I had the firm conviction that, just as the case for Klaus Barbie had been reopened in Munich, the case for Jean-Baptiste de Bonnery's disappearance had been reopened in my mind. This time I was determined to find the answers. I laid the newspaper articles in the suitcase and closed the lid.

"Merci, Eternité. Merci." Then I headed to the shower to get ready for my date.

| *twenty-three* |

As I shaved, seven years of my personal history bumped
around inside my head. The Jean-Baptiste de Bonnery part of my life
had changed very little. I'd received no word, no letter, no information
at all about my father. Every once in a while, Mama left Atlanta alone
to visit an old friend somewhere, which seemed suspicious to me. At
first I imagined that she had a lover. But she kept that picture of the
three of us right beside her bed, and I took it as a silent reminder of
her conviction that Papa would return someday and started wondering
if she were in fact going to visit him in some secret hideout in some
unnamed place. But I never had any proof.

Mama and I first returned to France in the summer of 1966. We
spent three weeks in Lyon at the château. The moment I saw Mamie
Madeleine, she hurried to me, held me tight, kissed my cheeks forcefully, and she cried, really cried, something I'd never seen her do
before. We visited old friends and our favorite restaurants, and our
taste buds were revived by the French cheeses and bread and four-
course meals prepared with pride by the Lyonnais chefs, who had their
reputation as the practitioners of the world's greatest gastronomy to
defend. When I came back to Lyon that summer after two years of
being away, I was home. And yet, of course, I did not feel at home at

all. That was to be my fate—to live in two places and belong fully to neither.

During those three weeks I constructed wooden boxes to hold the rather impressive collection of swords and knives and daggers my father and I had collected over the years when we traveled as a family to Spain. Papa had always promised that this collection would belong to me someday. I used his tools to make the boxes, and holding the saw and the drill and the hammer brought his memory back more than the bottles of wine Mamie brought up from the *cave* before every meal. I felt relieved that I could still feel his presence with me in the old château.

I graduated with honors from Northside High School in 1968 with the craziness of assassinations in the States and student riots in France as a sobering background. Throughout my last three years of high school, I sang in the youth choir at Second-Ponce de Leon Baptist Church. We traveled across America for two weeks each summer, performing God-inspired musicals to young people high on everything available and longing for a substance that would last. Ace McClary and I had even had roles as Jesus' disciples in *Godspell* our senior year. He played Simon Peter and I played John. The God part of my life had really happened. I did find my Father, the heavenly One, and it did matter, a lot, deep inside.

In the campus group of Christian students to which I belonged at Vanderbilt, we talked a lot about pilgrimage. My pilgrimage had settled into what looked to me like a pretty clear path—studies, more studies, and one day a professorship. But we talked also about the way God doesn't allow us to see too far down our life's path, because we need to trust Him one step at a time.

Here on the same day, two vital people from my past—people from whom I had safely distanced myself for the remainder of my growing-up years—had wandered onto my path at Vanderbilt. Eternity had appeared in person. But my father's implied presence seemed just as authentic. They were back. I had a fleeting desire to call Grandma and tell her what I was thinking, ask her to pray for this evening. She would. She would take out her prayer notebook and write down my request in her shaking hand.

Instead, I towel-dried my face, noting I'd nicked my chin and placing a tiny piece of torn toilet paper over where it bled, as Papa used to do. Then I took out my own prayer journal—yes, I had followed Grandma's example—and wrote *November 13, 1972—my date with Eternity.*

I chuckled to myself and then felt a chill run through me. On the one hand, the words seemed hokey, clichéd, ridiculous. But on the other hand, they sounded deeply spiritual and in a way, final. Who wanted a date with eternity? I flipped through the journal, glancing at the pages and pages preceding this one with lists of prayer requests and answers.

At that moment I knew I did not want to have an answer to Eternity. It terrified me to open that closed drawer, perhaps a Pandora's box. It could lead my thoughts away from my studies, my goals. And Papa? How could I peek inside the drawer I had sealed shut with so many colliding emotions: bitterness and respect, disappointment and hope, anger and love?

I closed the journal, stuffed it next to my Bible, went across the hall to my suite mate's room, and said, "Okay, where did you say you put the tux?"

"Right here, dummy. Have you even tried it on?"

"Yeah, last week. The pants were a little big in the waist, but it'll do."

"And shoes? Did you find shoes? No way your Longfellows are going to fit into mine."

"Great, I forgot about shoes."

For the next half hour I walked from suite to suite in a T-shirt and black tux pants and black socks, until at 7:05 I finally found a pair of black dress shoes that fit.

Eternity Jones was created to wear evening gowns. Tall and slender, black hair pulled into a loose bun, those sultry eyes highlighted with makeup, she took my breath away when she greeted me in the foyer of Debbie's dorm. She couldn't help turning heads that night, wearing a sparkling dark blue dress that clung to her all the way down to her hips where it swished out into a satiny full skirt that fell to her ankles.

The sequins on the dress glittered like hundreds of twinkling stars, as if she were wearing a universe that I desperately wanted to be part of.

"Wow!" I said. "You look great!"

She blushed. "I borrowed it from a friend at UNC. I feel absolutely silly in it."

"Not silly. Stunning."

"Well, wow back. I told you a tux would become you."

We rode in the back seat of the car belonging to Debbie's date, Fred. The dance was held at an old mansion in a fancy part of Nashville. We made small talk with Debbie and Fred, sat with them for dinner at a round table covered with a white linen tablecloth, fine china, real silverware, and a silver candelabra, its candles flickering in the dusky room.

Eternity seemed happier, less intense than the girl I remembered. She smiled more easily and laughed often. I mentioned it to her when Debbie and Fred left the table to dance. "You seem a lot more . . . I don't know, peaceful."

"I am."

"Are you in love?" I blurted.

She tilted her head, considering my question. "I guess you could say that."

I wished I hadn't asked.

"But it's not what you're thinking. It was thanks to your grandmother, Emile. She's the one who forced me to ask questions about my life."

Then I knew what she was going to say.

"You know how she is—we'd have these big discussions out on her porch, about the meaning of life. And of course we went to your church, and Blithe and Jake were baptized and everything. It all got me thinking." She glanced toward the dance floor. "I read the Gospels for myself, and I fell in love with Jesus, and everything changed."

I could do nothing but stare at her.

She started laughing again. "Oh, dear Emile. I've shocked you again."

I wanted to hug her, to shout, *Eternity, that's wonderful!* But for a second I was speechless, and the moment passed, and she misinterpreted my silence.

"Don't worry. I'm not in a cult. I promise. I go to a church with a lot of normal people." She waited for me to respond, but I hesitated a moment too long, and Eternity, as always, finished her thoughts.

"What about you, Emile? Do you have a special girl? I bet the girls are crazy over this blond-haired, blue-eyed Greek god on their campus!"

"Right. Sure. That's exactly what they think." We both laughed a bit awkwardly. "No. No, I don't have anyone special."

"Why not?"

I didn't answer immediately, but this time Eternity kept quiet. Finally I said, "I guess I never found anyone who understood the French part of me."

"Ah."

"There was one girl I really liked, but I don't know. I feel different. Oh, I can't explain it."

"You don't have to. I was there when you first landed in America, remember, French Fry?"

I smiled at her use of Ace's old derogatory term. Coming from her lips it sounded like a compliment. "Yeah. Yeah—you get it."

The band was playing Elton John's "Tiny Dancer," and the students, swaying together on the dance floor, belted out the chorus, "'Hold me closer, tiny dancer . . .'"

Distracted, I said, "You know, I spent the year after high school in France, doing my obligatory army service."

"Really? I thought you gave up your French passport."

"I did in 1965, but the laws kept changing. At eighteen I got to choose my nationality, and I chose French. So that meant I had a year of French military service. While some of my friends were being drafted for Vietnam, I did my little stint in the South of France. Not bad, I guess."

"You'd never been back before then?"

"Oh, yes, I had. Three times with Mama. But this time I lived there. I visited Mamie Madeleine in Lyon as often as possible. I thought about staying there to study, then decided against it and came here. But I get back every year or two."

"Good for you. Good for you, Emile."

We settled back in our chairs.

"Do you dance, Eternity?"

"A little."

"Then let's dance."

Her eyes lit up.

"But first, I have to take off these shoes—they're too small for me."

"Well, if you can do it, so can I. My feet are killing me too!"

We left our shoes under the table and danced for an hour, until the band took a break. I liked feeling her hands in mine, and I liked it when she was close for the slow songs and I could smell her perfume. I felt stupidly thankful that I'd grown tall enough for Eternity to be able to rest her head on my shoulder.

During one of the slow songs I closed my eyes and became lost in the past, with images of Northside High School and Second-Ponce de Leon Baptist Church and the trailer village and Anjaco Road and my "collection" flickering across my mind, almost as if they were dancing themselves. When the music stopped, I felt disoriented for a moment.

"Emile," Eternity teased. "What's the absentminded professor thinking about now?"

I took her hand and led her back to a table. "Stuff," I said. "All kinds of things from the past. I think I'm lost in some time warp, Eternity. I'm sorry."

"It's okay."

"Let's go outside," I suggested abruptly.

She shrugged and agreed. We put on our shoes and left the dance with its loud music and the raucous laughter from students drinking too much, and walked out into the cold night air. Neither of us had a heavy coat. "Are you freezing, Eternity?"

"Yes, completely. But I like it out here. Clears my head."

The party showed no sign of slowing down, but we were ready to leave. Eternity found Debbie and told her, and I called a taxi to take us back to Vanderbilt. When it let us off at school, I took her across campus and into the divinity school, whose doors were always open. I fixed us two cups of coffee.

"Coffee at midnight. I'm impressed," she said, holding the mug between her hands and letting the steam warm her face.

"The nerdiest guys come here and study through the night. We rigged up our coffeepot so we can stay awake."

We found an unlocked classroom, sat across from each other in the dark, and talked the night away. I took off my bow tie and unbuttoned my collar, and Eternity let her hair down and sat with my tux jacket wrapped around her.

"Those articles about Klaus Barbie were amazing."

"I know. Somehow I thought they might have something to do with your father. I'm probably crazy."

"Not at all. I agree."

"You've never heard anything else about him?"

"No. I mean, of course I've talked about him with Mama and Mamie Madeleine. But I've never heard directly from him."

"But they have?"

"I don't know. I got tired of trying to figure it out—it was too . . ." I almost said *infuriating*, then changed my mind. "Too painful."

"Yeah, I can believe that. Your Mamie Madeleine never hinted at anything more when you were living in France?"

"Remember, my grandmother was a *résistant*. She learned a long, long time ago how to keep her mouth closed. If she knows something and isn't supposed to tell, then she never will."

I didn't want to talk about my father. Klaus Barbie, Nazi hunters, and newspaper articles were fine, but talk of my father led to anger. I didn't want to feel anger on this night. I changed the subject. "When did you make faith a real part of your life, Eternity?"

She shrugged, pulled the coat around her more tightly, sipped her coffee. "As I said, it started way back on your grandmother's porch. And after we moved away, I wrote your grandmother long letters. I'd asked her about all kinds of things, and she always pointed me back to the Bible."

I guess I had always known that Grandma was keeping up a correspondence with Eternity, even though I wasn't. Now, for some reason, I felt ashamed and wished we had continued to write.

"I thought about heaven a lot. And about Jake. And I finally figured out what your grandmother meant about storing things up in heaven. In heaven there's gonna be a 'safe room'—just like Jesus says. The good things, the important things, will be there, waiting for us. There'll be a book about the stars and a play by Chekov and some sand from Tunisia. And poetry. Lots of poetry. It'll all be there waiting for me. And Jake will be there. I think his room will be right next door."

Her voice cracked; she cleared her throat and gave an awkward smile. "You probably think I'm nuts, Emile. I don't understand it either, but I have a vision of what it will be like. The hard things, the sacrificial things that didn't really work out the way I'd hoped, even all the suffering—it will all count somehow—in God's way of seeing. And He'll store those things like pearls in my room in heaven."

I had a vague, disturbing memory of Eternity dreaming about her biological father and me feeling sorry for her. But the dream she was describing to me now was different and alive and almost believable, simply because I could tell that she believed it.

"And we'll have the rest of our lives—our *after-lives*—to see anything and everything we ever wanted to see or know. It'll all be okay." She paused. "I'm sorry, Emile. I'm babbling. You must think I'm insane."

I shook my head no, but nothing came out of my mouth.

"Your grandmother was the first one to show me there is a purpose to life, to help me understand that waiting is an essential part of maturity, to give me a glimpse of hope for the future. . . . I wish you'd say something, Emile. You just keep staring at me as if I'm a lunatic. Please tell me what you're thinking."

What was I thinking?

"I don't think you're nuts, Eternity. It happened to me too. I did what Dr. Swilley said too—soon after you left. And I can't believe I never told you."

She sat up straighter, scooted her chair closer to mine, and whispered, "Tell me now."

So I told her about the summer camp in 1965 and Ace and the

mission trips and the campus ministry and the pilgrimage idea. I'd probably been going on for a half hour when Eternity just burst into tears and started crying hard, at the same time shaking her head back and forth and lifting a hand to reassure me that she was not having a nervous breakdown.

Fortunately my suite mate had insisted I tuck one of his white handkerchiefs into my pocket, and I handed it to her. I thought maybe I should hug her or hold her, and I wanted to, but I decided against it.

Finally she was able to speak. "I'm sorry, Emile. I, I don't know why I'm crying. I'm glad for you, and I'm scared . . . of coincidence, and why I'm here right now."

I understood exactly what she was trying to say. I felt it too—a divergence in the path I had planned out—a *bifurcation* as we said in French—something surprising me and getting in the way. Or was it a coming back together of two lives? And what in the world were we supposed to do with it?

I awoke suddenly at eight o'clock. Eternity was still asleep in the chair beside mine, my coat around her shoulders, her head leaning on the small desktop, her long black hair draped over it.

"Hey. Hey, you. Wake up." I touched her shoulder lightly.

She opened one eye. It registered surprise, then she grinned. "Good grief. Is it morning?"

I nodded.

"We must have talked all night!"

"We did. Most of it, anyway. You fell asleep in the middle of my story about Apollo 11."

"Sorry." She yawned, stood up and stretched. "This is the most uncomfortable dress to sleep in. These sequins make me itch!" She ran her hands through her hair. "Well, Debbie's gonna accuse me of being a loose woman—that's for sure." She blushed. "Don't pay any attention to me. I've gotta get back to the dorm. She's probably worried."

Nobody was out on campus at eight o'clock on Sunday morning. I walked her to Debbie's dorm. I did not want to say good-bye. I felt a sharp pang, a cold chill.

"When do you leave?"

"Tomorrow, right after church." She grinned sheepishly and glanced at her watch. "I guess, actually, that's today—in a few hours."

"Could we meet up in Atlanta then? Go see Blithe, as you suggested?"

I hated the urgency in my voice, afraid it would scare her away, scare her back onto her own separate path.

"Yeah. That would be good." She squinted, considering. "I think that would be good."

"Where are you going for Thanksgiving? I'm sure Grandma would love to have you and Blithe come over."

"I'll have to check with Blithe and her foster parents." She gave me back my coat and reached for the door. "Well, Emile."

My urgency increased. "Would you mind if I wrote to you occasionally?" My voice rose the slightest bit. My face reddened.

She turned back around. "I'd like that, like it very much, Emile."

She took my hands in hers and, with the intensity of the old Eternity, said, "Thanks for the date, Emile. It was really, really great to see you again." She gave me a kiss on each cheek.

Life changed for me over the weekend—or maybe it came back around. My mind was filled with Eternity Jones, and I wanted with all my heart never to lose touch again.

Dear Emile,

Merci encore for the date. It was very fun to catch up and so surprising to find that in many things we are still on the same page. I will be in Atlanta for Thanksgiving and having our meal at Blithe's foster parents. But if you wanted, maybe we could get together on Friday and visit Blithe. I'd love to see your mother and grandmother too.

Love,
Eternity

Dear Eternity,

The pleasure was all mine. *Tu m'as épaté!* I felt like I'd found a comrade in crime and a friend again.

Grandma is thrilled with the idea of you coming for dinner on Friday. Leftovers, she assures. If Blithe would like to come, we'd all be so glad. Grandma's phone number is still the same. Want to give me a call when you're in Atlanta? I can come pick you up, if you'd like. That way I'd get to see Blithe too, if she doesn't come to dinner.

A bientôt,
Emile

———

I drove my old Plymouth out to Blithe's foster home in Roswell. Chilly autumn had gone on a brief vacation and Atlanta registered at seventy-five degrees that afternoon. Eternity greeted me in the driveway, wearing jeans and a tie-dyed T-shirt.

The house was a comfortable light-brick ranch style, tidy and clean but without the cozy feel of family that Grandma's house gave off when you first stepped inside. I wondered if Blithe was happy here. She came from down a hall and met us in the den. She smiled at me shyly, half hiding behind her sister as she had done all those years ago.

The angel was growing up. She still possessed an ethereal beauty with her soft blond curls and pale blue eyes. Her face had lost the roundness of childhood; she was slender and graceful. But the innocence was gone. During my two-hour visit, she did not once break into laughter; she barely even smiled. In many ways she reminded me of Eternity at her age—efficient, businesslike, obsessive, determined, and much too old for her years. My cherubic Blithe had indeed evaporated.

"She doesn't feel like coming to your house," Eternity apologized as we walked out to the car.

"That's okay. Some other time." I leaned out the window of the Plymouth and waved to Blithe, who was still watching from the doorway as I started to back out of the driveway.

Suddenly she ran down the sidewalk and alongside my window with a strange intensity on her face. But all she said was, "It's too bad you don't sound French anymore, Emile. I always liked it when you sounded French."

The house on Anjaco enveloped us in its friendly arms that evening. Mama had a cassette tape of James Taylor humming in the background. Grandma glowed with the pleasure of rekindled friendships and awkward children now grown up. She had aged a bit in the past seven years, her shape a little rounder and her hair a lighter shade of gray, but she still walked with a brisk step, and her eyes were bright and filled with warmth.

While Mama finished preparing dinner, Grandma ushered us out into the backyard, saying, "I want to show you something before it gets dark."

The oak and maple branches trembled, naked, in the unseasonably warm breeze. Crisp brown leaves covered a flower bed where flashes of white and purple and yellow pansies peeked through.

"Remember when Jake was determined to plant an acorn?"

Eternity's face broke into a smile. "He was sure he'd have a tree sprouting up the next spring, just like the strawberries and daffodils."

"Well, it wasn't the next year, but look now."

A small, spindly oak stood near the strawberry plants.

"The faith of a child. Unless a grain of wheat dies . . ."

Eternity reached for Grandma's hand. "Thank you, Mrs. Bridgeman. Thank you for putting up with me and discussing life out on that porch and believing in me and caring. I needed someone like you in my life at that time. God put you there for a purpose."

Grandma patted Eternity's hand. "No accidents with God. It was my great pleasure. And I needed you and Jake and Blithe and dear Emile. Needed you all to remind me of what youth looked like."

The old jealousy was gone, replaced by a gentle contentment as I watched Eternity with Grandma.

Mama called then from the kitchen, "Dinner's ready!"

"He's turned into quite the gentleman, your Emile," Eternity teased when I seated Mama at the dining room table, giving her a kiss on the cheek.

"Yes, all grown up now. Fortunately we get him back home every once in a while." She reached for my hand and squeezed it.

Mama had aged a little too, I supposed, but she embraced the beginnings of middle age with a calmness she had never exhibited before. Still sharp and capable, but perhaps she had less to prove now, I thought. Perhaps she was becoming like Grandma.

In their motherly ways, both Grandma and Mama bubbled over

with information for Eternity. They talked of their visits to see Mr. Davis and Blithe, of their sadness at Ma's death, of Dr. Swilley and Second-Ponce and Northside High School.

Then came their questions for Eternity. How was she doing at college? What were her favorite courses? How did she like writing for the paper? Did she have a boyfriend? On and on the questions went, and Eternity answered with grace and ease.

I sat back and enjoyed the conversation, once again the lone male, the observer, the outsider. On this evening, I didn't mind. If I could have worked out my life so that for years to come the four of us would sit at this very table and share good food and pleasant conversation, I would have. I wanted to reach over and take Eternity's hand and clasp it tightly for a long, long time.

"Leftover pumpkin pie!" Grandma announced happily, and when we were all eating it and smacking our lips and agreeing it was heavenly, she asked another question. "You're a year ahead of Emile in school now, aren't you, since he spent that year in France doing his army service?"

"Yes, ma'am."

"So you'll graduate in May with a degree in journalism. Then what?"

"I have a few ideas—maybe I'll keep working at the paper in Chapel Hill, or maybe I'll do something else. I've toyed with the idea of going back overseas."

"I go to visit Jake's grave occasionally," Grandma said, as Mama served the coffee.

"Thank you," Eternity said. "That means a lot. Blithe's foster mother takes her too, and I go every time I'm up this way. I drive by the trailer village first and stop in to see Mr. Davis, and then we ride together in his pickup truck to the cemetery.

"It was cystic fibrosis, Jake's disease. Did I tell you? They haven't found a cure, but some of the children are living longer now. Someday it will be eradicated." She swallowed, breathed in deeply, and blinked her eyes twice. Cleopatra's eyes. "Or maybe we'll have to wait till heaven for that."

Small talk followed, then Mama and Grandma cleared the table, and Eternity and I were left sitting there alone.

"Can I see your room, Emile? I just need to see it."

"Of course."

Eternity had not one ulterior motive in seeing my room, I knew . . . knew with a pinched disappointment. She merely wanted to visit the past. I followed her up the stairs, watching her long slim fingers on the wooden railing.

"It hasn't changed. The dormer window, the little attic space, the yellow wallpaper. I'm so glad it's still the same. It's comforting somehow."

"Yes, I guess it is."

"I know this just seems normal and silly to you, but to me, Emile, to me, this is where my life actually began, sitting beside you and watching Blithe and Jake construct a Lincoln Log cabin and then rush out into the garden to plant bulbs. That was the beginning of my life."

In many ways, Eternity, my life began here too. Maybe I was just too blind to see it at the time.

———

Eternity spent the weekend at Blithe's, and they both agreed to come with us to church on Sunday. Except for mentioning the fact that Ace had made some sort of spiritual decision at that summer camp in 1965, I hadn't told Eternity just how much he had changed, how he was now considered one of the "cool college guys from Georgia Tech" who helped out with the youth group. I knew she didn't keep up with the McClarys, by her own choice. But it was another of my dumb ideas—something I hadn't grown out of—expecting her to run up to him that morning at Second-Ponce, throw her arms around him, and say, "Wow, it's great to see you, Cousin Ace!"

We literally almost ran into Ace after the morning service. He was carrying a stack of hymnals, not looking where he was going. Eternity, Blithe, and I came out of the sanctuary and found him smack in front of us.

"Hey, Emile," he said. Then he saw Eternity.

"Remember this girl?" I asked lightheartedly.

His face drained of color, then became a bright red. "Sure. Sure.

Hi there, Eternity. Been a long time."

Second-Ponce had been renovated since the Joneses' last visit, so when Blithe asked me where she could find the nearest restroom, I said to her, "I'll show you."

But when I came back moments later, Eternity's stance had changed. Her face was tight and hard and intense, and she was nodding at Ace, who seemed to be relating something very important. Everything in Eternity's posture indicated she wanted to end the conversation.

Ace's face had turned an even brighter shade of red, and he was sweating around the collar. ". . . sorry for what I did back then," he was saying. "I, I always meant to tell you or write you, but I couldn't . . ."

Her eyes were narrowed and she showed not one ounce of compassion for whatever Ace was struggling to apologize for. Then he caught sight of me, nodded at Eternity, and walked away, reaching out his hand quickly and shaking mine. "See ya later, Emile."

"What was that all about?" I asked her. "You look awful."

"Nothing. Nothing."

"You're shaking, Eternity! Are you all right?"

She turned on me, eyes blazing. "No! No, I am *not* all right at this moment," and she fled down the carpeted hallway toward the women's restroom.

In that moment, snippets of the past flashed in my mind—the bruises on her arms, her insolence with Mr. McClary, her hatred of Ace from all those years ago.

"He hurt you, didn't he? Way back at Northside?" I asked Eternity as we walked to the car, while Blithe was talking with Grandma and Mama.

"I can't talk about it."

"Okay. That's fine."

"Blithe and I need to get on home now. My ride back to Chapel Hill is coming to pick me up after lunch."

I drove them to Roswell, trying to make small talk and failing miserably. When they got out of the car, Eternity said, "Don't worry about me, Emile."

"I'll try not to." This was not the way I had planned to say good-bye. "I'll write, okay?" She nodded, but didn't meet my eyes. "Bye, Blithe. Send me a letter, okay? Your sister has my address."

I saw a flicker of interest in Blithe's blue eyes. "Okay. Maybe I will."

Dear Emile,

Sorry for the way we left last month. Some things are too hard to explain. But my reaction toward Ace was all wrong. So much for forgiveness. I'd appreciate prayers on that subject—it's a big one for me. Sometimes it seems like there is just way too much to forgive, and man, that makes me feel so rotten. God forgave me. Why can't I do the same for others? I mean, I think I forgive "mentally," but emotionally my heart just seems raw. Any insights on this?

Hope Vandy is treating you well. I've decided to apply for a Fulbright to teach English in French schools. The application takes forever, and then I have an oral interview. I wish you were here to take the interview for me.

Love,
Eternity

Dear Emile,

Bonjour! I'm taking French this year. All eighth graders have to take a language. Most girls choose Latin, but I chose French for you. It was fun to see you at Thanksgiving. 'Terni was right—you sure did get taller! I like your long curly hair. Will you send me a picture of you? Here's one of me—it's not very good, but it was my school picture.

Bye,
Blithe

Dear Eternity,

It was so good to be with you over Thanksgiving. Good luck on the Fulbright!

I'm sorry about Ace. And well, as far as forgiveness is concerned, I guess I feel like the things you've lived through are a whole lot harder than what I struggle with.

I tend to get stuck on the idea of *what* I'm forgiving. Take my father. I don't know if I should forgive him for having an affair or for leaving me without explanation or for being a coward or maybe I don't need to forgive him at all. And I go around and around analyzing things. But Jesus never said, "Forgive when you know what was done or when you understand why." He just said keep on forgiving. So I have to stop analyzing and just get down to the brass tacks of forgiving. The cerebral part does that much better than the gut.

> *Avec toute mon affection*
> *en Christ,*
> Emile

Dear Blithe,

Thanks for your letter. Well, this is the only picture of me I could find. It's a bit old, but I look basically the same. It was great to see you. Keep studying French. *Je suis fier de toi.*

> Hang in there,
> Emile

Dear Emile,

Wow! Thanks for your letter. What you said struck a chord with me. I mean, I do know what Ace did to me, and I understand why— he was a big fat jerk at the time—and now he has changed and asked me to forgive him. All that was so convicting that I decided I *have* to choose to forgive even if I don't feel one bit like it. I guess, to use your words, I need to be cerebral about it first and trust the emotions will follow.

Keep praying . . .

> Love,
> Eternity

Dear Eternity,

Glad you are moving forward in the forgiveness category. I will keep praying.

I'm in the midst of studying Emily Dickinson in my American Traditions in Literature class. Read this poem a few days ago and thought of you, obviously, for several reasons. Remember you had underlined the whole thing in your *Immortal Poems* book?

> *Exultation is the going*
> *Of an inland soul to sea,*
> *Past the houses—past the headlands—*
> *Into deep Eternity. . . .*

Okay, off to study. Any news on the Fulbright?

Emile

Dear Emile,

If I get the scholarship, maybe you could come over and we could visit Lyon, do a little research, see your grandmother. Someday I have to meet the infamous Mamie Madeleine.

Your sweet Grandma Bridgeman sent me brownies in the mail. I loved getting to see your family. It was good and hard and just right for now, I guess.

Bye,

Eternity

Dear Emile,

I'm going to be in the school play, *The Sound of Music*, and I am playing the von Trapp sister Liesl. Will you come see it? I have one solo and I'm scared to death. Here are the dates of the musical. . . .

Love,

Blithe

Dear Emile,

I'm going to France! I'm going to teach English in a small school in Versailles and look for a newspaper job in Paris. Can you believe it? I will give you all kinds of scoops, dear French Fry. Do think about joining me there, okay?

And guess what? I wrote Ace a letter. I told him I forgave him. It made me feel . . . um, it made me feel lighter. And thankful too.

Love,

Eternity

| *twenty-four* |

I saw Eternity twice before she left for France in the summer of 1973. The first time was at *The Sound of Music* in April. We sat side by side watching angel Blithe play Liesl, impressed by her strong yet sweet soprano voice.

"She's happy again," I whispered to Eternity during the second act.

"I know," Eternity whispered back, squeezing my hand contentedly. "This has been a godsend, this part in the musical." I considered the irony of the situation, attending this play while the past memories of *Hamlet* haunted me. The memories fizzled suddenly, replaced by my accelerated pulse with Eternity's hand in mine. I did not want to let it go, but she gave one more squeeze, a sincere smile, and put her slim hand back in her lap.

The second time I saw her was at the end of May at her graduation from UNC. My classes were out and I was back in Atlanta, living with Grandma and Mama for the summer. We drove to Chapel Hill for the ceremony, along with Blithe and Mr. Davis. When I told Eternity *au revoir*, she pecked me on the cheek and said, "I'm counting on seeing you at some point. You have a whole year to get over to France. Okay?"

I rolled my eyes, grinned, and said, "We'll see."

Then she added, "Pray for me, Emile. Will you do that?"

"Of course."

True to her prediction, she began writing articles for a small American newspaper in Paris called *The Paris Insider*. She sent me clippings of each one, the subject matter ranging from Vietnam to Vichy to Watergate to art exhibitions at the Louvre and expats dining in Paris. But the subject she kept close to her heart was the investigation of Nazi war criminals. A letter that came in late September was all exclamation points.

> Emile,
>
> The Lord has put me at the right place at the right time! I've met people involved in the hunt for former Nazis. I've gotten interviews. I have so much news! Enclosed are three recent articles I wrote. I know most Americans won't even bother to read them, but you must! I know you'll be interested.
>
> When are you coming to France? We could meet in Lyon, stay with your grandmother. You can show me around those *traboules* I've always wanted to see and meet some of the people who are Nazi hunters. Who knows? They may have news.
>
> Hope to see you soon!
>
> > *Bisous* as they say over here,
> > Eternity

I wondered if she was assuming we would just remain best friends, bosom buddies, private investigators. I couldn't tell if her heart was involved, but mine was. I contemplated hopping on a plane and joining her, but I had classes to finish and a job. I reasoned that going to France at this time did not fit into my schedule, my pilgrimage.

Still, I read her articles with a growing sense of anticipation and longing.

> The Paris Insider
> September 1973
>
> ### PORTRAIT OF A BRAVE COUPLE
> By Eternity Jones
>
> Last year in Paris, Beate and Serge Klarsfeld received a suspicious package at their home. They took it to the local

police, where an X-ray examination revealed the detonator, explosives, and nails of a large homemade bomb. Undeterred, the Klarsfelds continue their tenacious battle for justice—tracking Nazi war criminals. What inspires this brave couple to risk their lives time and again in this cause?

Serge is Jewish. His father, Arno Klarsfeld, served with the French Foreign Legion and was captured by Germans in 1940, but escaped to the "Free" Vichy Zone in southern France and settled with his family in Nice. The family was relatively safe in Nice, where the Italian occupation zone protected Jews from arrest and deportation to the East. However, in September 1943, Mussolini was overthrown and Italy's alliance with Germany ended. When Italian troops withdrew from Nice, SS teams commanded by Alois Brunner entered the city to hunt down Jews. Serge's father, Arno, was arrested by the SS as his wife, Serge, and his sister listened, hidden in the back of a closet in their apartment. Arno Klarsfeld was deported to Auschwitz and gassed.

Beate, a German from Berlin, came to Paris as an au pair. There she met Serge, a student at the Sorbonne. The couple married in Paris in 1963. Serge began work with the French National Radio and Television Organization (ORTF) and Beate with the Franco-German Alliance for Youth, a friendship organization newly set up by President Charles De Gaulle and Chancellor Konrad Adenauer.

... In 1971, the Klarsfelds intensified efforts to track and unmask unpunished Nazis, among them Klaus Barbie, chief of the Gestapo in wartime Lyon.... Beate, along with two mothers who lost their children during the raid of the village of Izieu in 1944, is responsible for a campaign launched in France and West Germany last summer to reopen the case of Barbie, twice condemned in absentia by French courts but never caught. Acting on secret information that Barbie was living in Bolivia but had taken temporary refuge in Peru, Beate traveled to South America twice last year to publicize demands for his extradition....

The Paris Insider
December 1973

INDOMITABLE BEATE

By Eternity Jones

> Returning to La Paz with Itta Halaunbrenner, whose hus-
> band, son, and two daughters were killed on Barbie's
> orders, Beate Klarsfeld has renewed her efforts to force
> Klaus Barbie's extradition for trial in France. The two
> women chained themselves to a bench near Barbie's
> office in central La Paz with protest placards and suc-
> ceeded in generating press attention despite police
> harassment before they returned to Paris.

Then a letter arrived in January of 1974.

Emile,

You are not going to believe this! Serge Klarsfeld went to South America to try to organize the kidnapping of Barbie and bring him back to France for trial! Apparently, he flew to a remote site in the Andes with another activist and met with other conspirators; the group was counting on help from Bolivian officers who oppose the current regime, but then there was some kind of coup in Chile that messed up their plans.

Okay, so it didn't work, but did you get that? "Other conspirators" were working with him to get Barbie. People living in remote places in South America. Could your father be involved? Don't you want to find out? I really think you should come.

Eternity

So I went to France for two weeks in March, missing a week of school and then using the spring vacation of my senior year at Vanderbilt, 1974. I flew to Paris and took the train to Lyon.

Eternity met me at the Lyon Part-Dieu train station in the middle of town. "Emile!" The smile, the kisses on each cheek. "I'm so glad you came!"

"Bonjour, Mademoiselle." I felt happy, confident, even expectant.

"You must be exhausted. How was your flight?"

"Not bad. Jet lag hasn't hit me yet."

How strange, how very strange to be in this familiar setting with Eternity. We hauled our backpacks downstairs to the metro and rode it, making a change to another line.

"Bus next," I said. "And then we'll have a little walk to get to the château."

The bus let us off at the bottom of a hill with a sign indicating the beginning of the village, St. Romain au Mont d'Or. The entrance up the hill to the village took us past a natural spring that cascaded over the golden stones, famous in the region. A ten-minute uphill walk brought us to the center of the village with its cobblestone narrow streets, ancient stone homes with yellow and green wooden shutters, pansies quivering in the breeze, an old twelfth-century church—actually no more than a chapel—and the adjoining château.

"Oh, Emile. Emile, it's, it's amazing. It's so—so French!"

"Built in the thirteenth century."

"And you grew up here. You grew up in the midst of history. Just think of all the other people who lived in this place before you!"

Eternity had discovered another world, and everything was fresh and real and exotic and ready to be discovered by her journalistic mind. She took photo after photo, then scribbled notes feverishly in a little pad as I watched.

"What is it exactly that you are trying to capture, Eternity?"

"Oh, hush, and let me work. You're just here for the fun, but I have work to do."

"I came because I was invited."

She was exasperated. "You don't care anymore, do you? You don't care about finding your father."

"Not particularly. I figure if he'd wanted to be found, he's had ample time to contact us. Maybe you're right—he's dead."

"Maybe he lives right here in Lyon."

"I'll kill him if he does."

"Aha! Not quite so indifferent after all."

Of course not. I wanted to explain to her that I certainly did not come to France for fun—that I dreaded any and every thing I might find out. That I came because I felt pushed into it by Eternity. Drawn to it by her as well.

The de Bonnery château sat in the middle of the village, three stories high and designed like a square with the courtyard in the middle. Centuries ago, a moat probably surrounded the building, but now there was merely a road on one side, and behind, Mamie's sprawling garden. The whole bottom floor was once a stable, and Mamie and Papy had never updated it. You could walk inside, brush away years of cobwebs, and come upon a horseshoe that had been hammered out for a steed from the fifteenth century.

I opened the huge oak door to the château without knocking, but when we walked into the courtyard filled with Mamie's climbing rose-bushes, not yet in bloom, a part of me melted, as it always did.

"*Coucou*, Mamie! We're here!" I called out.

I hadn't seen Mamie Madeleine for nearly two years. She looked frail, vulnerable, though still impeccably dressed.

I caught her in a big American bear hug and she didn't object, as she would have years ago.

"Silly child," she scolded happily in French. "What a delight to see you again, *mon amour*." Her voice cracked slightly with emotion. "And this must be Eternity. *Enchantée*. So good to finally meet you." The last phrase she pronounced in heavy English.

"Wonderful to meet you, Madame de Bonnery. I've heard so much about you for so long." Eternity took my grandmother's hand and shook it warmly, then embraced her with the kisses on each cheek. "And this is for you." She handed my grandmother a brightly covered package of Godiva chocolates.

"Godiva! My favorite. Thank you, dear." Then, "*Allez, les jeunes!* Come inside. You must be starving."

Every visit with Mamie smothered me in the past. Walking into the old château, the smells of years ago assaulted me—a vague musti-ness combined with bleach and percolating coffee. Strong coffee. Mamie had laid out her silver tea set in the small *salon* she used for receiving guests informally. Tea steeped in the silver pitcher. On a sil-ver platter sat delicious breads purchased from the *boulangerie*, a slab of real butter, and Mamie's homemade jams.

"I hope you're still hungry for *petit dejeuner*."

Eternity settled into an antique Louis Philippe chair with faded red upholstery. She had a cup of coffee, then one of tea, tried a slice of each bread plus ate a *pain au chocolat*. She chatted with Mamie in adequate French and immediately accepted Mamie's offer to show her around the château.

As we went from room to room, Mamie explained each piece of furniture and work of art in minute detail while Eternity feverishly took notes. In her mind, I guess, she was Nancy Drew and I was Tintin, investigating each room with its uneven floorboards and stone walls, ancient fireplaces and high ceilings.

"This is the coolest place I've ever seen!" she whispered to me periodically. "I can't believe you lived here."

My room had stone walls, a fireplace, and a huge oak armoire that went from floor to the twelve-foot ceiling. A big window—poorly insulated so that it let in air all winter long—gave a view to the fields and rolling hills beyond. On another wall of my room hung four handmade wooden boxes with glass fronts, which held my knife collection.

"You never told me you collected knives! There must be fifty of them here. Swords, sabers . . ."

". . . a switchblade." I retrieved a small silver pocketknife from one of the boxes.

"The switchblade hidden in Tintin?"

"The very one."

"Oh, Emile. No wonder you have such a big imagination. You grew up in a castle and had a regular armory in your room."

"Thanks to numerous trips to Spain. All the weapons used to be made in Toledo. Now it's filled with tourist shops overflowing with copies."

Eternity wasn't really paying attention. She punched the catch to release the switchblade and whispered, "Tintin."

"I made these boxes in the summer of 1966—it was therapeutic."

She perked up at that. "Why?"

"I used my father's tools. In an odd way, he was with me as I built these things. You see, I have tried to work through all my emotions dealing with him. I've been practicing forgiveness, even if I never understand."

Somehow, admitting this to her in person was harder than writing it in a letter.

She had the right response. She reached over and took my hand,

and our eyes met. "I know you're working on it, Emile. I know it's not easy. Thank you for coming."

Later in the evening, Mamie found me in my room, sitting on my bed and holding the switchblade. "I like your *Eternité*, Emile. She is a lovely, bright girl."

"Yes. Yes, she is, Mamie."

"You like her quite a lot, it seems?"

"Perhaps too much."

"Give it time."

"You sound like Grandma Bridgeman."

"Yes, well, your American grandmother and I have become good friends. We write long letters. We share ideas."

My two grandmothers had met when Grandma came to visit me during my year of military service. Amazingly, they had gotten along famously, to use one of Grandma Bridgeman's words.

"Emile, tomorrow we'll take Eternity on a tour of Croix Rousse and visit the important places of the Resistance. Would she like that?"

"Very much, I'm sure."

She turned to leave, then hesitated, staring at the switchblade in my hand. "Don't tear yourself up with memories, Emile. *S'il te plait*. I hope you can sleep."

The prospect of playing tour guide gave Mamie a new bounce to her step. She wore a beautiful bright blue silk scarf twirled around her neck and a long cashmere coat over her pantsuit. Dear aristocratic Mamie.

We took the bus and then the metro, emerging from underground at a colorful square bustling with people. Mamie began her commentary immediately, a mixture of broken English and French.

"This is the heart of the Croix Rousse neighborhood, Eternity. The *marché* here is very famous, open daily. Lovely and picturesque."

We strolled through the streets, admiring the stands overflowing with fruits and vegetables and early spring flowers. The boxes piled high with strawberries and asparagus made me think of Jake.

"Come, come," Mamie commanded, leading us away from the merchants. "Now you must see one of the most beautiful views over Lyon."

We followed her to a spot high above the gardens of the Montée de la Grande-Côte. Down below us was a steep, cobbled road and red tiled roofs, seemingly stacked one on top of the other. Off to the right in the far distance flowed a slice of the Rhône River.

"There's Fourvière way up on the hill over to the right." I pointed out the white basilica.

"It's breathtaking. All of this!"

Mamie continued on her tour back through the marketplace and onto a street where she pointed out houses from the seventeenth century. Eternity and I ambled along obediently, like schoolchildren out for a field trip. She told us about the silk weaving industry that peaked here in the mid–1800s. We traipsed up and down narrow streets and into tiny parks that gave other breathtaking views of the city below.

"Now for the *traboules*." Mamie winked at me. "The *résistants* weren't the first to use the *traboules* as secret hideouts, Eternity. The Protestants and Catholics hid from each other back in the sixteenth and seventeenth centuries too."

She stopped in front of a small shop. "Look back up the hill. That's where we first started our tour, way up there. Now we are by one of the most famous *traboules*. This shop is where Eugene Pons, a printer, lived and printed subversive literature. And we used this *traboule* to secretly transport the presses and other materials."

Beside the former printing shop was a heavy, imposing wooden door with a round brass handle in the center. We stepped through it into a dark tunnel that soon opened into an inner courtyard.

"This is the typical *canut*—silk weavers—building, the soul of the Croix Rousse."

We followed Mamie through a labyrinth of secret passages twisting through the buildings. The foul odors for which the *traboules* were also known accosted us.

"See what I mean, Eternity. It stinks."

"Yes, but with this much history and intrigue and secrets, I can stand the smell." She scribbled something in her notepad.

Mamie stopped in front of a row of wooden mailboxes attached to a wall right inside a doorway. "We left packages—secret information—in this box, and they were almost immediately picked up by someone else, another *résistant*. One such mailbox was exposed by traitors. The *résistants* continued to put messages in it, and the *boches* came, read the messages, and put them back. For a time, the *résistants* did not know this was happening. That's how Jean Moulin was arrested."

Near the end of Mamie's tour, we went into a silk boutique where the young man, whose family had been in the scarf-making business for generations, explained the whole process. Canopies of joined silk scarves floated above us, waiting to be cut. On the printing blocks on long tables, other scarves were laid out in every color. In the shop upstairs, I purchased a beautiful brightly colored scarf for Eternity.

She put it around her neck immediately and said, "Oh, Emile. It is the perfect gift."

Our tour ended when we stepped off the metro in Caluire and took a bus to a small, tree-lined parking lot.

"We stop here, children. A very important landmark. Do you know it, Emile?"

We walked over to a high stone wall. Peering inside the gate, we saw a courtyard leading to an elegant square house, three stories high, covered in ivy.

"Yes, I visited with Papa. It's the house where Jean Moulin was arrested."

There it was, just as I remembered it, and on the wall a plaque that could be read by every passerby: *On June 21, 1943, Jean Moulin was arrested here.*

Eternity had arranged a meeting in Lyon with a man—she called him M. Terrat—who had supplied her with information about the previous summer's foiled kidnapping attempt of Klaus Barbie. I thought it appropriate that our meeting was near a *traboule*, in the restaurant where Mamie had eaten with Papy shortly before their arrest.

M. Terrat was small, round, and balding, with an intense expression. We ordered drinks, and he gulped his down quickly, offering

small talk for a few minutes, then a story about Lyon during the Occupation. He lit a cigarette. I slid a photo of my father over in front of
him and watched his face.

M. Terrat reached for his glasses, put them over his nose, and studied the picture. His face betrayed nothing, but by the amount of time
he held the photo, I felt sure he must know something.

After a few minutes he cleared his throat. "This is your father, you
say?"

"Yes, Jean-Baptiste de Bonnery. His parents were *résistants*, and my
father helped out too, as a preteen and teenager. He has many stories
of those activities. This picture was taken almost ten years ago."

I couldn't bring myself to ask the next question, so Eternity did.
"Have you ever seen this man?"

"Yes." More clearing of the throat. "Yes. I knew him."

"You *knew* him?" I blurted.

Eternity filled in immediately. "Do you have any idea where he is
now, M. Terrat? Was he part of the plan to kidnap Klaus Barbie in
South America?"

M. Terrat looked at Eternity with what I later understood to be
compassion. At the time, it seemed like a lack of concern or interest.
"No, he was not a part of this plan, Miss Jones. He was not."

"Do you know where he is now? Do you have any idea?" I asked.

He didn't answer directly. "You say you haven't seen him in almost
ten years?"

"Yes. That's right. He disappeared on the night of September 22,
1964. That's the last time I saw him."

The image of Papa's hand covering the hand of the woman in the
café flashed before me. "The month of September 1964 was the last
time I ever saw him."

"I'm sorry to say it, son, but I cannot help you. My best advice is to
forget about trying to find him. I don't think you will have any success."

"Are you saying he's dead? Is that it?"

He stubbed out his cigarette. "I'm sorry. I have no more information to give you." He handed me back the photograph.

I struggled to control my temper. "Almost ten years, and it is always the same response! You *do* know something! Tell me—anything! What do you know?"

M. Terrat, unperturbed, didn't respond.

Eternity took over. "I've been researching the story of the Nazi hunters for articles I've written for an American paper based in Paris. I've met the Klarsfelds and others. Perhaps you could just answer a few questions for us. You understand that we are both naturally eager for any information."

M. Terrat nodded, allowing Eternity to continue.

"Could you please just tell us the last time you saw Jean-Baptiste de Bonnery?"

"The last time I saw this man"—he nodded to the photo—"was in Bolivia, where he was being tried for crimes against the Bolivian government. It was six years ago. He was heading to prison. He was not in good shape." He looked at me. "I believe it would be best for you to think of your father as dead. I am sorry." He stood, shook our hands, and started to leave the restaurant.

Eternity and I sat in shocked silence. Then she recovered and headed after M. Terrat. "What does that mean? Crimes against the Bolivian government?"

M. Terrat stopped, stared at me, and said stiffly, "Ask your grandmother."

That night I gained insight into Eternity's genius as a reporter. Mamie had fixed us a four-course meal, the fire was crackling in the fireplace, classical music played on the stereo. Our conversation started and stopped, each of us preoccupied.

Eternity and I were still recovering from the information about Papa. I couldn't bring myself to broach the subject with Mamie. But after dessert, Eternity the journalist addressed my grandmother in a professional tone, asking her questions as if she never doubted for a moment that she would receive an answer.

"Emile and I spoke with a man today, M. Terrat, who said he saw your son Jean-Baptiste on his way to a Bolivian jail six years ago. He was accused of crimes against the government. Do you have any idea what this means, Madame de Bonnery?"

Mamie's face tightened imperceptibly. "Perhaps. Perhaps I do."

I thought she grew old in that moment.

"There are missing pieces to this puzzle; perhaps you have found another one." She settled onto a small Louis Philippe couch and motioned for me to join her. "The night he told you good-bye, Emile, your father sat on this very same couch and tried to explain his life to me and to your mother. He was terribly afraid. Your father was never a man to show fear. That night I saw fear in his eyes.

"I had suspected for years his activities. Jean-Baptiste had a mind for intelligence work. I never knew if he was with the French or the Germans or the Americans—or perhaps all three. He was like a *traboule*, twisting in and out, much of his life hidden and secret as he looked for former Nazis. His motive was revenge. He lived for it. He made mistakes because of it. He was haunted by a past that no one should live. I have wondered why some of us are allowed to keep living when it means only continued suffering. I have wondered this."

We were facing each other on the small sofa, and I almost wanted to plead with Mamie to stop. This confession was costing her too much—the strain accentuated every wrinkle on her face, left deep pools of sadness in her eyes. It reminded me too closely of Mama's conversation with me the night after I'd discovered the microdot on the watch, the night I had held that wadded paper with Papa's message to me scrawled across it.

"That month of September 1964 he became unusually restless. I knew he was concealing something dangerous. He's my son—I could read it in his eyes. So I asked him one night, 'Jean-Baptiste, what are you planning?'

"'I have to leave, Mama. It's different this time—I will be gone indefinitely.' That was all he said, until the night before he disappeared—the night I saw the fear in his eyes. That night he said to me, 'I'm going. Please, send them away, protect them. Protect yourself.'

"I told him I was not worried for myself, I had lived through a lot. He asked me to help you and your mama get away. I thought he was overreacting, being paranoid, but he showed me notes he had received. The house was being watched. He'd had death threats. So he left, Emile. For your sake, for mine, and your mother's. Don't hate him any longer. It will not help. He did what he thought was best."

She stared at me for so long that Eternity finally asked, "And since that night? Have you heard from him?"

Mamie breathed in deeply; her hands, cupping a mug of *tisane*, shook slightly. "Yes. I heard from him twice. First, in the summer of 1966, shortly after you and your mother visited, Emile. He was in South America. Then almost a year later, in 1967. I didn't hear directly, but several friends—old *résistants*—told me about his arrest in Bolivia. We wrote the government, then your mother and I went down there. We searched through every prison and never found him."

"*What?*"

She set down the mug, spilling a little of the *tisane*. "I know, I know, we should have told you, but you were finishing high school. It was so very disturbing, with no guarantee of news. Your mother and I . . . we thought it wiser to say nothing. Every year or two we'd get our hopes up, only to have them crash around us.

"This M. Terrat was telling you the truth. Jean-Baptiste disappeared to protect you because he had information about Nazis in South America. He went there, knowing of the danger. He must have been in trouble, perhaps someone betrayed him, I don't know. I imagine former Nazis caught up with him. Barbie has worked with that awful dictator Banzer for years. They pinned some horrible crime on Jean-Baptiste and left him to rot in some Bolivian jail! But we never found him. We looked and looked. We had lawyers, very good lawyers.

"I imagine they shot him and left his body in a field. We will never really know." Her eyes filled with tears.

I felt myself sinking into the sofa, wanting to disappear back into August of 1964, before the threats, before the evening of the wristwatch and the conversation on the couch, before the next day in Vieux Lyon with my father's hand on the hand of the beautiful young woman.

———

It was Eternity's suggestion. We rode the funicular up to Fourvière, walked inside the huge, mosaic-filled basilica, and lit a candle for Papa, in his memory. Mamie prayed and cried, and I held her, and then we walked into the daylight and looked out over Lyon, the trees all green again and the two rivers far, far below and the smell of renewal in the air. Something in the act was cleansing and right.

| *twenty-five* |

The day before Eternity was to leave for Paris, I took her to a little restaurant across the river from St. Romain, on the banks of the Saône. We sat outside, warmed by the late March sun. Eternity had the silk scarf I had given her wound loosely around her neck, and it lit up her face with color. We watched the sun twinkling on the water, the breeze tickling the trees. Every once in a while a loud *slap* startled us, and we looked to see white swans poised in flight on the river, their oversized wings smacking the water, their long necks stretched out straight as they gradually gained height.

Something about how we were sitting at the table reminded me of the day I met her, in the cafeteria at Northside High. I had been fascinated and intrigued by her, intimidated and entranced and ultimately grieving for her, for her life and all she had suffered. I had always known that Eternity Jones would survive, and here she was—beautiful, intense, confident, caring. I reached out and took her hand.

She raised her eyes, shielding them from the sun with her other hand. "Are you sorry you came? Sorry for the things we learned about your father?"

"No. I'm not sorry I came." We let the silence warm us. "But I think we've talked enough about my father."

"Yes." She reached across the table and brushed the hair from my face. "You're right, Emile."

"We need to talk about us now, Eternity." My heart was hammering in my ribs.

Her face clouded, and she let go of my hand. "You're right. It's time." She took a sip of coffee, then set the cup in its saucer. "I know you care about me. I know you would like our relationship to move forward, to become more intimate, I suppose. I know." She shook her long mane and buried her face in her hands.

"I can't, Emile! I won't let myself care for you like that. I could care, I could love you. I *do* love you, but I can't be tied down! I want to live my life. I'm going to be a reporter, a journalist, a very good one. I'm on my way, and this is what I really, really want." She touched my hand again, then drew hers back and balled her fists.

"You are going to be the best professor in the world, Emile. You're going to live on a campus with ivy-covered buildings and teach and help and care. But I can't do that. I am going to travel and see, and I am not going to stop for a long, long time, and it just wouldn't be fair to have a relationship. It would be doomed."

"Why?" I demanded, surprised—no, shocked—by her reasoning. Then I felt a tinge of anger. "Why would it be doomed? We understand each other. We love each other. Why?"

A single tear slid down her right cheek. She gave a sad smile. "Oh, Emile. You see through me, don't you? You're right. It's not my job or yours that stands in the way. It's something much more insidious and scary and . . ."

She closed her eyes and struggled to find the words. "How can I explain it to you, Emile? The part of me you see here, the part that is happy and motivated and has found my calling, that is only a part. It's healed. But there's the rest of me, the little girl who remembers all that was done to me, to my siblings. The little girl who grew up way too fast. I'm terrified of that part. I'm so messed up in my head over those boys and men that I doubt I'll ever be normal."

"God can heal anything!" I regretted saying it so quickly, almost as a cliché.

She was shaking her head, crying, pushing her hair out of her eyes.

"Maybe. Maybe someday that part will be healed. I believe in miracles. But it hasn't happened yet."

A nearby duck squawked to her ducklings, and we turned to watch them parade behind her into the water.

"It's strange how it works, Emile. Most of the time, the horrible wounds are pushed way, way down deep in me, buried inside somewhere so I can't feel them. But every once in a while they rise to the top; there they are, like a corpse, like Ophelia floating in the river. And I think I will die. I want to die. The last time I felt that agonizing pain was when Ace McClary apologized to me. I don't want to look at that stuff. Not now. I can't."

I had not prepared myself for her confession. "But you forgave him! We discussed this! Surely you could see someone, Eternity. A psychiatrist or . . . I don't know, a pastor. Someone who can help you continue the process you've begun. I'll go with you. I'll wait. I can wait." I reached across the table to hold her hand.

She pulled it away, staring at me and shaking her head. "Do you know how it feels inside my heart when you touch my hand? At first I feel desire, and then I'm terrified and repulsed. I won't let my past destroy you. I love you too much for that, Emile."

My insides cramped.

She continued. "God can heal anything, and maybe He will someday, but He hasn't yet, and it's too hard and painful and deep. I can't look at my awful past right now. But I'm doing well. If I stay busy doing what I love, I don't have to think about it. I have to stay busy, Emile. That's how I want it right now." Her face had become determined, tense; almost, but not quite, condescending.

"Then why did you invite me here?" I was surprised by the anger in my voice. "Why did you keep insisting on seeing me? If you knew what I was feeling and you knew it was impossible, why did you string me along?"

She stirred her coffee, rubbed her hands over her eyes, and sighed. "Because I love you, Emile. I have always loved you. When I was with you at Vanderbilt, I felt like I'd gotten my better half back. It was as if all the years in between Northside and Vanderbilt were minutes—a few minutes, and we picked up again, still on the same page.

"It was foolish. Selfish. I wanted to believe I would be okay, that I could love you the right way. I shouldn't have pursued it, pursued you. But it's just—we understand each other. I, I prayed it could work out. I really did."

"You know, you might have let me in on your thought process a little earlier in the game." I met her eyes in a way I never expected to look at Eternity Jones. I felt disappointment and anger.

"I'm sorry, Emile," she whispered, her eyes filling again with tears. "You're right to be angry. I hate myself for saying these things."

She looked off into the distance, as if to strengthen her resolve. "But I can't promise anything else. It terrifies me to think of true intimacy. I won't hurt you in that way. I'd rather you hate me than live with me and regret it for the rest of your life." She turned to stare at me, pleading with her eyes.

"Let's live our lives. There's some gorgeous, bright girl for you, someone who can appreciate all of your idiosyncrasies and absolutely adore the French part of you and stand by you and love you. I know there's someone just right for you."

I know it too, I thought, looking straight at her.

"But it isn't me, Emile. I'm so sorry. It isn't me."

We held each other's gaze for a long moment. I wanted to freeze time, as John Keats had done for his lovers in "Ode on a Grecian Urn." But the next minute I was waving to the waiter and paying for our drinks and standing up. Numbness overtook me. We walked to the car in silence. Two swans glided in perfect harmony over the river.

I know I drove her to the Part-Dieu train station the next day. I think she kissed me good-bye on each cheek. I cannot remember the rest, except for thinking to myself, *Off to save the world. That's my Eternity.*

She was running, and to be honest, I didn't think she was running from me. She was running from her past, as she had plainly said, from the shadows of men whose memories had chased her for so long.

I wanted to hold her close and say, "You're safe with me, Eternity. Safe." But since I could not, I sent her off with this prayer: *I'll always be waiting for her, Lord. Let her heal. And when she decides to come back, let me be here.*

That afternoon I drank a whole bottle of the fine red wine I'd bought to drink with her on our last night together. I threw up and woke with a horrible hangover, which seemed a fitting antidote for heartbreak.

Later I found her note slipped under the pillow in my room.

> *Listen, Emile, I'm sorry I have to go. But I know that you of all people understand. I love you. I care. But I just can't be who you need me to be. And I don't know when we'll see each other again. Please, please promise me that you won't wait for me. Find that gorgeous girl and marry her and have a bunch of kids.*
>
> *I have a promise for you, too. I will find out what happened to your father in that Bolivian jail. You may never see me again, Emile, but I will do this one thing for you. I promise.*
>
> *Love,*
Eternity

Mamie found me in my room, staring out the window at a magnolia that had erupted into huge, bright pink and white blooms. "Emile, go home. Finish your degree. You will teach. Later perhaps there is life here. This girl is not for you; this city isn't for you—not now. Go home. Go back to America, for now. It will be okay."

I contemplated Mamie Madeleine, once again all alone in the château. But she was right. I needed to go home.

The Vanderbilt campus should have delighted me—the daffodils tossing their heads in sprightly dance, as Mr. Wordsworth said, the trees in bud, the girls dressed in their miniskirts. I avoided student life by hiding in the basement of the art history building, staring at slides of obese Rubensian women and cursing my existence. I had successfully compartmentalized my life—perhaps not intentionally, but still, it worked. But the compartments entitled *Jean-Baptiste de Bonnery* and *Eternity Jones*, after lying dormant for eight years, had been disturbed.

She had shown up—walked right onto the campus of my life and taken up residence. She had blown apart that tight compartment and sat in front of me for all the world to see. I had not asked for this.

The staff leader of our campus group said once, "Don't go trying to dredge up your past. Who wants to look at all that pain again if it isn't necessary? But if it comes knocking on your door, you are probably going to need to invite it in and have a discussion over a good meal."

Well, there. That's what I had done. I had looked it over. Looked *her* over. I liked what I saw. I thought this was a turn in the path, a good choice. I was less sure with my father, but I was willing to peek, willing to crawl out of that foxhole in France and see what was over the hill, even if it meant ugly realities like betrayal and unfaithfulness.

Even if it meant accepting my father's death.

But after all the time and emotional energy invested in these two relationships, everything remained a mystery. Nothing was accomplished except ripping the scab off the wound and letting it bleed and bleed and bleed. And what good had that done? Now I was furious with Eternity, and I was mourning a presumably dead father. I felt more alone than ever.

Outside Vanderbilt's beautiful red-brick library, seven stories high, I stood on the vast lawn alone, with only the moon looking down on me. The campus worship service was over and I felt like a hypocrite, singing those hymns and choruses with all the anger boiling inside. I threw my arms into the sky and shook my fist at the heavens. "Now what am I supposed to do? Just forget them again?"

I stared up into the black sky and saw only a melon slice of white moon and a handful of stars. Silence and mystery. Grandma had always said that suffering etched character into God's people, making them stronger, better, holier, more useful to God and man. I had believed her for many years, but I did not see it on this night.

Maybe what you should be looking for isn't Eternity or your father but the emotions they provoke. Maybe that's what God wants you to deal with right now.

Who had said that? Someone had spoken it out loud, I was sure. No, I had *felt* rather than heard the words. A chill spiked through me, like a gust of wind. The conviction that truth had floated out in the April air for me to hear did not leave me, even as I walked across campus to the Towers and let myself into the suite. Three of my suite mates were watching a rerun of *Hogan's Heroes* on TV.

I went into my room, got out my prayer journal, and simply wrote: *Okay, then, what? Now that I am in this situation, now that my heart is bleeding, what do I do next? And when You answer that question, Lord, could You please also tell me* how?

Late one night before my last exam, the one on the history of the Reformation in Europe, I was drinking a cup of coffee in the divinity school, reading over my notes, when I came to a quote from Martin Luther. *"I have held many things in my hands, and I have lost them all. But whatever I have placed in God's hands, that I still possess."*

In an instant, I remembered a scene from my youth back at Grandma's house, shortly after Eternity and Blithe had been sent to foster care. I was angry, and Grandma took my hands in hers and slowly pried open my balled-up fists.

"I know it seems wrong and cruel. But this is what you must do. Let go. Give up the control, Emile. Be mad, grieve, accept that you cannot figure it out. Give up."

"Giving up is weakness!"

"This time it will be strength."

"How?"

"You must give up, not out of resignation, but out of trust. Trust that God knows and cares and will let you in on all the secrets you need to know in His time."

I shook myself out of the memory, sipped the coffee, and, heavy-eyed, turned back to my notes, but I could no longer concentrate. I walked outside to clear my head. It was a starless night.

"Okay, Eternity," I said aloud. "Live your life. I won't be angry with you any longer. I forgive you for not being able to . . ." *To what? Heal?* "For needing time and living your own life and setting me free. And you, Papa. I forgive you for being eaten up with revenge and for running away. I'm moving on. Without either of you."

I walked circles around the divinity school, quoting Scriptures I had memorized years ago. *"The anger of man does not achieve the righteousness of God. . . . Do not anxiously look about you, for I am your*

God. . . . I will not fail you or forsake you. . . . Be strong and courageous.
Do not tremble or be dismayed, for the Lord your God is with you wher-
ever you go."

I cannot say that the anger disappeared. Perhaps dissipated is the
better word. I felt a scattering of the emotions, a lessening of a need
to control and an opening up of all that had been stuck inside.

———————

I graduated from Vanderbilt with honors in the spring of 1974
and enrolled in their master's program in literature for the following
fall. I spent the summer between in Atlanta, back in the gray shingled
house on Anjaco Road. On this visit, my first matter of business was
with Mama. I had shared very little with her by letter or phone, or
even when she came for my graduation, of my time in Lyon. I wanted
to speak with her face-to-face and see her reactions to my questions.

I took her out to eat at a restaurant at Lenox Square called The
Magic Pan. We ordered the specialty, crêpes, which seemed a fitting
meal for a discussion about my time in France. I told Mama about
Eternity's discovery of the Klarsfelds and their attempt to arrange Barbie's kidnapping, and then I told her about our meeting with M. Terrat and his claim to have seen Papa in Bolivia in 1967—on his way to
jail.

Mama was nodding, her finger tracing the outline of her eyebrow.
"Mamie Madeleine told you, didn't she? We looked for him, Emile.
We looked in every putrid jail we could find. I couldn't tell you. I
could not get your hopes up. It was too disturbing, too horrible."

"But you know he's dead, then?"

She nodded.

"Oh, Mama, you should have told me that! Years ago."

"Yes. Perhaps. But Emile, I had no proof of his death, and I
couldn't bear for you to go down there looking for him. I knew you
would. I was afraid I would lose you too. It was all so twisted in my
mind."

I pushed aside my plate and reached across the table, taking her
hand in mine. "And if you know he's dead, Mama, why do you refuse
to date other men? Why do you live here like an old spinster—with

Grandma? Two widows! Why don't you build another life?"

She pulled her hand back. "Because I still love him, Emile. I'll always love him, and I don't want another life." Her eyes did not meet mine. "I guess I like the thought of giving back to my mother the years we lost. I have no desire to remarry. Emile, you are young and bright, and life is opened before you. Let this rest."

"Eternity will never let it rest."

"Then she can keep pursuing the Nazis. You study and live and find someone to love. Please, Emile. I'm so proud of you."

"It didn't work with Eternity, Mama."

"I gathered that by your silence. I'm so sorry."

I could tell she wanted to say something else. I saw the motherly pain on her face, the desire to make things easier, better for me.

"How are you doing?"

"Ups and downs. It's hard to forget. I had my hopes up."

"Yes. It is always more painful when we get our hopes up, isn't it?"

———

I worked at an advertising agency that summer during the day and waited tables at night, my goal to earn enough money to pay for part of the master's program at Vanderbilt. I attended Second-Ponce de Leon Baptist Church on Sundays and volunteered at the church gym, helping to coach a summer soccer league. Griffin, who had graduated from the University of Georgia the year before, came back to Atlanta for the summer to work before starting grad school. He helped with the soccer team, as did Ace, who had recently graduated from Georgia Tech. I found it pleasantly ironic that the Mexican, the Frenchman, and the redneck racist of yesteryear were all working together in a church gym, coaching kids from rough family backgrounds.

Ace and I were alone in the gym, mopping the floor one Friday in late June, when he said out of the blue, "I was awful to Eternity, Emile. I regret it every day of my life, what I did to that family. I added shame to their misery. And I can't ever make it right."

Unsure of what to do with this information, I mumbled, "You tried."

"Too little, too late." He kicked the wooden bleachers, and they made a racket. "I should have gone to jail—for what I did to her and what I did to Edward Hasty. I should be rotting there right now."

Ace McClary, the picture of athletic prowess, stood leaning on a mop, trembling. "She forgave me, Emile. She's an amazing woman— she forgave me."

"Then accept that forgiveness, Ace. Accept it as the gift it is." I patted him on the back.

I thought we were done with the conversation, but Ace needed to say one more thing. "Emile, I was awful to you back then too, and I never had the guts to say I was wrong. I'm sorry. I really am."

He reached out his hand hesitantly. For that brief instant, Ace was the underdog. He was once again that puffy-faced teen, crying at the campfire.

I took his hand. His grasp was strong, desperate. I looked at him, and he gave me a pained smile.

"Ace, I forgave you a long time ago." I pumped his hand firmly, smiling with confidence. "It's over," I said. "It's done."

───────

My feelings for Eternity ebbed and flowed, but I knew the intensity would gradually fade—even though, because of her profession, I heard from or about her rather often. She came back to the States and worked as a journalist; she was in the news. *Reporting* the news, that is, objectively yet courageously—whether it was the Supreme Court's *Roe vs. Wade* decision on abortion or the aftereffects of Watergate or a seemingly minor political squabble in Georgia. Her letters to me during the mid-seventies were sporadic, but probably every three months at least, I'd get an article with her byline in my mailbox, sent with good intentions by Grandma or Blithe or Mama or even Eternity herself. So the wound never did have time to heal.

Eternity could not love me as a wife, and I eventually began dating other women. But in the recesses of memory, Eternity was with me. I pictured her in Boston, where she did a stint at Harvard, or in Paris again, where she spent two years, or in South America, where I was sure she traveled, probably on some clandestine mission. Someday she would heal, too. Someday she would let her heart be vulnerable, and another man would fill it. I could have waited for her forever, if I had thought she would wait back.

When she kept looking for news of Papa, I knew those articles were her way of showing me the love she couldn't give in any other form. Often I was tempted to grab a pen and scribble an angry letter—*I don't give a rip about what happened to my father. He's dead. But you are alive. You are still a possibility. If you could only give the emotion you put into your journalism to me, oh, Eternity, it could work. I know it could.*

But I never wrote her those letters. Instead, I gave her news of my master's program, told her about the private high school where I taught French part time, about my "starving student days" as I tried to pay bills. I sent her two articles I had published in literary magazines. When I enrolled in the PhD program, still at Vandy, she wrote, chiding me that I was in love with country music and for that reason refused to leave Nashville.

In 1979 I purchased a little house not far from the campus; I told her that halfway through my doctoral program I had begun teaching several classes at a small university forty-five minutes from Nashville in a town called Murfreesboro. I told her about those first classes as a teaching assistant and how right it felt to be communicating the truth in literature to my students.

I wrote about Mama launching a summer program to take North-side students to France and about Grandma's brush with skin cancer and the way she had to wear special sunscreen on her face and neck—in addition to the straw hat—whenever she was out in her garden.

I told her about the Christian student group I sponsored on campus and the fresh faith of the kids and the way they challenged my own faith. And I told Eternity that Blithe, now nineteen, had suddenly picked up her pen in the summer of 1978 and started writing me long letters once a month.

But I never told her that I was still waiting for her. And gradually, once again, our correspondence waned and then stopped completely.

October 1980

Hey, Emile, I was thinking about coming to visit you next

weekend. I've got a break from college and thought it might be fun to catch up.

What do you say?

Speak soon,
Blithe

Dear Blithe,

It would be my pleasure to see you! The only snag is that there's a symposium at Vanderbilt this weekend, and I have two lectures to give on Saturday. You're welcome to attend, but they may bore you to death. At any rate, I'd enjoy taking you out for dinner Saturday night.

Looking forward to it,
Emile

I hadn't seen Blithe in five years, and in my mind she was still a young teen. So when we met on Rand Terrace on a Saturday morning that fall, my shock was great. Her hair was still fluffy and blond, but worn in a sassy style. She dressed provocatively, with a tight T-shirt and her miniskirt hitched up high to show off her long, slender legs.

"Hey, Prof!" she said, and the tone was familiar, flirtatious. She touched me easily—my shoulder, my hand, my face, with her fingers. She laughed, but not a carefree laugh. Perhaps a rehearsed laugh, one she'd learned for a play.

I struggled through small talk over a cup of coffee, my thoughts flitting from my lectures to our shared past in Atlanta and then screeching to a halt in front of this strange young woman sitting across from me.

Blithe attended both lectures, the one on faith and the modern classics and then a debate on faith and fiction.

"Sorry to have bored you, Blithe," I commented as we left the lecture hall.

"Not bored, Emile. You did a good job. You know your stuff."

We ate dinner at a cozy restaurant near campus, but the conversation I had imagined with Blithe did not come to pass. She was not interested in discussing faith or literature.

She ordered a vodka and Coke, drank it quickly, and ordered another. She ate quickly too, then talked loudly about school and weekend parties that ended with her passed out in some guy's room. She seemed intent on communicating shocking information. I listened quietly, an old gnawing pain gradually spreading throughout me.

"Hey, is there anywhere we can go for a drink?" she asked.

"You've had several drinks already."

She laughed and reached across the table, kissing my hand. Then she began to play with my fingers.

I pulled my hand away. "Blithe, what are you doing?"

"Trying to seduce you, darling. Do you mind?" She leaned over the table as if to kiss me.

I pushed her away. "Blithe!"

She pouted. "Can't you tell I've grown up! You're not afraid of me, are you? Come on, Emile. You're not still waiting on Eternity, are you? She isn't coming back. Get over her."

I paid our bill and we walked outside and crossed the street onto Vanderbilt's campus. "What's happened to you, Blithe?"

She laughed her scary laugh and slurred her words. "What happened to me? Don't you know, Emile?" She grabbed on to me again. "How dare you ask that question when you *know* the answer!"

She plopped herself down on a bench and motioned for me to join her. "I was in the room, trying not to hear, when Eternity was raped one awful night. My mother beat me, time and again. Then I watched her kill my brother—swatting him like a fly. Little by little I died, Emile. That's what happened to me. And no God in heaven did one thing to stop any of it!

"It was Jake's idea about being baptized and all. I knew he never would have walked down that aisle alone, so I went too. For Jake. I believed, Emile, but it was Jake's idea." Then she whispered, "And look what happened to poor Jake."

She took out a cigarette and with shaky fingers lit it. "And the voice I heard over and over and over in my head just kept saying it was all my fault. Ma's voice, screaming at me, telling me everything in our awful, screwed-up life was my fault.

"So I decided I'd just go for the fun part of life. Don't worry. I'm doing well in school. I party hard on the weekends, but I keep my grades up. I won't lose my hard-earned scholarship. But I will not live with those accusing voices. I have to drown them out, Emile. Won't you help me?"

I literally felt sick to my stomach, seeing Blithe so calloused and destroyed, talking about her life as if it were a cheap, trashy novel. "Oh, Blithe," I whispered, a catch in my throat. "I'm sorry. I'm so sorry."

"Don't be sorry. It's just life."

"It wasn't your fault, Blithe."

She blew the cigarette smoke away.

I grabbed her by her shoulders, as if I could shake every horrible memory out of her. "It was not your fault. You hear me? Look at me, Blithe!"

Her eyes brimmed with tears.

"You grew up in a horrible situation, and terrible things happened. It's okay to be mad about it. It's okay to be furious with Jesus. He can take it. But deep inside, Blithe, there's still that pure heart of yours. Once you've run out of ways to be angry, come back, okay? Will you promise me you'll come back?"

We sat on that bench from dusk till pitch night, and she held on to me for dear life, bawling her eyes out. I held on to her too, praying, *Show me what to do, Lord. Show me what to do.*

And the only answer that came was *Hold her for a while longer.*

The next morning I walked her to her Honda Civic, putting her small duffel bag in the trunk. "We'll get together again, Blithe. Okay?"

"Thank you, Emile. I'm sorry I was so awful. I must have freaked you out completely. You always thought of me as an angel, didn't you? Well, I guess you can tell I've plummeted."

"I guess we all have to plummet before we realize how much we need to get under bigger wings. Find shelter there. Will you promise me, Blithe, that you'll find help? Someone to talk to at school?"

"Can't I keep writing you? You understand."

"Sure. Sure you can. But find someone at school. Someone wise."

She kissed me softly on the lips, burst into tears again, and hugged me tight. "We'll never be normal, will we, Emile? Eternity and me?"

"Shh . . ."

"I wish she could love you. She doesn't deserve you, Emile. But I wish she could."

She put on her sunglasses, got in the car, and drove away. As I watched her leave, I thought to myself how Eternity continued to love me through her work, but Blithe had shown up in person and, from somewhere in her tormented soul, loved me desperately as the big brother and the nameless father and the idealized lover she did not have.

That night I dreamed a dream I had had before. I was standing in Grandma Bridgeman's yard—actually, I was kneeling. I think it was to plant a bulb or maybe to dig up a weed. But the *me* that was above and looking down on the *me* that was kneeling realized I wasn't gardening. I was praying. Crying, petitioning, begging. I couldn't see my lips moving, but I somehow knew the distress and I felt chilled and afraid, wanting to find out what was causing me to sob, and at the same time, not wanting to know.

Then it hit me like a forceful intake of cold wind. Jake. I was petitioning for Jake. Where was he? The *me* in the air circled the garden and searched, while the *me* on my knees remained there crying and praying. Jake. Where was he? Then I saw him, lying completely still on the ground, by the strawberry plants.

I ran to him, but Blithe got there first and then Eternity, and they were pulling on him and begging him to wake up. Then they saw me standing there and grabbed me, crying, weeping.

Suddenly I was hurtling toward something, being drawn—no, pushed—I couldn't tell. But moving fast and smoothly through another dimension, something bright and full. And as I hurtled through this undefined space, my mouth was open and I was pleading with Eternity and Blithe to come with me, come along. Then someone was rushing toward me, pulling me and lifting me up toward myself, yes, but not myself, toward something fuller and better and brighter.

| *twenty-six* |

On a dreary evening in January 1983, I was watching the evening news, alone in my Nashville home, hungry and tired from the day's work. I had finished my PhD and gotten the job I'd always dreamed of, teaching at a small Christian liberal arts university in Nashville. I enjoyed interacting with the students and helped coach the men's and women's soccer teams. Occasionally I taught classes as a visiting professor at Vanderbilt. And I dated women, several fine women, strikingly pretty, caring, supportive women, each in her own way. Why couldn't I ever get up the nerve to ask one to be my wife?

I was eating a piece of leftover pizza and wishing it were *blanquette de veau*. The story came near the end of the NBC program. Jessica Savitch, the news reporter, was standing in a town square, talking excitedly over the commotion around her. "It appears that the infamous Butcher of Lyon, Klaus Barbie, has been located here in La Paz, Bolivia. Living under the assumed name of Klaus Altman, the former Nazi official who was responsible for thousands of assassinations and deportations during World War II has at last been located, after having disappeared nearly forty years ago. . . ."

I tried to concentrate on what she was saying, but my breathing came hard. I scooted close to the TV screen, caught a glimpse of the monster, and shuddered. *Maybe now it can be over. Finally, it can be over.*

I dialed the phone number in Atlanta automatically. "Mama, turn on the news! Hurry!"

"We're watching, Emile," she whispered.

"Maybe finally we'll get more answers at last."

"Maybe, son. Time will tell."

I wanted to remind her that time did *not* tell. At least in this matter, time had kept secrets, many secrets.

Then it was Grandma Bridgeman's voice I heard, the voice of twenty years ago. *"Emile, you know there is more to life than looking for answers. Some answers you will never find—some you will. As long as the most important question is answered, the 'not knowing' of the others doesn't seem so unbearable."*

Of course I was thinking about Papa, but at the same time I was thinking of Eternity, wondering if she was down in Bolivia, if she had helped them locate the Butcher. *You may never see me again, Emile, but I will do this one thing for you. I promise.*

I could not eat stale pizza or grade finals or anything else. I sat as if in a trance while the TV screen switched to a commercial. *I did what you said, Grandma. I gave it up. I gave it over. Left it for years. But it is back.* I got off the couch, grabbed my raincoat, and headed for the door as if I could just drive to the airport and catch a plane from Nashville to Bolivia.

What was I thinking? But I had to do something.

I went to my study and took out the thin hardback comic book. Tintin, my boyhood hero. I let the book fall open to the middle, stared at the mutilated pages, squeezed my eyes shut, and said out loud, as if in prayer, "Let it be over. Please let it be over."

I thought about how Eternity had held the switchblade when she visited the château in 1974. I had long since brought it back with me to the States, and I kept it, along with *The Black Island* and every other treasure, no longer hidden, but displayed inside those handmade wooden boxes I had retrieved from the château. On one bookshelf I had my complete collection of hardback Tintin comic books, all twenty-three volumes. Beside them I kept a photo album—the kind with the clear plastic over sticky pages—in which I had stored every newspaper article written by Eternity over the past ten years that gave information about Nazi criminals or the Resistance or the Klarsfelds.

I took the album off the shelf, leafed through it, and began reading the articles, the ones that were her voice to me since we'd said good-bye in the spring of 1974 at the Part-Dieu train station in Lyon.

1975

BEATE ON THE MOVE

By Eternity Jones

Beate Klarsfeld returned to the Middle East to campaign in defense of the Jewish communities in Syria and Iraq. In Cairo, she disclosed that Hans Schirmer, head of the Euro-Arab cooperation program, had served as second-in-command of Hitler's international radio propaganda service. Klarsfeld was arrested when she visited Beirut and was expelled from Lebanon. . . .

September 3, 1978

KLAUS BARBIE, "BUTCHER OF LYON," UNREPENTANT

By Eternity Jones

Seen in Bolivia and brought in for questioning in La Paz, Klaus Barbie (living under the assumed name of Klaus Altman) was completely unrepentant about the mass crimes of torture and murder he committed during the Second World War. One witness said, "He stood there with a cynical grin on his wicked face, his eyes cold and hard as marbles. He is a monster, not a man. . . ."

December 14, 1978

FROM VICHY, WITH LOVE?

By Eternity Jones

The Klarsfelds have launched a concerted effort to break the immunity enjoyed for more than thirty years by former Vichy officials who worked with the Nazis to organize the deportations of Jews from France. Their focus is on René Bousquet, Vichy's chief of the National Police. . . .

1979

KLARSFELDS CONTINUE BATTLE, OPPOSITION HEATS UP

By Eternity Jones

As a result of Serge Klarsfeld's accusations, René Bousquet has been forced to resign from the board of the Indo-Suez Bank and many of his other posts, and Jean Leguay was the first person to be indicted in France for crimes against humanity. . . .

There has been a new attempt on the lives of the Klarsfeld family: a time bomb completely destroyed their car and damaged twenty others parked near it in Paris. . . .

1979

LISCHKA TRIAL IN GERMANY

By Eternity Jones

Kurt Lischka, Herbert Hagen, and Ernst Heinrichsohn are on trial in a German court in Cologne for their crimes against Jews in France. Among the lawyers in the courtroom is Serge Klarsfeld, representing hundreds of Jewish families whose members were deported to their deaths by the three former Nazi officials. . . .

August 1981

MEMORIALS BY KLARSFELDS

By Eternity Jones

This could be called "The Year of Memorials" for Serge and Beate Klarsfeld. In March the Klarsfelds organized the first one-day pilgrimage to Auschwitz by French Jews; two planeloads of members of deportees' families made the sad journey to Poland. In June the families and the Klarsfelds dedicated a monument to Jews deported from France in Roglit, Israel. It bears the names, birthplaces, and dates of the 80,000 French victims. Around the monument, 80,000 trees have been planted as a Forest of Remembrance. . . .

I closed my eyes, replaced the album, and waited for the inevitable. I had a strong conviction that Eternity Jones would show me what to do next.

Barbie's arrest gave me the perfect opportunity to tie current events with literature of the past. One day in late January I changed my lecture, and instead gave a talk about Dietrich Bonhoeffer.

"Bonhoeffer was a German pastor who was heavily involved in opposing Hitler's treatment of the Jews," I told the class of sophomore students. "He was arrested in April 1943 and ultimately hanged for his part in a failed conspiracy to assassinate Hitler. During his first year of imprisonment, he wrote fiction and poetry as well as letters to his family."

I wanted my students to know the courage of one man in the face of Nazism. I wanted, I needed them to read of hope, of the resolve that results from true faith, even as images of Klaus Barbie and his heinous crimes flashed across their television screens night after night.

On that day, I stood before the class and read Bonhoeffer's poem "Who Am I?"

". . . Am I then really that which
other men tell of?
Or am I only what I myself
know of myself?
. . . Am I one person today and tomorrow another?
Am I both at once?
A hypocrite before others,
and before myself a contemptibly woebegone weakling. . . ?"

The students did not speak when I finished reading the poem. Did they see the tears in my eyes?

"The apostle Paul described this battle with self in the seventh chapter of his epistle to the Romans. Throughout history, those who hold to the Christian faith have written of their struggles, their questionings. I find great comfort in Bonhoeffer's conclusion: 'O God, I am Thine!'"

To my assignment that they write a poem describing their struggles with faith, my students wrote the testimony of their hearts.

Eternity was right. I loved my profession, especially when faith, history, and literature blended in such an obvious way.

I continued my teaching routine throughout the end of January and the first week in February with an eye on the television and the newspapers. Over the next few weeks there was no shortage of information about Klaus Barbie. What was revealed shocked and angered the American public.

Eternity's articles, held together with a paper clip and tucked into manila envelopes, reached me quickly. One more batch of love letters, written on newsprint . . .

February 8, 1983

FORMER U.S. INTELLIGENCE OFFICER
SAYS BARBIE HIRED BY AMERICA
By Eternity Jones

Arrested on January 25, Klaus Barbie, former head of the Gestapo in Lyon, was put on a plane to French Guyana on February 5. There he was arrested and sent to the destination he dreaded most: France. Since the statute of limitations on Barbie's war crimes convictions has run out, France will put him on trial on a new charge, crimes against humanity.

Even as Barbie was being arrested in Guyana, an American professor, Erhard Dabringhaus, was giving an interview on NBC TV. Shocking millions of TV viewers, Dabringhaus said that after World War II, U.S. intelligence had employed Barbie, paying him $1,700 a month. How did Dabringhaus know this? Because as a U.S. Army Intelligence (CIC) officer, he had been Barbie's handler in conquered Germany in 1948. According to Dabringhaus, the U.S. financed Barbie's escape to Bolivia. . . .

February 1983

THE RATLINE
By Eternity Jones

It has long been suspected by high officials in France and America that Klaus Barbie, along with dozens of other Nazis, was smuggled out of Europe through a ratline.

"Ratline" is a nautical term referring to the rope ladder reaching to the top of a ship's mast—considered the last place of safety when a ship was going down. The term was used for the different operations and networks that carried out the rescue of some of the worst mass murderers in European history, including Klaus Barbie.

In 1946, Kurt Merck, a former member of the Abwehr, was engaged by the U.S. as a spy. As a member of the regular German army, and not the SS, Merck did not have war crimes on his head. In 1947 Merck proposed that Barbie be hired by the U.S. Army's Counter Intelligence Corps to run a network aimed at spying on the Communists. His proposal was accepted.

Whether through incompetence or deliberation, the CIC never looked into Barbie's past. No matter how Barbie got admitted, the fact is he was very important to the counter intelligence and knew more about the Americans' methods and way of working than did many of their own agents.

Eventually French intelligence agents, while seeking Barbie's arrest on charges of torture and murder, picked up his scent. But in 1949 the CIC contacted a Croatian priest, Dr. Draganovic, who ran a Vatican ratline that helped hundreds of Nazi SS officers escape from Europe. In 1951, this priest arranged papers and transportation for Klaus Barbie to flee from Germany to Italy, and from there to Argentina and Bolivia. . . .

Tucked in among the newspaper articles was a letter from Eternity.

Dear Emile,

As you can see, my up-until-now personal interest in Barbie and his story has now turned into a full-time job. Klaus Barbie's name is mentioned everywhere. I hope it isn't too painful for you to read these things. Well, of course it is painful. What I mean is, I hope I am not being insensitive by sending you my articles.

I pray that life is treating you well.

Love,

Eternity

The day that Barbie arrived in France, the famous newspaper *Le*

Monde proclaimed *He Is Going to Pay at Last!* The French government had finally captured Klaus Barbie, and he was going on trial for his crimes against humanity. Yes, perhaps it was over. I let out my breath. I put Eternity's articles in the album with the others. The waiting had paid off.

But the rest of February left me chilled, and not because of the abundant snow that surprised the campus. She had finished her mission. Eternity Jones owed me nothing else.

Spring hovered around the corner. In April I was presented with a small award for my writing and research on eighteenth-century French poets. And I was dating a woman who seemed to like me a lot. Why, why did I feel that sudden sadness, as if the book was completed but I didn't like the last chapter?

I had prayed for it to be over when I'd heard the first report on NBC. Never before had I felt so disappointed in an answered prayer.

But I was wrong—in Eternity's mind, Barbie's arrest was not the end, but simply the last act before the climax and denouement. She kept her word—filling my mailbox with articles sent from Lyon, where she was on assignment with *The Paris Insider* to cover the Barbie trial.

February 1983

THE BUTCHER IN PRISON

By Eternity Jones

The old man appeared to be just another typical prisoner, reading newspapers, cleaning out his cell along with the other men. In fact, Klaus Barbie, 69, who was imprisoned in Lyon this week, was extraordinary in every way: a sadist, a murderer, a man who had aptly earned his nickname 'The Butcher of Lyon' for his reign of terror during World War II. During his two years in Lyon (1942–44) he reveled in torturing Resistants, thought nothing of tearing a baby from his mother's arms and dashing him on the floor, or locking one hundred teenagers into their schoolhouse and burning it down with dynamite. . . .

> Two weeks ago, when handed over to the French
> police by Bolivia's new government after three decades
> in exile, Barbie was as unrepentant as ever. "What is
> there to regret?" he told an interviewer. "I am a con-
> vinced Nazi . . . and if I had to be born a thousand times,
> I would be a thousand times what I have been. . . ."

The preparations for the trial dragged on and on, month after
month, article by article from every newspaper imaginable. Of course
I read them all. But four years would pass before Klaus Barbie would
finally be brought to trial.

Blithe kept her word as well. She wrote me letters. Many, many
letters. And she got help—from a psychologist, from a pastor's wife,
from a group of Christians on her school campus. At first her letters
were all about venting her anger. Getting it out. But gradually, I read
hope between the lines.

She graduated from college in 1981 with a degree in marketing,
worked for two years with a company in Ohio, and then went to business school in the Northeast. We did not see each other, but her letters
arrived from time to time.

September 28, 1986
Hey Emile,

I've landed a job in Atlanta! I'm so excited to be coming home—
back to the South, where people talk slowly and winter is mild. I
hope we can see each other sometime. Will you come to Atlanta for
the holidays? Will you stay at the house on Anjaco? Eternity is stuck
in France with the Barbie trial. Could we get together? I won't
pounce on you, I promise.

Love,
Blithe

We met at Cumberland Mall in the late afternoon in mid-Decem-
ber, the day I arrived in Atlanta after giving my last exam. She had
Christmas shopping to do, and we agreed to look around before dinner.
I saw her from a distance, standing with her back to me, looking

down at the fountain. She was wearing faded jeans and had on a puffy blue coat. I recognized her by her hair—that soft, fluffy blond hair. She turned and spotted me and waved enthusiastically, her face lighting up in a smile that reminded me of her angel days, so long ago.

We strolled around the mall, engaging in small talk. She purchased several gifts, then we went across the street from the mall to a steak house. She took off her coat and was wearing a light blue sweater, the color of her eyes, and a simple strand of pearls. She looked elegant and pure.

We ordered steaks and salads and talked about her master's program, her new job, my classes, the course I was preparing on modern European literature.

Halfway through the meal, Blithe commented, "This is a little different from the last time we got together all those years ago—when was it, 1980? I know we've written about it, but I just need to say in person that I'm sorry I was such a jerk."

I wiped the napkin across my mouth. "No problem, Blithe."

"Thank you for insisting I get help. Thank you for being my dartboard for a while."

I closed one eye, feigning injury. "It was rough, but hey, I survived."

"You don't want to talk serious, do you, Emile?"

"What do you mean?"

"Are you still waiting on Eternity?"

Her question caught me off guard. "Waiting on Eternity? What do you mean? She's great about sending me her articles, but we haven't talked in years."

"That's not what I meant. I want to know if you're still in love with her."

I felt uncomfortably hot. Blithe was right. I wasn't interested in a deep discussion, especially not about Eternity Jones.

"I'm not still in love with your sister. Who knows if I ever was? Why do you ask?"

"Because you seem to be waiting around for something. Or someone."

I shrugged. "What do you want me to say? Haven't found the right woman, that's all."

"Do you date?"

"Sure. In fact, I just ended a relationship that lasted almost six months. That was a record for me." I heard the bitterness in my own voice.

"Why'd you end it?"

"Aren't you nosy, young lady?"

She didn't smile.

"She didn't have the disease that Eternity and I talked about on the very first day we met."

Blithe frowned. "What in the world are you talking about?"

"She didn't have *culture*. A wonderful woman—but she never could understand the other part of me."

We said good-bye in the parking lot, and she drove away in her little car. As I was walking back to mine, it struck me, the whole meaning of this evening, the questions, and the confessions. Blithe wanted to know if I was fair game. Men are obtuse.

I called her the next week, asked her to attend Second-Ponce de Leon's Christmas pageant with me. We spent time together during the Christmas holidays, seeing old movies, driving around neighborhoods we liked, admiring the Christmas decor. During the whole month, I never touched her, never held her hand or even kissed her cheek. I hadn't forgotten Eternity's words, which seemed to apply equally to Blithe—"*When you touch me, first I feel desire and then fear and repulsion.*" I had determined that Blithe would make the first move.

On our last date before I returned to Nashville, she leaned over and kissed me on the mouth. "Thank you for waiting on me," she whispered. "I won't hurt you, Emile. I'm okay now. I won't play with your heart. I promise."

| *twenty-seven* |

I sat in my study, head in my hands, staring at the opened envelope on my desk and the letter beside it, which I had just read for the third time.

"Emile! Are you coming? We're going to be late. That wouldn't do—to have the honored guest, Professor de Bonnery, showing up *en retard.*"

I was thankful for Blithe's cheerfully reprimanding voice calling from downstairs, calling me to the present, breaking the tightness that had been creeping across my chest.

You could just wad it up and throw it in the trash can.

The thought surprised me, astounded me, and I answered myself aloud. "Impossible! Not after all these years! I need to respond."

So it was settled. I would answer the letter. But not yet.

Blithe could not see it. I grabbed *The Complete Works of Shakespeare* off the shelf and thrust the envelope and its contents inside the heavy volume.

First I'd go downstairs and out the door with Blithe to the dinner party. But later, when I was alone, I would come back to this room and sit at this desk and read the letter. Then I would know what to do.

This was how I consoled myself as I closed the door with a glance at the switchblade and *The Black Island,* my "treasures" that hung so innocently on the study wall.

When we returned from the evening out, I drove Blithe to the house of a friend, who was putting her up for the weekend. Blithe rested her head on my shoulder in the car and said, "Your speech was perfect, Emile—humor, intellect, humility."

"Fooled them all, didn't I?"

I pulled into the drive and parked the car. She kissed me softly on the mouth. "You seem very preoccupied for a professor who's just been given a rather prestigious award and named head of the department. You okay?"

"Yeah. Just a bit tired—maybe it's all the attention. And I have some work to catch up on."

"Tonight, Emile? Isn't it a bit late? Surely it can wait until tomorrow." She gave me one of those dog-eyed pleading looks that women have mastered through the ages—a look that sometimes might be read as a precursor to seduction, and at other times just a pout. I did not have the mental resources to decipher it at the moment.

"I have to, Blithe. I'll pick you up for church at nine, okay?" We walked to the door, and I kissed her forehead.

She encircled my waist with her arms and, leaning on my chest, sighed, "If you insist."

I had never been able to explain to Blithe how I felt about Eternity. Perhaps it was because I wasn't sure myself. Of course, I never wanted Blithe to feel she was a side dish—that since I couldn't have the main course, I had chosen her. So I generally avoided the topic altogether. Our relationship was rocky enough without the added burden of her older sister.

Somehow, in spite of my attraction and true concern and love for Blithe, and hers for me, something about it always felt . . . unhealthy. As if I were dating my little sister, or maybe as if Blithe were holding on to me as a father. But I had no real conviction from above, no "word from the Lord," as the pastor of my Nashville church would say, as to what I should do. I *did* have pages in my prayer journal filled with my rambling thoughts, my deep questioning.

One thing was sure: neither Blithe nor I had told Eternity about us. That felt heavy and unhealthy, too.

Back home, I looked for the envelope on my desk, impatient to see if the letter was real or if I had imagined the whole thing. It took forever—an eternity, I thought smugly—for me to remember where I'd put it. I truly was an absentminded professor. I chided myself when I finally located it, hidden appropriately between the pages of *Hamlet* in my Shakespeare anthology.

There it was, the envelope addressed to me in Eternity's unmistakable cursive.

Dear Emile,

Bonjour from Lyon. Yes, it's me.

I know I don't write much, but this time it's different, my friend. They've set the date for the Barbie trial—May 11. I really think you should be here—both you and your mother. Your Mamie Madeleine is going to testify. I went to see her a few weeks ago, and she told me she had called and asked you to come. Maybe you'll think it's none of my business, but Emile, I think you need to be here with her.

We don't have to see each other, if that would be too hard. But come for your grandmother, please. I can't tell you the exact dates she'll testify. This trial is going to be drawn out—you've read the papers. I don't think you will regret it. Maybe afterwards it really will be over for you. All of it.

If you want to get in touch with me, my address is on the back. If I don't hear from you, I'll understand. I always have.

Eternity

Once again I felt slightly reprimanded by Eternity. Of course I was planning to attend the trial. I had talked to Mamie about it several times, but since the date kept getting pushed back, I had never given a definitive answer. I jotted a note to myself to make the plane reservations on Monday. I would be there for my grandmother.

The room drew in around me, assaulting me with a lifetime of memories—of treasures and spies, families lost and found, and of two sisters whom I loved.

Who is Blithe to me, Lord? I am so confused. I want to have a life, a family. I am tired of these questions.

No answers, only questions, but of one thing I was sure. When I got to Lyon, I would call up Eternity Jones. I would see her again.

In the meantime, I talked with Blithe almost daily and with Mama and Mamie at least once a week. And I reviewed the latest articles about the Barbie trial.

November 14, 1986

SERGE KLARSFELD REPRESENTS VICTIMS

As a lawyer for more than 120 associate plaintiffs in the Barbie case, Serge Klarsfeld has assumed a key role in the four-year preparation of the trial. He has documented the diplomatic conflict between French and American authorities who, from 1948 to 1951, protected Barbie against demands for his extradition from the U.S. zone of Germany to face trial in France. . . .

January 23, 1987

WHY THE FOUR-YEAR DELAY?

Klaus Barbie's trial seems destined to be postponed. The main reason is infighting among the prosecution. Barbie has committed so many crimes that there are thousands of people who want to press serious charges against him. Each of the forty lawyers prosecuting Barbie represents a different set of plaintiffs. . . .

March 21, 1987

BARBIE, D-DAY MINUS 51

The trial of Klaus Barbie will take place in the Lyon's Palais de Justice, beginning on May 11. . . .

I gave my last exam on the last day of April, drove to Atlanta, and spent the night at the house on Anjaco with Grandma and Mama. My plane was scheduled to leave at four in the afternoon on May 2.

Late in the morning I went outside to the garden with Grandma. At eighty-five, she could no longer get on her knees to weed and plant, but she still pruned the rosebushes with her shears. As I watched her, I got a painful longing inside. Her health was failing. Mama and I were afraid to leave at the same time for the Barbie trial, so I was leaving a week ahead, and Blithe, who loved Grandma like the grandmother she never had, insisted on coming to stay with her while we were both away. Still, my heart ached as I mowed the grass and glanced over to where Grandma, straw hat in place, stood beside the garage and clipped the rosebush climbing up the trellis.

When I turned off the lawn mower, Grandma motioned me over to the little wrought-iron table and chairs where she liked to sit and drink iced tea. She balanced herself by holding the back of the chair, then sat down stiffly.

"Do you expect to see much of Eternity while you're in Lyon, Emile?"

I shrugged and sat down beside her. "I'm sure we'll see each other."

"She knows about you and Blithe, of course."

"No."

"I see." She patted my hand.

I covered hers, wrinkled with its protruding blue veins, protectively with mine.

"I rarely write to Eternity. I didn't see the point in mentioning it. And I certainly don't want to hurt Blithe."

Grandma's lips quivered into a smile. "Blithe is a beauty and a feisty young gal who just may be worthy of you. You needn't worry about Blithe. She'll be fine here with me." She took a long sip of iced tea. "It has been my great, great pleasure to watch you grow up, Emile. I have no complaints." She made a face. "Except perhaps that you should cut your hair." She chuckled then.

"I only want to remind you that you have been waiting an awfully long time. Blithe is a delightful woman. But you must tie up the other end, dear. You have to let it go. Let Eternity go, Emile."

I sighed. "I don't know what to expect, Grandma. I don't know exactly why I'm going. Of course, to be a support to Mamie. But I'm afraid I'm hoping for something else, too." I could not bring myself to state it plainly.

Grandma had never needed anything to be stated plainly.

"Emile de Bonnery, look around you. It is spring. Everywhere, new life. You go to this trial, and then you come home. You hear me? Let go of the winter once and for all, and come back and enjoy the spring."

"Thank you, Grandma."

I went upstairs, sat at the desk by the dormer window in the yellow bedroom, and graded exams until late in the night. William Wordsworth's "Tintern Abbey" was one of the poems the students had analyzed for the exam. On every mimeographed copy of the exam I read the first lines from the poem and imagined Mr. Wordsworth was speaking of my return to Lyon, to St. Romain, to the rushing rivers.

> *Five years have passed; five summers, with the length*
> *Of five long winters! And again I hear*
> *These waters, rolling from their mountain-springs*
> *With a soft inland murmur. Once again*
> *Do I behold these steep and lofty cliffs. . . .*

By the time I had marked the last exam with a fat red *B+* and placed it in the envelope with the rest of the exams, to be mailed back to Nashville, I was ready. I even felt a certain excitement for what awaited me in Lyon.

Mama and Blithe drove me to the Hartsfield International Airport, and I kissed them both good-bye.

"I'll see you in a week, right, Mama?"

"Yes. Thanks to Blithe, I'll be there. She's a pearl, your Blithe."

Blithe rolled her eyes and gave Mama a hug.

"An angel," I said, touching her face softly. "I'll call you tomorrow," I promised them both.

"Emile, tell Eternity hi from me," Blithe said. "Tell her I miss her. I'll write soon." She did not, of course, say, *Tell her how you and I feel about each other. It's time, you know.*

———

I called Eternity the day after I arrived in Lyon and arranged to meet her in one of the popular little restaurants, a *bouchon* in Vieux Lyon. She got there before me, and I rushed in, feeling haphazard and small, as I did on the first day I had met her.

"Emile!" she called out brightly.

I smiled, extended my hand, then wondered if I should hug her. What was the appropriate way to greet a woman whom I'd loved, whom I hadn't seen in over ten years? More than twenty years of a friendship, and I was still baffled by her.

She hurried to my side, pecked me on each cheek in true French fashion, then stood back, her heavy-lidded eyes appraising me. "Oh, you look marvelous, Emile. You are so *you*. The disheveled professor. Emile! Don't look so astonished! Say something."

I cleared my throat as she grabbed hold of my arm. "Our table's over here."

We sat down, and I fumbled with my glasses, took them off, put them back on. This was true *déjà-vu*.

"I'm sorry, Eternity. I don't know what to say. It's just so . . . it's just so good to see you again."

"Yes. Yes, isn't it? I feel the same way."

"You look great," I managed. She did. Her hair was still black, shoulder length and shiny. She was wearing a gray pantsuit and had dangling earrings, the new fashion, I had noticed. She was sleek and slim, at ease with herself. But there was the same intensity about her. Those eyes still surprised me, deep and penetrating underneath the heavy lids.

Typically, she did not waste time on small talk. "Thank you for everything you've done for Blithe, Emile."

"Of course." I gave her a quizzical look. "She seems much better, doesn't she?"

"Yes."

I tried to change the conversation. "And what about you? Are you better, Eternity?"

"Yes," she said, nodding. "I believe I am. Thirteen years is a long time, isn't it? Yes, I am much better in my head than I was back then. I treated you poorly, didn't I? I've always felt awful about it."

"I forgave you eventually." I gave her a half grin.

"And did you find that gorgeous girl I told you would be waiting somewhere?"

My mouth went dry, and I nodded. "Maybe." I had not planned to bring up my relationship with Blithe so quickly. But I couldn't ignore it now. "Eternity, I need to tell you something and ask you something else."

She frowned. "Fire away."

"It's about Blithe. I . . . we . . . we're seeing each other. Spending time together." I felt pained.

"Are you saying you're dating?"

"Yeah. Yeah. That's pretty much it. And so, I, well, I thought it'd be good to discuss it with you—make sure you don't have a problem with it . . . with us."

A range of emotions passed over Eternity's face: shock, surprise, disbelief. "Do you *love* her?"

"I care for her deeply. I don't know what's next, but I don't want to keep on if, if you are against it."

Her face reddened. "I don't see that I have much to say about it. You're both adults." That familiar defensive edge had crept into her voice.

"True, but . . . Well, anyway, now you know."

I could tell she was angry.

"Now I know."

I needed to get up; I felt warm, feverish. I had not expected this reaction. "I'm sorry. I guess I should have told you when we started seeing each other. I thought maybe Blithe would—"

She interrupted me. "How long have you two been *dating*?"

"Not that long. Since December. Blithe got in touch with me when she moved back to Atlanta in the fall."

Eternity studied me.

"Are you mad?"

"No. Not mad. Surprised." She looked away. "Well, maybe a bit hurt, disappointed. Kind of a shock, finding out my kid sis is dating my best friend."

"Eternity, I'm *not* your best friend!" It came out unplanned, as with all of my gaffes. "Best friends talk together more than once every ten or fifteen years! They share things. All I know about you is what I read in your articles."

I sighed, took off my glasses, and traced the outline of my nose with my fingers. "This isn't going too well, is it? I'm sorry. I think I'm a little on edge. Blithe, Mamie, the trial. You." I glanced up at her.

"No, it's my fault. You're right. We don't know anything about each other, really, do we?"

"No, not much." I cleared my throat for the third time. "But I want to hear. How are you? Are you seeing anyone?"

She hesitated, took a breath. "Actually, yes. Seeing someone rather seriously, I think. His name is Jacques."

"He's French?"

"Yes." She blushed again. "Yes. I met him in Paris years ago. We were friends and then, well, I guess—you know—things developed."

"I see."

"I wanted to introduce you to him last year, when you came to Lyon. Blithe told me you were coming over to see your Mamie. But in the end, I didn't call you." She made a face. "The truth is, I didn't want to hurt Jacques. I had talked of you so often when I first met him. My stories were filled with you. So long ago, but still you. And I was afraid, I was afraid if I invited you, well, he might be hurt or jealous, or see it wrong."

She sat back in the chair, heaved a sigh, and ran a hand through her hair. The waiter placed the menus in our hands. She glanced his way and murmured, *"Merci."*

Her accent was perfect Parisian.

"I have never figured out how to explain our friendship, Emile. Not to anyone else. I talk of you constantly, and now, of course, Jacques just laughs and tells me I was silly to worry. He insisted I write to you."

I stared at the bright green menu, concentrating on the words *Special du midi, 60F.* I wanted to ask her *why* she talked of me constantly, but all I said was, "I'm sorry I didn't keep in better contact. I didn't think it was appropriate—after how we left things. You told me never to—" I cleared my throat—"I was afraid to open up something that had been closed. Afraid that I would need you." I shook my head. "I can't explain it. I've never known how."

She reached across the table and brushed the hair out of my eyes as if I were her little boy. "I went to see Blithe after she got out of the clinic a few years back. When I hugged her, and she melted in my arms, and we cried, later, later that's when I understood how I loved you, Emile. It was a safe love. You were my brother. Our brother. You saved us."

I clamped my lips together and nodded. "You've always been the woman with the words."

The waiter was hovering, polite, but perhaps impatient. We studied our menus in silence, ordered, and handed them back to him.

"You look beautiful, Eternity. Better than ever."

"That's what Jacques says." Her cheeks reddened again. "He says I've aged like a fine wine. More body, fuller, richer." She laughed. "It makes aging sound attractive!"

"How long have you known him?"

"I met him seven years after you and I parted at the Part-Dieu station in Lyon in 1974." Her face was beet red now. "It took me a long time to heal, Emile."

I thought she looked guilty, or repentant, I wasn't sure which.

"You know I went back to Paris in 1980 to do reporting. That's where I met Jacques. In a little Baptist church in Paris. He's older than I am by eighteen years. A widower. A wonderful and godly man."

"You found a father figure," I said, without thinking, almost to myself.

Eternity looked at me, astonished.

"I'm sorry—I don't know why I said that—it's none of my business."

"It's okay. He is quite a bit older."

I had flustered her, such a rare emotion for Eternity. "Never mind. I'm a bit older than Blithe too."

We both sat perfectly still. In an effort to redeem myself, I asked, "So, do you have more information about the trial—what it's going to look like?"

"Yes." She looked relieved. "I'm always doing this, aren't I? Coming back to you with information? You must hate me for it. Opening old wounds."

"I trust you, Eternity. You don't give me information unless it's important."

She took a deep breath. "How does Mamie Madeleine look to you?"

"So old. Feeble. But determined. I even think there is a kind of excitement in thinking justice may come at last."

"It's about time. The whole thing has been enmeshed in red tape for four years now. Oh." She reached into her purse. "You know I can't see you without producing some scoop. I thought you'd like to see this."

She spread several pages from a Lyon newspaper out on the table. On one page was an article entitled *Former Résistants to Testify at Barbie Trial.* On the adjoining page were photos of men and women, with brief paragraphs beneath explaining their roles in the Resistance. I stared at the picture of Mamie Madeleine, taken when she was a young woman, doubtless for some high society function. She looked beautiful.

> *Marie-Madeleine de Bonnery directed the French intelligence network known as Les Alliés de Lyon, along with her husband, Pierre. Under their leadership, Les Alliés placed nearly 3,000 agents in most of the cities and large ports in France. The organization provided the British armed forces with vital information about German defenses in Normandy prior to the D-day invasion. Pierre and Marie-Madeleine, along with their son Jean-Baptiste, were arrested two months before the D-day invasion and eventually sent to Auschwitz, where Pierre de Bonnery perished.*

In one paragraph in a French newspaper I had just learned more about my grandparents' work in the war than during my thirty-seven prior years of existence. I examined the other photographs, reading the fine print underneath each one.

The awkwardness broken, Eternity scooted her chair beside mine. "I think Serge Klarsfeld is representing something like a hundred of the former *résistants* who were Barbie's victims."

Her voice faded into the chatter of the restaurant. My vision became blurry as I stared at the newspaper and its photographs. I could not hear anything at all. I was trying to focus on the picture of a beautiful young woman with dark hair and laughing eyes. I had only seen her once before, for ten seconds, but I was sure this was the woman at the café with my father.

> Andrée "Dédée" Gresselin was twelve when the Allies parachuted into Normandy. Daughter of a resistance worker, she worked alongside her parents to cut the vital telephone line from her town, Cherbourg, which resulted in blacking out much of Normandy's communication. . . .

"I have to see her!" I said out loud.

"See who? Emile, you're pale. What is it?"

"It's her, Eternity. The woman I saw with my father. The one in the café right before Papa disappeared."

"How can you be sure?"

"Eternity, you of all people can understand that there are some images from our past etched into our minds so clearly that they never go away."

She nodded. "Yes, of course you're right. If she's testifying at the trial, she must be around here somewhere. I'll help you find her."

———

Eternity went into reporter mode. She had no difficulty locating Dédée Gresselin and setting up a rendezvous two days later. We met at another *bouchon* in Vieux Lyon, the three of us.

Dédée was small, energetic, with dancing eyes. Twenty years had dimmed her beauty, but I still recognized her as the young woman whose hand had been under my father's.

I held out my hand and introduced myself to her in French. "I'm Emile de Bonnery. Thank you for seeing me."

She gave a pinched smile, almost as if she were in pain. "Emile. How good to meet you finally."

"You know who I am?"

"Yes, of course. You're Jean-Baptiste's son."

My pulse began racing, and I felt the color drain from my face.

Eternity reached over and touched me on the shoulder. "Are you all right, Emile?"

I nodded, but I thought I might vomit. My skin felt clammy, my vision once again blurred. I sat down and wiped a handkerchief across my face.

The woman began to speak softly, kindly. "Shall I tell you about my involvement in the Second World War? In the Resistance?" She seemed intent on putting me at ease.

"Yes, please," Eternity said.

"My parents and brothers and I lived in Cherbourg—do you know where that is?"

I cleared my throat. "Of course—the tip of Normandy."

"I was just a girl at the time, but my parents and brothers and I were all involved. In preparation for the invasion, London had drawn up detailed D-day plans that called for the French Resistance fighters throughout the country to paralyze the French railway system, cut the roads, flood the canals, sabotage the power stations, and mount attacks on the fuel and arms depots. General de Gaulle helped organize this strategy with the Allies. Instructions for carrying out the plans were contained in 325 'personal messages' to be broadcast by the French-language service of the BBC on the eve of D-day. Each message, mean-ingless to the Germans, was the go-ahead for a specific *maquis* or Resistance group somewhere in France.

"So all during the months of April and May of 1944 we waited, my parents and I and thousands of other *résistants* throughout France, by our concealed radio sets—listening for a few words that would change our lives and help decide the fate of our nation.

"It was at 9:15 on the evening of June 5, 1944, when the lead ships of the invasion fleet were almost within sight of the Normandy beaches, that a BBC announcer began to read the vital messages, each of them twice over. He read the messages for almost an hour, slowly, calmly. But long before he had finished, many *résistants* were already creeping from our homes to perform our duty—all of it bent on caus-ing some prearranged havoc for the Germans."

Dédée began to whisper the words to me, "*The centipede is a mammal . . . The crocodile is thirsty . . . I hope to see you again, darling, twice at the Pont d'Avignon . . . You may now shake the tree and gather pears. . . .* That was ours, our sign to go and cut the telephone lines in Cherbourg. I was very young during the war, but I already knew I would continue this kind of work when I grew up. And I did."

"You knew my father?" I finally got out.

"Yes, Emile. I knew him quite well. In many ways we were alike—involved in the Resistance as children and called into intelligence work as young adults."

"When did you first meet him?"

"Long after the war. I was studying in Paris and involved in different things. So was he."

"Intelligence work?"

"Yes. We only met briefly at the time. Then he moved to the States in 1949, I believe. I didn't see him again until he moved back to Lyon with your mother. I met you, too."

I could not help myself. "Were you his lover?"

"No. No, Emile. I wasn't his lover. I was simply his colleague. An undercover colleague, of course."

I didn't believe her.

"Emile, your father has always loved your mother. Trust me. As far as I know, he's always been faithful to her."

"But I saw you with him! In the café—the day he disappeared!"

"Yes. He knew you would be coming that way. You needed to see us, needed to believe that he was involved with someone else."

"Why would he want me to think you were his lover?"

"To give your mother an excuse to leave Lyon. You know that, Emile."

I bristled at her condescending tone.

"Your father thought through every option, Emile. He is the most detailed man I know. This option was the best."

It was only then that I realized Dédée was referring to my father in the present. "Why do you say *is*? He's dead. He died in a Bolivian jail."

"He is not dead, Emile. Only presumed dead. He is coming to France tomorrow, and he is going to meet with you."

The room began to spin. I started perspiring profusely, wiping my handkerchief across my face. I cleared my throat and croaked out, "Please don't say these things if they're not true! You're throwing out answers to twenty years of pain. I hope you know what you're talking about."

Dédée leaned over and touched my hand. I drew it away quickly. I did not trust this woman.

"Emile, I'm sorry to shock you. You couldn't have known earlier. None of us knew. Don't you see? We've come out of the woodwork, miserable, terrified, starving mice. The fat cat—the Butcher—has been caught. It is safe to come out."

She glanced at Eternity. "I'm glad we've met. I was planning to get in touch with you, Emile. Your grandmother let me know you were coming."

I stared at her, uncomprehending.

"Be patient, Emile, and you will see."

When she left the *bouchon* fifteen minutes later, I watched her walk away on the cobbled streets. At any minute I imagined her turning into a doorway that led to a *traboule*. Papa was there waiting, the pitiful mouse in the stinking passageway, hidden away for so very long. Tomorrow I would know.

Eternity had lost her professional air. "Emile, I'm sorry. I had no idea. I'm sorry. Tell me what you want me to do."

"You've done enough, Eternity," I said abruptly. "The rest is up to me. That's all." I got up from the table and walked off, feeling disoriented, leaving her there to stare after me.

| *twenty-eight* |

How many times throughout my teenage years had I imagined the reunion between my father and me? He would suddenly appear, and we would regard each other from a distance. Then, with a cynical smirk on his face, the cigarette smoke lazily curling around him, he would motion to me, and we would embrace. Later, in my imagined safe room in the château, the smoke still hazy around us, he would confide all his secrets, tell me more fascinating stories, Papa and I as accomplices, as allies, as friends.

Gradually, as months turned into years and the years to decades, I lost this boyish image of our reunion. Now, at thirty-seven, with Dédée Gresselin's revelation fresh in my mind, I dreaded this appointment more than I had dreaded anything in my life—more than the first day of school at Northside, or Ace McClary's fist, or even my meeting with Eternity just five days earlier.

Dédée had given me directions to an old library in the center of town with only two instructions, "Be there on time, and come alone."

I went into the building and down the ancient stone stairs, worn smooth in the center by centuries of feet, into the room on the right at the bottom of the steps. A rectangular table with an ancient-looking machine sitting on it was against one wall. The only other furniture in the room were two plain metal chairs with a small round table between them.

I arrived first, heart racing, a thousand questions colliding in my mind. Five minutes later, with one knock on the door, my father entered.

He was much smaller than I remembered, a slight shaking to his stance, his hair, still abundant, now silver. He was well dressed in a dark gray suit. He did not smile. His eyes were faded and tired. "Hello, Emile," he said in a quavering voice. "Hello, son."

I was standing with my arms crossed tightly across my chest. "Hello, Papa."

He held out a tentative hand, and I shook it. We were strangers. I had no idea where to begin. He nodded to the chairs, and we sat down.

"So. You're back," I said.

"Yes. Back in time to see justice given. Finally." Each breath seemed a struggle.

"Where have you been?"

"Where have I not been?" His whole torso was shaking now. "I've seen it all, Emile. The atrocities of the Nazi regime, the cover-ups, the lies, Bolivian jails . . ."

"You've always been in intelligence work?"

"Of course. Always."

"For whom?" My voice was accusing, hard.

"Whom have I not worked for? It was the French police first. Then the Americans—for a while in Germany, and then in the States, where I met your mother. Things heated up a bit, so we came back to France. But you can never escape your past—it always catches up to you and then runs ahead and turns to face you, to betray you." He took a pack of Gitane cigarettes from his coat pocket and offered it to me.

"No, thank you."

He retrieved a cigarette, produced a lighter, and with a trembling hand lit the cigarette and inhaled deeply. His face, once so sharp and handsome, looked gray, like his suit. "I saw too much, Emile. Too much horror as a young teen. It possessed me, and I swore I would get revenge."

"You abandoned us!"

"Yes."

The rage boiled over, twenty years of rage. "All you can say is *yes*? Yes, for leaving us, ruining our lives, changing everything?"

"Did I ruin your life, Emile?" Cigarette smoke curled between us.

I thought of Grandma Bridgeman and her house on Anjaco, of Northside High School and Second-Ponce de Leon Baptist Church, of Vanderbilt University. And I thought of Blithe and Eternity.

"No," I admitted. "I survived. We survived. But you abandoned us, with no explanation. They told me you died in a Bolivian prison! And now you're suddenly here."

He inhaled slowly, so slowly I thought he might never let the air out.

"I know I owe you an explanation. You're the one who never knew the whole truth."

"Mama knew? She knew and didn't tell me?"

"She knew and *couldn't* tell you. She has lived with that." He seemed resigned. "Think of it, Emile. She tried to tell you—in her way."

I knitted my brow, recalling conversations with my mother. Her words from the day I had discovered Papa's microdot message to me echoed in my mind. *"You want your father to be a hero. But suppose he was just an ordinary man, some good, some bad. Brave, daring, smart, but also vain and careless. Suppose he wanted to do the right thing, but suppose he was motivated by hate and revenge and it was too strong. . . ."*

"Mama knew where you were hiding? All these long years, she has known?"

"At times she has known."

"And you never cared about us, never came to see any of us."

"I've seen Janie." He flicked the ashes onto the floor.

"When? When did you see her?"

"The first time I saw your mother was in 1969. I believe Mamie told you she had heard from me in 1966. And you know that she and Janie came and searched for me in the Bolivian prisons."

I nodded, my eyes accusing him. I remembered the day Mama came into the house on Anjaco, her eyes shining, humming a pretty tune. I was sure she had heard news of him.

"They didn't find me on that first trip to Bolivia. It wasn't until the fall of 1969 that your mother finally found me."

"You did this together! You disappeared, and Mama knew, and you let me suffer and wonder for all of my life!" I was thirteen again, or maybe eight, trying to hide the tears as I had when I first saw the hole in the Tintin book.

Slowly it dawned on me, the part of the puzzle I had never considered before. "Mama was part of it."

"She was involved in intelligence work at one time. Yes. Crazy life, isn't it, son? We brought you into a crazy life."

Never in all my years of trying to figure out the mystery of my father had I considered that my mother too might be involved in intelligence work.

"When it became apparent that I was going to have to disappear in the fall of 1964, I tried to divorce her. I wanted to give her a way out, a new start. She loved me too much, Emile. We loved each other too much."

"This is unbelievable!" I pulled my hands through my hair, wanting to yank out every memory, all the lies. My face contorted. I stared at my father, disgust on my face. I could have been staring at Klaus Barbie. "I'm glad you loved each other. You obviously didn't give a rip about me!"

My father tossed the cigarette butt on the floor and crushed it out with his shoe. "What do you want from me, Emile?"

"I want you to suffer!" I seethed. "I want you to suffer as I have!" I pounded the table with my fist, then jumped up, knocking over the chair. I stood far off, in the corner of the room. Hate was pulsing in my temples, and it frightened me.

One silent tear slid down the rutted indention in his right cheek. "Do you think I haven't suffered, son?"

His question stabbed me in the gut. At not quite sixty, he looked seventy-five, the marks of pain embedded on every inch of his face. The man I had known as my father had vanished, the arrogance gone, the cynicism too. Pitiful, broken, twisted, ill. That was my father, sitting at the table, hacking with a cough as he smoked a Gitane.

I felt an overwhelming softening, a pity. I *was* eight again, staring at the cut pages of *The Black Island* and hating him with my whole heart, then listening enraptured with his story, my hands holding the switchblade. My emotions teetered from hate and deception to love and pity and perhaps even respect.

I sat back down.

He reached into his suit pocket, fumbled, found a white cotton handkerchief and rubbed it across his forehead, which was glistening with sweat. I watched the patchwork of wrinkled skin, the thick blue veins popping from his hands, hands that could have been Mamie Madeleine's, that shouldn't have been his.

"Do you have time for one more story, Emile? Just one more? It will be my last."

I tasted bile, swallowed without saying a word. I did not want to hear another spy story.

"In 1964 I was working for the CIC when I accidentally discovered that the United States had hired Klaus Barbie in the late forties to be a counterintelligence spy, and then smuggled him out of Europe. I felt betrayed. I wanted out. Fury was nothing compared to my emotions. The man who had ruined my family had been protected by the very people I was working for!" His voice rose, hoarse. "I had contacts who had gained top secret information about CIC activities. These people suspected that Barbie was hiding in South America.

"I volunteered to go and see, in a sense spying on the CIC, for whom I still worked. I was afraid for you and Mama. I didn't trust anyone—not the U.S., not France, and of course not the former Nazis. I knew I could be gone for months. That's when I wrote you the microdot and had it fixed to the watch. I wanted you to know, son."

I thought I saw a flash of compassion and regret cross his face. "Then, while I was still planning the trip, I began receiving death threats—against me, Janie, Mamie, you. I had no idea who they were coming from. All I knew was that the danger had suddenly escalated, and now it involved my family. So Dédée and I staged the disappearance and Mama went back to the States. I thought I would join you soon—within several months."

I interrupted him, but my voice was calmer. "Do you realize that my last view of you was with another woman, and I've lived wondering about that and keeping it from Mama and Mamie all these years? I've lived with the memory of your look of indifference."

"Yes, yes, I know." He took out another cigarette and ran his hand through his silver hair. "I hoped you would eventually find the microdot. At least you would have that." He lit the cigarette, inhaled, then blew out the smoke with a sigh of resignation. "I'm sorry, son! I tried to explain. There are times in life when you realize there is no way you can win. People are going to get hurt. The people you love the most."

He looked me in the eyes. His were tired, tinged with red; mine bore into him, daring him to make things right.

"Dédée was my cover, and we have both paid for this for many years. Again and again, I have paid for that day. We both trusted Rémi—the man who called me the night I gave you the watch—with intelligence information. He warned me of danger, supplied the information about Bolivia, found a way to get me to South America.

"So I went—right into his plan. I'd barely been in Bolivia for a month when Hugo Banzer's men came looking for me, caught me, pinned crimes on me. And once again I found myself in front of Klaus Barbie, my torturer from twenty years earlier. He smiled when he said, 'History repeats itself.' He was still using the same tactics as before. And there was Rémi with him, watching and helping."

My father's face twitched uncontrollably for a few seconds. He stared straight ahead, concentrating, as if he might break under the pressure of some heinous memory. "I was taken to another prison. Held there for a year before I came to trial. They circulated the story of my imprisonment and then my murder."

He reached into his coat pocket and took out an old razor. "In the best of all worlds, Emile, you would have known sooner. Much sooner." He unscrewed the handle of the silver razor and hit the handle against the palm of his hand. A tiny piece of film slid out.

"We used this old microfilm reader back during the war," my father said, walking over to where the machine sat on the table. He flicked on a switch in that dark library room, slid the film under the lens, and the magnified picture revealed pages from Bolivian newspapers dated from 1966 and 1967: newspaper articles in Spanish, the beaten face of my father, a death certificate.

"Your mother found me. She got me out of that hellhole after seven long years. It's a place where you rot, Emile. Do you remember the story I told you of Lucie Aubrac during the Resistance—how she saved her husband by kidnapping him when he was being transferred from one prison to another? Your mother did that for me."

My head was swimming. An image of me sitting next to Papa on the bed in my room in the château flashed in my mind. He was trying once again to captivate me with a story.

"The former Nazis, now working undercover, had murdered several of their own. Anyone with information about Barbie's previous crimes eventually disappeared. The story of my murder was circulated . . . and believed. I thought the best thing I could do for you was to stay away, let you think I was dead."

I stood up and paced about the room. "Serge Klarsfeld's father died in the camps! But when Klarsfeld sought justice for his father's death—and for thousands of others—he did it without abandoning his family. They worked together—even his children!"

Papa covered his face with his hands. "Emile, I cannot judge another man's actions. I won't try to justify myself. All I can tell you is that I was still working undercover. That was my job, and when you were threatened, when my mother and your mother were in danger, I chose what seemed best to me.

"I saw my father and mother tortured by Klaus Barbie. I was tortured. I saw awful things that I have never shared with anyone, ever." He swallowed hard. "I never got over all of these things, Emile. I will go to my grave with them.

"But you had another chance. I knew that my little Tintin would come looking for me if he could. I was not about to let them find you, let them force you to watch me die, make you and your mother a bargaining chip for the future.

"Perhaps I was wrong, Emile. I ask your forgiveness."

My legs were shaking, almost as much as my father's. I felt chilled to the bone. I said nothing. I could not look at him.

"I want you to know that I am proud of what you have become. I am very, very proud of you."

I could not even find the strength in my body to acknowledge this compliment.

"I know it is too much to ask to walk back into your life." He held his hands out, resigned. He reached into his suit pocket and handed me a small plastic photo album.

I opened it brusquely, struggling again between rage and pity.

The album was filled with photos of me growing up, of me in college, of me with Grandma and Mama, with Griffin and Ace and children from the soccer teams, of me in my graduation robes from high school and college and receiving my PhD.

My father was still talking. "Eventually your mother would come to visit me wherever I was hiding. I was always hiding, Emile. Working and hiding and wondering when the past would catch me again. It was not really a life. I admit I was motivated by revenge. But there was something else, something stronger. I could not let you suffer as I had. Janie and I decided that you should not ever have hope of finding me. We didn't want you to come looking. We wanted you to have a normal life."

"You should have let me choose!"

"Perhaps . . . who can know? Answers are not always obvious."

"And Mamie?"

"I wrote to Mamie regularly. She managed the estate, sent money to Janie, helped pay for your education. It killed her not to see me, but she knew the risks, she knew the protocol. And then, thanks to the Klarsfelds and others, the secret was gradually leaked out, the Butcher caught, the trial set. It was finally safe for me to come home."

I was only half listening. In the album I had found a picture of me with Eternity when we were in Lyon in 1974. We were standing in front of Mamie's château, smiling at the camera, looking carefree.

"It was Eternity who kept looking for you, long after I had given up."

"Yes, I know. She is a good reporter, that girl."

"She knew about you?"

"No, no. But I knew about her, about all those people who were looking for me." His tired eyes softened with a look of gratitude.

It sliced me in two, and I felt repulsed by my anger, my distance in the presence of my father. His suffering enveloped the whole room. I thought I would choke on it.

"Oh, Papa," I said, meeting his eyes and clasping his hand tightly in mine. "I'm so sorry." It was all I could get out. I was afraid I would cry, sob, here in front of this stranger who was my father. I needed to go back home. Where was home?

But so much of me wanted to go out and find Eternity, wanted to hold her and cry and thank her for finding him. Then I wanted to scream at her for the very same reason.

My father stayed at a hotel that first night—some sort of debriefing, he explained to me. I thought it would surely take him the rest of his life to be debriefed from the hell he had lived through. When I reached the château, I went into the *salon* and phoned Mama.

All I said was, "Mama, I found him. Found Papa. He's here in Lyon. He's alive."

"Thank God," she whispered into the phone. "I'm on the next plane, Emile."

That was all.

Then I dialed Blithe's apartment.

"Blithe, I've found him."

"Found who?"

"My father."

"Your father? I thought he was dead."

"Yes, that's what I was told."

"Oh, Emile."

"Mama will leave immediately."

"That's no problem. I can go to your grandmother's house tonight. I'll take good care of her. Don't you worry."

To her credit, Blithe tried to understand, over the static in the phone lines, but she was not the one who had walked these twenty-three years with me. She was not the one with whom I had shared the deepest secrets of my adolescent heart. She did not remember Tintin or the stories of the treasures, because I had never told them to her.

I had learned long ago to distrust my emotions; nonetheless, their magnitude on the day that my family was reunited threatened to suffocate or debilitate me. One minute I wanted to hate them all, wanted to disinherit myself from my mother and my father and Mamie Madeleine. The next I wanted to hug them close and thank them for surviving. And then later, I wanted to fall to my knees in tears and beg them to forgive me for my hard heart.

As I watched them there, Mama and Papa, embracing, crying, I think I envied their love, as I had the relationship between Grandma and Eternity way back in 1964. I stood off to the side of the big *salon* in the château and felt like an intruder. Mama was giddy, Papa had already lost ten years from his face, and feeble Mamie went into her garden and cut roses as if she were forty-five again, a spring to her step, something akin to laughter in her old, old eyes.

The next day I came back from a jog through the Mont d'Or and was surprised to find Eternity waiting for me at the château.

"I'm sorry," she said. "I know you don't need me anymore. But after all these years, I had to know how you're doing. You know I've prayed about this since high school, imagined a hundred different scenarios. I'm sorry I thought you were crazy, Emile. I'm sorry for so many things."

I leaned over, resting my hands on my knees and catching my breath. "It's all so very strange, Eternity."

We walked through the village, past the centuries-old houses built of golden-hued stones, down to the Saône. Silently we watched the river rush by, its waters high after weeks of rain. I explained my encounter with my father in vivid detail—his emaciated frame, his rasping cough, his years of imprisonment and hiding. And my volleying between rage and pity, hate and love.

"I'm ashamed of myself, Eternity. Where are love and compassion? Where is forgiveness?"

"Oh, Emile. Give it time. Surely with time . . ."

"Surely, yes."

"Does Blithe know?"

"I called her. She can't really understand, though. Not like you." I tossed a rock into the Saône and watched a few ducks scatter away as it splashed close by. "But I know she'll try."

"The trial starts tomorrow," Eternity said, as if changing the subject would change my mood.

"Yes. Thank goodness."

We walked back up the hill to the château in silence.

"I guess I should get back to the hotel," she said when we reached her car. "Big day coming up."

I furrowed my brow. "Thank you for coming by. It means a lot. I'm sorry to be so melancholic."

Before she drove off, Eternity said, "If you need to talk again, you can call, you know."

I hardly heard her offer. *I won't bother you and Jacques,* I said to myself. Outwardly I just nodded—a resigned, tired nod. I watched her go with an emptiness that was gnawing inside, as if someone were taking a knife and scraping out all the fiber and seeds in the interior of a pumpkin. If that same someone could have carved my feelings out of the exterior of the shell, drooping, mournful eyes and a bitter smile would be all that was left gleaming from the light of the candle inside.

Much is said in the Bible about finding joy in suffering, considering our trials as stepping stones to development of character. I figured someday I too would serve as an example of this truth. But not yet.

After I had showered, I joined my family in the *salon* where we sipped Muscat and ate pistachios and discussed the details of the Barbie trial as if we were an ordinary French family, reunited after a few months instead of twenty-three years. I did not have the mental strength to visit any more of the past or hear their explanations. We were depleted of energy, all of us, and after a light dinner of soup and cheeses, with long, awkward pauses in conversation, we made our way to the bedrooms, retiring early.

The awful bombardment of emotions that had overpowered me time and again in the previous two days left me with profound guilt, as if I were the Butcher of Lyon, on trial for my cruel, hard heart.

That night before the trial began, I made the phone call to the only one who might understand.

"Grandma?"

"Hello, Emile." Her voice sounded old. "Would you like to talk to Blithe? She should be showing up soon. After work."

"No, Grandma. I need to talk to you." My throat constricted, and for a moment I could not say a word.

"Dear, dear Emile. How I have prayed for you."

"Did you know too, Grandma? Did you lie to me all these years?" But before she could answer, I said, "Never mind. I don't want to know."

"Emile, darling. How baffling, all these strange occurrences. No, I didn't know their story until Janie explained it to me after she got your phone call."

"They all lied. Papa, Mama, Mamie. I know it was for a good cause—perhaps a great one—but I hate them for it."

"Yes, dear. It was a shock to you, I'm sure. And terribly confusing."

She could hear my heavy breathing, the weight of my silence. Still, she remained quiet for a long time.

Finally she said, very softly, "Emile, remember that life isn't that neat little puzzle with all the pieces in place. Remember, you don't need all the answers. This is your chance to love in spite of all that was wrong. Jesus will make a way, Emile. If you hold tightly, He will."

"But I feel such hate and then such grief and shame. And confusion. More than twenty years of lies. It's impossible to explain it."

Grandma was not in a rush. I could have been sitting on her screened porch, sipping iced tea.

"You know, Emile, when Janie showed up at my door after fifteen years, it wasn't easy. I had a lot of bitterness, so many painful memories. How her father had longed to see her before he died. But she didn't come then, and she didn't come after. So when she showed up with you, I couldn't love her at first.

"You, I could love, her precious son. But with Janie I just had to *act* like I loved her, that's all. I chose to show love in spite of all the pain and hurt of the past."

I was listening to Grandma, but what I was seeing in my mind were those first days in Atlanta—Grandma's kindness, her simplicity, and the way her eyes radiated love.

"The good thing about following Jesus is that His Word eventually seeps way down into your heart. And then, when you need to respond as He would, somehow that love blooms, watered by years of tears and tended by His Spirit. It blooms. Maybe not all at once, Emile. But eventually. He doesn't waste your obedience. It counts. It works."

I said nothing, but I was listening, begging God to let her words— His words—penetrate into my heart.

| *twenty-nine* |

May 11, 1987

Klaus Barbie's trial took place in Vieux Lyon at the Palais de Justice—the long, elegant court building with twenty-four stone columns along the front. Fourvière looked down from the hill behind. The day was sunny, a perfect spring afternoon. I got a lurching in my gut as I walked down the small cobbled side street from the metro to the courthouse, the very street with the café where Papa had sat with Dédée all those years and lifetimes ago.

I took in the scene that first day as if watching through a telescope from far, far off: the police all around the building, the journalists—including Eternity—swarming, the witnesses wearing tags over their heads to identify them, no longer a golden star but a badge of honor; they had survived. And the public, crowding outside the court building, gossiping, wondering, waiting for forty years of evaded justice to be made right.

I stepped inside the Palais with Mama holding on to my arm. She needed me beside her, and no matter my confused feelings, I was determined to support her through this trial. Papa and Mamie Madeleine had already taken seats with the other witnesses.

The courtroom buzzed with people talking. Hundreds of wooden folding chairs were set across the floor and in the balcony for the witnesses, the journalists, the families. The walls, papered in luxurious red with white wooden paneling underneath, the ceilings coffered and sculpted, and the large fluted columns all lent to the feeling of grandeur and expectancy. In these beautiful, hallowed halls surely justice would prevail.

Suddenly, silence. The leading judge came forth, President Cerdini they called him, serene and serious, along with the nine other assistants, all of them dressed in their formal legal attire: long, flowing red robes with *cravates* over black blouses. An air of tension hung in the room as Klaus Barbie arrived, handcuffed, escorted by two policemen.

He was thin and smallish, balding, his blondish gray hair long and scraggly; his blue eyes, the ones so many victims would describe as piercing, looked icy and transparent. But it was the sneer on his face that sickened me most. It was a thin smile "like the blade of a razor," as one of his victims would describe it. At seventy-three he was sharp and lucid and had the reflexes of a police officer. "Innocent, I'm innocent," he proclaimed again and again during the first days of the trial.

The victims, more than 150 of them, were there, along with the thirty-nine lawyers representing them. The families of the victims, we were there too. And of course the defense lawyers, M. Vergès and his associates, determined to prove that Klaus Barbie was not the guilty one, but rather France was, for collaborating with the Nazis in World War II and for subsequent atrocities in Indochina and Algeria.

The stage was set for a public spectacle—hatred, cruel memories, old wounds opened, countries' allegiances questioned—it was all a part of the Barbie trial. And the victims and their families forced to remember and relive.

The journalists came from around France and around the world, over eight hundred in all. Three hundred riot officers and policemen were present. For the first time in the history of a French court, the trial was to be videotaped. Otherwise, no cameras were allowed. Throughout the entire trial, there was the figure of M. Réné Diaz, the artist hired to record the trial through his sketches. He sat there, sketching, sketching, always sketching, the calm face of the judge, the inalterable Barbie, the feeble witnesses. Day after day, as the trial dragged on, the newspapers were filled with articles from a hundred pens and the sketches of one man.

During the first week there were no testimonies, only the lawyers, explaining the legal aspects. In the middle of the third day, before the crimes of which he was accused were read, Barbie suddenly refused to stay in the tribunal, insisting that he was Klaus Altman, a Bolivian citizen.

"I consider myself a hostage, not a criminal," he said in German. Perhaps it was his last act of insurgence, but for much of the remainder of the trial, Klaus Barbie would not appear in the courtroom, choosing to remain sequestered in his cell.

On the fourth day of the trial, with Barbie no longer present, Erhard Dabringhaus came forward and gave his testimony. He was now retired from university teaching and had traveled from Florida for the trial. He repeated his story, familiar to me from the articles I had read. In 1948, as a member of the CIC, Dabringhaus was given charge of helping two Germans, Barbie and Merck, with their work in Augsbourg. Gradually Dabringhaus caught on that Barbie was a war criminal. He asked his superiors about this, and they told him they still needed Barbie. In November 1948, Dabringhaus asked to leave Augsbourg and transfer to Stuttgart. He never saw Barbie again until the Butcher appeared on TV on January 29, 1983.

On the fifth day of the trial, the crimes against humanity for which Barbie was being tried were read out loud. Specifically, he was prosecuted for eight crimes, which included massacres of hostages, arrests, tortures, shootings, and deportations of both Jews and *résistants* to concentration camps. The last crime listed the arrest and deportation of fifty-five Jews, many of whom were children, from the village of Izieu.

Every day after the trial, the summary of the day's events appeared in all of France's newspapers. Throughout each day, Eternity sat in her chair and scribbled notes so that other people around the world could read the same news. I felt an inexplicable pride as I watched her from a distance: Eternity Jones, the girl with the alcoholic mother, the girl who raised her siblings and hid them in a safe room, the girl who drew the universe with her food and was determined to be a journalist. That girl, all grown up and professional, sat across the vast hall from me, noting the testimony of every witness, evoking the atmosphere of this long-overdue trial for Americans to read.

As I was leaving the Palais that fifth day, my head swimming with details of Barbie's atrocities, she found me. "Emile."

"Hello, Eternity."

"How are you holding up?"

I shrugged, shook my head. "What can I say? It's too complicated."

"I'd like to hear. Could we get a coffee?"

So we did. And for the following seven weeks of the trial, Eternity and I established a routine, so very natural, much like her riding the school bus home with me from Northside. Almost every afternoon we spent an hour at the café around the corner. Sometimes we talked about the trial, but more often we did not. We chose to leave the vivid, terrifying images at the Palais and speak of another life—our lives, catching up on the past and dreaming of the future.

"What are you reading these days?" she asked me one afternoon.

"I've been reading a lot of Bonhoeffer." I told her of the lecture in class and the poem. "I think I can relate to the poem even more now. His two selves are juxtaposed—the one the world sees and the one he knows inside; the courageous pastor, immovable in spite of circumstances, and the cowardly prisoner, terrified and questioning his faith. I feel his struggles. They were my father's. And they are mine."

"Everyman," she said, lifting her eyebrows.

"Exactly. The thing is"—and all of a sudden Eternity was my best friend again, and I was baring my soul to her—"the thing is that I don't know why it is so hard for me to forgive my father. He's been through a lot more than I have."

Eternity let me struggle for my words, not filling in the blanks or jumping ahead. I thought she had changed.

"Grandma always encouraged me to consider the weight of time on circumstances. So I've been reading Ecclesiastes—you know, 'for everything there is a season.' I found a quote where Bonhoeffer basically says the same thing as Solomon. Something like, 'Each thing in its own time. The essential thing is to order one's steps to those of

God, not to want to run several yards ahead of Him nor to stay behind.' It's strange—I guess I feel like I'm rushing to catch up with the Lord's steps, to accept this new reality, embrace it, be thankful for it, forgive where I need to and move on. . . ." I paused. "I'm babbling, aren't I?"

She nodded and said, "Keep going, Prof. I'm following. I like being privy to your thoughts."

On another day I asked her, "Are you planning to stay in France, Eternity?"

"I don't know. Jacques has made an offer." She laughed self-consciously. "If I accept, well, of course I'll stay with him in Paris."

"If?"

Her penetrating, sleepy eyes—dark brown, full of life and expression—met mine. "Sometimes I have second thoughts. I'm almost afraid."

I nodded. "I guess I understand. Why is it so hard for us to decide?"

That question always remained unanswered.

After one particularly trying day at the Palais, I mentioned to Eternity, "You've spent years of time and research, and probably heartache, on this case. You started out doing it for me, and I want you to know how much it means. No matter that I don't know how to deal with my family. That will come." I smiled. "Grandma has assured me of it."

"Your dear grandmother always seems to find the truth under the layers of pain."

"Yes, she talked about 'painful but redemptive experiences.' I hope this trial is that for the victims. For all of us. I pray it is. Anyway, I just want to say it: thank you. It seems so insignificant after all the time you've invested."

She reached out and touched my hand. "Emile, keeping my promise to you spurred me on during some very long and depressing nights. I don't think I would have followed it through on my own—not just the hunt for Barbie, but my whole career. I'm thankful I had that desperate force that pushed me, obliged me to keep going."

She never put a name on that "force," not in any of our conversations during the months of May and June. She didn't have to. We both knew it was love.

———————

During the second week of the trial, the victims were called forth to give their testimonies. One after another, they came; most of them old, very old, pain etched in their faces. I will never forget any of the testimonies, but those of the first day were perhaps the most difficult to hear. We, the audience, may have thought we knew of the atrocities that had taken place, but we were unprepared for the graphic horror. It overwhelmed us.

Complete silence fell over the court as the first witness told her story. Lise Lefèvre was small and wrinkled, in her eighties, and yet she held her head high. Pride and dignity flashed in her eyes, and her voice was shaking, but strong.

"I was a member of the Resistance and forty-three years old when I was caught on March 13, 1944. Three savages took me into the prison. During the night I managed to swallow some compromising documents, but not all of them.

"The next day I met Klaus Barbie for the first time. He was like a caged animal, with his shifting eyes. Barbie was enraged with me. He ushered me into a room where I noticed strange things on a table. The first torture was with handcuffs. These handcuffs had sharp claws inside, and every time I refused to answer a question, they tightened those cuffs, tighter and tighter until I was sure my fingernails would fall off. Then they hung me up by my hands. I cannot describe the pain.

"At midnight I was subjected to the bathtub. They stripped my clothes off and threw me into a tub of ice water. One of Barbie's men held my nose shut while another threw water in my mouth. Then my feet were bound together with a rope, and each time I refused to answer a question, they jerked me underwater until I nearly drowned.

"At other times they tied me on a table, my feet in one direction and my arms in another, and they stretched the table open; all the while Barbie was beating me with his riding crop. For nineteen days the torture continued.

"Finally I was attached naked to a chair and beaten with a ball of iron, which tore open my back. I fainted. When I awoke I found myself in a fancy *salon*, seated in a comfortable *fauteuil*. There was a rose in a vase on a table. And there was Barbie, with his piercing eyes and wicked smile.

"'I admire you,' he said. 'I wish our German women were as strong as you. But everyone talks.' Then he screamed, 'Send her away. Get rid of her!'

"I was put on the train to Auschwitz. Barbie found my husband and son and had them brought in and tortured too. Later I saw my son on the train to Auschwitz. He died in the camp. My husband died of typhus at Dachau—the last time I saw him was in a hallway in Lyon."

No one dared to breathe in the room; many were weeping. I felt so sick to my stomach that I thought I might have to leave.

Day after day and week after week, witnesses described Barbie's atrocities and then the horror of the death camps where he sent them, described men crawling like worms along the ground, having been shorn of every bit of hair on their bodies.

One victim explained, "I was sent to Ravensbruck with a thousand other women. Most of us there were *résistants*. We anticipated torture and execution, but we could never have imagined Ravensbruck. Arriving at midnight, we were greeted with our first view of the other prisoners. Their eyes were blank, they stared without seeing. The guards took all of our personal objects. They shaved us completely, humiliated us, terrorized us. We were no longer human beings. We were a sub-race of humanity."

And then it was Mamie Madeleine's turn to testify. She stood and walked slowly toward the microphone.

"Would you like to sit?" President Cerdini asked.

"I will stand," she replied. She stated her name and her part in the war—a *résistant* along with her husband and son.

"We were brought in for questioning on a Friday afternoon in late May, only weeks before the Normandy invasion. The three of us." Her voice cracked, and she wobbled slightly. "Our son, Jean-Baptiste, had been away, working as a *maquisard*. He had survived the terrible battle of Glières, was wounded, and came home for only a few days. That is when we were arrested."

She paused. "Barbie was a sadist. You cannot understand the extent of his perversion. He forced my son to watch me being tortured, naked. Then, when I would not talk, he beat my son, my husband. He hung us up by our wrists in those terrible handcuffs that tore into the skin, the bones, broke us. When we fainted, he woke us with ice water in our faces."

I felt tears flickering behind my eyelids; I struggled with Mamie to maintain a bit of dignity. I saw her falter, heard the catch in her throat. I wanted to run to her, throw my arms around her and tell her she was doing the right thing. My grandmother, always so stalwart, strong, courageous, was faltering under the weight of the memories.

"'You will talk or you will end up like your husband,' Barbie told me. That is when I glimpsed my husband for the last time. He had been beaten beyond recognition. We were all sent to Auschwitz, but on different trains. I was there for a year. I thought if anyone survived these horrors and told about it, no one would believe them.

"They gassed so many people that the ovens could not burn them all, even with that sickly smoke rising night and day, night and day. Eventually they began throwing bodies in ditches at night and pouring gasoline on top. They lit the gasoline to burn the bodies. One night we heard the most awful, bloodcurdling screams piercing the darkness. We learned the next day that they had thrown live children into the ditches, burnt them alive." Tears trickled down her face, but she continued.

"I am not finished," she stated emphatically. "This man, Klaus Barbie, is an animal, worse than any wild beast. He acted in full capacity of his senses. He tortured and killed for pleasure. Those of us who survived—we survived on the outside. But he killed us on the inside. We have fought hard to live, to move on. But no one must forget."

In my mind I saw Mamie Madeleine as one of the leaders of the Resistance groups in Lyon, efficient and determined. I imagined her before Klaus Barbie, tight-lipped and indomitable, refusing to be broken. Then I saw my grandmother after the war, desperate to rid herself of the unimaginable horror of Klaus Barbie's torture and the Auschwitz camps. I thought about the way she gardened, with purpose, resolve, determination, a maddening speed of clipping, raking, weeding. *To help her forget.*

Oh, Mamie, Mamie! I'm sorry! I wanted to scream it out to the whole congregation of people. But there was no need, for the faces throughout the courtroom revealed the breadth of emotions we all felt: hatred, fury, disgust for Klaus Barbie, pity and comfort for Mamie as we listened to her, and all the others, with a believing incredulity.

How did she survive, I wondered? What resolve did it take to come out of the death camps alive, having first endured over two weeks of barbaric torture by Klaus Barbie?

I glanced at Mama. Her face was pale, her brow beaded with sweat, tears in her eyes . . . tears for the mother-in-law she hated and loved, the woman who had made her life a trial. Did she understand more of this woman now, watching her feeble steps as she descended the podium?

During the third week of the trial, the main topic of discussion was the roundup of forty-four Jewish children who were being kept at a camp in the village of Izieu. Someone in the camp was an informant, and the children were denounced. Sabina Zlatin, principal of the Izieu school, took the stand, and with her voice breaking, said, "Barbie always claimed he was concerned only with *résistants* and *maquisards*. But he arrested these children. The children were innocent."

On May 26, President Cerdini required Klaus Barbie to come back to the court and answer for the crimes of which he was accused. His face hard and eyes bright, Barbie showed no remorse, not one faltering expression of guilt. Each time, after the crime was read and President Cerdini asked him to speak, he replied in German, "I have nothing to say."

At last Papa was invited to the witness stand. As he stood to give his testimony, I wanted to run to him and hold him tightly and tell him I forgave him for his lies.

"I was young, barely sixteen, when the Gestapo arrested my mother, my father, and myself. I had returned from Glières. Perhaps I was followed. Somehow we were all three denounced." He glanced in the direction of Mamie Madeleine and said, "I have never known braver people than my parents. They risked everything for the cause of freedom.

"At the Gestapo headquarters, after a night in the cells, we were brought in before Klaus Barbie, all three of us together. As my mother has told you, Barbie gained pleasure in forcing us to watch the others being tortured. Eventually, he took us alone, one by one. He was always in his shirtsleeves and held a riding crop that he would snap while questioning his victims. Then he punctuated his demands with blows from a blackjack or a rough cudgel or a simple two-by-four. Vicious blows to every part of the body. He only stopped when you lost consciousness. Then he woke you up with kicks to the belly, the kidneys, the crotch. If that didn't work, he threw you into a tub of ice water with cubes floating in it. After the tub, the blackjack again, which made your skin swell up. Then he injected acid into your bladder."

I recognized the familiar twitch on the left side of Papa's face, and for the first time I realized where it had come from.

"Day after day he tortured me. I would not speak." Papa's fists were balled tightly at his sides. He was blinking his eyes. "I tried to protect my parents. My mother was worn down, my father almost dead when Barbie put us on the train to Auschwitz."

I looked over at Mamie. She was slowly moving her head back and forth, and crying.

"Auschwitz was a factory where more than two thousand persons were gassed each day. At night you could see the fumes. We younger ones tried to help the morale of the older prisoners. But every night, fathers who had not been able to protect their children, who knew their children were part of those evil fumes, rising, rising, those fathers would run in the night toward the barbed wire fences, try to climb out, knowing they would be gunned down. In the morning we saw them hanging there, looking like autumn leaves.

"I did not know if my parents were still alive. We had been separated. I wondered if my father was one of those dead leaves. He had suffered so terribly and had seen me tortured."

A lone sob escaped his lips. "It is hard to talk of these things. My son is here, my mother, my wife. What I am about to say will hurt them." He looked pleadingly toward us, and my heart rammed into my ribs.

"From Auschwitz, the inmates were marched to Ravensbruck. You have heard perhaps of this death march, where only two thousand of the twenty-five thousand people who began the march arrived alive. We walked in the freezing cold with nothing to eat or wear. One day, a short ways from me, I saw him, my father, walking in a line of men, a different convoy. All skeletons, wearing rags, nothing more, no boots, trudging along, half dead. I recognized my father by his height—he was quite tall. For one moment our eyes locked, and my father nodded ever so slightly to me.

"A guard saw and approached me. 'That is your father?' he asked.

"'Yes,' I answered. The guard yelled something in German and then instructed me. 'Go, you may hug your father. It's okay.'

"Slowly the two of us walked toward each other. But before we could embrace, a guard forced my father to kneel down, and with me only inches away, he shot my father in the head."

A gasp went through the crowd. My grandmother reached out as if to grab something for support. Several people near her caught her as she slumped forward.

"I ask you, men of the court, what happens to a teenage boy when he watches his mother and father brutally tortured, and then sees his father murdered before his eyes? What happens? He dies too. I died inside that day and have spent the rest of my life seeking revenge. My father is no longer here. Please, give him the justice that is so long overdue."

Papa left the podium with his silver head high, standing erect, but he could not hide the emptiness and pain shining in his eyes.

It was after midnight—the early minutes of July 4, 1987—when the verdict was brought in by the jury after six hours of deliberation. A huge crowd waited outside the courthouse. Those inside stood to their feet as the judge and jury came in. Then everyone took a seat.

Klaus Barbie was led back in, his hands in handcuffs. He stood as the verdict was read: guilty of crimes against humanity, sentenced to life imprisonment in Montluc prison in Lyon. As those present applauded, Barbie remained unperturbed, as did his lawyer, M. Vergès. Outside the courthouse, horns honked, people cheered.

The victims had been allowed the right to express themselves. All of them, including my grandmother and my father, had kept their dignity up until the very end.

That night the people of Lyon celebrated the victory over Nazism.

| *thirty* |

Out in the streets of Vieux Lyon, with the noise of celebration around me, I caught sight of Eternity. She started moving through the crowd toward me.

"Thank you again for never giving up," I said to her, with difficulty.

"You know I did it for you, Emile. Just as a way of thanking you for all the times you saved my life."

"I did nothing."

"You cared. And you gave me hope, by introducing me to life. Real life. A real family. Remember what your grandmother told us? Some things are worth looking for. Some answers we will find. I found the main one, and then I guess you might say I was pushed along by the Spirit to find this one."

She nodded to where my father was standing with Mamie and Mama. Then she leaned over and gave me a soft peck on each cheek. "I need to be going, Emile. But this time, let's keep in touch."

"This time we will," I said through the catch in my throat.

Back at the château, I crawled into bed and lay awake for hours. I could not rid my mind of the images of Mamie and Papa standing at the podium, testifying of unspeakable horror. In the middle of the night I sat up in my bed, clutching my stomach. My eyes were dry, but inside I was grieving for their pain. Papa was right—the images would haunt me until I died. If I could vicariously feel such intense pain, what did he experience?

I decided then that it didn't matter that his reasoning for leaving me was misguided. The point was to move forward, living, forgiving, as Grandma had said on the phone. I had nothing to prove, neither did he. My father was brilliant, brave, paranoid, selfish, afraid, courageous, misled, cowardly, proud. All of the above. And he was even heroic—a strange heroism, where he left those of us he loved to fend for ourselves, believing he was protecting us from a danger he could not name.

He had needed revenge, and at last he had obtained it. Klaus Barbie would pay for the crimes he committed against these thousands and thousands of victims. Barbie was not remorseful or broken, but he would pay. Papa's father, and so very many others, had at last been avenged.

I pondered this until the sky outside the window paled with the first light of day. My father was actually on a road moving forward. Healing was possible. Perhaps with Klaus Barbie's sentence, he could let the awful burden go. Perhaps in some way, his twenty-three years of erring and searching had been justified and acknowledged.

I came to another conclusion during that sleepless night—something I had acknowledged many times before, but which seemed clearer now. Victims could move on, but deep down they were still victims. Maybe there were parts of us that would never recover from the injuries of the past. And maybe that was all right, because we could still be useful in our maimed and injured state.

"For when I am weak, then I am strong." I grabbed on to those words of the apostle Paul. Yes. Yes, of course.

It was true for Eternity. Years ago she tried to tell me the same thing as my father. She was too hurt to live normally, to endanger another relationship. She did not see a way to rid herself of the memories of the boys and men who had used her and scarred her, of a mother who terrorized her and her siblings. But she could still live, move forward, and find healing little by little. And she had done this.

Eternity Jones had survived and triumphed.

Why they had both thought that leaving me would protect me, I couldn't say. It seemed warped. And yet, I loved paradox in Scripture, in literature. I had to accept it in real life. Hadn't Grandma told me to ask the question, "Now that I'm here in this mess, Lord, what do You want me to do about it?" Not *why me?* but *what next?*

The people who surrounded me were all, as I was, simply flawed humans with good and bad, hope and treachery, lies and truth. All flawed, and all worthy of redemption. In the working out of life, some things healed and others were left to bleed. But even the open wound served its purpose. The pain brought forth an array of emotions and actions and passions that otherwise would have remained hidden. I had witnessed a small representation of humanity allowed to grieve, allowed to vulnerably expose their suffering. Surely I could rebuild a life of love with my family.

The day after the trial ended, I spent the morning at the *marché* not far from St. Romain. I purchased *foie gras* and goat cheese and a succulent *pintade* and new potatoes and carrots and baby onions. I drove into the Beaujolais and bought several bottles of wine from a *cave*. I brought them back to the château, and I prepared a meal. *A Meal.* I even smiled to myself, thinking of Ace's taunt. I set the table with Mamie's fine china and crystal, and called them to dinner, Mamie and Mama and Papa.

I lifted my wineglass high and gave a toast. "To my family. For surviving." I asked a short blessing on the food.

Papa held the wineglass up and swirled the liquid around and around and then, as it coated the sides, he stuck his nose in the crystal glass and inhaled. "Son, you have chosen a fine young wine."

His face seemed less wrinkled. I glimpsed a hint of that long-ago French pride, a flicker of a smile on his lips.

Mama reached over and grabbed my hand and his. Looking at Mamie, she said, "For so many years all I thought of was getting away from here. But tonight, this is the only place on earth I want to be."

Somewhere in the middle of our meal, after we had finished the first bottle and our cheeks were rosy from the red wine and the warmth of a July evening, I began to laugh. Then Mama giggled, and Mamie said, "Emile, this is divine. How on earth did you learn to cook like this in America?"

———

I don't know if spies have badges they turn in when they retire. All I know is how my father and mother reacted. They slept for days, barely leaving their old bedroom on the second floor of the château. Of course, they were not always sleeping. They celebrated a strange love story that had somehow weathered almost thirty-eight years.

I planned to head back to Atlanta a week after the Barbie trial ended. Mama told me the morning before I left, "We've decided to stay here for a while. Until your father gets stronger."

"Stay, Mama. Rest." I thought of Grandma sitting on the porch and waiting for her Janie to come home. "I'll take care of Grandma."

They were all there at the château, Papa in between Mama and Mamie, when the taxi came to take me to the airport. Mama rushed to hug me one more time.

"Will you be okay, sweetie?"

"I'll be okay, Mama. I promise." I held her tightly, kissed her cheeks, which were wet with tears. Then I kissed Mamie. "You're very brave," I told her. "I'm proud to be your grandson."

She shooed me off with a scowl, then grabbed me again in an embrace. "Don't stay away too long, Emile."

Lastly, I shook Papa's hand and met his eyes. "I'm glad you're back, Papa. I forgive you."

He nodded. I hesitated, and then hugged him around the neck, very briefly, but for that moment I was sure I felt something akin to love.

———

Eternity's article appeared in the newspaper the morning I left for the States. I purchased it and read it on the plane, thinking to myself that this time, at long last, the story *was* over. The Butcher was in jail, my father was back in my life, and I had found Eternity, several times over. If things worked out with Blithe, I wouldn't lose Eternity again. She would stay in my life, part of my family.

I read her words with a sweet nostalgia, her last love letter to me.

> July 8, 1987
>
> ### TINTIN, A SWITCHBLADE, AND BARBIE
>
> By Eternity Jones
>
> For over twenty years I have followed the trail of Klaus Barbie. It all started for me with the fascinating story of a fourteen-year-old boy whose father had disappeared, leaving his son a clue in a microdot message attached to a wristwatch. . . .

Eternity told my story and my father's from 1964 up to the present. She mentioned the switchblade and Tintin, the oilcan and the thumbtack tin and every other "treasure." I read her words with a lump in my throat. Her story ended with this paragraph.

> Sometimes we report on events because it is our job, and sometimes we do so out of obligation to society's pressure. But occasionally we use our journalistic resources because we are pushed along by something bigger than ourselves, searching for some eternal truth that at the same time has become personal. My involvement in the Klaus Barbie trial is such a case. Thanks to Tintin and a wristwatch, I have witnessed the best and the worst of human nature. And I have learned this lesson. Love will triumph, in the midst of the Holocaust and in the soul of one broken family.

During my first two weeks back in the States, I split my time between Atlanta and Nashville. I had decisions to make, decisions about Blithe and me, about my teaching career, about my family. During the four-hour drives back and forth from Atlanta to Nashville, I listened to a variety of books on tape—*Bleak House* and *Huckleberry*

Finn and *The Cost of Discipleship*—and I held conversations with God.

A long, complicated chapter had ended; a new chapter needed writing. It was a tired but true metaphor for my life. I knew the main characters in the new chapter: my parents and my grandmothers. My commitment for this part of the story was to them—their health, their healing. I wanted with all my heart for their stories to end peacefully, filled with good meals and flaming sunsets and walks beside tranquil rivers or on the sidewalk of Anjaco.

They all deserved a respite.

Of course, I longed for the new chapter to have other characters in it, too. My wife. My children. If I had shared my analogy with my family, each member would have pointed out the fallacy in dedicating my time to the past generations. Each, Mama and Papa and Mamie and Grandma, would have urged me to keep moving forward. They would have insisted on my pursuing my relationship with Blithe and having it end in marriage.

But this was the conversation I had most often with God. I was stuck in Ecclesiastes, and the appointed time for our lives was simple: "A time to heal . . . a time to laugh . . . a time to sew together . . . a time to love . . . a time for peace." This was my family's time.

One evening as I was once again reading the passage in my Bible, I focused on the way I had underlined it several times over in different colors of ink. The verse I had underlined most often, circled, and even annotated with angry words off to the side, said, "A time to search and a time to give up as lost." That time was over. Finally over.

I let my eyes travel several centimeters down the page to another verse I had underlined. "He has also set eternity in their heart." Beside it, in a moment of great frustration, I had scribbled *This is a sick pun!* I remembered the exact day I had written that note. I had recently returned to Vanderbilt after my two-week stay in France in the spring of 1974. Eternity had made it very clear that she did not want a relationship with me. In my depressed state, I had read the book of Job and then Ecclesiastes. Vanity of vanities. Ah, how I felt it!

And then, right smack in the middle of chapter three, after identifying a time for each activity, Solomon makes the statement about God setting eternity in the hearts of men. He was saying that every human has a soul, has a knowledge of God, but I saw it as extremely personal. God had set Eternity in my heart, and I was having the darnedest time getting rid of her.

I read it again, circling it absently with a pencil, wondering about the girl with the Cleopatra eyes, wondering if I should call her and ask her for advice about Blithe. And in the deepest part of me, I wondered if I was ready to admit the truth. "There is a time to search and a time to give up as lost."

The backyard was bathed in late summer light, and there was the slightest remnant of a breeze. Grandma sat in the chair near the rose-bushes; she was wearing the straw hat and had covered herself in sun-screen. I'd fixed her a tomato and mayonnaise sandwich, chopping up the fresh basil and sprinkling ground pepper on it, and brought her a glass of sugary iced tea. She took a sip of tea and set the glass on the wrought-iron table. Then she smiled at me, and I helped her put her gnarled hands into the gardening gloves, and she began potting a geranium.

She had fallen twice recently, while I was in France, but we hesi-tated to move her to a nursing home. She loved Anjaco so much. I had decided to move into the house to care for her, at least until the end of the summer. I was actually considering leaving my beloved Nashville and taking a teaching position at Georgia State, so that I could stay on. I had no confidence in my talents as a nursemaid, but I knew I wanted to be near Grandma.

I heard the phone ringing and hurried inside to answer it. Blithe had promised to call as soon as she finished work. We were meeting at a restaurant for dinner.

I picked up the phone. "Hey there . . ."

"Hi, Emile." It was Eternity.

"Oh, hi! Wow, I wasn't expecting to hear from you. You okay?"

"Yeah. I just needed to hear your voice, see if you made it home okay."

"Yep. Got home fine. Been running around between Atlanta and Nashville." I cleared my throat and tried to think of something to say.

"Blithe and I are going out in a little while."

"Give her a hug from me." She sounded nostalgic.

"Sure. But you know, you should come see her sometime. She misses her big sis."

"Yeah. I should come. Sometime. Maybe soon."

"How's Jacques?"

"Okay. Pretty good, I guess." She hesitated. "I broke it off with him."

"What? I thought y'all were serious."

"Yeah, well, you were right. He was more of a father figure to me."

"Now wait a minute, Eternity," I said. "That was a silly comment I made on the first day we met. It didn't mean anything."

She gave a long sigh. "You said out loud what I'd felt in my heart for several months. I knew it wasn't love—not the eros kind of love, anyway. When I got back to Paris, it was so clear to me. All of a sudden so clear."

"I'm sorry, Eternity. I don't know what to say."

"It's okay. It's the right thing. I know it. Anyway, it's been pretty lonely around here the past week or two. I always feel deflated after a big story is over. And this one—Klaus Barbie and your father and all—well, it took up so much of my time, my thoughts for so long . . ."

"I can never thank you enough, Eternity."

"No, don't start on that. I just needed to hear your voice. I'm not even sure why. It just seemed important. I guess I got used to being with you again."

"Yeah." I did not know what to do with this information. "Well, it's great to hear from you, and if you decide to come back to Atlanta, there's room for you at Grandma's or at Blithe's. You know that."

"Yeah . . ."

"Bye."

Blithe and I were seated at Houston's—her favorite restaurant. She loved the big salads and the cheese toast. I found the atmosphere a bit loud and the lighting way too dim. I put on my glasses and stared at the menu.

"You okay, Emile?" She was dressed in a sweatshirt and blue jeans, looking very much like the angel of yesteryear.

"Oh, yeah. Sure. Just feeling a bit disoriented tonight. 'Sow your seed in the morning and do not be idle in the evening, for you do not know whether morning or evening sowing will succeed, or whether both of them alike will be good.'"

She frowned. "Oh, dear. There you go quoting Ecclesiastes. What's wrong, Emile?"

I kept hearing Eternity's voice in my mind. "I'm sorry, Blithe. I think I'm bad company tonight."

"You talked to Eternity today, didn't you?"

I set down my fork, pushed my glasses up on my nose, and asked, "How did you know that?"

"She told me she was going to call you."

This came as a surprise. "You've talked to her too?"

"Yeah, we've been running up these crazy phone bills lately."

"Well, that's good. I told her she needed to get in touch with her little sis more often. Did she tell you about Jacques? That she broke it off?"

"Yeah."

"Have you ever met him?"

"No. But she told me about him. I think she's right. He was a father figure to her. I've felt that all along."

"Really?" I shrugged. "I don't know, Blithe. I feel like I spoke out of turn and put an idea in her head. I feel rotten about it."

"I think you spoke the truth, and as soon as Eternity heard it, she knew what was right."

"Maybe so." I took my glasses off, put them down, and ran both hands under my eyes. "You women are confusing. I can't figure you out." Then I blurted out, "For instance, am I a father figure to you, Blithe? Do you see me like that?"

She reached across the table and took my hand. "Kinda . . ."

I felt my face drain of color. "Are you serious?"

She leaned over, her elbow resting on the table, one hand pushing a fork around on her plate. "Oh, Emile, you've thought it from the beginning. I didn't want to admit it, though. Then Eternity started calling me during the trial. We talked a lot about the really awful things from our childhood. And the way we saw men. She's the one who brought it up first—needed to ask my opinion about Jacques.

"But I knew it applied to me too. What I'm saying is, I think I needed you too much. I begged myself onto you. I idolized you. I'd given Eternity years and years to catch on, and she didn't, and so I moved in on you. But maybe, well . . . maybe it's not the best fit." She frowned. "Do you know what I mean?"

My temples were beginning to throb. Of course I knew what she meant. I'd struggled with it for six months now.

"I know you don't know how to tell me. But it's okay. I figured it out. What do you think I did all those nights I was here with your grandmother? We talked. We talked about long ago and you and Eternity and me and life and forgiveness. You don't have to explain. On the phone I heard it in your voice; every time you called me from Lyon, I heard it. Everything my sister had done for you. You needed to be sharing it with her, not me. I was just the kid sister, the little girl, with a crazy crush on the handsome prince who tried to save my life—who did save it, and my brother's, and Eternity's many times."

"Blithe, I care about you a whole lot."

"I know that, Emile. I've never doubted it for an instant."

I could tell that Blithe felt relieved with the confession. I simply felt numb.

Maybe it was because I grew up in a women's world that I lacked self-confidence with the fairer sex. Blithe had read my thoughts, had heard something in my voice, first across the phone lines, and then that evening across the table. After all these years, I was still in love with Eternity Jones. I knew I had looked forward to our hour at the café every day in Lyon. I knew it felt like *Paradise Found* to sit with her and discuss life. I knew I felt I had gained my best friend back. I did not feel we were betraying Blithe or Jacques. Never had I considered stealing her away. She had healed. So let the poor woman enjoy a healthy relationship with a man, albeit an older one.

I had let go of Eternity a hundred times. A thousand times. I had admired her, applauded her from a distance, prayed for her, and concluded that allowing her to live her life without me was the ultimate sacrifice and proof of my love. But now, again, there was a choice, an opening. I did not want to go through rejection again, so I approached this matter in the way I had learned to handle all the questions and decisions in my life. I would wait and trust.

I would wait for time to tell.

———

It was God's Spirit, blown across the pages of Solomon's advice, that pushed me to my decision. I had analyzed the times and seasons and admitted my confusion and was reading straight through Ecclesiastes for the fourth time in a week when I came to another familiar verse that made me laugh out loud. In fact, to use another old metaphor, the words literally leapt off the page, as if the Lord were saying, "Get it, Emile? This is my message to you now."

There it was: *"Two are better than one."*

In that minute, I knew what I needed to do. I dialed her number. It was the middle of the night in Paris, but this could not wait.

She answered in sleepy French, *"Oui, allo?"*

The connection was clear, and I spilled out my thoughts. "A long time ago you asked me not to pursue you. And I didn't. You healed, you met Jacques, you developed your career. We found each other again and got along well, but I never said a thing. I thought you were taken. I thought I was taken. Now, it looks like things have changed for both of us.

"So here's the thing, Eternity. Maybe you are completely uninterested in me. But if there is anything romantic in your thoughts, then tell me. Not right this second. Think about it. Pray. I'm going to be as honest as I know how to be before God and man—or wo-man: I love you, Eternity Jones. I want to marry you. We've both grown up a lot. Heck, we're nearing middle age. So, please, Eternity. Think about it. And I'll call you back next week."

I hung up before she had a chance to say one word.

Five minutes later the phone rang.

"Emile, you hung up on me." The tall girl with the Cleopatra eyes was reprimanding me once again, but this time her voice betrayed excitement and longing.

"It was Blithe who called me in Lyon, who told me I was the biggest fool on the whole entire earth. 'You're not going to settle for a father instead of a lover, Eternity. You've got a Father and so have I— and He's the same. You know that. He's the same. Emile doesn't want me—he wants *you*. And you have been waiting for him all your life. He won't chase you anymore.'

"The truth is, I started missing you the second we said good-bye after the trial. I've been so stupid. I learned something at the trial, Emile. I want to live. I want to move forward. I know I'm not completely healed, and maybe I never will be. But if those people, those victims of Barbie, can keep living, can make a life out of ashes, then so can I. And all I know is that you are the only man I want. Every day in that café, I grew more and more convinced of it. Only I thought it was too late. . . ."

───────────

I picked her up at the Hartsfield International Airport and we drove on I–75 through Atlanta's late afternoon traffic. I got off at the North Avenue exit, and we went into the Varsity and ordered onion rings, two chili dogs, and a frosted orange to split between us. We stared at each other, touched hands, let go, laughed a lot.

When we got to Grandma's house, I opened the car door and helped her out. She flashed me a grin. I encircled her waist with my arms and lifted her off the ground. She laughed her low, smooth laugh and kissed me on the mouth. We stood there, for who knows how long, on the little incline in the driveway of the house on Anjaco Road with the rustling leaves applauding us. We stood there, locked in an embrace, making up for years of lost time.

Finding out the truth about Papa had been worse than the waiting. So painful. But finding out the truth of Eternity was heaven on earth. We did not want an elaborate wedding. There was too much we had missed out on, too much to catch up on. We married in the chapel in Second-Ponce de Leon Baptist Church on a hot afternoon in late

September of 1987. Dr. Swilley, long since retired, agreed to officiate.

Mr. Leroy Davis, wearing the biggest smile I'd ever seen on his face, hobbled down the aisle with Eternity on his arm. When Dr. Swilley asked, "Who gives this woman to be married to this man?" he said, "I do, and her heavenly Father does, too." Then he took his seat on the front row of the chapel right beside Grandma, Mama, Papa, and Blithe.

Griffin came to the wedding with his beautiful Mexican wife and a brood of children. "It's about time, you crazy amigo," he whispered to me.

Ace was there too, along with his wife and three children, and I'm pretty sure I saw tears in his eyes.

When Dr. Swilley said I could kiss my bride, I did, for a long, long time, until all the wedding guests began to clap and then to cheer.

Blithe wished us well with a self-satisfied grin on her face. We kidded her that she was trying to take credit for a story God had been writing long before she had a clue. "Then maybe I was the final link in the chain so that you two airheads would wake up to reality," she teased.

I whispered to my new wife, "Wake up to Eternity—now that's what I'm looking forward to," and the freckles orbited again and the subtle wrinkles danced around her eyes.

| *epilogue* |

*There is a time
to love. . . .*

"Accepting to forget is admitting our indifference."

"I am convinced that the dead will speak. We can't bring the dead back and make it right. But we must keep the memory. We couldn't stop the first death but we must stop the second death. The first is the killer's fault, the second is ours."

—Elie Wiesel, winner of the Nobel Peace Prize, writer and deportee

"Memory is the root of deliverance as forgetfulness is that of exile."

"If the echo of their voices diminishes, we will perish."

—Quotes on the wall of the Museum of the Resistance and the Deportation, Lyon, France

October 15, 1992

**RESISTANCE MUSEUM TO OPEN IN
BUILDING USED BY KLAUS BARBIE**

By Eternity Jones-de Bonnery

Two days of celebrations and speeches are planned for the inauguration of the Resistance Museum, a new center for the history of the Resistance and the Deportation. Mayor Michel Noir, whose father was a World War II deportee, will open the memorial tomorrow at ten o'clock. Nobel Prize Winner Elie Wiesel will also be present. . . .

The center is set up in the Gestapo's former building and the headquarters of Klaus Barbie. In this place where Barbie tortured so many, the walls can finally speak. . . .

March 1993

Eternity and I have lived at the house on Anjaco Road ever since our wedding. It was our privilege to care for Grandma for four years, until she passed away last winter at ninety years of age. She died peacefully, with a smile on her face, in her bedroom with her family around her, all of us: Mama and Papa, Eternity and me, Blithe and her husband, Clay. Grandma even got to kiss the great-grandchildren two days before she died.

We're remodeling the house now—all except for the bedroom upstairs. I wanted at least to change the yellow wallpaper, but Eternity would not hear of it.

After Eternity reported on the opening of the Resistance Museum last fall, I knew immediately what to do with my collection.

Today, Papa and I walk together to the museum with a cardboard box filled with the "treasures"—the newspapers, the thumbtack tin, the pen, the bicycle pump, the hairbrush, the oilcan, and the wristwatch. My father's gifts to me, my gift to the memory of history, so that none of the story will be forgotten.

We are in the open square surrounded by plane trees, a slight breeze rustling their new green leaves. Above, the French flag flies proudly, waving to us—blue, white, and red. We make our way to the building where the tortures took place, now transformed into a museum.

Later, Papa and I drive to the cemetery and stand beside the graves of my grandparents. I read the headstones: *Pierre de Bonnery,*

1900–1944, beloved husband, father, Résistant; Marie-Madeleine de Bonnery, 1902–1992, courageous until the end.

Eternity and I go with Mama and Papa to the old château in St. Romain. It too is being renovated, having been divided into five different apartments and sold to French couples with an avid interest in historical preservation. Mama and Papa are keeping one of the apartments for themselves.

We take a walk down to the Saône River. Mama, delighted with her role of grandmother, pushes our baby daughter, Maddy, in the stroller. Eternity has her arm looped through my father's, and our four-year-old son, Jacob, holds tightly to his other hand. My father is talking rather animatedly with Eternity.

He turns to me and calls out, "Well, you never told me that story, Emile, son! Fighting the bullies at school with dirt and then teaching them French."

We arrive back at the château where Eternity and Mama prepare dinner for the children. I start a fire. Papa begins to tell me about the wine he has chosen for the meal. Soon Eternity is sitting beside Jacob with the baby on her lap, and they are making a beautiful mess out of Jacob's dinner: broccoli trees, an applesauce moon, rice stars, and ground-up hamburger, which has become the earth.

After dinner, Papa takes Jacob's hand and they walk toward my old bedroom, where the children will sleep. I want to give Jacob a kiss, so I follow. Eternity's hand catches my arm, and she holds me back, nodding to Jacob and my father, deep in conversation.

"Can you tell me one of your stories, Papy? Just like you told my daddy? A story of the war?"

I turn to Eternity, make a face, and whisper, "He's too young for a war story."

Eternity kisses me on the mouth and says, "You're one to talk!"

Papa ruffles my son's hair and smiles. "Of course I can tell you a story, little Jacob." He walks to the bookshelf and retrieves a thin, hardbound book.

I wait by the bedroom door and watch. They are sitting side by side on my son's bed.

"Have you ever heard of Tintin?"

Jacob nods.

"Wonderful stories, son. Someday soon you'll be old enough to read them. But in the war we used books like this one to carry secrets. . . ."

As his story unfolds, my father opens *The Black Island* to the middle, where the pages are cut. We couldn't give that book away. We needed it for the next generation. To remember. Into eternity.

| *Acknowledgments* |

Writers of fiction get their inspiration from people, places, books, experiences—anything that gives a glimpse of something that *could have been*. This story sneaked up on me and tapped me on the shoulder as I discovered the city of Lyon and her history. However, I would never have tried to tell the story from the point of view of a fourteen-year-old French boy were it not for my two teenage sons, Andrew and Christopher, who embody all that is wonderful about "third-culture kids"—being raised in one culture while your parents hold passports to another. Thanks, guys, for being so *you*. What a delight.

I am indebted to the staff at the Centre d'Histoire de la Resistance et de la Déportation in Lyon, who let me poke around on many a day, and am especially thankful for the free access to the Centre de Documentation, where I spent many hours gleaning information.

Special thanks to:

My parents, Jere and Barbara Goldsmith, for all your help and support and for setting me straight about Atlanta time and again. To Mom for all the descriptions of Northside High School way back when, and to her great group of friends who helped when she wasn't sure. Also, as always, thanks for your enthusiasm, energy, and the hundreds of practical ways you help.

Daddy, for lending me the Time-Life book on the Resistance, which sparked my imagination for the "treasures," and to those who provided tidbits of information about weapons, microdots, and *traboules*: Thom Shelton, Kathy Brooks, Howell Williams, Robin Grant, William Crawford, Maurice Fusier, Didier Moreau.

My grandmother, Allene Massey Goldsmith, for being my Grandma Bridgeman.

The rest of my family, all of you, for your faithful encouragement, support, and so much more: Jere and Mary Goldsmith, Glenn and Kim Goldsmith, Alan and Jay Goldsmith, Harvey and Doris Ann Musser, H. A. and Rhonda Musser, Steve and Janet Granski, Scot and Carol Musser, Bill and Beth Wren.

Cathy Carmeni, Kim Huhman, and Bob Dillon, who all three happily stepped in to play the role of pre-editor and offered invaluable insights.

My friends in Lyon who have prayed and encouraged me as I write: Lori Varak, Karen Moulton, Michele Philit, Chery Stauffer, Liliana Mornet, Vivianne Perret, and many others.

Trudy Owens, Odette Beauregard, Laura McDaniel, Val Andrews, Margaret DeBorde, Kim Huhman, Cathy Carmeni, Marcia Smartt—for being there for me and praying for my writing career throughout so many years.

Cheryl Stauffer for Keeping up the Web site and gently encouraging me into twenty-first century cyberspace.

My new agent, Chip MacGregor; thanks for believing in me—I'm looking forward to working together.

Dave Horton for your steady faith in my writing and your wise insight. I owe you a great debt. As always, *Merci mille fois*.

LB Norton—working with you across cyberspace makes the editing process a delight. We are a team, and my stories are clearer, sharper, and (hmmmm) shorter because of you!

All the staff at Bethany House Publishers.

My readers—thank you for taking the time to read, encourage me, and spread the word.

Paul, my master spy and partner in crime, who makes me laugh when my characters are threatening mutiny and holds me close when the story seems too hard to bear.

The Lord Jesus for finding me before I even knew I was searching. I am so excited about spending eternity with You!